NEVER DARE A
DRAGON

ASHLYN CHASE

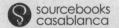

sourcebooks
casablanca

Published by Sourcebooks Casablanca, an imprint of Sourcebooks, Inc.
P.O. Box 4410, Naperville, Illinois 60567-4410
(630) 961-3900
Fax: (630) 961-2168
sourcebooks.com

Printed and bound in Canada.
MBP 10 9 8 7 6 5 4 3 2 1

To Massachusetts firefighters.

*I lived a block away from the fire station as a kid,
and they always had time for a smile and wave.
I knew they were keeping us safe every time the
sirens blared and the trucks rolled out.*

*Now, as an adult, they still make time to meet
with me, take me on tours of their stations, answer
questions about their equipment and policies, and
give me great ideas to make my stories even better.*

*Thanks, gentlemen and ladies.
You're the best of humanity.*

Chapter 1

"PRIDE OF MIDTOWN. NEVER MISSED A PERFORMANCE?"

Someone with a deep, sexy voice was reading the FDNY patch on Kristine Scott's dress uniform. She swiveled enough to see a dark-haired, devastatingly handsome Boston firefighter—a lieutenant, from the insignia on his uniform. He was admiring not only the patch but also *her*. She was tall, five-foot-ten, but he was taller.

The after-funeral crowd noise obliterated anything but close conversation in the firehouse, and yet she didn't mind his proximity. Not one bit.

"Yeah. I guess you wouldn't know what our motto means, being from Boston and all." She picked up a canapé from a long folding table.

He smiled—and, oh God, he had dimples.

"Enlighten me," he said.

She chewed and swallowed the little cracker before launching into her explanation. "We're located in Manhattan, close to Broadway but in an affordable neighborhood, so a lot of actors live in the area."

"Affordable? In Manhattan? Even a mere Bostonian like me knows that's like finding a unicorn in Central Park."

She chuckled. *Damn. So sexy, except for that hideous Boston accent.* "I work in the second-oldest fire station in the country. The area is known as Hell's Kitchen. Maybe you've heard of it?"

"Shit. Only as a horrible place where hundreds of thousands of immigrants died of nasty diseases."

"Yeah, that was a long time ago. We're becoming gentrified and fairly disease-free these days."

He looked her up and down. "Now there's a relief."

"And what is that supposed to mean, Boston?"

"Oh, nothing." He heaved a deep sigh. "You live in Manhattan, and I live in Charlestown—the part of Boston where Old Ironsides is docked. You don't care about that. The point is…it would never work." His sad smile spoke of resignation.

"Oh? Were you thinking of asking me out?"

That devastating grin of his returned. "Is there any chance you'd consider moving to Boston?"

"Ha! Nope," she said, trying to sound casual. Not that she'd date a firefighter *anywhere*.

"Then we have an insurmountable problem. I can't leave Boston because of family obligations. And you can't—or won't—leave New York. I guess we might as well break up now."

She hoped her disappointment didn't show, but she had a sinking feeling she didn't hide it well enough.

As if he'd just come up with a solution, he snapped his fingers. "I know. Since we can't date anyway, why don't we tell each other all of our annoying habits right off the bat? That way we won't worry about what might have been."

She couldn't help letting out a loud laugh. Probably inappropriate after a funeral, and several nearby firefighters turned toward them. *Oops.* "Sorry," she mumbled.

"I'll start," her potential ex said. "I forget to floss about ninety percent of the time."

Playing along, she crossed her arms. "Ugh. That's disgusting. Don't you know that's the only way to brush between your teeth?"

He simply showed off his pearly whites and said, "Your turn."

"Okay… I wear granny panties."

"No way!" He cringed and recoiled. "Haven't you ever heard of that not-so-secret store? If we were dating, which we're not, I'd get you a gift certificate."

"Ah. There's another thing that would annoy me. I want to be accepted exactly the way I am."

He let out a snort. "You're not wrong, but a little sexy something for your man to uncover goes a long way."

"Hey. I'm a firefighter. You don't want to floss your teeth? I don't want to floss my butt—I'll leave that to the girls who slide down a different kind of pole."

He laughed "I guess it might be inconvenient on the job."

She shrugged one shoulder. "You think? Well… It's your turn again."

"Okay. When I'm home, I can be a slob. I leave my clothes in a disorganized pile," he said.

"That's ridiculous! You must have to keep your area at the fire station neat. Why not at home?"

He smirked. "Because I can. Your turn."

One of the nearby firefighters interrupted before she had a chance to respond.

"Hey, Jayce. If you're flirting, that's the worst I've ever seen."

He laughed and slung his arm around the other firefighter's shoulder. "This is my brother Gabe, who should be minding his own business."

"I was about to say the same thing as Gabe," another firefighter chimed in.

"And that's my brother Noah. Same goes for you, buddy."

The family resemblance was hard to miss. Tall, dark, and good-looking, every one of them. But there was something special about the one they called "Jayce." His brown eyes were darker—almost black, and full of mischief—and he had killer dimples. Suddenly she realized she and he hadn't even introduced themselves.

"So, is Jayce short for Jason?"

"Nope. My given name is J-a-y-c-e. And who have I had the pleasure of breaking up with?"

"My name is Kristine. Kristine Scott. They call me Scotty."

"Hey, Fierro!" a firefighter called to the group.

"Yeah?" the three men answered at once.

"Your dad and the chief are looking for you."

"Wait," Kristine said. "The firefighter we memorialized today was named Fierro. Are you related?"

"Yeah. He was my younger brother," Jayce said. "A probie."

"Holy fuck," she muttered. "I've been joking and laughing with the deceased's brother?"

"Guess so," Jayce answered matter-of-factly.

"How can you be so callous?" The words were out before she could think about them. *Oh well. Since we're being totally honest…* "It's a good thing we're breaking up before we even get started. That kind of insensitivity just blows." She found a hole in the crowd and stomped off before he could object.

He called after her. "Hey, pride of Midtown."

She stopped and turned around.

He sidled up next to her. "Do you know which is the oldest fire station in the country?"

She shook her head.

"You've been standing in it for the last fifteen minutes."

"How do you know I've been here for fifteen minutes?"

"I noticed you the minute you walked in." He grinned. "Can I get your phone number?"

Still miffed, she answered, "Yeah… It's 911."

He winked and then strode off, leaving her without the satisfaction of a dramatic exit.

How infuriating! But she couldn't help admiring his gorgeous ass as he walked away.

Leaving the firehouse, Kristine shivered in the January wind and made her way to her car in the Prudential parking garage. On the way there, she ran the gamut of emotions. Her outrage gave way to sympathy. She tried to give Jayce the benefit of the doubt. Some people coped with grief through denial. Maybe that was what he was doing. However, she had a feeling that wasn't all of it. He was too charming. Too polished. He seemed totally comfortable in his own skin. Usually that would be a turn-on. But today of all days?

Something was off about that whole funeral. The only one who seemed truly devastated was the firefighter's fiancée. She tried to be brave, but tears shimmered in the corners of her eyes. Occasionally her head dropped and her whole body shook as if she were literally racked with sobs, but no sound came out. She was a firefighter too—probably doing her best to be brave. *Just another reason to stick to my vow of not dating firefighters.*

And it wasn't just Jayce who was acting like it was a normal Tuesday and not the solemn day they were burying his brother. All the brothers she met seemed to be taking it rather well. Their only complaint about Jayce's flirting was that he was doing it wrong? *What the hell?* Of course, she wasn't inside the church during the service. Thousands of firefighters from all over the country attended, so only family members and those closest to them were allowed inside. Maybe they got their tears out there.

Still…smiling and joking? If that had happened at the 9/11 funerals, somebody would have been pounded into Ground Zero… Her mind was definitely boggled.

"Scotty! Wait," a familiar voice called.

She stuck her fist on her hip and waited for Donovan, the guy she had carpooled with. *Damn.*

"Jesus, Scott, were you about to take off without me?"

"Sorry," she mumbled. "I thought you could get a ride from any of the other hundred FDNY attendees."

"Well, it would have been nice if you'd told me that you were leaving."

She chewed her lip and popped the passenger side door open with her key fob. When they were both seated inside the tiny rented sports car, he scrutinized her.

"What's wrong?"

There was no hiding emotions from guys you lived with almost as much as your family.

"It's nothing." The universal code for *I don't want to talk about it.*

"Bullshit. Did the funeral hit you that hard? Enough

to make you want to get the hell out of town without even telling me? Did you run into someone you knew?"

"No. Nothing like that."

"Then what?"

She backed out of the parking space, turning the rented Corvette toward the exit without explaining herself.

"Are you on your period?"

She stomped on the brakes. "You are never, ever, ever allowed to ask a woman that—ever!"

He leaned away with his hands up. "Okay, okay. Don't shoot."

She resumed her exit from the parking garage with a bit more speed than was prudent. Donovan glanced over at her a couple of times but didn't say another word.

—◆◆◆—

Jayce and his brothers found their father and mother among the crowd. The chief was nowhere in sight.

"What did you want, Dad?"

"Me? Nothing. Why?"

"Miguel said you and the chief were looking for us."

The brother in question spoke from behind them. "I was saving your ass. Do you even know how inappropriate your flirting with a girl at your brother's funeral is?"

Their tiny mother stepped forward. "You were flirting with someone, Jayce?"

He heaved a sigh. "Yeah. I'm sorry. There was this drop-dead-gorgeous redhead, or strawberry blonde, kinda golden-red—whatever—with the most incredible turquoise eyes... We got to talking."

"And laughing," Miguel added.

Jayce shot him an angry look designed to shut him up.

Mrs. Fierro placed a soothing hand on Jayce's arm. "Well, I'm not upset about it at all. I want all my boys happy, and that means settled down with a good woman." She glanced around at her fidgeting sons, except Miguel—the only married man in the bunch, naturally.

Mr. Fierro pulled Jayce closer so he could whisper, even though all of his supernatural sons could hear him. Obviously he didn't want their human mother to overhear. "You know I want to retire in the Caribbean, and your mama refuses to leave until you're all married off. Flirting is fine, but remember where you are. We're all aware that Ryan is alive, but no one else knows that, including Chloe."

Jayce glanced over to where his brother's fiancée, in her dress uniform, leaned against her own big brother, Rory. He seemed to be propping her up. Most firefighters had seen some horrors, but few had had to watch helplessly as the person they loved most burned to death in front of them.

"Whatever you do, don't let it slip to that poor girl," Antonio Fierro continued. "She's devastated, and we can't let her know Ryan has reincarnated. She'd never recognize him in his new form, and, well, you know what would happen…"

"Got it. Message received," Jayce whispered back. He stepped away and said, "I think I'll go to the restroom and see if I can muster up a few tears." Just thinking about what that cute NY firefighter said to him was enough to dampen his mood.

Mrs. Fierro smiled at her son as he kissed her on the cheek and excused himself. She had a not-so-hidden agenda, and all of her remaining sons knew it well. But the chances of finding a lover who could stand the shock of what he really was seemed slim to none. Some girls might like to know that if the worst happened, a blazing bird would rise from its own ashes—and several weeks later their lover would return to human form. But telling the truth about their supernatural natures could have devastating consequences. Ryan had learned that with his first fiancée, Melanie. The only reason she hadn't screamed it to the world was her fear of being locked up and labeled crazy.

The brothers had to avoid telling a potential mate until they were a hundred percent certain the love they shared was strong enough to survive such a revelation. Miguel had gotten lucky. Sandra adored him, and she always would. And as much as his mother teased his father, she'd throw herself on a sword for him. The Fierro men treated their women like the rare treasures they were.

Jayce bypassed the restroom and stepped outside. Some of his fellow firefighters were smoking. Knowing how many fires were started by unattended cigarettes, he thought the habit weird, but the stress of the job was too much for some to manage without a vice. He knew doctors and nurses who smoked too.

"Jayce!" His buddy Mike strolled over to him. "I know I said it before, but I'm really sorry about Ryan. He was a good man and, from what I've heard, a great firefighter. No one could have survived that backdraft."

"I know."

Yet somehow Chloe managed to survive. She had said she was thrown clear of the blast, but with two floors of a high-rise completely engulfed in flames, her escape was a miracle. Jayce didn't believe in miracles.

She said she had been knocked out and really didn't know how she had made it out alive. The theory was that she was thrown into the stairwell and had fallen onto a safe floor. When Ryan could tell his side of the story, they'd find out what really happened.

Even with a mystery like that to puzzle over, Jayce's mind kept returning to the beautiful, redheaded, granny-panty-wearing FDNY firefighter. He doubted he'd ever see Kristine again. If he did, she'd probably still think he was some kind of cold, heartless monster.

Mike squeezed Jayce's shoulder and wandered back to the butt can, where he crushed out his cigarette. When he returned he said, "There's a great buffet in there. Want to get a bite to eat?"

Jayce sighed. "I don't think I can."

Mike nodded. "I understand, man."

He really didn't. The firefighter brotherhood was good for understanding a lot of things, but only his biological brothers could possibly know what he was feeling right now. Fortunately there were a lot of them, so support was never far away.

As if conjured, Luca, the youngest Fierro brother, stepped outside. "Hey, Jayce. The captain is about to make a speech."

"Shit. Another speech?"

"I guess he didn't want to be outdone by the chief."

Luca and Jayce returned to the fire station where Ryan and their father had worked. It was time for the brothers to brush up on their acting skills.

Acting. Everything reminded him of Kristine, even after only a ten-minute conversation. *What the hell is wrong with me?*

—⁓—

Two days later, Kristine was back to work at her fire station in Hell's Kitchen, back to studying for the lieutenant's exam. Her life seemed on track, but something was missing.

Her mind had returned over and over again to that bright smile and those dark eyes glinting with naughtiness. She kept telling herself to forget about the handsome Boston lieutenant. When he had mentioned her transferring to Boston, she had thought about it for all of one heartbeat. Then she remembered everything she would be giving up in New York.

If she went to Boston, she'd have to go through the fire academy all over again and start at the bottom rung as a probie. During their early days on the job, a firefighter was on probation, therefore the term "probie" became common slang, like "rookie" for a brand-new cop. The technical term was FFOP—Firefighter on Probation. That was no better. Either way, it seemed like a slap in the face after all she'd been through. And with only a few months left to finish her degree in fire science, she had a better chance for a promotion to captain or chief someday. Not to mention that her mother depended upon her half of the rent.

Years ago, Hell's Kitchen had been a tough neighborhood. Mother and daughter were dragons—not as vulnerable as humans, so they felt safe enough there. Then in the early '90s, the middle class began moving in and gentrifying the area. Kristine and her mother had lived there all that time and had watched their rent go up, up, up. With no father to help or pay child support, her mother had had to work two jobs—while pursuing an acting career. Kristine vowed she would never forget that. It still took two salaries to live there, but only one of them would be her mother's. Amy Scott had finally landed her dream job. She taught at a nearby acting school.

Even though Kristine had grown up among actors, artists, and writers, she hadn't inherited the need to express herself publicly. Despite being paranormally gifted, she had been a sheltered kid—and that was fine with her. As a little dragon, she'd never felt like she fit in. She was happiest when reading in her room overlooking Ninth Avenue.

She knew she wasn't supposed to talk about shapeshifting or demonstrate what she could do, ever. When she grew up, she realized there was something special she could do with her powers other than just protect herself. Because she was fireproof, she would make an ideal firefighter. She could protect her community.

She loved the job. Only a handful of women worked for the FDNY, and half of them were on ambulances. She was one of the few with the strength and fortitude to do the heavy lifting required of a firefighter on the front lines.

She had proven herself to be the equal of any man in her battalion. They respected her and depended upon her to have their backs. And as much as she cared about her fellow firefighters, she could never see herself falling in love with one of them. She would worry constantly, knowing what he was up against as a mere mortal.

One ordinary Thursday, her battalion was gathered around the long kitchen table, eating lunch and watching *Judge Judy* on the wall-mounted TV, when the tones rang out. They all rushed to their turnout gear, suited up, and jumped into their usual roles.

Kristine rode next to Donovan on the ladder truck. When the truck pulled up to the high-rise office building, smoke was pouring out of two large broken windows on the fourth floor. A police cruiser was already there, getting people to clear the area for the fire apparatus. So far nothing seemed unusual.

Kristine and Donovan followed the captain into the building to locate the seat of the fire. Alarms were blaring, and people were filing down the stairs. When the firefighters came to the fourth floor, they located the office they had seen from the outside. The captain pounded on the door and yelled, identifying them as the fire department.

When there was no response, the captain instructed Kristine and Donovan to take off the door with the ax and halligan bar. Two other firefighters from the engine company rushed up behind them hauling the hose. One of them broke into the firebox on the wall. As soon as the door was breached, flames shot out from the hole.

They had the right place.

When they got the door open, the captain barked out, "Scotty, stay with me. Donovan, go above and see if anyone is still up there."

"Yes sir," he said and dashed to the stairs.

The captain didn't need to tell Kristine to step aside. When the pressurized water hit the fire, steam filled the hallway. The guy carrying the hose entered slowly, bathing the place in water. Between the smoke and steam, firefighters had to go in blind and look for survivors or people who weren't that lucky.

"Scotty, stay beside me."

Kristine followed the captain's orders, even though she knew he was in more danger than she was. He kept one gloved hand on the wall to avoid becoming lost. She placed a hand on his shoulder and walked a few feet to his right. Even a dragon could barely see through this.

Her foot hit something dense but soft. Squatting down, she felt a leg. "I've got someone," she said. Hauling the person up by the arms, she tossed his torso over her shoulder and made her way back to the door.

She heard the captain shouting into the radio that she was coming down and to have EMS ready. Something felt off about the body she was carrying. She had to adjust its position to account for an uneven distribution of weight.

When she finally made it to the street level, the EMTs were there to meet her, but as she emerged, their eyes bugged out of their heads.

"You're covered in blood!" the female EMT exclaimed.

She glanced down and saw that it was true. She squatted down, braced the victim's back with her hand, and gently laid the headless body onto the sidewalk. Startled, she jumped backward and gasped.

The cop who had been redirecting traffic ran over. "What the hell?"

The chief strode over and set his hands on his hips. "As soon as we put the fire out, you can have your crime scene."

"Jesus," muttered the male EMT. "The coroner won't have any problem identifying cause of death."

The captain's voice crackled over the radio, alerting the chief that he was coming out with another body.

"You don't have to go back in there, Scotty. You've got to be pretty shaken up right now."

"No, sir. I'm fine. I'd like to go back in there and help where I'm needed."

The chief smiled and nodded.

On her way back in, she passed the captain, carrying a second body in the same condition. She didn't take the time to find out if he knew what was going on; she just rushed up the stairs faster.

I wonder where the heads are.

When she reached the fourth floor, the steam met her as soon as she opened the fire door. She rushed through it and worried about her mortal coworkers, who could be standing in boiling water.

If she had to shift, her thick scales would protect her, and her alternate form's wings wouldn't show because her turnout gear covered her up to the neck. She only had to worry about her snout protruding and interfering with her breathing apparatus. Fortunately, she wasn't huge like the dragons of Hollywood. She was five-foot-ten as a human or dragon.

The fire was almost out, and she could see that the walls of the room were still intact, as was the ceiling. Apparently they had stopped this fire from traveling very far. The building's sprinklers may have helped slightly. She suspected that the fire was meant to cover the crime scene—and that the location of the bodies would prove to be where the fire was set…deliberately.

Even in New York, this was unusual. Not that fires weren't accidents—faulty wiring, an unattended cigarette, deep-fried turkeys—oh yeah, plenty of accidents. They had their fair share of arson too, but it was usually to defraud an insurance company. Not to cover up decapitations.

As the smoke and steam cleared, she glanced around

the room, casually looking for a couple of male heads. The other two firefighters seemed blissfully unaware of the unusual circumstances. Just thinking about it, bile rose to her throat. She didn't envy the cops their jobs, especially after something like this.

She couldn't help wondering if this sort of stuff happened in Boston too. It probably did, but maybe on a smaller scale.

Boston again. When would she stop thinking about what it would be like to be a firefighter in Boston, working with a particular sexy firefighter she couldn't seem to get off her mind? She loved New York. It made every other city she'd ever visited pale by comparison.

———— ᨆ ————

Two months later, Jayce and Gabe were back at the Back Bay firehouse on Boylston Street, filling in for the firefighters who were marching in the big South Boston St. Patrick's Day Parade.

As the two sat in the kitchen, drinking coffee, Jayce couldn't help feeling guilty because his whole family had avoided Chloe. Any one of them could have given away Ryan's secret in a moment of compassionate weakness. But now she was right there in the building— somewhere. Maybe she was avoiding them too.

That girl had loved his brother so much. He'd heard that she looked like a zombie ever since the funeral. According to his sources, she was going through the motions at work and keeping to herself. Avoiding her any longer seemed cruel.

"C'mon, Gabe. Let's find Chloe and at least say hello."

"I know we were supposed to leave her be, but you're right. Enough is enough."

At that moment one of the station's regular firefighters walked into the kitchen and headed for the coffeepot. "Hey, guys. Thanks for filling in. I'm Lieutenant Streeter, by the way."

The Fierros stood and shook the lieutenant's hand as they introduced themselves.

"Uh, we'd like to give Chloe our respects. I understand she's working today. Do you know where we might find her?"

"She's probably in her room. Second floor, toward the front. Next to the bathroom with 'ladies' written on it with Magic Marker."

"Thanks, Lieutenant," Gabe said.

Jayce and Gabe headed up the stairs and found the room. They knocked, and something thudded, as if a heavy object had hit the floor. Jayce glanced over at Gabe, who gazed back, eyebrows raised. Just then the door whooshed open and Chloe smiled at them.

"Hi."

"Hey there, Chloe. We just thought we'd say hello since we're working here today."

"Jayce? And Gabe, is it?"

"Yep. Two of the famous Fierros," Gabe said, trying to sound chipper.

"I think I heard something heavy fall on the floor," Jayce said. "Is everything all right?"

She smirked and hesitated. She almost seemed to be thinking about how to answer the question. Jayce remembered she could be a bit of a smart-ass.

"Oh, quite. I just dropped me dictionary," she said with her lilting Irish accent.

"I'll get it," Jayce said as he started inside, his

gaze searching for a book on the floor and not finding one.

"Leave it. I'll get it later." She opened the door wider. "Come in, come in. I don't have much room to sit, but there's a comfortable armchair in the corner for one of you, and I can bring over the desk chair for the other."

"I'll get it, Chloe," Gabe said.

"Don't be silly. I'm closest to it," she said. "Besides, I don't want to be treated any differently. Certainly not because I was in love with your brother and you think I'm a fragile little girl."

The brothers laughed nervously. "No. There's no danger of anyone thinking that, Chloe," Jayce said.

She stopped on her way to the chair and turned slowly. "There's not? Why not? I'm a girl, and I've been in a terrible state since your brother died."

Gabe's face fell; the situation was becoming decidedly uncomfortable. Jayce kicked at the old wood floor. "Of course. I'm sorry."

"Sorry? For what?"

"For not…you know…" He looked to Gabe for help, but his younger brother just shrugged.

She tipped her head to the side and waited. Jayce wished he could find the right words when he needed them. Instead, he just spoke the truth. "I—I don't know what to say, Chloe."

"I think that's why it took us so long to check on you," Gabe added. "None of us knew what to say."

"And why is that?" She folded her arms but didn't look angry.

Shit. They should have sent flowers or something. But no one disobeyed their father, and Antonio Fierro had issued his edict. Leave her be until Ryan could decide what to do about her. And he wouldn't be back in human form until—well, any day now.

"I called your mother a couple of times, just to ask how she was doin'," Chloe continued. "She sounded all right. I figured your mother was gettin' through it because she had a lot of support. I would have liked some too."

Jayce groaned.

"We figured you were, you know…okay," Gabe said.

"But you didn't ask. How could you know?"

Jayce began to fidget. "Yeah, you're right…"

She waited, but he didn't finish his thought. He just tried to get past her to the desk. "Let me get that chair."

She stepped back, and when he rounded the end of her bed, he couldn't help noticing the back half of a naked man trying to jam his big frame under it.

"Oh!" he said. "Oh, I didn't realize…"

She batted her eyelashes innocently. "Didn't realize what?"

"That you had company." He pointed to the figure on the far side of her bed.

She crossed to the door and shut it. Gabe followed his brother's gaze. The two of them stared at the form of a man, buck naked, wriggling out from under Chloe's bed.

When Ryan rose and turned around, Chloe must have seen his brothers' wide eyes and known that they'd had no idea he was there "in the flesh." She grabbed a bath towel off her dresser and tossed it across the bed to her lover.

Gabe whooped and hugged Ryan briefly. He backed away and let Jayce shake Ryan's hand.

Grinning, Ryan set his hands on his towel-covered hips and addressed his girl. "Yup. No dust bunnies under there. You passed inspection, Chloe."

All three brothers burst out laughing.

Mr. Fierro burst through Chloe's door and dropped a paper bag on her bed—he must have discovered Ryan was no longer in their home. Upon seeing his son, alive and healthy, he sighed with relief. "I knew you'd come to her first." Then he asked him, "How much does she know?"

Ryan smiled at Chloe with pride. "Everything. She knows everything."

"And she's still standing?" He grabbed Chloe up in his arms, whooped, and gave her a huge impulsive hug. Jayce was impressed when she didn't cry out or act like he was squeezing her to death. Instead, she laughed and gave as good as she got.

When he'd put her down, he strode around the bed to his recently reincarnated son and shook his hand. "Welcome back."

Mrs. Fierro appeared in the doorway, huffing and puffing. "Thanks, Antonio."

"Sorry, love. I couldn't wait to see if Ryan was really here."

His wife strode around the bed. "Neither could I. It's just that some of us don't have such long, strong legs." She winked at Chloe, who was also petite. Ryan had said more than once how impressed he was with her ability to keep up with any man.

Mama Gabriella hugged Ryan hard, and he returned the hug more gently. As they stood there, his towel fell off. Chloe closed the door while everyone laughed.

"I guess I should get dressed," Ryan said casually.

His mother passed the paper bag to Ryan and stared at Chloe, who just smiled and shrugged.

"I think she's seen it all before, Gabriella," Antonio said.

"I guess so."

Ryan unrolled the paper bag and slipped on his tighty-whities. Then he pulled the fire department T-shirt over his head. Mrs. Fierro had stacked everything in order of dressing. Mr. Fierro smiled with pride at his wonderful wife. Jayce also couldn't help noticing the loving looks Ryan was exchanging with Chloe Arish.

They were a match. Jayce would bet his beak on it—and he couldn't help being a little envious. He had played the field long enough, and there was only one woman he couldn't get out of his head. A certain FDNY firefighter named Kristine Scott.

That's when he made up his mind. He was going to take a well-earned vacation—in Manhattan.

Chapter 2

JAYCE HAD DONE A LITTLE CHECKING ON THE FIREHOUSE HE planned to visit. "Pride of Midtown" didn't even begin to cover it. This particular station had lost fifteen firefighters on 9/11. More than any other. Its firefighters were considered experts in high-rise rescues, so they had been among the first on the scene.

As for the part of the patch that said "Never missed a performance," well, what Kristine had said was true. The station was in the heart of the theater district. Jayce passed the acting school as he walked around the neighborhood. He almost missed it because it looked like a church.

But the firefighters' performances were worthy of more incredible awards than a Tony or Emmy. In one recent year they responded to more than nine thousand calls between two companies. How they managed to do that blew his mind.

He had hoped this trip would put Kristine out of his mind by seeing her again, but as just a normal woman. Unfortunately, it looked as if his plan might backfire with his respect for her already growing.

He had checked in at a nearby hotel and deposited his stuff in his room. He'd brought only enough for a week's stay, and the place was so small he could touch both walls with his arms outstretched. Suddenly, he was glad he hadn't decided to spend two weeks there. Now it was time to stop puttering around and seek out the woman he had come to visit. He didn't know if his presence would be welcome or not, but there was only one way to find out.

Bravery came in many different forms.

Fortunately, Jayce was an extrovert. He usually excelled in social situations and could charm the pants off almost any female. He hoped Kristine had forgotten about his chipper mood at Ryan's "funeral." He felt that enough time had passed and he could let his personality shine through now. She might actually enjoy him.

Hands in his pockets, Jayce stood outside the second-oldest fire station in the country. He gave his appearance a quick mental check. Hair clean and slightly tousled. Recent shave. Well-worn brown leather jacket and blue jeans with no holes or rips.

He took a deep, fortifying breath and walked past Engine 54 into the open bay. Ladder 4 was absent, so they might have been out on a call. Not knowing if Ms. Scott was assigned to the ladder, he'd just have to find out when he breezed in and asked for her.

No backing out now. A tall guy wearing an FDNY T-shirt was checking some equipment near the inside door. Jayce approached, and without waiting for him to look up, he smiled, stuck out his hand, and said, "Hi. I'm Jayce Fierro, a firefighter from Boston."

The guy faced him and shook his hand. "Hey, Jayce. I'm Lieutenant Jack Mahoney. Welcome to Hell." Jack gave him a knowing grin.

"Yeah, I'm impressed with what I've heard about the Hell's Kitchen firefighters." Then Jayce cleared his throat and got down to business. "Do you happen to know where I might find Kristine Scott?"

"Yeah. She's inside. Probably in the kitchen. It's her turn to clean up after lunch. I'd take you there, but I've got to finish this equipment check before we're called out on another job."

"Yeah, I hear that happens frequently here."

"It hasn't been too bad since the weather's warmed up. Only two or three jobs a day."

Jayce nodded, knowing how many fires were caused by poorly attended woodstoves and fireplaces. In the inner city, they even had to worry about homeless people starting small fires in or near abandoned buildings to stay warm.

"Just point me toward the kitchen, and I'll see if she's there. If nothing else, I can make myself a cup of coffee and see if it's as bad as ours."

The guy laughed. "Sure. Our kitchen is in the back on the right. Help yourself."

Jayce found the place and opened the door quietly. A redhead with a ponytail, wearing a black FDNY T-shirt, didn't turn around. He leaned against the doorjamb, arms folded casually, and watched her as she rinsed dishes and loaded the dishwasher.

Eventually, she must have felt she was being watched and whirled around to face him. Sudsy water dripped off her rubber gloves. "You!" she exclaimed, and her turquoise eyes widened.

"Hey there, Kristine." He stayed where he was and aimed his most charming grin at her.

One side of her kissable lips curled in the half smile he'd seen before—and couldn't forget no matter how hard he'd tried.

"Jayce, is it?"

"You *do* remember me."

"How could I forget? We only broke up a few months ago. So what are you doing here?"

He shrugged. "I was going to come up with something clever, like saying I wanted to get back together, but honesty is more my style. I'm on vacation this week. I thought I'd finally ask you out. Will you have lunch or dinner with me when you're free? Maybe you can recommend some sights I should see while I'm here."

She leaned against the counter and studied him for a moment. "Sure, but first I want to apologize."

"For what?"

She stared at the floor. "For being so mean to someone who had just lost a loved one." She raised her eyes. "I figured out later you were probably dealing with your grief in your own way. Maybe acting like nothing was wrong was helping you get through the day."

He smiled and nodded. "You're forgiven. And if I somehow upset you—"

"No. You didn't. A fellow firefighter's funeral is always an emotional powder keg. I think I was just caught up in all the beautiful things that were said about your brother, and the tragedy affected all of us."

"I totally get that. He was a good man." Jayce almost said "still is" but caught himself in time.

"So, that dinner... When were you thinking?" she asked as she removed the rubber gloves.

"I can probably be more flexible since all I really want to do is go to a taping of a late-night TV show I like, but it's filmed in the afternoon. What's your schedule like this week?"

"I'm coming off my rotation tonight at six, and I have

the next seventy-two hours off. I have a dentist appointment tomorrow, but after that I'm free."

"That should go well. I mean, since you floss and everything," Jayce teased.

She laughed. "Yeah. I expect a gold star on my forehead for that."

Her merriment seemed to bubble up from her toes. Jayce liked it much better than some of the cute but fake giggles of the girls he usually dated. "So, how about tonight? Where and when can I pick you up?"

"Um…"

Her hesitation began to concern him. Did she not want to give him her address? "Or we could meet at the restaurant," he added.

She smiled and seemed to relax. "Yeah. That would work better for me. There's a selection of international restaurants right here in the neighborhood. Where are you staying?"

"Not far from here."

Suddenly the tones rang out.

"Damn," she muttered. "What food do you like?"

Recognizing the need for a quick decision, he said, "Thai."

"Great." She began running toward the kitchen door. "There's a Thai place right around the corner on Ninth Avenue."

He held the door open for her. "Eight o'clock?"

"Fine," her voice called out as she disappeared around the ladder truck.

"See you there," he yelled after her.

"So, what does this 'friend' look like?" Amy Scott asked her daughter.

"I'll tell you that if you give me a hint as to what my father looks like."

Amy sighed.

"I don't know why you won't tell me a damned thing about my father." Kristine aimed an angry look at her actress mother as she got ready for her dinner out. Still not sure what the evening held, she'd just called it "dinner with a friend" instead of a date.

"We've been over this a thousand times, Kristine. You don't want to know."

Kristine stomped her foot. "Yes, I do, dammit!" She hadn't meant to start a fight, especially not as she was getting all dolled up to go out.

Her mother started straightening the items on Kristine's dresser. "You look awfully nice for a casual dinner with a friend. Little black dress. Black pumps. Gold earrings…" Her mother plucked a cologne bottle off the dresser and handed it to her daughter. "Here. I imagine you might want this too."

Kristine sighed. "I know what you're doing."

Amy gave her an innocent stare. "Oh?"

"Actually, you're doing two things at the same time. You're changing the subject, and you're trying to figure out if this is a date." She swiped the bottle out of her mother's hand. "Very clever, but it won't work."

With the perfume in her hand, Kristine muttered "Why not?" and spritzed a small amount of the light floral Victoria's Secret scent on her neck. Yes, she had visited the store Jayce had suggested but walked out with only the fragrance.

Her mother gave her a sly smile. "Where did you meet him?"

"That's it. No more changing the subject! It may have worked when I was little, but it won't work now. Tell me about my father. Something. Anything!"

Her mother heaved a deep dramatic sigh. Always the actress.

"We've had this argument for a decade! I know you feel you have a right to know, but don't I have a right to keep my private life private?"

Kristine snorted, and a tiny curl of smoke escaped her nostril.

"Please try not to be angry with me. After all, it's 'you and me against the world…'" Amy sang the opening lines to a song they used to sing together when Kristine was growing up. Her mother's professionally trained soprano voice was as pitch-perfect as ever.

"Mom. Just stop it. My theories might be worse than the truth. For instance, were you raped?"

Amy gasped and slapped her hand over her heart. "Absolutely not!"

"Well, good. There's one worry out of the way."

"Honestly, Kristine, you need to just give it up. Any knowledge about him won't do you any good anyway."

"How do you know?"

Amy tossed her hands in the air. "I just do."

"Mother! That's the parental equivalent of 'because I said so.' I'm an adult, dammit. Stop treating me like a child who can't handle the truth. I want to know something, no matter how ugly."

"Well, I wasn't raped."

Kristine had just about had it with this stupid

argument. She was fuming—literally. If she didn't calm down, she'd probably greet Jayce with skin so heated, it would radiate right through his jacket, *and that wouldn't be suspicious at all*. She grabbed her purse and sweater and marched to the front door of the apartment.

Amy followed slowly, looking dejected. That sad face was just more acting. Kristine was sure of it, so she shot her mother a parting glare and slammed the door on her way out.

She tried calming down by walking around her neighborhood for a bit. She'd lived here ever since she could remember, although she had been born in a hospital on Long Island. Why there? She didn't know. Of course, her mother wouldn't answer that question either.

Try as she might, staying angry with her mother was difficult. The woman had worked as a waitress and taken acting gigs on Broadway any time she could get a bit part. Kristine had to admire her. She had never been made to feel like she was getting in the way of her mother's dream of acting, even though she may have been. The widow who lived in the apartment next door was a nice person and had watched Kristine when her mom had to work. Kristine was always taken care of.

She had essentially been a good kid. She came home from school on time, did her homework, and tried not to give her mother too much to worry about. Of course, it helped that Amy knew her dragon daughter was strong and fireproof with heightened senses and could protect herself. Theirs had always been a solid relationship. Kristine had only one problem with the whole arrangement—two, actually. Who the heck was her father, and was he partly responsible for her secret abilities?

Did he even know about her? Since she'd had to form her own theories, she had to assume he probably didn't. Was he still alive? When her mom said it wouldn't matter now anyway, that made Kristine think he had probably died.

She had to stop thinking about it. Otherwise she'd never calm down enough to meet Jayce for dinner. Maybe this was a mistake, but since three days were all they had, she didn't think there was much danger of getting overly involved with the handsome Bostonian. And she needed a fling—badly. It had been a long time since she'd been with a guy. Actors were a worse relationship choice than firefighters, so the local options were slim.

She took a couple of deep cleansing breaths and forced herself to get out of her own head and look around. At almost eight at night, restaurants were well lit and plenty safe simply because of the number of people out and about. The continuous noise of traffic was like the city's heartbeat. It always reminded her how alive Manhattan was. The occasional blast of a horn or siren was like that live entity letting out a shout.

The laughter of people exiting a bar lightened her mood. Maybe she'd be laughing in a few minutes too. Jayce Fierro was a charming guy with a good sense of humor. She might not know him well, but she'd been able to glean that much already. She was looking forward to spending some time with him.

At last she felt human enough to go meet her…date? Whatever this was, she wasn't going to worry about it. She vowed to simply have a good time and let whatever happened happen. She dodged pedestrians and made her way to the Thai restaurant, hoping Jayce would be there. The very last thing she needed tonight was to be stood up.

Happily, she saw him leaning against the building, watching the people across the street. Sometimes she engaged in people watching too. One of her silly enjoyable pastimes was to sit at her favorite café that had windows at ground level and check out people's shoes as she sipped her latte.

Tonight Jayce was wearing boots. Nice ones. Not the shit-kickers most firefighters wore even on their days off. And though he still wore jeans, with his hands in his pockets, she could see he had paired a dark-gray wool blazer with a white dress shirt. Good. He seemed to be treating this as a date too.

She sighed in relief, knowing she wasn't overdressed.

He turned as if he sensed her gaze on him. His dark eyebrows arched, and a smile lit up his handsome face. If his reaction was any indication, he liked what he saw too.

"Well, hello," he greeted her. "You look…gorgeous!"

Kristine laughed. Even if he didn't mean a word of it, she was thrilled to receive a positive review. Boy, did she need a compliment! Fortunately, he seemed sincere.

"You're not too shabby either," she said, smiling.

He swooped in, gave her a kiss on the cheek, and extended his elbow as if he were escorting her to a fancy function, not just taking her on a…possible date. Probable date. *Oh hell. Just call it a date and be done with it, Kristine.*

"I didn't know the name of the place, but I did some reconnaissance and made reservations."

"I'm sorry. I should have given you the name."

"No apologies necessary. I didn't have any particular plans, and walking around aimlessly is one of my favorite things to do."

She laughed again. "Aimlessly, huh?"

"Sure. You know. Go where the mood takes you." He held the door for her. "Sometimes I find awesome things I'd never have discovered if I'd stuck to a plan."

"I think that's called serendipity." She passed him and entered the restaurant.

"Good to know. I've been calling it dumb luck." Leaning close to her, he whispered, "Maybe meeting you was a kind of serendipity."

His velvety voice and warm breath on her ear created an instant sensation she hadn't felt in a long time—damp panties. *Whoa.* She almost groaned as she remembered she had worn her satin granny panties. She figured it could be a joke if he ever got that far; meanwhile she'd be in no danger of showing panty lines in her figure-hugging dress.

He escorted her to the hostess and gave his name. She wondered how he had gotten such an unusual name and filed the question away to ask in case their conversation stalled. Somehow she doubted it would.

When they were shown to their seats, he pulled out the chair for her, and when she was seated, he helped push her in. Kristine wondered where that totally unnecessary action had come from. In olden times, had furniture been so heavy and females so frail that it took a gentleman to be sure they made it to the table?

Regardless of the stupidity of some customs, his good manners were greatly appreciated. At work, Kristine wasn't exactly treated like "one of the guys," but they had no problem using the most vile profanity in front of her or letting a door slam instead of holding it for her. It was nice to be treated respectfully, like a classy woman, for a change.

Jayce leaned forward. "You really do look beautiful tonight."

She felt a blush warm her cheeks, but it wasn't due to the dragon within. She was unsure how to answer multiple compliments. "Thank you" seemed like the right response, but it could become redundant around a guy like Jayce.

"I used to work here after school a few years ago," she said to change the subject. "The place has classed itself up, but the menu is about the same. Do you know what you want, or should I make a few recommendations?"

———

Jayce knew what he wanted, all right, but it wasn't on the menu. At least not the menu in his hands. He closed the long tablet. "Why don't you order for both of us?"

"Are you sure? I mean, what if you don't like something in it or if it's too spicy?"

"Don't worry about it. I love anything hot and spicy." He winked at her and then almost groaned aloud. *Try not to be too obvious, Fierro.* He cleared his throat and added, "If it doesn't walk off my plate, I'll eat it, and I'm sure I'll like it."

She chuckled. "And if it does walk off your plate?"

"I'll take a video and post it on Facebook."

She laughed aloud. He really did love that throaty sound and the way her smile almost split her face. Even at rest, her sensuous mouth was wide and her full lips were…kissable. *Very* kissable.

A waiter appeared, and Kristine ordered a bottle of wine as well as their dinners. She'd picked choices with three chili peppers next to them on the menu. He quirked a half smile. If she was testing his honesty, she was about to find out how much a firebird loved its food hot. Fortunately she could stand the heat too, or she wouldn't have ordered it.

Another waiter appeared with a pitcher of ice water and filled their glasses. They smiled at each other, as if both were wondering who would reach for the water first during dinner.

Jayce wasn't as competitive as some of his brothers. Maybe because as the biggest, he was assumed to be the best. Ryan was especially competitive, but that may have been due to their messed-up family dynamics.

Ryan was actually the oldest—until he'd met with a near-fatal accident at the age of seven. Jayce had been only five, but after witnessing the family secret in action that day, the image was burned into his brain. Literally. Mommy and Daddy quickly explained what was going to happen and dumped lighter fluid on his big brother— then lit him up. Ryan didn't yell or scream. He just sort of went to sleep, and they watched until there was nothing but a pile of ash left. Then the ashes stirred…and the brilliant phoenix arose.

Jayce startled himself out of his reverie. Hopefully Kristine didn't notice that he'd gone elsewhere for a few moments.

"What were you just thinking about?"

Shit, she noticed. "I was wondering if you have a boyfriend." *Good save, Fierro.* He'd wanted to know that anyway.

Her smile began to appear, and then she schooled it quickly. "Not at this time, no. You?"

"No. I don't have a boyfriend either…or a girlfriend," he teased. The truth was that no one compared to her in his mind. He was well aware he came off as a player. That didn't quite match the reality. He simply couldn't find an open-minded lover with the right chemistry whom he could trust completely. He liked the clean slate he had with an out-of-towner like Kristine.

She tipped her head. "You're single? How can that be? You're handsome, charming, have a heroic job… I don't get it."

He shrugged. "I've done my fair share of casual dating. What can I say? I'm picky." He hoped she'd be satisfied with that answer and realize he was complimenting her at the same time. "What about you? A gorgeous woman with a sense of humor? How are you still single?"

"Well, I can't say I've done a lot of dating…casual or otherwise. I'm not seen the same way you are, being a female in an almost all-male profession. Some men think I'm gay. Some think I'm an overzealous feminist with something to prove, and that's threatening to them."

"Well, then some men are stupid."

She laughed. "Tell me about it." Then she sat up straight. "But not all men are like that."

He'd let it slide. There was plenty of time to find out if she had some kind of deep-seated resentment toward men—later. "So, did you ever have a long-term relationship that didn't work out?"

"How did you guess?"

He shrugged. "Like I said, you're incredible. I imagine guys hit on you all the time."

"Ha. You imagine wrong."

That was good news as far as Jayce was concerned. Then he caught himself wondering why. This trip was supposed to burst his bubble. Make him not want her like he did. Unfortunately, his plan was backfiring big time. He wanted her more than ever.

"So…tell me about the one who got away," he said.

She took a deep breath, then seemed to relax and compose herself. "You were right about a sense of humor being important to me. I dated a comedian for a few years, and that's what attracted me to him in the first place. He wasn't especially good-looking. Shortly after I moved in, he moved on."

"Oh? Did he go to LA or Vegas?"

"No. He moved on to a blonde."

"Ouch!"

"I guess you don't approve," she said.

If he wasn't mistaken, there was a hint of hope in her voice. Being as honest as he could, he held her gaze. "No. I don't. That's why I don't get into relationships unless I'm sure—"

Her eyes widened. "Sure of what?"

Oh shit. What could he say? Sure that the woman of his dreams wouldn't freak out when he revealed his supernatural status? He was saved by the waiter bringing their bottle of wine.

~~~

The rest of the dinner went well. In fact, Kristine was surprised by how well it was going. She hadn't dated a guy like Jayce in a long time. Their connection seemed to be almost instantaneous. It was just too bad he was a firefighter—and lived three hours away as the Acela train flies. Actually, a quick plane ride would reduce the commute to only an hour and a half, but the hassle and time it took to go through security would make the trip even longer.

Walking down the wide sidewalks of Times Square, hand in hand, sure made her feel as if the trip might be worth the hassle. His hand was warm and rough. For once she wasn't concerned that hers were the same way. No hand cream could stand up to a firefighter's routine. Wet gloves, rough weather, unbearable heat... All of that detracted from the soft, supple skin she longed for.

They had decided over dinner to visit the top of the Empire State Building. Jayce had never been there before, and Kristine had only visited with friends—never a date. It was supposed to be romantic. She'd never understood why. Probably because her cynical ex-boyfriend thought it was hokey. As she glanced over at Jayce, he glanced back, and they smiled. One thing she wasn't seeing in him was a city dweller's pessimism. Its absence was a refreshing change.

Eventually, they arrived at their destination, and as luck—or the stars aligning at the right moment—would have it, they stepped into an elevator with no one right behind them. The doors whooshed closed while they were still alone.

She spun toward Jayce with a hand over her mouth. "I guess that wasn't very nice of me. I probably should have waited."

He stepped right into her space. "I'm glad you didn't."

As the elevator began to ascend, he leaned in and captured her mouth with his firm lips. She looped her arms around his neck, and he pulled her close. She immediately opened her mouth, and their tongues found each other and swirled together. Kristine wasn't at all sure her light-headed feeling was due to the elevator traveling so fast. Unfortunately, she felt as if she were falling instead.

Don't think about it. Whatever happens happens... She seemed to have found a new mantra. She heard the ding of the elevator doors opening, and they were greeted by chuckles and a wolf whistle.

"Yeah, yeah..." Jayce said, but he was grinning and holding Kristine's hand as they made their way off the elevator.

When they spotted a space at the building's edge that was fairly deserted, they walked over to it with no hesitation.

"You're not afraid of heights, I guess..." Jayce said to her.

She laughed. "I'd be in deep trouble if I were." Not only was she a firefighter in a company that specialized in high-rises, but she was a full-fledged, fire-breathing, wing-soaring dragon. She could hover at this height and enjoy the view.

Speaking of enjoying the view...

Jayce turned his back on the dazzling city lights and kissed her knuckles as he stared into her eyes. She felt as if her insides were melting. A deep shimmer in his eyes must have been reflecting the lights. Or not. His eyes seemed to glow for a moment, and then he quickly turned back toward the city.

She took her first good look at the city lights as well. *Dear Lord.* At last she realized why people thought this place was romantic. At night, so many lights against the velvet black sky were more beautiful than Christmas. Some even seemed to twinkle like stars. Below, white headlights and red taillights trailed through the landscape, but the sounds of the city were far away.

A chilly breeze ruffled her hair. Jayce enveloped her in a side hug. If she felt a chill, it was forgotten in favor of his warm, strong body alongside hers. Everywhere they touched, merging heat radiated through her. *Wow*. How she'd missed this! Or had she ever had this feeling?

Good Lord, Kristine… Get ahold of yourself!

"So, Jayce… What do you think of the view from up here?"

He turned her toward him and said, "I think the view right in front of me is as beautiful as it gets." Leaning in, he delivered another toe-curling kiss, and she realized she was a goner.

Chapter 3

JAYCE WASN'T SURPRISED HIS COCK WAS HARD AND straining his zipper. That happened whenever she smiled at him. But this feeling—this instinct to mate—was almost overwhelming.

He didn't want to scare her, and if he wasn't careful, he might. A stray lock of strawberry-blonde hair was blowing across her eyes. He reached out and tucked it behind her ear. Instead of leaning away and fixing her hair herself, she actually leaned into him.

Was he getting the go-ahead signal? Since when had he ever had trouble figuring out what a woman wanted? Some girls gave mixed signals, but he didn't think she was doing that. For whatever reason, he sensed she was as ready to go to the next level as he was.

There was only one way to tell. He held her gaze and let her know how he felt. "I don't want this night to end."

"Neither do I," she said breathlessly.

Leaning close to her ear, he whispered, "It doesn't have to."

She turned her face toward the city and chewed her lip, as if trying to make up her mind. He waited as patiently as he could.

At last she said, "I live with my mother."

"And I have the tiniest hotel room ever built," he said, trying to lighten the mood and take the pressure off. She chuckled as he'd hoped she would, but he wanted to make sure she didn't think he was trying to discourage her. "But…I think I can squeeze you in, if you want to spend the night together."

"I—" She took a deep breath and let it out with a whoosh. Her gaze dropped to her toes. "I really shouldn't."

He made an effort to keep his disappointment from showing. "I understand. You barely know me. There's the distance—"

"No. It's none of that."

When she didn't elaborate, he told himself to back off. To not pressure her. If she wasn't ready, she wasn't ready. But he could have sworn…

"I should tell you that I made a vow."

Shock rippled through him. "You're a firefighter and a nun?"

She belted out a laugh. "God, no! I just meant that I vowed not to sleep with firefighters."

"Oh." He chuckled at himself. "I see. And why is that?"

"For one thing, living and working together is stress-ful enough. Add in spending our spare time together, and there's no separation at all. If we ever had a fight, it could not only affect our cooperation with each other, but could make our coworkers uncomfortable. Considering what we do, staying on good terms with everyone is highly recommended."

"All good points. But I don't hear anything that applies to the two of us. We'd never end up in the same firehouse or even on the same job in a city-wide disaster."

"I know, and that's the only reason I'm consider-ing…" She gazed out at the city again.

Waiting for her to make a decision was killing him. He was just about to say "Never mind, there's no hurry," when she grabbed his face and took a deep breath.

"Okay, yes. But I might only go part of the way, and I can't stay all night."

"Good enough." Without another word, they grasped each other's hands and headed for the elevator.

Jayce wanted her badly, but he was also having some niggling second thoughts. He pretty much stayed out of relationships, but he wasn't a love-'em-and-leave-'em kind of guy either. He glanced over at her a couple of times, and she looked up at him shyly. Maybe "part of the way," as she put it, was a wise decision.

He was tempted to offer to wait, but his body wanted to slap him just for thinking it. Why this girl made him want her so much he couldn't fathom. There were women who could rival her in the looks department, but that wasn't the deciding factor. He'd dated models and a couple of beauty queens, so if looks were all he needed, he could have proposed to any of them.

No, there was also the absolute need to find an open-minded woman he could trust, who would trust him completely in return.

By the time they reached his hotel room, he was good and confused. And yet she seemed to have convinced herself to go full speed ahead. She was yanking his shirt out of his jeans and pushing his jacket off his shoulder at the same time. Her anxiety made him chuckle, but he wondered if she was trying to get it done before she could talk herself out of it.

"Relax, Kris. There's no need to rush."

"Oh. I thought you wanted this."

"I do. Don't get me wrong. I do...very much. But I don't want you to feel pressured or hurried."

"Am I hurrying too much?" Her expression said she was taking this the wrong way.

He grabbed her elbow and led her to the bed two steps away. "No. But sit down."

She remained standing and crossed her arms. "If you're going to say you've changed your mind, do it now. I don't need to hear any fancy explanations. If you're just not into me, you're not into me."

"Huh? I *am* into you." He smiled and then winked. "Or I will be, if you'll give me a chance."

"Oh...*oh*! You, um, need a few minutes?"

"What? No." He laughed. "I'm good to go. I'm just making sure that this is what you want."

"For fuck's sake..." she said under her breath.

Obviously she didn't know what to think of his gallantry. Maybe she'd never experienced a man being considerate before. He didn't want her to get the wrong idea and think he was backing out. Far from it. At last, he tackled her and pulled her down on top of him.

She came up laughing. "Women aren't the only ones who give mixed signals."

"I guess not. I'm sorry." He rolled her onto her back and loomed over her. "I'm very into you. Maybe so much that I got a little scared."

Her brows shot up. "I've never heard that one before."

"Because it's not a line." Before she could comment on his embarrassing burst of honesty, he dipped his head and devoured her mouth. She returned his passion, and they rolled across the bed. As the heat built, he needed to get his clothes off. He should never have stopped her as they were entering the room.

He reached behind her back and lowered the dress's zipper. Slipping it off one shoulder revealed a pretty lavender lace bra. Maybe she had been joking about the granny panties.

Getting the rest of the dress off her was a bit of a trick. She seemed fine letting him remove the dress from the other shoulder and pop her bra open, but that's where her cooperation ended. She didn't lift her bottom, so he couldn't pull the dress down and off. He couldn't yank it up over her head either. He tried to slip his hand inside, and she batted it away.

Fine. He'd lavish attention on her breasts until she was ready to move forward. As he suckled, she moaned and arched into him. There was no question in his mind that she was enjoying this.

Finally, it occurred to him what the problem might be. He rose up on his elbows and stared down at her. "Kristine, are you wearing granny panties?"

"Um…" A blush stained her chest and worked its way up to her cheeks. "Yes."

Jayce leaned back and laughed. "Oh, honey. You don't have to worry about that. I was just giving you a hard time that day in Boston. It was just part of the fun."

"Really? You don't mind?"

"It's certainly not a deal breaker. I like you too much."

"Well, that's a relief, because I like you too."

"I propose that we give this long-distance thing a try. After all, it might work out, but we'll never know unless we give it a shot."

"I accept your proposal." She immediately broke eye contact and blushed.

—⁓—

Later Kristine practically floated into her apartment after her date.

On the lookout for her mother, she crept to the bathroom. She didn't want to go into details, and her mother would have grilled her. She just wanted to bask in the glow of adoration for a little while. It had been a long, long time since any man had treated her this well. She knew the high wouldn't last, but by God, she was going to enjoy it while it did.

Her mother must have gone to bed early. She never went to bed before eleven, and she usually read for a while. It was after midnight when Kristine tucked herself in and turned out the light without waking her. At that point, she'd considered her night a complete triumph.

Would he really call her today like he said he would? Or was it a one-night stand? She'd given him her landline number just in case her mobile phone's battery died.

Crap. Now she'd obsess about it all day. Oh well, at least she had a dentist appointment to take her mind off him. She mentally rolled her eyes at herself. Yeah, right. Like anything would get her to stop thinking about Jayce Fierro.

On her way to the dentist, her phone rang. It was only 9:30 in the morning. It couldn't be him. It must be her mother, wanting to interrogate her over the phone since she didn't get a chance to do it in person.

Well, she couldn't avoid her mom forever. She dug her cell phone out of her jacket pocket. Her phone had its own case with the absolute necessities in it: credit card, cabbie cash, and a spot to tuck business cards if she was ever offered one. It took her a minute to answer, and she was almost to the subway. That gave her the perfect excuse to cut the call short.

"Hey, Mom—"

"Mom?" asked a sexy male voice on the other side of the line. "I've been called a lot of things, but never 'Mom.'"

Oh my God! It's Jayce. She giggled as she realized her mistake. "I—uh…I thought…"

He laughed as a combination of relief and mortification washed over her.

"I'm pretty sure I know what you thought. Don't worry about it. Your cell phone probably didn't recognize my number. I'll have to program it in when I see you again."

He wants to see me again. Yay!

"I know you have a dentist appointment, but I was wondering if you were free for lunch. We can get sticky buns and destroy all your hygienist's hard work."

She loved his sense of humor. Just the right amount of irreverence. "I'm going to tell her you said that."

"And get me in trouble with the ADA? You wouldn't."

"Yeah, you're right. You're probably already walking a fine line with them for not flossing."

"So where and when do you want to meet?"

She wanted to say "Right here, right now," but that would sound desperate. "How about if I call you when I'm done?"

"That works."

"Same number you just called me with?"

"Yup. Or I could just go with you…"

"Huh?" *Now who's sounding desperate?*

"Turn around."

Kristine halted and whirled around. Another pedestrian on his cell phone almost walked right into her. He mumbled some profanity, then swerved around her. About twenty feet behind him a familiar tall, dark, and smirking guy sauntered up to her.

"Were you following me?"

"Nope. I was heading toward the TV studio and recognized you as you were crossing the street two blocks back."

She didn't know how to feel about this "coincidence." If he had been following her around, that would be a little creepy.

He gave her a quick kiss on the cheek. "I figured I'd see if I could get two tickets."

They resumed walking at the city clip they both seemed used to. The explanation sounded reasonable. But… "Why didn't you just call and ask them?"

"I did. They said first come, first served. I was going to call you when I got there and ask if you were interested. Then I saw you and thought I'd have a bit of fun."

"You're all about having fun, aren't you?" She didn't mean to sound so judgmental.

He shrugged. "Firefighters work hard, so we should play hard too. The more fun we can have during our time off, the better."

"Like what we did last night? That kind of fun?"

"Ha! I wasn't talking about that. Like I said, I'm picky."

She was relieved to hear he wasn't bed-hopping. "So, what else do you do for fun?"

"I own a fishing boat. My brothers and some of the guys I work with enjoy fishing. We don't go after the big fish. We're not equipped to land swordfish or tuna or anything like that…mostly mackerel, but there's nothing like being on the water on a nice summer day."

The subway entrance loomed ahead. "I'm getting on the subway here," Kristine said.

He slipped his arm around her waist and swooped in for another kiss…this one a toe-curling, tongue-seeking, hot lip-lock.

"Whew." She stepped back and shook her head to clear the daze. "I'll tell my hygienist to hurry."

Jayce was glad he went early to pick up the tickets. They were almost out. Kristine had called to say she wanted to stop at home before going for sticky buns—or possibly a salad.

His phone rang, and he was happy to hear the ringtone he had already programmed in for Kristine: "Too Hot."

"Hey, hot stuff. You ready?"

"Um… Actually I have to cancel. I'm really sorry."

What? "Cancel? Did I freak you out this morning? Running into you really was a coincidence."

"Oh, yeah. I know that."

But maybe she didn't believe it. Rather than jumping to conclusions, he asked, "Then why?"

"I—it's my mother."

"Is she sick?"

"I can't talk right now."

"Okay. I can tell something has you upset. I'm here for you if you need me."

"Maybe it would be better if you just spend the rest of your vacation doing the tourist thing. Then just go home and forget about me. We knew a long-distance relationship wouldn't work anyway—"

"Whoa. You're not making sense. We agreed to try it. Something is very wrong. Tell me what's going on."

"I can't." Her voice wobbled. Then the call disconnected.

"Shit!" He cursed out loud and then glanced at the pedestrians within earshot. No one even blinked.

How could he pretend he hadn't heard the desperation in her voice? He'd go to her apartment and demand to know what had her so spooked—but he didn't know where she lived. He didn't want to ask her firefighter buddies in case she already thought he was a stalker. He tried the Internet, hoping some information might lead him in the right direction. There was nothing. What the hell could he do?

A little rule-breaking might be in order.

He jogged to a nearby parking garage and made sure he wasn't being observed and there were no cameras to record his actions. Then he stripped, stashed his clothes behind a large cardboard box, and shifted into his phoenix form. His tail feathers were too colorful to be ignored, even in New York, so he found a pile of dirt and rolled in it. Fortunately, if he needed to refresh his camouflage, there was no shortage of it.

Now that he was less ostentatious, he flew to the Hell's Kitchen firehouse. Kristine lived somewhere in the area. He could scope out the neighborhood from above, hoping to spot his beautiful redheaded firefighter coming out of an apartment building. If nothing else, she was due back to work in a couple of days.

A couple of days. If he had been able to groan in phoenix form, he would have. He'd age like a regular bird. Three days in a bird's life was approximately one year in a human's. However, with a lot of flying, the aging process ramped up even more. At the moment, he was willing to age two or more years if it took all week to find her. Something was drastically wrong, and he had to know what was frightening her.

He flapped his powerful wings, gliding on the wind. He only hoped that when he finally found her, he wasn't too late.

Kristine lowered herself onto the couch with a thud. How long had that note been on the floor? She tried to remember the last time she saw her mother. Had she knocked the paper off the sofa table when she tossed her clutch there?

"I was getting ready for my date last night, and she seemed fine then," Kristine mumbled. "I was gone for about five hours…"

Remembering how she'd thought she was lucky to have dodged her mother's questions around midnight, she wondered if her mother had even been in the apartment. Right now she'd give anything to see her mother—even if she wanted to know every last detail of her date.

Kristine focused on the note in her shaking hand.

We have your mother. Do not call the police. Your mother will be okay as long as you don't do anything stupid. We don't want your money. Just a favor only you can do. Wait for our call.

Had they already called while she was out at the dentist—or flirting with her new boyfriend? Would they think she was being uncooperative, not answering the landline when they called or, worse, doing something "stupid" like having the police set up recording equipment and wiretaps?

"Oh God!" Kristine dropped her head in her hands and began to cry. "I don't know what to do."

Suddenly the phone rang. She grabbed the receiver sitting next to her and said a rushed "Hello."

"Are you alone?" a male voice asked. She suspected the caller was speaking through one of those voice modulators.

"Yes," she answered.

The voice, sounding like it was coming from underwater, asked, "Have you called anyone? Spoken to anyone?"

"No."

"Are you sure? The line was busy a few minutes ago."

"I had to cancel an appointment."

"So you did talk to someone. You lied."

"No! I didn't mean to lie. I just thought it wasn't important. I didn't say anything about the note to anybody. I swear."

The phone call ended abruptly.

Her hand flew to her mouth. *What have I done? What if I just caused them to hurt my mother?*

She was worried enough already. If she knew Amy Scott, she'd be wailing and throwing herself on the floor. Icy chills traveled down her spine as she realized no kidnappers would put up with that. Her mother must be bound and gagged.

Kristine wanted to wail and throw herself on the floor too. But she had to keep it together.

The phone rang again. She grabbed it.

"Did you learn your lesson?" the odd voice asked.

"You'd better not have hurt my mother!"

"She's still alive. Not happy at the moment, but alive."

Dear God. If she's giving them a lot of drama, Lord knows what they'll do to her. "Let me talk to her," Kristine demanded.

"Certainly. After you've done what we ask you to do, you can talk to her all you like."

She wanted to yell "No. Now!" But she took a deep breath and tried to sound logical. "How do I even know you have her?"

"You don't."

"Then why should I do…whatever it is you want me to do? What is it, by the way?"

"As a firefighter, you have access to many businesses in the area."

She had a sinking feeling but didn't dare lie again. "Yeah…"

"We simply need you to retrieve something from one office building after hours."

"I could lose my job!"

"Or you could lose your mother. Your choice."

Dear Lord… "You know it's not going to be easy to do that without getting caught, right? Most places have cameras."

"Well, that's where your special skills come into play. We not only know who you are, we know *what* you are," he said in an ominous tone.

His implication stopped her words in her throat. Was

he talking about her being a dragon shifter? How could he possibly know that?

"I—uh…I don't know what you're referring to."

"Smart girl. You didn't try to deny that you're fairly unique. Not exactly one of a kind, but probably one of a tiny handful—your mother being one too."

Oh crap. He knows our secret, but how? Her mother was the one who impressed upon her the need to keep their supernatural natures absolutely private. She wouldn't have told anyone—unless maybe under torture…

"I demand to speak to my mother. Right fuckin' now!"

"Oh, you want Mommy's permission to talk about your powers?"

"Kind of, yeah."

"Okay. We'll put her on the phone, but only for a second. Not long enough to exchange any secret signals or anything."

Secret signals? "What does that mean? We don't have any secret signals."

"That's good. You won't be chatting long enough to use them anyway."

Kristine had heard of family members who'd picked a code word to indicate they were in trouble and to follow certain previously agreed-upon instructions. Such tactics were usually used with little kids. Right now she wished she and her mother had some kind of code in place. They'd have to set something up later, *if* her mother came home.

"Honey?" Her mother's voice came over the phone.

"Mom? Are you all right?"

"I'm okay," she said, her voice trembling. "Do whatever they say. I'm afraid they'll—"

Then the monster who had her mother came back on the phone. "See? She's okay…for now. We're watching your place. If we see cops or any kind of monitoring equipment entering the building, she's toast."

"But what if they're here for someone else? There are a dozen apartments in the building!"

"Not my problem." He ended the call.

Kristine slid to the floor and cried her eyes out.

Chapter 4

JAYCE HAD SPENT THE BETTER PART OF THE DAY FLYING OVER and searching Hell's Kitchen. His vision was sharp, even at night, and he had no plans to quit. The only reason he'd have to pause, and only briefly, would be to grab a bite to eat. Rat wasn't his favorite meal, but he'd spotted some scurrying down a side street. Hopefully he wouldn't have to resort to that.

As he was thinking about his empty stomach, he caught a break. Kristine exited a building on Eleventh Avenue. It wasn't a pretty area, but it was certainly convenient to the places she and her mother frequented. Kristine had told him that her mother was now an acting coach at an acting school on Ninth Avenue. Kristine was a firefighter on Eighth. Did her mother need her rent that badly?

As he followed Kristine from above, he thought about how her neighborhood compared to his refurbished condo in gentrified Charlestown. It was on the river, and even though it was a ground-floor unit, he had access to a deck and a great view. He could walk to his firehouse on Beacon Hill. Granted, it was a longer walk than hers…

Speaking of walking, where was she going?

She was making impressive progress, walking at a good clip and heading toward Times Square. Then she cut over to Madison Avenue. Stopping in front of a tall building that could house anything from businesses to apartments, probably both, she eyed it carefully.

She also peered up and down the street, searching for who knows what. Then she walked around the nearest corner and eventually studied the same block from the back. *What could she be looking for?*

Jayce continued to circle high above her but not high enough to escape notice. Through a ninth-story window, someone pointed to him and ran off for a moment, only to reappear with binoculars. He flew higher and checked his tail feathers in another window. Sure enough, the dirt was mostly gone, and his bright-yellow and red tail feathers were peeking through.

He headed for the roof and found some grime to roll around in. Hoping he hadn't lost Kristine, he hopped onto the edge and peered over. She seemed to be heading home.

Now that he knew which building was hers, he could shift quickly, redress, and hopefully find an apartment labeled "Scott." Although, if her mother was an actress, she might not go by her real name. He'd just have to follow Kristine as closely as he could without getting caught. Maybe a light would go on in one of the units and he'd spot her inside.

He knew he was grasping at straws, but at this point he'd do whatever it took to locate her place and get her to let him in. Then he landed near the cardboard box where he'd left his clothes…only there was no cardboard box. Or clothes!

Shit!

～∿～

Kristine had returned to her apartment and was beginning to cook dinner by rote habit. She wasn't particularly hungry. As she ruminated over her mother's and her situation for the hundredth time, a knock at her door interrupted her thoughts. "Who the hell could that be?" she muttered.

Realizing it must be a neighbor since no one buzzed from the outside, she wiped her hands on a towel and strolled to the peephole. When she saw Jayce standing there, she almost dropped the towel.

How did he… Mixed feelings swamped her. On the one hand she was angry he hadn't listened to her and left her alone to deal with her problems. On the other hand, she was *glad* he hadn't listened and badly needed him to hold her and tell her everything would be all right.

After a few seconds of hesitation, she opened the door. He probably wouldn't go away if she didn't at least talk to him. Just as she was about to ask him what he was doing there, she took a good look at him and gasped. He was wearing a pink sweat suit several sizes too small. His face was smudged with dirt, and his hair stood on end. "What happened to you?"

He glanced down at himself and casually asked, "What? You don't like my new look?"

She grabbed his arm and yanked him toward her. "Get inside before anyone sees you." After slamming the door shut, she stared at him.

He looked like he was trying to suppress a smile. "I was going to tell you I lost a bet, but I really do want to be honest with you. I had a slight accident."

"An accident?" Her anger fled, quickly replaced by concern. "Are you all right?"

"I'm fine. But I was worried about you and may have been distracted. Are *you* all right?"

"Yeah. I—I'm fine."

"Sure you are…" His sarcasm was hard to miss.

As she was about to argue, her phone rang. This time it was her cell phone. "Hello."

The underwater voice said, "I trust you came up with a plan…" Her mother must have given them her cell phone number. Maybe that was a good thing and meant her mother was still alive.

How the hell did they know I was finished scoping out the place? Oh yeah…They're watching me. She glanced at Jayce, took a deep fortifying breath, and willed herself to stay calm. "It's possible, but it's not going to be easy."

"If it were easy, we'd do it ourselves."

How could she make them understand how tricky it would be? "Look, by 'not easy,' I mean there are many, many things that could go wrong."

"Like?"

Shit. How could she talk to them without Jayce figuring out what was going on? Her hesitation left her caller to fill in the blanks.

"Are you thinking you might be seen by people or by cameras?"

"Uh—both, and if anyone is carrying a phone—"

"But there are no security cameras on or pointed at the building?"

"N—not that I could see…"

Jayce tipped his head, and she knew he was listening to her side of the conversation. Before he could overhear the other voice, she strode away and put the couch between them.

"You sound nervous. Is anyone else there?"

"No!"

"I don't believe you. Hang up. I'll call back on Skype and have you pan the room."

"Ah. Okay…" She disconnected the call and told Jayce in a hurried voice, "You have to leave."

"No. Not until you tell me what's going on."

Her phone rang again, only this time it was the Skype tone. *Shit.* "Hide!"

He ducked behind the couch.

"Stay right there. Whatever you do, don't move," she said.

"Hello," she said to a black screen. The caller must have placed tape over the camera on the other end. "If you can see me, then I should be able to see you."

"We're calling the shots. Now walk around the room with the camera facing out to prove you're alone."

Doing as she was told, she panned the room from her vantage point.

The monster still wasn't satisfied. "Move around. I want to see the *whole* place."

"You want to see the whole room?" She took a deep breath, hoping Jayce would race to the bedroom. He didn't, so she began walking around the room, avoiding the back of the couch.

When she had finished, the caller growled. "That's not the whole place. Let me see behind the furniture and in the kitchen. Under tables. Under beds. In closets…"

"Yeah, fine." She turned toward the kitchen, hoping to get there without revealing the hiding spot behind the couch. She glanced back over her shoulder and was surprised to see a pile of pink clothes on the floor behind the couch *but no Jayce*.

She panned behind the couch and headed to the kitchen.

"I guess you're a slob, leaving your clothes on the floor like that." He laughed. Heard through the voice modulator, his laugh sounded absolutely evil.

"I was getting the laundry together," she said, wondering the whole time where Jayce had gone and realizing he was now naked. Did he strip, go to her bedroom, and try to find something that fit? How? He didn't have time. She was just relieved she hadn't exposed her man to the asshole who had her mother.

Since when had she begun thinking of him as *her* man?

After she toured the kitchen, she had to show the caller the bathroom, pull back the shower curtain, open the linen closet, and finally expose the bedrooms— including the closets and under the beds. *Where the heck did Jayce go?*

"Okay. I guess *maybe* you're alone. Now go back to the living room and point the camera at the door. I want to make sure no one tries to sneak in or out."

When she returned to the living room, the pile of pink clothes were still on the floor, but they looked as though they stirred slightly. *What the heck?*

Jayce tried not to move a feather under the pink sweat suit now that Kristine was back in the living room. With his supernatural hearing, he was able to follow both sides of the conversation. Piecing things together, he figured that somebody had something precious to her, or she'd never agree to do whatever risky thing she was being asked to do.

This afternoon she had said something about her mother needing her. Did her mother's well-being depend upon Kristine carrying out some nefarious mission? Fuck. That was it. Someone was probably holding her mother hostage until she met their demands.

She was receiving specific instructions. She was to go into the building she had scoped out earlier and find a law office on the thirteenth floor. There was a file the caller wanted retrieved before the secretary or PA had a chance to transfer some sensitive information into a computer. The file was to be delivered the following day. That meant Kristine had to break into the office, swipe the file, and—*what's that now? They want her to light it on fire—with her breath?* Oh, come on. It couldn't be that bad...

Shock passed over him as he realized they'd chosen her for a reason. She wasn't a mere human firefighter. Could she be like Ryan's Chloe? A dragon?

When at last Kristine was able to disconnect the call, she spoke loudly, "Jayce? Where are you?"

A full-grown naked man rising up from under the pile of pink clothes would be a shock, but she had some kind of secret too. He mulled over his choices for another second until he heard her coming toward him. Just as she lifted the sweatshirt, he rose to his full six-foot height.

"Jayce!"

He stood in front of her motionless and allowed her mind to adjust to what she had just seen.

"Wh—What *are* you?"

He crossed his arms and said, "I'll tell you my secret if you tell me yours."

She hesitated, but didn't fall over in a dead faint. He had to give her credit for that.

She pointed at the now-flat pile of clothes on the floor and then lifted her hand, indicating his full-size body. "Obviously you must be a shapeshifter of some sort."

"Uh-huh. And you are?"

She worried her lip. "Also a shapeshifter. I—I'm a dragon."

Instead of the shocked reaction she probably expected, a slow smile spread across his face. "So is my sister-in-law."

"Really?" She sounded like the shocked one.

"Yeah. The family just found out recently. It was actually a relief. Because of our secret, my brothers and I have the worst time finding open-minded women, but Ryan finally got lucky. Chloe's a great girl, and when we learned she was actually a paranormal too—"

"Wait. Chloe and *Ryan*? Wasn't he the brother you were burying?"

Jayce winced. "Have a seat. I'll explain."

Kristine gazed at him doubtfully.

"I can put on clothes, if that's what's distracting you—do you have anything that might fit me?"

She chuckled. "I think I can do better than pink sweats. Give me a second."

While she was gone, he strolled around the apartment, staying away from the windows. It was a typical older layout. Not the open concept that renters preferred now, but a separate kitchen and dining area off the living room on one side, and a hall that must have led to bedrooms and baths on the other.

When Kristine returned from one of the back rooms, she produced an FDNY T-shirt that looked closer to his size than hers and a pair of matching navy-blue sweatpants.

As he put them on, he wondered who they had belonged to but didn't have the heart to ask. Maybe she'd had as poor luck with men as he and his brothers had been having with most women.

He looked down at himself. "Perfect fit."

"Keep them," she said.

He smiled, trying to lighten the moment. "I might keep them on your roof, if you don't mind. The garage where I left my clothes and cell phone wasn't the best place, apparently." He ambled over to the couch and sat in the middle of it.

"Oh. Your stuff was stolen?"

"Yeah. I guess that qualifies as an accident. I didn't plan on it happening. I'll explain." He motioned her over, extending his arm for her to cuddle under. Happily, that's just what she did.

Her warmth made sense now. All women were warm, *eventually*, but Kristine's hands and feet were always warm. Most women's were not. Some had feet that were like blocks of ice until they'd had time to warm up under the blankets—or on him.

Jayce turned her face toward him and leaned in for a long, hot kiss. She reciprocated for only a moment and then pushed him away and said, "Not now. I have a major dilemma, and I can't be making out with you instead of handling it."

With effort, he tamped down his lust. "Let me help you," he said.

"You can't. The only thing you can do is get me into more trouble." She raked her hand through her shoulder-length reddish-blonde hair. "How much did you hear?"

"Everything."

"Both sides of the conversation?"

"Yup."

"So, I guess whatever kind of shifter you are comes with amplified hearing?" she asked.

"And eyesight and strength and speed…" In other words, he could *help* her. Not just get in the way. He hoped she'd see it that way. "And the icing on the cake? I'm almost immortal. My kind live to be about five hundred years old. If we die before we're supposed to, we can become reincarnated in fire."

"Fuck. Is that what happened to Chloe and Ryan?"

"Ryan, yes."

"That's handy… Well, not for me." Her shoulders sagged. "I'm being forced to do something against my will to save my mother. We're fireproof and hard to kill, but we're not immortal."

"Your mother's a dragon too?"

"Yes. That doesn't mean she's not in danger. Are you going to be some kind of justice-obsessed vigilante who insists I not give in to their demands? Will you try to talk me into getting the police involved?"

"Not at all."

She scrutinized him carefully. At last she let out a deep breath. "Good. They have my mother, and she must be immobilized somehow. I won't do anything to put her at risk."

He nodded. "I won't do anything you don't want me to do, but I can help. For one thing, I can fly."

"So can I, but in this case it's not a help. It's what they want. Because I can get into the building with the fire department proximity card and then fly from the roof, they think I won't get caught."

Jayce laughed. When she scowled at him, he said, "They think a full-sized dragon flying around New York City won't attract attention?"

She dropped her head into her hands. "I know. It's insane. I've had it drummed into me that most humans would never handle the fact that paranormals live among them. Now these asshats not only know about it, they want to use it."

"Who are these criminals you're dealing with?"

"I don't know."

Jayce stayed quiet for a few minutes. He wanted to give her time to scan her memory for possibilities before he started throwing all kinds of shit out there. She rubbed her temples as if she had a headache. He pulled her into a hug, then rubbed slow circles over her back.

"Do you know for a fact that they have your mom?"

"Yes. They let her talk to me earlier. I mean, she only said 'I'm okay' and 'do whatever they say,' and her voice was kind of shaky, but I have to believe they'll keep her alive until I do what they want. It's after that…" Her voice became very soft. "I wish I knew how to make sure they'd let her go."

"Maybe that's where I can come in."

She gazed up at him with hope. He didn't know what the hell he could do. He just wanted to do *something*. He felt helpless sitting there, listening to her confusion. Although that was *all* he could do for now. He had to take this slowly so he didn't spook her. "Do you know when this is going down?"

"Tomorrow, I think. They said there was something being delivered to an office tomorrow, and they want it before it has a chance to get scanned or retyped into a computer. I'm supposed to use my fire breath to burn the lawyer's office and whatever else is around it. If it were just the one file that disappeared, that would throw suspicion on them."

"Got it." He rubbed her arms, and she seemed to relax a bit. As long as he didn't try to tell her to do anything heroic, she'd probably be okay.

"So, what can I do to help?"

She stared at him. "Help? Nothing! If you show up at all, they'll know I told someone, and my mother will be killed. You can't help!"

"Relax," he said. "They'll never know I'm there. As far as anyone thinks, a bird is just a dumb bird. As long as I cover up my colored tail feathers with some dirt, they'll tune me right out."

"Won't that interfere with your ability to fly?"

"I'm not a normal bird, remember? Even in our alternate form, we're stronger."

"I don't know, Jayce. If you see something happening to me, can you resist shifting in order to help me? Or are you just going to peck someone to death?"

He chuckled. "I can do either or both. Just don't ask me to watch someone hurt you and do nothing."

She shot to her feet and walked to the door. "That's what I thought." Opening the front door, she said, "It's time you went home—to Boston."

"Fuck," he muttered under his breath. But he had to leave without a fight. The woman had enough to deal with until he could come back to her with a solution.

—∿∿—

Jayce flew back to Boston without the help of an airplane. He had to call a family meeting right away. The trip took him about an hour and a half, and he was exhausted when he landed on his parents' roof. He shifted and then opened the attic skylight and slipped inside. They kept a pile of clean clothing in a trunk for just this kind of emergency.

At last he was dressed and took the stairs two at a time, locating his mother in the living room. "How fast can we get everybody here?"

"What's going on, dear?" Gabriella asked.

"It's better if I tell everyone at once."

His father ambled into the room. "Hey, Jayce. I thought you went on vacation. Aren't you supposed to be in New York City?"

"I was, but something came up. I need to call a family meeting as soon as possible. Can you get everybody here right away?"

"I think we can reach everyone but Ryan. Let me start the phone tree and see what happens." Antonio left the room, and Jayce imagined he was using the old kitchen wall phone. His father must have seen many changes in his seventy-five years, and maybe that's why he resisted some of them.

"Mom? You knew I was going to New York to see a girl, right?"

Mama Fierro smiled. "I thought it was something like that. Is she okay? Are you? Is everything between the two of you all right?"

Jayce chuckled. "She's fine, I'm fine, and everything between us is fine, but not everything is fine."

Gabriella Fierro shook her head. "I don't pretend to

understand, but I imagine you're going to tell us what that means."

"Yes, when everyone's together."

His father came back into the living room and sat on the sofa. "Miguel and Sandra are calling the others. They'll be here in a few minutes. Now what's all this about?" He patted the spot next to him, and Mrs. Fierro sat next to her husband.

"I'd really rather just tell you all at the same time. It's a long story, and I don't want to go through it again and again."

Confusion etched his father's forehead. "Okay. What can you tell us that won't need repeating?"

Jayce paced the length of the living room and back. "Well, there's good news and bad news. The good news is I found a special woman, and she knows what I am. She's not freaked out, but she needs my help, and I don't know how to help her."

His mother gasped. "She knows you're a phoenix? Already?"

"Yeah. She has her own secret, but it isn't mine to tell."

"She'll fit right in," Gabriella said, smiling.

"It sounds like you're getting distracted from what you really should be doing, Jayce," his father said.

"What on earth are you talking about, dear?" Gabriella asked. "Did you hear what he said about finding a *special* woman? What could be more important than that?"

"Oh, I don't know…maybe learning to lead this family? I still want to move to a warmer climate one of these days."

Jayce tossed his hands in the air. "I don't know what's so hard about running the family. You'd think we're the Mafia or something."

His father rolled his eyes. "There are seven of you. And now two in-laws. How often are nine people going to agree? There has to be a head of household to keep the peace."

Jayce was just about to disagree when a knock sounded. He strode to the door and opened it.

His second-younger brother, Gabe, stepped into the entryway. "What's going on? I heard there was some kind of family emergency." Gabe hurried into the living room, kissed his mother on the cheek, and shook his father's hand.

Jayce was about to close the door when another Fierro jogged up the steps of the South End brownstone. Noah straightened his arm to prevent the door from closing and pushed his way in.

"What's going on?"

"Come in. I'll tell you when everyone is here," Jayce said. He turned to his father and asked, "Is Luca home?"

Antonio hit himself upside the head. "Luca! I knew I forgot one." He stood up, walked over to the basement door, and then yelled downstairs, "Luca, get up here. Something important is going on—not that I know what it is."

"Do you really need to bother Luca?" Gabriella asked. "He has to study for school. He's having his finals soon."

"When are you going to stop babying him?" Jayce and his father asked at the same time.

Gabriella straightened. "I am not babying him. I just

want him to do well in school, and whatever is going on probably doesn't have anything to do with him."

"In other words, you're babying him," Jayce said.

A soft knock at the door was followed by Sandra and Miguel striding in. "What's the big emergency?" Miguel asked.

"Is that everybody?" Antonio asked.

Gabriella narrowed her eyes. "We have one more son…Dante, remember?"

Mr. Fierro smirked. "I knew I was missing somebody else. You see, Jayce? There are so many of you it's impossible to keep track. That's why the family needs someone in charge."

"And why that someone needs *a wife*," Mrs. Fierro added.

"Dante will be here in a minute," Noah said. "He's just getting a girl's phone number."

"Oh good," Gabriella said.

"Oh God," the Fierro patriarch echoed. Then he turned to her and winked. She poked him in his big, meaty arm.

"Let's gather around the dining room table," Jayce said.

Gabriella jumped up. "Good idea. I have some tiramisu left from Sunday dinner, and I'll make coffee. Sandra, would you set the table?"

"Sure."

"Thanks, Mom," Jayce said. He slung an arm around Noah and another around Gabe and walked them into the dining room. Luca was just pounding up the stairs to join them as Dante was the last to barrel through the front door.

Jayce glanced over his shoulder at Dante and called

out, "Before you ask what's going on, come into the dining room and sit down. Do you want some of Mom's tiramisu?"

"Are you serious? When have I ever said no to tiramisu?" Dante strolled into the dining room and took his place toward the end of the long wood table.

When everyone was gathered except Gabriella, who was making coffee in the kitchen, Jayce decided he would let them in on what he could.

"I was in New York visiting that FDNY firefighter I met at Ryan's funeral."

"You mean Ryan's fake funeral, right?" Sandra asked, as she spread napkins around the table in front of everyone and placed a spoon on each.

"Of course."

"I thought she wasn't speaking to you," Noah said. "She seemed mad, as if you were really breaking up."

Jayce smiled and shrugged. "Things change. I went to see her while I was in Manhattan on vacation. All is forgiven."

"So did you call us all here to tell us you have a girlfriend?" Dante asked. "That ain't news, bro. You get more tail than any of us."

"Dante! Really!" their mother called out from the kitchen.

His brothers chuckled.

"No, smart-ass. That isn't the news. She may need my help, and I don't know what to do."

Mr. Fierro cleared his throat. "So instead of trying to figure out how to solve problems so you can lead your brothers, you want to drag them into solving someone else's problem?"

"You want me to lead by example, right? Well, Dad, that's what I'm doing. I'm just more democratic about it than you are. When someone we care about needs our help, I thought we banded together to help."

"So you care about this girl?" Miguel asked.

"Yeah. I do."

"I never thought I'd see the day when you'd get serious about a woman. I thought you were the perpetual playboy," Mrs. Fierro said as she reentered the dining room with tiramisu and plates on a tray. "Antonio, will you please serve this while I get the coffee?"

Antonio rose and took the tray from her, albeit reluctantly.

"So, this girl... What can we do?" Noah asked, looking at Jayce.

"That's just it," their father said as he dished up dessert. "He doesn't know. He wants you to tell him." He gave Jayce the stink eye.

"I have to swear you all to secrecy first."

"Jesus. What the hell have you gotten yourself into?" Dante asked.

"Swear none of this information will leave this room," Jayce demanded, resolute.

All the people in the room raised their right hands and swore themselves to secrecy. Jayce nodded. "Her name is Kristine Scott. It's kind of a long story, so get comfortable..."

Chapter 5

A FEW AGONIZING HOURS LATER, KRISTINE'S PHONE RANG, and she pounced on it. The kidnapper explained that he wanted her to go to Central Park. There was a bridge as part of the jogging trail through the woods, and nearby behind a rocky outcropping, she'd find a *murse*.

"What's a murse?"

The kidnapper sighed. "It's a man-purse. Like a messenger bag, but thicker. It's made of heavy leather. Very manly. And this one is fireproof."

"Okaaay—"

"Hey, don't get fresh. It's spring and might rain. I don't want the papers you're going to steal for us to get wet."

So, "us" means there's more than one of them. "From that building on Madison Avenue?"

"Yeah. You're not as dumb as I thought."

Kristine was tempted to give him a piece of her mind. But when dealing with her mother's kidnapper, who probably thought he was smarter than everyone, it might be smart to play dumb.

"Okay. Tell me what you want me to do."

Kristine received her orders. She'd have to show up at work when she wasn't expected or needed, and that was a little suspicious right off the bat. But she couldn't think of another way to do this. She had to get the proximity card.

Some older buildings in the suburbs left keys to the outer doors in the trusted hands of the local fire department. Or there was a locked box on the wall outside, and the fire department had a key to all the boxes in that area. In the city, anyone who wanted to get in could and would break into one of those boxes, so there was a special access card. Protected by none other than the captain himself.

Now Kristine had to hope the proximity card was in the kitchen drawer in the firehouse as it usually was and not in the captain's pocket. He had been known to accidentally go home with it on occasion.

Strolling in at 9 p.m., she waved to a couple of surprised firefighters having a card game. They had been playing for money, but paused. One of them asked, "Scotty, what are you doing here?"

"Hi, Alex. Hey, Murphy. I was out for a walk and had a hankering for coffee, but then realized I'd left my wallet at home." She chuckled at her lame-ass excuse and hoped they'd buy it.

The one called Murphy eyed her with suspicion. "You wanted coffee, and you came here? You could have walked a couple more blocks to get your wallet. Sounds like an excuse to me. Does it sound like an excuse to you, Alex?"

"It sure does… Maybe she misses us."

"Or did you lose all your money playing against this asshole?" He tipped his head toward Alex. "And you're here to win it back."

The other guy laughed. "Get your coffee and sit down. We'll deal you in."

"Thanks, but I'd rather hold onto my paycheck."

Alex bellyached, "Aw, c'mon. I haven't got quite enough for my Gold Coast mansion yet."

"Are you sure about that?" Murphy asked.

The banter wasn't unusual, so Kristine felt she hadn't tripped any alarm bells among the guys. That was good. As soon as they went back to their game, she surreptitiously glanced over at the drawer that held the card she needed.

The tones rang out. The guys rose and stuffed their money into their front pockets, leaving the cards where they were.

"I guess your summer house is gonna have to wait a little longer," Murphy said as he exited the kitchen.

"Don't touch our cards, Scotty!" Alex called over his shoulder.

"I won't." She pretended to sip the coffee and casually listened to the announcement. A possible gas leak on Eleventh near the ports. Good, she'd be able to avoid her cronies on her way to Madison Avenue. As soon as she heard the trucks rolling out, she grabbed the card from the drawer and stuffed it in the flat fanny pack she had hidden under her sweatshirt. She didn't want to risk losing it by tossing it into the kidnapper's murse.

As a dragon, she couldn't exactly fit into her sweatpants. She did what Jayce had suggested earlier and left a pair of sweats on her roof…right next to the ones he'd left there. When she'd spotted them earlier, she'd smiled. Realizing he might be coming back despite her tossing him out on his ear made her feel wonderful. She had been abandoned by the most important men in her life and was beginning to wonder if she could trust any man to stick by her when the going got tough.

Kristine had to hurry. The sooner she got this over with and returned the card, the better off she'd be. If someone noticed it was missing, they'd probably assume the captain had it. Unless it was the captain looking…

She really couldn't get too caught up in the "what ifs" or she'd panic and blow the whole thing.

—⁓—

Jayce wasn't sure he should be doing what he was doing. If Kristine found out, she'd probably rip out his tail feathers. But he had to do *something*. She had no idea what she was up against. It could be one human or a whole pack of werewolves. She needed backup—a lot of it.

That's why six phoenixes followed him, soaring above the New York skyline. Every one of his Boston brothers, including rule-following Miguel, was defying their father and getting involved.

Papa Fierro had lectured Jayce on his responsibility to the family. Jayce was to take over for him someday, and he'd better start becoming responsible…lead by example, put family first, and blah, blah, blah… Jayce believed that's exactly what he was doing right now.

Of course they had their mother's blessing. She said Jayce had changed, and she suspected the woman he called Kristine had everything to do with it. She kissed each of her boys and whispered a short prayer with her hands over her heart…and then distracted the old man so they could get as far away as possible before he found out and decided to take off after them.

Before Jayce left New York, he'd found six black sweat suits and stashed them on an adjacent roof—just in case he needed the cavalry. He'd had to find a secondary hiding place since Kristine had stashed some black clothes next to his dark-blue FDNY sweats. He didn't want her to know he might be bringing his whole family to her rescue. She'd kill him—or want to.

He'd had only one idea on his way to Boston, and it was a bit mad, but his brothers were on board. That's all that mattered. They landed where he did…on top of the building next to Kristine's. When the brothers shifted, they put on the black sweat suits, and then Jayce flew to the next rooftop to shift and change into his. He pointed them toward the door to the stairs, and they jogged down to the sidewalk.

He gave two of them the address of the Madison Avenue building that Kristine had visited that night. They were to keep an eye on that building's entrances. He asked three more to keep an eye on Kristine's building. And his little brother Luca went shopping with him. He needed a very special item to complete his plan.

After they bought what they needed, they checked with the brothers at Kristine's apartment building. They hadn't seen her exit. He returned to the roof, stashed what he'd just bought, and shifted into his winged form.

He flew to the Madison Avenue building and saw his brothers—one in front of the building, one across the street. As he swooped over each one, they just shook their heads to let him know they hadn't seen her either. So he returned to the apartment building in Hell's Kitchen and flew by Kristine's windows.

There she was on the couch, speaking on the phone and nodding. He landed on her windowsill and watched. After a few minutes, she hung up and then dropped her head in her hands. Her whole body shook as if she were crying.

Jayce knew she would be upset if he were to get involved, but he was glad he'd made the decision to do something whether she liked it or not. He couldn't stand to see her like this.

She rose, straightened her clothing, marched to the mirror over the fireplace, and looked at her tear-streaked face. She wiped at her tears and disappeared around the corner, probably to go to the bathroom and pull herself together. Jayce's heart broke for her.

Soon she exited the building and was on the move.

Kristine jogged to Central Park as instructed. She was unsure if she'd find the right place. She finally found the rock with the murse behind it. Lifting it, she realized it was heavier than she thought, but the long strap would make it easy to put around her dragon neck, and her dragon strength wouldn't have a problem carrying it from the building on Madison Avenue to her building in Hell's Kitchen. The trick would be making sure nobody saw her as a dragon. With so many tall buildings and many apartments with curious onlookers using telescopes, it would be almost impossible not to attract some kind of attention. All she could hope for would be that whoever reported seeing a full-size dragon flying around the city would be considered a nutcase.

Looking both ways for anyone using the jogging trail or coming out of the woods, she found that she was alone as far as she could tell. Just out of curiosity she glanced up. There was a bird in the trees above her, but she couldn't be sure if it was Jayce because she hadn't seen his other form. She hoped it wasn't. This mission would be hard enough without interference.

If she could carry fifty pounds on her back up several stories of a burning building, she could certainly handle this stupid murse. It wasn't balanced very well, so she wore it cross-body, with the bulk of it resting against her butt. Then she jogged out of the park, which took several minutes.

It was quite dark and pretty late, so she figured a lot of people might have gone to bed. It was a weeknight, and she prayed most people wouldn't be partying into the night. They might call New York the city that never sleeps, but some people worked for a living and had to go to bed at some point. Fortunately Madison Avenue was mostly dedicated to daytime businesses.

Several minutes later she arrived at the target building, huffing and puffing. She checked up and down the street. Cabs drove by, but not a steady stream of them. She'd just have to work to avoid headlights. She retrieved the card, walked up to the front door, and scanned the pad, and, thankfully, something clicked. Then she snuck inside, closing the door behind her. She didn't think anyone saw her.

Jogging up thirteen flights of stairs rather than using the elevator and possibly alerting a security guard, she found the office with the lawyer's name on it, and then she had to get in. She opened her fanny pack, found the card again, and slid it into the spot between the door-jamb and the lock, and sure enough the door popped open. "I'm surprised people don't update their locks in this day and age. Someone could easily break in," she muttered while at the same time realizing the irony of her words.

Leaving the door open, she strode in, found the pile of mail, and started going through it. She was looking at the return addresses for the one she needed. At last she found it. It was a PO box, but it was the right one. A PO box on Long Island. *Interesting*.

The mystery of her birth and parentage seemed to be coming into play—maybe. If she knew whom she was dealing with, she might be able to complete the puzzle. Is that why the kidnapper—*kidnappers?*—knew who and *what* she was? She shrugged off the thought, knowing it was a stretch. Clearly her father was on her mind.

Opening the envelope, she slid out the papers. She wasn't supposed to, but she couldn't help being curious. Besides, there might be a clue as to where her mother was being kept.

It was a contract, all right. *And oh my God*. It was a contract to kill someone. "Holy fuck," she whispered. Stuffing the contract back into the envelope and making it look as if it had never been opened, she tucked it into the murse. Now she had to make it back up to the roof… but the kidnappers wanted a fire started. How the heck was she supposed to do that? She was a firefighter. That went against every ethical bone in her body.

And then she thought of her mother. Carrying out the kidnappers' instructions to the letter might be the only way to get her mother back. The building wasn't much higher than the floor she was currently on. She could shift into her dragon form, scoop up her black jeans and jersey, blast the place with fire, and then jog to the nearest staircase. After padding up three more stories to the roof, hopefully it would be unlocked or she'd be able to punch her way out. Like she told the monster on the phone, a lot could go wrong.

She looked around for a logical place for a fire to start. To look innocent, it would have to be an electrical fire. With no one in the office, anything else would be suspect. There was one outlet with a lot of extra electronics plugged in, and she figured that might be looked at as an overload. It would have to do.

She shifted and blew fire on that section, making sure the wall caught. Then she spread her fire breath up to the ceiling until that caught too. Then she torched the desk as she grabbed the murse and her human clothing and backed out of the room. She made sure the door locked behind her, hoping to put it back the way she'd found it and minimize the damage to one room.

Now she had to get out before the smoke alarm went off. She flew to the nearest stairwell, managed to open the door even in her dragon form, flew up to the top floor, and then found the door to the roof. There was a lock on it, but it was on the inside and hooked up to an alarm. She shrugged. Oh well…the smoke alarms would sound soon anyway. She broke the lock with her dragon strength. Pushing her way onto the roof, she was shocked to see seven birds clutching black satin sheets in their talons. Three on each side of the door.

Holy shit. Jayce had come to her rescue after all, and it looked like he brought his brothers. She slipped between the two rows of birds, which took off when she did, their black sheets shielding her from both sides as she flew through the night.

She landed on her apartment's roof, grabbed her

clothing, and raced around to the opposite side of an air-conditioning unit. One of the birds dropped out of formation and landed on her roof. The others flew to the next building. As soon as she'd hopped into her clothing, she ran back to where Jayce stood, holding the FDNY sweats she'd given him.

His brother-phoenixes landed in two straight lines, holding the sheets in their beaks, and then they rose up as full-sized men, covering their nakedness with the black sheets held between their smiling lips. Jayce waved to them, and they waved back. They shifted again, dropped the sheets, and flew off.

As soon as Jayce and Kristine were both dressed, they made their way to the rooftop entrance and quietly jogged down the stairs to Kristine's apartment on the third floor. The fanny pack had served her well, holding her keys and phone.

"I take it those were your brothers."

"Yup. You guessed it," Jayce said.

Kristine fiddled with the lock until the door opened and they were able to scoot inside, closing it behind them with a soft click. She threw herself in Jayce's arms and breathed a heavy sigh of relief.

"I can't believe we got away with that. At least I *hope* we did," she said.

"Do you mean as long as nobody saw a group of weird-colored birds flying in formation and thought it was strange enough to take a picture…"

She leaned away and stared into his eyes. "That's exactly what I mean. I couldn't see anything except the sky in front of me. Did you notice anyone staring out their windows or grabbing their cameras?"

"I don't think so." He gently rubbed her arms up and down and then escorted her to the couch.

Kristine sank down, and he sat opposite her on the coffee table, holding her hands. "So what happens now? Do you wait for the kidnapper's instructions, or do you already know what he wants you to do?"

"I'm supposed to wait for him to call." She bit her bottom lip and avoided his gaze.

"What aren't you telling me?" Jayce asked.

"Nothing!" Kristine took a deep breath and let it out. She let go of his hands and flopped against the back of the sofa. Closing her eyes, she mumbled, "I didn't tell you this before, but they said they were watching me. That makes me nervous as far as what they've seen. Like…have they seen you?"

"What do you think?"

"I don't know." Kristine sat up and faced him. "If they have seen you or they saw the little stunt up on the roof, I imagine I'll hear about it." She rubbed her temples, as if she had a headache.

Just as Jayce was about to say something, her phone rang. She dug it out of her fanny pack and answered with a nervous "Hello?"

"Did you get it?"

Kristine straightened and seemed to be pulling herself together. "Yes, I have it. It's in the murse. How do we exchange this for my mother?"

After a brief hesitation on the other end of the phone, the monster said, "Not just yet. We'll talk about that in the morning."

Kristine shot to her feet. "Tomorrow? Do you mean to tell me you're going to hold onto her another night?"

Jayce watched her pace past the windows. If anyone was watching, they'd see she was obviously upset.

The voice on the other end of the phone just said, "You'll receive instructions tomorrow." And the click on the other end signaled he had hung up.

Kristine threw the phone on the floor. Fortunately, it hit the thick rug and not the hardwood.

Jayce rose and approached her slowly, until he remembered he had to stay away from the windows. "He didn't say anything about seeing you with a bunch of birds and sheets."

"That's right, but he didn't say where my mother was either."

Jayce stood with his hands in his pockets, unsure if he should reach out and comfort her or stay back. He waited a few moments, and eventually her posture sagged. She picked up the phone and returned to the couch. When she sat in the middle, she left enough room for him to join her. So he snuggled next to her and put his arm around her shoulders.

"I just wish this would end." Kristine laid her head on his shoulder.

"I agree. You've done what he asked you to do. There must be a reason they have to wait until tomorrow." He began rubbing her arm, trying to soothe her.

"I can't imagine why. What if something's wrong with my mother?" Kristine leaned over and dropped her head in her hands. "I feel so awful. The last words I said to her were not very nice."

"You had a fight?" Jayce asked.

Kristine frowned. "You could say that. I was demanding to know something she's always refused to tell me.

I thought she was keeping it to herself just because I was young and she didn't think I would understand. All these years later, as an adult, I figured she could tell me anything. But she still refused. I blew up at her and stormed out."

Jayce rubbed her back gently. "You couldn't have known that this was going to happen. You'll see her again, and I'm sure you'll be able to forgive each other and get past it."

"I hope you're right." She leaned into him, and they shared a hug.

Jayce ran his hand over her loose light-red waves, planting little kisses along her jaw. "I'll be right here if you need me. It will be all right," he whispered.

Kristine hugged him harder. "I wish I didn't have to wait until tomorrow. The suspense is killing me."

He cupped her face between his hands "I can think of a way we can pass the time and release some tension…" He held her stunning turquoise gaze. He didn't know how open she'd be, but he'd never know if he didn't broach the subject.

She snorted. A tiny curl of smoke rose between their faces. "Are you one of those guys who thinks you can fix everything with sex?"

At least she was smiling. Jayce smoothed her hair away from her face and tucked it behind her ear. "No. Did I say anything about sex?"

She laughed. "Don't pretend that's not what you meant and that *I'm* the one with a dirty mind."

"Sex isn't dirty. Not between two people who care about each other."

Kristine hesitated. She seemed to be mulling

something over. At last she rose, holding his hand in hers until he followed.

She led him to the second door on the left at the end of the hall. Opening the door, she allowed him into a very girly bedroom. It wasn't teenage girly—maybe he should call it womanly or feminine. One wall behind the queen-size bed was painted lilac.

The main thing that stood out was the bedding. The top blanket was like a sumptuous cream-colored fur from some animal that didn't exist...or if it did, it would have to be about ten feet tall. He had to conclude that it was faux fur, not the hide of the abominable snowman.

Lots of unnecessary pillows rested against the shabby white headboard. She closed the door behind him, and he wondered why. They were alone. Perhaps it was just out of habit. That made him wonder if she'd brought men here before. The look she gave him as she came closer was a little shy, so if she had entertained in this room, it hadn't happened very often.

She caressed his chest, and his arms enveloped her automatically.

"So, what were you thinking we should do to blow off steam?" she asked and leaned forward to nuzzle his neck.

He couldn't help chuckling. "I'm sure we'll think of something." He walked her backward until they both fell onto the bed, and he rolled her on top of him. Their lips found each other easily. This time the kiss wasn't as much passionate as tender...loving.

A gentle agreement.

"Kristine, are you sure you want to do this? And please don't joke around by asking what I mean. I need to know."

She took a deep breath and held his gaze. "Let's play it by ear. I could use the closeness. I don't know if I need the whole shebang. Yes, it would relieve tension, and I have plenty of that. But I don't want to force anything."

He nodded. "Got it. No *she*-bang."

Jayce just held Kristine, letting her take the initiative. She knew he wanted her. But did she know how much he desired and craved her?

Her lashes fluttered, but she let him kiss her eyes. Holding and stroking what he could reach, he hoped his touch soothed her. At least it seemed to. He could feel her relax in his arms.

She brushed his hair out of his eyes. His stubble had grown, and he hoped it didn't scrape her. Little nibbles and tastes of his neck and jaw didn't seem to put her off.

He wanted to explore and worship her body, leisurely, and perhaps this was the best time to do that. He would just have to be sure he didn't drown in his own desire.

She parted her lips and let him feast on her tongue. The flood of passion eventually consumed them both, and she sucked his tongue, reveling in his attention as if it were what she needed to breathe. He tried to hold himself back so he didn't just ravish her. But the restraint he was showing was about to kill him. He caressed her rib cage, swirled his tongue with hers, massaged her shoulders, and snuggled. Eventually he cupped her bottom and nuzzled her neck.

"I'm not wearing granny panties," she whispered.

"From what I gathered, you're not wearing any panties." Jayce trailed his finger down her abdomen. Her black jersey had ridden up to her midriff without any help from him. Pausing at her belly button, he gave it a little swirl and then found the snap to her jeans and popped it open.

He waited to let her continue if she wanted to. She opened the zipper with one hand and at the same time yanked open the tie of his sweatpants with the other.

It seemed that they were going to do this. He whispered words of adoration in her ear. She began to inhale deeper, and as he moved her jeans over her bottom, she raised it, allowing him to strip her down and reveal her precious secrets to him. "Do we need protection?"

"Not on my end," she said.

"Nor mine."

She wiggled out of the black jeans and moved his sweatpants over his hips. It was all he could do not to let out a growl when she touched him. She grasped his member and teased his erection. He almost choked, begging her to stop for a moment until he could get rid of the offending garments—all of them. Soon her top and his sweatshirt hit the floor, and they were finally able to romp without clothes in the way.

He trailed his tongue around her nipple and she gasped. When he took her breast between his lips and sucked deeply, she arched and moaned. He didn't wish to torment her with long, drawn-out foreplay, but he knew she needed the maximum release he could give her. When he had thoroughly suckled that breast, he moved to the other and teased it just as thoroughly.

Eventually, he moved down her torso, trailing kisses along her heated skin. She hissed and gasped as he bestowed his loving attention on her sweet spot below. He instinctively knew how to touch her. And she touched him the same way, skyrocketing the electrified sensations to his cock.

He wondered if she knew how torn he was. His erection swelled even further, if that were possible. The strain of holding himself in check was difficult. But he didn't want to succumb to his lust until she was right there with him.

He leaned back to pull out of her hand and moved down beside her legs. He bestowed little kisses on her upper thighs as his finger trailed down her abdomen. Her thighs trembled. He glanced up at her face, which was flushed. When he reached her clit and flicked his tongue right there, she jerked and then grasped his hair and tugged.

"Do you not want me to do this?" he asked.

She laughed and let go of his hair. Instead she grabbed his shoulders, giving them a squeeze. "No, I don't want you to stop. I was just holding on for dear life."

He chuckled and relished watching her enjoy the pleasure he was giving her. When he knew she was close, he eased up. He really wanted her to tumble over the edge with him. He was confident in the feelings he could elicit because she was so responsive.

"Don't stop," she rasped.

Okay…we'll go for two.

He flicked her bud rapidly and repeatedly while she thrashed and convulsed, bucking and arching—almost lifting right off the bed. She screamed as she clenched the sheets and vibrated.

He didn't stop what he was doing until she shoved him away. Her body melted into the mattress as she panted.

As much as he wanted to just drive into her and

pound her with his steel-hard cock, he still held himself in check, crawling up beside her slowly. He kneeled at her side, brushed her sweat-soaked hair aside, and kissed her forehead, her nose, and finally her lips. She cupped the back of his head and crushed him to her as she drove her tongue into his mouth, and then, just as abruptly, she let go. Her arms fell to her sides, and she gazed at him with a look of wonder.

"How did you manage to do that?" She breathed heavily.

"Do what?"

"Take me right out of my body," she said. "I felt like I was floating above the bed. That's never happened to me before."

"Maybe you just needed the right guy."

She smiled up at him and parted her thighs in invitation. "I can't promise to do anything that monumental for you, but it's your turn, and I want you to take it."

"Are you sure? I don't want you to feel obligated."

"Just to be perfectly clear," Kristine said, "I want you to fuck me silly."

Jayce chuckled. "I guess you can't be clearer than that."

He placed himself at her V. "I want you to come with me wherever I go. Be it out of body or just to a nice hilltop climax. We go together."

"Like wine and cheese." She chuckled.

He couldn't help laughing, and perhaps he needed a moment to regroup, so he leaned back on his heels and said, "I'm going to bring you to the brink before I take my own pleasure."

He let his hand roam while his lips kissed a path

down to her curls. She wiggled when he got to her clit, but she didn't squirm away. She twined her fingers in his hair and breathed deeply while he brought her close.

When she was trembling but hadn't shattered yet, he pushed her legs open wider and positioned himself between her thighs. He plunged into her wet warmth and buried himself deep in her core. She sucked in a sharp breath.

"Are you okay?"

She sighed. "More than okay. Please…"

He didn't have to ask what she wanted. He just rocked in the age-old rhythm, loving the feel of her warmth and sliding eagerly in and out of her tight, slick channel. Braced on one elbow, he didn't lower himself completely. He left enough room between them to find and rub her sweet spot with his thumb. She immediately arched and moaned, grasping the sheets again.

As the tension built between them, he watched her carefully. The intoxicating rhythm was overwhelming. At last they both shattered. She screamed as the sensations took them somewhere indescribable.

Her muscles clenched his cock, and wave after wave of incredible release shook him to his core. He rode every last aftershock.

His own fulfillment was complete. He'd had a staggering orgasm. As soon as he'd floated back to earth, he embraced her and rolled onto his back, allowing her to decide if she wanted to withdraw and lie beside him or stay coupled.

She stayed. He couldn't believe the beauty of that act. His hunger and longing for her were sated at last, which didn't mean he didn't want more. He would want this passion over and over again, whether it drove him to madness or ecstasy. When she gazed into his eyes, he saw sparkling pleasure and satisfaction, mirroring his own gratification.

There were no words between them. There were probably no words to express this euphoria—this elation. She turned her head to the side and laid her cheek on his heaving chest. They stayed like that for several long minutes. There was no doubt about his feelings for her. He loved this woman and would do anything to protect her.

She rolled up on her elbow and grinned. "Ready for round two?"

Chapter 6

AFTER MAKING LOVE FOR A SECOND TIME, KRISTINE LAY IN
the warmth of Jayce's arms and basked in the afterglow.
She needed to know a little more about this guy. Who
was he? *What* was he?

"Jayce?"

"Yeah, hon?"

Even the endearment was strange for her. She had
been called Scott or Scotty for so long, it felt strange
when anyone called her Kristine again. The only one
who called her *hon* was her mother, and now…

"Jayce…"

"Mmm?"

"Can you explain what phoenixes are? You and your
brothers are supernatural, obviously, but what are your
unique abilities—exactly?"

Jayce caressed her hair and held her in his arms,
breathing steadily. After a short hesitation, he said, "We
have an advantage as firefighters, like you have. My kind
may not be fireproof, but if worst comes to worst, we can
reincarnate from the flames. We are known as firebirds.
The phoenix is not as mythical as some people think."

"So you call yourselves firebirds?"

Jayce turned her face so he could see into her eyes.
"What my family and I call ourselves doesn't really
matter. What matters is what you and I call each other—
I'm referring to what we have together."

Kristine squirmed uncomfortably. What did he mean by that? She pulled away from his arms and sat up, using the sheet to cover her breasts.

Kristine wasn't feeling shy, exactly. She just didn't know how to respond. "What do you mean when you say 'what we have together'? What do you want me to say?"

Jayce propped himself up on his elbow and tugged the sheet. "Please don't be shy around me. After what we just shared, especially."

Kristine let the sheet drop, watching as he appreciated her chest, which was a little on the small side—according to her mother. She was just as happy not to have huge boobs getting in the way of her active lifestyle. "All right. I'll try not to be shy. It's more like self-consciousness than shyness, anyway."

"What do you have to be self-conscious about? I hope you're not talking about your body. It's beautiful, just like the rest of you."

She laced her fingers with his and worried her lip. At last she took a deep breath and launched into it. "I have a hard time trusting men. I know that may sound ridiculous since I'm putting my life into the hands of my fellow firefighters every day, but that's not an emotional thing."

Jayce stared at her for a moment. "I think I understand what you're saying. Of course emotions can run high during a fire, but those aren't romantic feelings. I think that must be what you're talking about as far as trust is concerned. Am I right?"

Kristine rubbed his knuckles with her thumb. "To an extent, yes. But it's not just that. I think being abandoned by a father I never knew is part of the problem."

Jayce's brow furrowed as he held her gaze. "Explain, please."

Kristine sighed. "Remember how I said I had a fight with my mother, just before she disappeared?"

"Yes, I remember."

"The fight was about my father. I don't know why he wasn't in my life, and she won't tell me. All I know is that she absolutely does know who he is because, in her words, 'I'm not a slut.'"

"Why won't she tell you?" Jayce asked.

"She won't even tell me that much. It's frustrating as hell. I feel like a part of me is missing, even though she has provided for me in every possible way."

"I can't imagine what that would be like. I have a big, boisterous family…half Italian, half Spanish. A mother and father, six brothers, and two sisters-in-law. And we're close. We try to keep our schedules the same so all of us can get together for as many Sunday dinners as possible. Recently my parents had to buy a new dining room table to accommodate everyone."

She chuckled. "It must be wild when you all get together."

"That's just it—our father keeps it from becoming too crazy. He rules the roost, pardon the pun, but in a gentle, loving, and joking way. Sort of like a benevolent dictatorship. Although he's been a lot more serious lately—especially with me. When they move to the Caribbean for retirement, I'm supposed to take over as head of the family."

Kristine smiled sadly. "And that's why you can't leave Boston."

"You remembered." Jayce rubbed her knuckles with

his thumb. "I'd like you to come to Boston and meet everybody at one of our Sunday dinners."

Kristine ran her fingers through her hair. "I don't know if that would be wise. I meant it when I said I couldn't leave New York. My mother is here for the duration because this is where her job is. It's not like there's another Broadway anywhere. And not only is she my mother and my roommate, she's also my best friend."

Jayce nodded. "I thought as much."

"Then why do you want to pursue things between us? It seems impossible. You have your family obligations in Boston, and I have mine in New York. Just because I only have one person to think about and you have, like, a million doesn't mean that my situation is less important than yours."

"Of course not. I never said that, and I wouldn't." A sly smile stole across Jayce's face. "But just because it's impossible doesn't mean we shouldn't pursue this anyway."

Kristine couldn't help chuckling. "I wish I had your optimism."

"So will you come home with me and meet my family sometime?"

Kristine heaved a big sigh. "After this is all over and my mother is safely home—"

"That goes without saying. Family comes first. Always."

Kristine admired his values. They seemed to have that in common too. Why the hell couldn't they be together? He was perfect. He was everything she needed and wanted.

"We have to get you out of this hopeless mind-set," Jayce said. "So what can I do to help? Make you a cup of coffee? Take you out for some rocky road ice cream? What do you need?"

Kristine gave him a sad smile. "Not coffee, my nerves are shot as it is. Ice cream sounds good, but I don't want to go out, and I don't want you going out either."

"Why not? I'm willing and able, just as soon as I get some pants on."

She nuzzled his neck. "You are just about the sweetest firebird I've ever known, but the kidnapper may be watching. How about if I make us some cocoa?"

"Cocoa sounds great. I think we need to stop calling this asshole the kidnapper. We need to give him a less respectful name."

Kristine slipped out of bed and strolled to the closet. "Like what? Dick?"

Jayce laughed as he rolled to the edge of the bed and stood up. "I was actually thinking more in terms of dickhead, shit-for-brains, or fuckwad," he said.

Kristine thought about how she could swear with the best of them at work, but she didn't want to be "one of the guys" with Jayce. "How about Donkey Pizzle?"

Jayce laughed hard. "Much better. More unique but still irreverent. Do you know where my pants went?"

She donned her fluffy pink bathrobe and wondered what he thought about all her girly accoutrements, but on the other hand she really didn't care. This room was her domain. This was where she could express herself and enjoy who she really was—not the generic room at work. "On the floor, of course." She pointed to the pile of clothes on the opposite side of the bed.

"Oh yeah, we got in on the other side, didn't we?"
His bold grin reminded her of the passion that swept
them away earlier.

Damn. If only she could grab hold of Boston with one
hand and New York with the other and then mash them
together somehow… Oh well. She'd just have to enjoy
whatever time they had.

The following morning, Jayce sat at Kristine's kitchen
table, sipping coffee. She was on pins and needles, waiting for the kidnapper to call with instructions. Jayce
admired the way she had been holding herself together
all this time.

But she was starting to lose it.

"What if they've seen you? I don't understand how
they could be watching me and not have seen you." She
paced back and forth across the kitchen, not touching the
breakfast Jayce had made her.

"Sit. Eat. You're driving yourself nuts."

Kristine whirled on him. "You think sitting down will
make me any less nuts? I thought they would've called
by now."

"Pacing won't make Donkey Pizzle call faster."

Kristine let out a sigh, and her posture sagged. "I know,
you're right. But I can't stop wondering why they didn't
want this exchange to happen last night. Wouldn't it be
easier to hide in the dark? What if something's wrong?"

Jayce thought about it and deduced that the kidnappers might be playing a mind game. If that were the case,
it was working. Kristine was more unbalanced than he'd
ever seen her.

"What if they think I disobeyed them? They could have taken it out on her. What if they—"

Jayce rose, moved to the chair on the opposite side of the table in front of her untouched omelet, and pulled her down onto his lap.

He linked her hand with his. "I don't think anybody has seen me, or Donkey Pizzle would've said something last night. To be honest, I don't think anybody is watching you at all."

"How can you say that? You don't know… How do they know I'm home? They only call when I'm home."

"But you wouldn't know they called if you weren't here. It's not like they're going to leave a voicemail."

She heaved a huge, frustrated sigh.

"Okay, maybe someone is watching from outside," he said. "But I stayed away from the windows, and I really don't think anybody can see in from the street."

"Unless they live across the street on the third or fourth floor…"

He rubbed circles over her back gently. In as quiet and calm a voice as he could manage, he said, "I know you're anxious. I am too. We'll get through this."

She draped her arms around him and leaned her cheek against his forehead. "Thank you," she whispered. "I don't know what I'd do without you right now."

Jayce cut off a piece of her omelet and fed it to her. He didn't dare mention that he was going to follow her all day in bird form. On the other hand, if she looked up and saw him, she might have a fit right there in public.

No. He knew she wouldn't put him in danger or do anything to put her mother in jeopardy. He'd have to risk it. But what could he do if she did run into trouble and needed him? Come to her rescue in another pink sweat suit three sizes too small?

Whatever he did, it would probably require some last-minute thinking. He liked knowing what to do. Even in a fire when he had to make decisions on the spot, there were protocols to follow, which helped. There were no protocols for this.

At last the phone rang, and she bounded off his lap, rushing to the counter where she'd placed it. Jayce was thankful for his supernatural hearing. He didn't even have to lean in close to follow the conversation.

"Hello?"

"Are you ready for the next set of instructions?"

"Yes. I've been ready since last night. Why didn't—"

"Shut up and listen."

She paused with her mouth still open and then quickly interjected, "I was just going to say I have to go back to work tomorrow. This has to be over soon." When he said nothing, she sighed and said, "All right. I'm listening."

"Take the murse back to the spot where you picked it up in the park. You didn't open the envelope, did you?"

"No. Of course not."

"You say 'Of course not,' like ninety-nine percent of people wouldn't do exactly that."

"Well, I'm not about to place my mother's life in jeopardy. I'll do what you say in order to get her back."

"Good. That's very wise of you."

"Will she be at the park?"

"No. As long as you carry out your part of the bargain, you'll see her when you see her."

She cursed under her breath. "How do I know she's alive?"

"Hold on." A moment later Donkey Pizzle said, "You can say hello. That's it."

"Mom?"

"I'm here." Her mother didn't sound as anxious as Kristine was. Maybe she was being treated better than her distraught daughter imagined.

"Are you okay?"

Donkey Pizzle said, "She's fine. In fact, she's being treated very well. Cooperation is rewarded."

"Then you'll return her as soon as possible because of my cooperation."

Donkey Pizzle laughed. "You sound like you're the one giving the orders. You're not. Remember that. Now get that package to the park. If it takes longer than an hour, your mother will pay for your negligence."

"I'm on my way," she said.

The click on the line indicated that he had hung up and she'd received all the instructions she was going to get.

"I have to go." She disappeared for a few moments and came back wearing her sweats and sneakers. "Will you wait here for me? Please?"

Jayce didn't want to lie to her. "I'll stay out of sight."

She frowned and looked like she was about to argue. Then she checked the clock on the kitchen wall and said, "I've gotta go." She slung the murse over her head and jogged to the door. "Please stay right here," she begged and then let herself out, locking the door behind her. Jayce heard her footsteps running down the stairs.

As soon as he was sure she was on the sidewalk, he left the apartment, knowing he couldn't relock the dead bolt. He rushed up to the roof, stripping off the sweatshirt before he got there. He shoved open the door and shifted while he still had the pants on. The door caught the bottom of the pants as it closed but not the bird that flew out of them.

He had to stay well behind and above her. Now that she knew what his alternate form looked like, she'd recognize him. It took him a few seconds to roll in the dirt and cover his tail feathers. When he took to the sky, he saw Kristine disappear under the trees. Good. The leafy-green foliage in the park would provide cover for him.

He knew where she was going because he'd followed her before. She had to jog all the way to the opposite side of the park, so it was a good thing she was in shape. She'd make it in an hour, but Donkey Pizzle sure hadn't left her much room to spare.

He scanned the other people strolling, jogging, and lounging on benches. Even the bum who looked like he was passed out under a pile of newspapers could have been spying on her, making sure she was alone.

Jayce was relieved when she made it to the rock and placed the murse where it belonged. He hoped her mother was where she belonged too—at home. There would be hell to pay in Hell's Kitchen if Kristine got there and the place was empty.

Kristine looked all around as she placed the murse behind the rocky outcropping. Before she reemerged from behind the rocks, just to be thorough she glanced up and saw nothing...at first. And then off in the distance she caught sight of the exact bird that Jayce became when he shifted. He rested high in a tree but in plain sight. *For Christ's sake, maybe he is stalking me.*

Kristine sent him a glare and then jogged out of the park, knowing he was going to follow her all the way back. She was both comforted and irritated. She had asked him to stay in the apartment. What if her mother returned and couldn't get in?

When she reached her building, Jayce was nowhere to be seen. She realized he was probably on the roof changing back into his clothes. Or maybe she was mistaken and the bird she saw was just a bird. She'd know when she got inside. Unlocking the door quickly and running up the stairs at top speed, she reached her apartment at the same time Jayce did.

"I knew it! I knew you couldn't do as I asked."

"I'm sorry, but I'm not sorry. I had to be sure you were safe."

Kristine unlocked her door, walked in, and tried to slam the door in Jayce's face. He stuck his foot in the way, and the door bounced open.

"Argh!" She was beyond frustrated. "Mom?" she called. Racing through the apartment, she checked every room. When she didn't find her mother, she began checking closets and under beds. "What the hell? Where is she?"

When Kristine returned to the living room, Jayce stood just inside the door.

She jammed her hands on her hips. "Aren't you supposed to be on vacation? Shouldn't you go see Rockefeller Center or visit the Met or something?"

Jayce glanced at his feet and kicked the floor. "Kristine, I think you know that this isn't just a vacation.

I came here to see you, and that's what I want to do. I want to see you safe. I can't leave until I'm sure that you are."

Kristine glared at him for a few moments, saw the sincerity in his eyes, and wandered over to the couch, where she collapsed. Throwing her arm across her eyes, she started to cry. Jayce was at her side in a flash and tried to gather her into his arms, but she pushed him away. "I can't deal with you and this at the same time. Please just leave."

Jayce hesitated. Kristine rolled toward the back of the couch and hid her face in the pillows. A few moments later she heard the door open and click shut. Jayce had left her.

She burst into tears and cried harder than she ever had in her life. She was letting out feelings of disappointment, abandonment, and loss, all at the same time. Even though crying usually made her feel like a weakling, this time it was cathartic—and necessary. She felt as if she'd break if she had to stay strong a moment longer.

When she had finally pulled herself together, she sat up, plucked a tissue from the box on the coffee table, and blew her nose.

Her phone rang.

"Shit." She grabbed the phone, took a deep breath, and answered, "Hello." She was surprised at how normal she had made her voice sound.

"I have another job for you."

"Where the *hell* is my mother?"

At that moment, the door opened quietly, and Jayce tiptoed back in. She wondered if he had gone any further than just outside the door. He was probably listening the whole time. As much as that irked her, she was actually glad he hadn't deserted her. His quiet strength was exactly what she needed. She had to stop pushing him away. He didn't seem like he was going to leave anyway. That in itself was oddly comforting.

The asshole on the other end of the line said, "Again with the demands? You should know by now that cooperation is the only way to get what you want."

"But you're not holding up your end of the bargain. You're not giving me what I want at all. I want my mother back."

Jayce moved toward her but didn't come within touching distance, and she was grateful for that. She needed to concentrate on what the dickhead was saying. She could fall into Jayce's arms later.

Donkey Pizzle said, "Why would I give up my leverage? Don't bother answering that. That was a retro... reorertical..."

"Rhetorical question?" Kristine supplied.

"Yeah. You have to do one more job before I return her, and I'll let you see her as your reward for doing this job."

Kristine gazed up at Jayce. He nodded and stepped behind the couch, shrinking down so he couldn't be seen.

"Fine. Let me see her."

"Hang up, and I'll call you on Skype," he said.

Kristine disconnected the call and waited. She thought Jayce would say something, but perhaps he didn't know what to say. She didn't know what to say to him either.

The Skype sound came through, and she tapped the video button. A moment later she saw her mother sitting at a dining table with a fluted glass of orange juice in her hand—or perhaps it was a mimosa. She looked clean and well-dressed, but the clothes were not her own. *Did they buy her a whole new wardrobe?*

"Mom? Are you all right?"

Her mother nodded. "I'm fine, honey."

"Are you being treated well?"

Amy glanced off to the left of the screen. She may have been checking someone's reaction or direction. An anxious male voice was babbling something about a ship being boarded.

"I'm okay, honey. Just please do what they say, and I'll be allowed to come home very soon."

The Skype call disconnected. That's all she was going to see of her mother, but it reassured her that she wasn't tied up.

Jayce rose up behind the couch. "Did she look all right?"

Kristine huffed. "She looked better than all right. She was well-dressed and sipping a mimosa. It looked like she was even wearing makeup."

"Did you recognize the surroundings?"

At that moment, the phone rang again. Kristine answered immediately.

"Hello," said a computerized voice. "We're taking a survey—"

"Agh!" she screamed and poked the *end call* button. Then she gave in to a fit of giggles. She peeked at Jayce, figuring he must think she was insane. He just smiled. In a way, it was handy that he had supernatural hearing and she didn't have to explain everything she heard on the other end of the line.

When the phone rang again, she prayed it wasn't a telemarketer, a charity, a survey, or any other kind of intrusion. Didn't people know her mother's life hung in the fucking balance?

"Hello."

"Who did you talk to just then?"

"It was a computerized call. I hung up right away."

"What did they want?"

"My participation in some kind of survey."

There was no response on the other end for a few moments. Then the underwater voice said, "Don't you hate that?"

She almost giggled again. *How inappropriate would that be?* "Uh, yeah. I do."

"I hope you know I'm going to have to check the room again to be sure there's no police or surveillance equipment."

She sighed. "Sure. Why not?" She waved Jayce toward the front door.

He nodded and strode over to it. When the phone clicked off, he opened and slipped around the door. He managed to close it behind himself before the Skype call began.

Kristine knew the drill. She walked Donkey Pizzle all through the apartment, under beds, and in closets. The shower curtain was already open, so she didn't have to do that again. How long had it been since she'd showered? *Sheesh.*

"Satisfied?" she asked as soon as the tour was complete.

"For now," Donkey Pizzle answered. "You'll need to memorize the address I'm about to give you. Don't write it down."

"Okay." She hoped it wasn't complicated. Her stress

level might affect her memory, and the location was probably where she was supposed to go to meet his next set of demands.

"1483 Park Avenue. Repeat that."

"1483 Park Avenue."

"Good. You're to wait until the middle of the night, then huff and puff, and set the place on fire."

"*What?*" she exclaimed.

"You heard me."

"But…you're aware that I'm a fire *fighter*, right?"

"Yup. But you're also a dragon."

"I have to work tonight."

"You can slip out, do what you're told, and get back before the dispatcher gets the call."

"No! I can't! I'll lose my job if I'm discovered."

"You'll lose your mother if you don't do as I say. Call in sick."

"Holy crap. That's a residential neighborhood. People could be asleep."

"It is. And, hopefully, they will be."

"Shit! I can't do this. You must know that."

"Didn't your mother tell you to do whatever I said?"

Kristine placed her elbow on her knee and dropped her forehead into her hand.

"Headache?" Donkey Pizzle asked.

"What the fuck do you think?" she growled.

"Oh now, now. That's no way for a lady to talk."

The door opened quietly, and Jayce peered around it. Then he snuck in and closed the door silently. She would have waved him away, but they were still on Skype and she could be seen. She couldn't see the caller, however. They must still have tape over the camera lens.

"Who are you looking at?" Donkey Pizzle demanded.

"No one," she said. "I was just staring at the window."

"Show me."

Jayce moved with supernatural speed to hide behind the couch.

Kristine flipped the phone around and scanned the side of the room where Jayce had been. "See?"

Donkey Pizzle's hesitation frayed her nerves even further, if that were possible.

At last he said, "All right. I'm going to hang up, but before I do, I have one more detail about the job you're *going to do* tonight."

She gulped.

"You need to fly up to the top floor at the back of that building. That's where the fire should start. See? No one but the target gets hurt."

"How do you know he won't wake up and run out of the building when the smoke alarms go off?"

Eerie laughter followed her question. Then he said, "Oh, don't worry. He won't wake up."

The call disconnected. "Shit!" Kristine threw her phone toward the back of the living room. As it whizzed by, Jayce popped up and caught it.

Chapter 7

KRISTINE DROPPED HER HEAD INTO HER HANDS WHILE JAYCE walked around the couch, settled next to her, and pulled her into his arms. Jayce tried to lend her his strength, hoping it would seep through his skin and into her.

"Are you all right, hon?"

Kristine shook her head. "Of course I'm not all right. Did you hear what he wants me to do?"

Jayce caressed her arm, trying to calm her. "I did. I can't help wondering when this is going to stop. He could keep having you do more and more dangerous things."

Her posture sagged. "I know."

Jayce had heard things in the background when Skype was open and wondered if she had too. "I heard waves lapping and seagulls crying in the distance. And someone mentioned a ship."

"Over the phone?" Kristine looked thoughtful and then raised her eyes to look straight at him. "Now that you mention it, I did too. How did you hear those things but I didn't register them?"

"You're stressed," Jayce said. "I imagine tunnel vision happens when you're anxious…just like it does sometimes when we're fighting fires. If there's a life-and-death mission to accomplish, the world around us can disappear while we're doing what's necessary."

"You're right. I don't know why I wasn't paying more attention to clues. I was so worried about my mother, seeing her alive and supposedly well was all I could think of at the time."

"That's understandable. Where do you think she might be—if you had to hazard a guess? If it's near lapping water and a ship, that sounds like the ocean. Or it could be one of the great lakes, if you think there's any reason she might be up that way."

Kristine rose and paced again. "The only place I can think of that might hold a possibility is Long Island. I was born there. If a ship was being boarded, maybe the Coast Guard has a record of it."

"Hey, that's a start…"

"I don't know… We've never had a summer home there or any relatives that I know of. I guess my mother lived there for a while, but she wouldn't tell me anything about it." Kristine heaved a giant sigh. "Of course."

"You had to provide a birth certificate for some of your IDs. What does your birth certificate say?"

"The certified copy showed my name at birth as Kristine Adaria Scott and my date of birth, and place of birth was listed as Good Samaritan Hospital in West Islip, New York. But where it said parents' names, only my mother was listed. That's when I found out her real name was Ainslee. She changed it to Amy Scott. Supposedly so it would be easier for Americans to remember and she needed a stage name. The only other items were a file date and certificate number."

"So no home address?"

"Nope. I had high hopes until I actually saw the certified copy. An address wasn't listed."

"Did you ever try to find *her* birth certificate?"

"I looked a few years ago. Since I knew her real

name, I thought I might be able to find relatives, and maybe one of them could tell me who my father was. But I don't know her birthplace. All I know is she's eight hundred years old—not that she'd admit to being a day over forty."

Jayce said, "It's still worth a try. You might find something if you use one of those ancestry websites."

Kristine snorted. A tiny curl of smoke reminded Jayce of what they were really dealing with. *Dragons*. His sister-in-law Chloe had told his family she was ancient and her grandparents had survived St. Patrick's purge by hiding in caves. Maybe Ainslee was born in a cave.

She'd also said she wasn't able to have children with Ryan. Perhaps dragons could only breed with other dragons. *Shit*. He hadn't thought about that yet. If he and Kristine wound up together, his mother would be disappointed. She wanted grandchildren. *Badly*.

He quickly decided he didn't care. He loved this woman—dragon or not. "If we can find your mother and free her, they'll have no more leverage. You can have your life back."

"Do you think there's any chance of that before the new mission I have for tonight?" Kristine finally sat in the armchair across from him.

"What else can you think of that might help us find her? Did you try calling the hospital? Maybe there's a nurse still working who worked there when you were born," Jayce said.

"I tried that. Apparently nurses don't stay in one job for long periods of time."

He was grasping at straws. "Maybe it's worth a trip to Long Island, along the coast?"

She rolled her eyes. "And do what? Drive around calling her name?"

"I can fly above, and you can drive below. If I see something, I'll signal to you."

After a long hesitation, she finally said, "I'd better rent a convertible. That way you can fly into the backseat and get dressed if I leave some clothes on the floor." A small smile tried to make its way across her face.

"Actually, a convertible isn't a bad idea. You can see a lot more that way." Jayce leaned back, stretched out his legs, and crossed them at the ankle, resting his feet on the coffee table.

Kristine pointed to his feet. "Now there's a bad habit you didn't tell me about when we were breaking up. You put your feet on the coffee table."

Jayce yanked his feet off the table and put them on the floor. "Sorry. I didn't know there was a rule against that in your home."

"There isn't. I was just heckling you."

Jayce was actually happy she was teasing him again. He sprang to his feet and said, "Let's go. You rent a car, and I'll meet you there. If I go now, I might spot the Coast Guard before they leave the area, which would narrow our search."

"So we'll concentrate on the area of Long Island facing open sea?"

"Yes. I can swoop low and look in windows after we meet up. Rent a convertible. I should be able to spot you if you take the route that runs right along the Atlantic side."

"How do you know there is one?"

Jayce laughed. "There's always a road right along the

coast in populated areas." He handed her the phone he had caught after she threw it.

Kristine nodded. "That makes sense. I'll grab your sweats. They'll be faster to get in and out of. Let's see where I can rent a convertible. I'm sure I can get a Long Island map from the rental agency."

He didn't wait for her to dial to set out on his journey. It might be fruitless. The chances of them happening upon her mother were almost nil. But Jayce knew they couldn't just sit around and wait. They both needed to feel like they were doing something that could possibly help.

Jayce jogged up to the roof while Kristine locked the door and ran down the stairs to the sidewalk. He rolled his tail feathers in the dirt, happy he didn't have bright-red and yellow markings on his wings, which would require muddying them too. Flying would've been more difficult…not impossible, since he was stronger than an ordinary bird, but tiring nonetheless.

He took off and sailed on the wind.

Even though they weren't supposed to, shifting and taking to the air and then floating on the wind currents was something he and his brothers enjoyed doing from time to time. That was why he owned a fishing boat. When they got far enough out to sea, where no one would see them, they took turns shifting and dive-bombing the water to catch fish in their beaks. It was a lot of fun on a hot summer day.

In bird form they aged more quickly, even faster in flight, so they had to be careful how often they did this. If their father found out, they'd be in trouble. But even knowing the risks, the joy and freedom of flying were worth it.

Jayce wondered how much he was aging on this trip. The flight last night took a few hours, from New York to Boston then back to New York, and there was some flight-time while creating the black sheet camouflage flight with his brothers. Then shifting this morning and watching over Kristine as she went to the park and back—well, that wasn't much.

Now he might spend all day in this form flying around Long Island looking for a redheaded actress. Fortunately Kristine had several pictures of her mother. There was a clear headshot of her lovely face. A few full-body pictures, some of her onstage. And even one in a bathing suit, looking curvaceous and supposedly alluring. Kristine's body was more to his liking. Athletic.

Jayce tried to avoid buildings as much as possible. They messed up the winds and made it more challenging to fly where he wanted to. So he soared over rooftops and water towers, enjoying a nice bird's-eye view of the city.

This meditation gave him time to reflect on his relationship with Kristine. He had never felt this way about a woman before. He was willing to do whatever was necessary to keep her safe—hang the consequences to himself. Most other women he'd dated appealed to him physically, but this connection was not just physical.

They were both firefighters, concerned about the safety of the citizens of their beloved cities—which were three hours apart as the Acela train flies, dammit. But the point was they had similar values, and that meant a lot. She was concerned about her mother, just as he was loyal to his family. Another double-edged sword.

The fact that he had already showed her his alternate

form and she had shown him hers seemed to mean they were *almost* meant to be. While he was home for the emergency family meeting, he'd told his parents. They were shocked he'd already revealed himself to Kristine. But when he'd said that she had a secret too and hinted it was like Chloe's special gift, they both relaxed immediately. They adored Chloe, even though she'd taken Ryan to Ireland to live. His brother was deliriously happy, and that, in the end, was what everybody wanted.

When Kristine described the background she had seen on the Skype call, it sounded as if her mother could have been in a very expensive home. Chances were the place was not in a crowded neighborhood, but a place with some privacy. If he could hear the waves lapping but no other sounds in the background but seagulls and one other guy, he imagined the place would be off by itself.

He swooped low over every estate within earshot of the beach and, trying not to attract attention, flew by large windows facing the ocean. When he saw women inside but couldn't get a good look at their hair color, he found a low branch to sit on until he was able to rule them out. If there was a possibility it might be Kristine's mother, he would fly in front of Kristine's windshield to grab her attention…when he found her car. Yeesh. He'd better move his tail.

At last he spotted her. While Kristine was halted at a stop sign, he flew down and rested on top of her windshield for a moment. That was his signal for "find a private spot and pull over to the side of the road." They probably should've talked about it sooner, but fortunately, she understood. When she pulled into a dirt road lined with trees, it looked like they were alone. He hopped into the backseat, then shifted and dressed.

"Did you find anything?" she asked anxiously.

"Not much. I saw the Coast Guard speeding away from what looked like a small cargo ship when I first got here. If that's the scene the guy was talking about, we're close."

"Good. Let's check out the homes with ocean views. I'll study the places from the street side, and you examine the beach side. If there's nothing right here, we can widen the search."

"Sounds like a plan." Jayce kissed her, shifted back into phoenix form, and rolled his tail feathers in some roadside dirt. Then he took to the sky again.

They spent hours combing the Hamptons and Montauk, which had the kind of oceanfront homes where Jayce thought Kristine's mother might be held. Eventually he had to change back. He had probably aged months in those few hours.

"Maybe it's time to get the authorities involved," Jayce said as they ate dinner at a sidewalk café in South Hampton.

Kristine gasped. "You can't mean that. I know what I've been asked to do is heinous—despicable. But give me a chance. I've been wrestling with how I can make it look like I've met their demands…but don't worry, I won't kill an innocent person. I couldn't live with that. Honestly, it sounds like the guy could already be dead. If not, I'll get him out first. I'll make sure the fire department gets a heads up just as soon as I'm sure I've done what Donkey Pizzle wants me to do."

Jayce shook his head but said nothing.

His hesitation bothered her. "You wouldn't say anything to anyone, would you?"

"I'd like justice, but I'm not a cop. I'm here for *you*, Kristine. My only thought is to make sure you don't get caught. When do you have to do this? What time tonight?"

"They didn't say."

"Why don't you go home after this, and I'll keep looking for your mother."

"Which, by the way, is still a long shot. We don't even know if we're near the right beaches."

Jayce seemed to be picking at his food. He'd had a margarita, and she wondered if the alcohol might affect him if he didn't eat.

"Are you gonna be okay to fly?" she asked, nodding at his empty cocktail glass.

He chuckled. "I don't think the FAA is going to ground me. Seriously, Kristine, I'll keep looking for your mom. Once it gets dark, I'll be able to see in lit windows, and chances are I won't be seen. We can leave my sweats behind a rock in the woods where I can go and change privately and then find a phone. I promise to call you if I see her."

"What phone?"

"I can grab a prepaid phone or use a pay phone— there are still pay phones in most public places. I'm sure if it's an emergency someone will take pity on me. Just answer even if you don't recognize the number."

Kristine leaned on her elbow and rested her chin in her hand. "That's fine. But what do you plan to *do* if you find her?"

Jayce scratched his head. "I think that's when we

should get the authorities involved. Kidnapping is a crime. Anyone in that house with any knowledge of your mother being held against her will should be arrested—at least as an accessory. I can ask for a SWAT team. They'll make sure your mother is safe before they storm the place."

Kristine closed her eyes. She tried to picture the scene Jayce had described. So far, she didn't see anything wrong with that plan. "Okay. I think that sounds reasonable. Promise me you won't do anything about it yourself. Just call the police and give them the address. Make sure they don't come in with sirens blazing." She leaned forward and whispered, "You know how they are sometimes."

Jayce laughed. "Yeah, they can be real cowboys. Don't worry, I'll make sure they know exactly what's going on." He took a deep breath and let it out slowly. "I do feel better having a plan we can agree on."

If you find her. Kristine didn't feel much better at all. They finished their dinner, and she paid with her credit card.

"I wish I had a couple of cards on me. I'll pay you back," Jayce insisted.

"Tell you what, if you find my mother, dinner's on me." She managed a small smile, hoping to make him feel better. "It's not like you can carry your wallet in your beak."

They walked hand in hand back to Kristine's car, and she wished they could enjoy the lovely evening. She would've loved to watch the sunset with him, holding hands on the beach. But logic dictated she should get back home. She had called in sick. If her shift came

around and someone called to check in on her, it would
be suspicious if she didn't answer. The captain had been
known to do that before when he was concerned and had
the time.

When they arrived at the car, she turned toward him,
and they held both hands for a moment. "I'd better get
back," she said.

Jayce leaned in and pulled her close to kiss her. He
only let go of her hands to wrap his arms around her and
hold her in his warm embrace. Any time his lips touched
hers the passion sprang up, and Kristine never wanted
that feeling to end.

When they tore away from each other, Kristine took a
few deep breaths, bit her lip, then said, "Man, what you do
to me… You'd better let me go, or I'll never get home."

"I know what you mean. If you don't hear from me
by eleven o'clock, wait for me. I want to be there to
protect you while you carry out your orders."

Kristine opened the car door and slid inside. "What
are you going to do? You can't hold a king-size sheet
open and shield me from view all by yourself."

"I can act as lookout. If I see anything, I'll give you a
couple of squawks so you can find a hiding spot."

She closed the car door and rubbed her temples,
trying to ease the headache that was starting. "Okay."

Jayce cupped her chin and leaned down. "I know it's
not ideal. What would be perfect is finding your mother.
I'm going to concentrate on doing that."

Kristine nodded. She was just about to drive away
when Jayce said, "By the way, there's one more thing I
think you should know."

Kristine groaned. *What now?*

Jayce tapped her nose. "I think I'm falling in love with you." Then he stepped away from the car, smiling.

Kristine didn't know what to say to that. She felt like she might be falling in love too, but this just wasn't the time. Instead, she rolled her eyes, took off, and checked her rearview mirror as she left him in a cloud of dust… but she could still see the cocky smile on his face.

As much as she felt it was inappropriate—maybe downright absurd at a time like this—she smiled to herself. How did the ludicrous man know that's exactly what she needed to hear? This was just like him. Her heart was a little bit lighter as she drove home.

―――∿∿∿―――

Jayce was more determined than ever to find Kristine's mother and return her safely home. As darkness fell, he was able to get closer to the homes, worry less about the color of his feathers, and worry more about finding this needle of a woman in the haystack of gorgeous oceanfront homes.

He flew by several palatial estates, some of which were very private with large grounds separating one from the next. There were a few more modest mansions sheltered by woods, hedges, or walls. Even those were multimillion-dollar homes.

He tried to remember that staying in bird form was aging him much more quickly than he would age as a human. His brother had reincarnated and reached his prime in a little over two months. *What will I look like in a week if I keep this up?* Then he shook that thought out of his brain, realizing that helping in this way was better than worrying about a few gray hairs.

At about 10 p.m. he was getting more and more worried he'd fail when suddenly he spotted someone sneaking out of a side door, leaving it open just a tad, probably so no one would hear it shut. He tried to get a better look and saw a woman wearing a black bathrobe. Rushing off on bare feet toward the beach, she seemed determined to get away. A dark scarf slipped off her red hair.

My God, that's her.

Jayce wasn't sure how to reveal himself without scaring her to pieces. If he shifted into a full-size naked man, she might freak. According to Kristine, Amy was high-strung, and he didn't want her screams to alert whomever she was running away from, so he followed her from above. She smartly ran along the edge of the water on the hard sand where the waves would wash away her footprints.

At one point far down the beach, she headed toward some woods. *This might be my chance to show her she's not alone and still have some cover.*

When she reached a spot where the woods were fairly thick, he found a low bush and landed behind it, and as she came toward him, he shimmered into his human form. She gasped but didn't scream.

"It's all right, Amy. I'm here to help."

"Who the heck are you?"

"I'm a friend of Kristine's. Are you all right?"

"Yes. I need to talk to her. Is she here?"

"No. She was. We've been looking for you all day. I need to let her know you've been found. She's about to do something she really doesn't want to because the jerk holding you hostage was threatening you, but your daughter was fucked either way. Sorry about my language."

She looked down at herself. "I'm not exactly dressed properly for a rescue, but I didn't know what else to do. Please tell me you have a fast car hidden somewhere."

Jayce groaned. "I wish I did. Kristine took the car back to the city. I have some sweats stashed, and I can carry them in my beak and meet you somewhere. Then we can find a way to call Kristine."

"Beak? Were you the bird that was following me?"

"That would be me. I'm Jayce Fierro, by the way."

"I *think* it's nice to meet you, Jayce. Since I don't really know you, I'm a little nervous about trusting you, but I don't have much choice right now."

"I promise you can trust me, and I'll tell you more about how I know Kristine after we're both dressed so we don't get arrested."

She gave him a weak smile.

"You seem to be well hidden. Wait here for me." Jayce shifted and took off. He went straight to the place he had left his sweats about two miles away. He didn't want to shift and take forever to get back to her, so he scooped up his clothes in his beak and carried them to the woods where he'd left her.

Jayce was no ordinary bird, and he was able to fly carrying a lot more weight than anyone would think possible. He could yank a full-grown man off the ground if necessary. Hopefully, if anyone spied a bird carrying men's clothing, they'd figure a skinny dipper was in for a surprise when he went to get dressed. Fortunately, the darkness would hide him from most onlookers.

When he landed, Kristine's mother, Amy, was trudging on foot through the woods toward civilization. He wondered if she'd decided not to trust him after all. He wouldn't blame her. She was a New Yorker… Probably even more suspicious and careful than a Bostonian.

Jayce found another rock further down the path, shifted quickly, and slipped on the pants. By the time he donned the top, he'd caught up with her.

"Okay, where do we go from here?" Jayce asked.

Amy hesitated and finally said, "It's been a long time since I've been out here, but I was heading toward the town center. I figured I could find some kind of pay phone, if they still exist."

Jayce smiled. "From what I saw of the towns around here, not much has changed in the past few decades."

"I know where there used to be a pay phone. Let's go there."

"How long will it take us? I told Kristine I'd call by eleven."

Amy glanced around. "It seems to be fairly deserted and dark tonight. It's not high season yet, so most of the summer people aren't even here. How do you feel about flying next to someone who also has a secret identity like yours? Well, not *exactly* like it—"

"I know about Kristine's secret. Is yours the same?"

She answered simply by sloughing off her black bathrobe, shifting into dragon form, picking up her robe, and holding out her talons to indicate that she would carry his clothing too.

Jayce grinned and pulled his sweatshirt over his head, then shifted and flew out of the sweatpants. She picked up his clothes and took off into the sky, flying higher than he usually did unless he was avoiding tall buildings.

At last, she found a rooftop on a dark street. The small town seemed very quiet. An outdoor ladder led from the rooftop down to the wraparound porch. They shifted and dressed quickly.

"I wish we could just fly back to Manhattan," Amy said, "but I'm apt to attract attention, being a dragon and all."

As Jayce chuckled, they sprinted toward the sidewalk. Only about fifty yards away Jayce spotted the phone booth. When they arrived at the old booth, Jayce nervously asked, "I don't suppose you have a quarter on you, do you?"

Amy pulled a heavy sock out of the pocket of her robe and smiled. "I may have borrowed a little money from my captors before I left."

Jayce laughed when she pulled a wad of twenties and a roll of quarters out of the sock. "Hallelujah. You really thought of everything."

"I planned this for a couple of days. I simply had to cooperate until they let down their guard. I knew they would. They're stupid and lazy. Still, it's strange that they never changed the combination to the safe."

"You know them? You've been there before?"

Amy stepped into the phone booth and inserted the quarters she needed, and as she dialed, she said, "I used to live there. Kristine doesn't know it, but I'll tell her everything when I get back."

Jayce knew how much that would mean to Kristine. She had been through so much, and she'd said that a hidden piece of her background caused the rift between her and her mother. Certainly it seemed like knowledge she deserved to have now.

Kristine answered on the first ring. "Hi, honey, it's me," Amy said.

"Mom! Where are you?"

Amy turned and smiled at Jayce. "I'm with a nice young man who says he's a friend of yours. Do you know someone named Jayce?"

Kristine burst into tears but managed to eke out the word "yes." Then she sniffed and said, "Please tell him thank you and to guard you with his life."

"Don't worry, honey. We're going to be careful. It might take a little while. We're still an hour away as the dragon flies."

Jayce said, "I wish we could take public transportation, but your mom is wearing a bathrobe, and I'd rather put some distance between us and her abductors, so I'm not too keen on waiting around for an Uber or taxi."

Kristine said, "I still have the car. I can bring some clothes to my mom and drive us all home."

"That sounds great," Amy said. "Bring me my blue sweater, the cashmere one. Oh, and my Isaac Mizrahi skinny jeans."

Kristine laughed. "Always the fashionista."

Amy's face blushed a bit. "Hey, a girl has to look her best even when she's running from her captors."

"Are you safe from discovery?" Kristine asked. "I want you to stay hidden, but I need to know where you are so I can find you."

"We're in Southampton. I'm not sure of the name of the street."

Jayce said, "Hang on, I'll run down to the corner and see what the sign says." He did that and saw they were on the corner of Main and Harrison. Then he ran back, took the phone, and relayed the information.

"I'll be there as soon as I can. Stay out of sight."

"We will, hon," Jayce said.

Amy raised her brows and looked him straight in the eye. He could imagine the wheels turning as she figured out his relationship with her daughter.

"I'll tell you all about it while we wait," Jayce said.

Chapter 8

"So, it seems we both have stories to tell." Amy settled into a rocking chair on the wraparound porch of a house that appeared to be vacant at the moment.

"It would seem so." Jayce sat in the chair next to hers.

She chewed her lip and stared out at the street.

"I'll go first," Jayce said. "My story seems a lot shorter than yours."

"Thank you. I'm afraid my story is a bit long and convoluted. To be honest, I'm not looking forward to explaining everything to Kristine."

Jayce crossed his feet at the ankles and stretched out. "I think Kristine will be more understanding than you realize."

Amy looked over at him. He seemed sincere, but how could she trust him? She didn't know this man, and she thought she knew all about Kristine's boyfriends. Could this be the guy from the other night?

Jayce steepled his fingers and said, "Kristine and I met a few months ago in Boston. There was an instant attraction, but acting on it at the time wasn't, well...appreciated."

"You mean to say that Kristine rejected you?"

Jayce smiled as if he were remembering the scene. "I don't consider it a rejection so much as just poor timing. You see, we met at my brother's funeral."

"Oh! I think I remember her saying something about that."

He looked hopeful. "Really? She talked about me?"

"In a matter of speaking. I heard her muttering to herself something about the only man to spark her attention recently was a jerk at a funeral. And something about how she had the worst taste in men and should just give up and become a nun."

Leaning back, Jayce laughed. "She did say something about taking a vow. Fortunately for me it wasn't a nun's vow. She had vowed not to sleep with firemen."

"So, it sounds like you're saying you're sleeping together."

Jayce looked over at her and simply asked, "Is that a problem?"

Amy thought about how this guy had saved her. If Kristine trusted him, knowing she wasn't all that trusting of men—at least when it came to romantic relationships—he must be a special guy. "No. No problem at all. As long as you treat her right."

"I'll let you ask her if she's being treated well. But to ease your mind, I care about her, maybe more than I should. We've only been together for a few days, and I'm already in love with her. I live in Boston, but we've agreed that making the effort to overcome the distance and our crazy schedules is worth a try."

Amy nodded. "So you're the guy... The one from Boston that she was muttering about."

Jayce shrugged. "Unless there was some other jerk she was attracted to who frustrated her by hitting on her at a really bad time."

Amy laughed. "I doubt that very much. Kristine keeps most men at arm's length. I'm sorry if that's my fault. I've told her nothing about her father for good reason." She took a deep breath, knowing she was going to launch into the story.

"Kristine's father was a very dangerous man. I was young and naive. We had a whirlwind romance during which he took me to Paris, gave me beautiful jewelry, and quickly moved me into his mansion in Southampton. He promised he'd help me with my acting ambitions, and he paid for private coaching." Amy worried her lip and began wringing her hands. "By the time I realized who and what he was, I was already pregnant."

"I have a sister-in-law who is also a dragon. She mentioned that she can only have children with another dragon. So she and my brother will never have any kids. Is that true?"

Amy nodded sadly. "I'm afraid so. I knew Kristine would be my one and only, and I couldn't allow her to be in danger all her life. Plus this man had become incredibly possessive, not allowing me to go anywhere without him or one of his most trusted guards. I felt like I was living in a prison. And if I tried to get away, he could shift into dragon form and come after me."

She looked Jayce in the eye and said, "He wanted me to get an abortion. He wanted me all to himself. I couldn't let that happen, so the first chance I had, I ran."

"How far did you get?"

"I managed to hitchhike my way to Hicksville. I found a job waitressing and saved enough money to pay for the delivery with a midwife in my little basement apartment."

"You must have had to use a fake name—"

"No. Not on the birth certificate. I didn't want Kristine to have anything that raised red flags hanging over her

head. I had planned to tell her that her father died before
we got married, so that's why she has my maiden name.
We couldn't get married anyway. We were…related."
She felt like she was sucking on a lemon. "I'll elaborate
on the bombshell after I talk to Kristine."

She sighed. "I still wanted to become an actress. I
took a stage name and began my career as Amy. By
that time we had moved to Hell's Kitchen. It wasn't the
nicest neighborhood, but it was all I could afford, and it
was right in the heart of the off-Broadway theater district. And being stronger than humans, I wasn't really
worried about our safety the way a normal woman
might be.

"I got a waitressing job that paid under the counter.
I did some acting in small productions. Meanwhile
Kristine grew up to be the most incredibly levelheaded,
well-rounded, intelligent girl a mother could ask for. I
wish I'd had the money to send her to college. If I had
stayed with her father, she could have gone to an Ivy
League school."

"Or not," Jayce said. "Did he even want her?"

"No. He didn't want any kids. I always wondered if
he'd have gotten past that. I guess I'll never know."

"So, is he the one who took you? Did he finally find
out where you were?"

"No. He's dead now. It was his goons. They just
picked up where he left off. I guess one of them caught
my last show and discovered a lot about my current
life—including my pride and joy. My dear daughter, the
incredibly brave firefighter."

"And he knew she had to be a dragon."

"Yes. My ex made no secret of it among his men. It

was one way he ensured their loyalty. One long blast of fire was all the threat he needed."

At last Kristine's rented convertible roared up to the house where they were camped out.

Jayce rose. "I'm glad we had the chance to talk alone. Whatever has gone on between you and Kristine, I'm not a part of that…but it's good to know the background. I'll wait outside your apartment while you talk. You'll each need to pack a few things and get out of there as soon as possible. I'll make sure you get to safety."

Amy took a deep breath. "Wish me luck, Jayce. I think we're both going to need it."

Amy was relieved when they arrived back at the apartment. She and Kristine sat on their couch. They faced each other, and Amy took her daughter's hands. "Thank you for everything you did for me, darling."

"Of course. What choice did I have? I would never leave you in danger."

Amy glanced up at Jayce, who was standing in the doorway. He smiled, waved, and quietly slipped out the door, closing it behind him.

"So, Mom, you said you were going to tell me everything. Did you mean it?"

Amy took a deep breath. Her thoughts were jumbled, but she had to somehow find the right words to explain to her daughter where she came from and to whom she was related. *Through a dragon hookup that turned into a highly dysfunctional relationship, I inadvertently created a daughter with… Oh God, how do I tell her about this? Will she understand the circumstances?*

"Mom, you know you can tell me anything. I won't think less of you. I love you no matter what."

Amy heaved a sigh. "I know, honey. But this is going to come as a shock either way." She just had to launch into it and let the chips fall where they may. "Your father was a gangster. I didn't know this when I met him, and that's not all I didn't know—"

"It's okay, Mom. That's not the worst thing I've ever heard. Tell me everything."

"Oh, honey. I've barely scratched the surface. First of all, he's dead now—and I'm not sorry to hear that. Unfortunately, he had minions, and they took over his businesses when he died…most of it was illegal and lucrative. I don't know if staying with him would've been better for you or not. I just know I couldn't live with myself if I did. I could barely look at him anymore by the time I left."

"When did you leave? Before or after I was born?"

"Before, darling. I couldn't raise you in that atmosphere. There's so much I have to tell you, and it's not going to be pretty."

Kristine nodded, probably to encourage her.

"As you know, dragons are supposed to be extinct, and in order to maintain that impression, out of necessity, we're pretty sheltered. I thought that meeting a handsome single dragon was the most incredible thing that could've happened to me. A dragon can only have children with another dragon, and I wanted children badly. But I also wanted a career onstage.

"Your father encouraged my acting career. He paid for my coaching. I only did a little acting in summer theater before I left Long Island. After that, the most acting I could do was to act like I hadn't a care in the world."

"I'm sorry you had to go through that, Mom. But I sense there's more."

"I'm afraid so. Okay, here's the worst part. Your father was my half-brother."

Kristine's eyes flew open wide. Then she purposefully schooled her expression, and Amy heard an audible gulp from her daughter.

"I shocked you."

"No. I'm okay. Please go on."

"I didn't know we were related at all. I grew up in Scotland, as you know. Your grandfather was supposedly the last dragon, and St. George was credited with killing the last dragon in Libya. The few dragons left ran and hid. My mother fled all the way to the Scottish Highlands. She was pregnant with twins at the time. She gave birth to a boy and girl in a cave, and shortly after that, another dragon heard the babies' cries and sought her out. The cave was high on a rocky face that wouldn't have been passable by a human. The new male dragon was your grandfather, my father."

Amy could see the wheels turning in Kristine's mind. She was putting two and two together, and it looked like she was coming up with four.

"So my father must've been one of the twins. You and my father happened to have the same mother but not the same father. Is that right? Did you know?"

Amy shook her head. "That's correct, and I *didn't* know. I didn't grow up with the twins. They were both sent to a relative in Canada. Nova Scotia, also known as New Scotland."

"But why?"

"It wasn't uncommon to send children to relatives

that had better circumstances at that time. The twins were troublesome teenagers, and he said they had to go. He sent the other two to an aunt in Canada shortly after I was born. He wanted to raise his own child—me—in relative peace."

"That was hundreds of years ago, right?" Kristine asked. "I thought only indigenous people lived in North America then."

"Yes and no. A few dragons made it to Canada after St. Patrick's purge and St. George's supposed victory over the last dragon. The dragons stayed largely hidden. We mature normally and then age slowly. Once we hit our prime, time really slows down."

"When people think we're sisters, you can't help gloating." Kristine gave her a sly grin.

Amy laughed. It broke the tension, and she was grateful for that. "You know me well. So, do you have any questions about what I've told you so far?"

"Yes. How did you both wind up in New York?"

Amy smiled. "New York is the city of dreams. We both had dreams…very different ones, apparently. But they were dreams nonetheless. I wanted to act, and your father wanted to be rich."

Kristine fidgeted. "I guess he didn't care how he got rich as long as it happened. What caused him to be like that? There had to be a reason."

Amy sighed again. "Dragons have traditionally been very fond of hoarding treasures. Our parents were no different. Of course, when he was sent away, your father lost all claim on the treasure in the hollowed-out mountain where your grandparents amassed quite a bit of gold, relics, and rare gems."

Kristine rested her elbow on the back of the couch and cupped the side of her head "Okay. I get that. So, was his twin sister the same way?"

"No. Not at all. She found someone special, and they stayed in Canada."

"Was he a dragon too?"

"I'm sure he must have been. By that time rumors of remaining dragons had begun in Scotland. Your grand-parents and I had to flee. In order to hide their treasure, they caved in the side of the mountain. Later on, I found out that your father had gone back there briefly. He knew about the valuables and tried to uncover their keep without success. He never told me the details of his participation in that whole debacle. He may have been thinking of going back again someday and may not have wanted anyone else to beat him to the spoils."

Kristine looked uncomfortable. "Mom, can we give him a name? I know you don't want me to know who he was, but is there a way we can talk about him without always saying 'your father'?"

Amy realized now that Kristine might not like the idea of claiming this man as her father, and giving him a name would allow them to talk about him without con-stantly pointing out the relation. "I don't feel comfort-able giving you his real name or even his alias. So let's make up a name for him."

Kristine surprised her by giggling.

"That's what Jayce and I did for your abductor. The guy had the upper hand and let us know it whenever he called, so we named him something that would take his power away. We called him Donkey Pizzle."

Amy laughed. "Very apropos. The right-hand man

was a donkey way back when I lived there. Now he thinks he owns the place. It was actually left in a trust." Amy had one more bombshell to deliver, and she didn't know how Kristine was going to take it. But her daughter deserved to know the truth—all of it.

"I imagine you want to know who the trust fund's beneficiary is."

Kristine shrugged. "If you want to tell me."

Amy didn't want to tell her daughter that she had struggled for years when she could have laid claim to dirty money. A lot of dirty money. "He put it in my name, Kristine. But I didn't want it. I didn't want anything to do with it."

To her surprise, Kristine sat up straight and leaned forward with her hands on her knees. "Good for you, Mom. I wouldn't want any of that money either. I'm proud of you for that."

Amy would have been surprised, except that she knew her daughter. She had raised a highly principled, wonderful girl. She couldn't be prouder. "I'm so glad you feel that way, honey. I didn't know if you'd be mad at me for refusing to make our lives a lot easier. We could have coasted *if* I could have lived with myself. I wrestled with the decision, believe me."

"I'm sure it wasn't easy. But you made the right decision. I wouldn't change a thing."

Amy scooted over until she could wrap her daughter in her arms and give her a long, warm, grateful hug. "I love you so much, Kristine. You've been the light of my life." She felt tears begin to burn behind her eyes. Before she let go, she heard her daughter sniff and knew she was deeply affected too. This bond they had forged was beyond any so-called normal parent-and-child relationship.

When they leaned away from each other, they grasped both hands and smiled despite their tears. Amy couldn't help being touched by her daughter's forgiveness.

"I understand now, Mom. I know why you didn't want to tell me who my father was. I'm not sure I would have been able to confess that to a daughter either. But I want you to know, if anything, I love you more."

Amy burst into tears. She couldn't help it. It was a cathartic cry, letting out emotions that had immobilized her and festered for years. She'd had no one to talk to about this. She couldn't shame the remaining family with this news. So she had disappeared from everyone's life, legally changing her name from Ainslee to Amy Scott and starting over.

—⁓—

Jayce was getting antsy standing in the hall, waiting for the women to finish their conversation. He really had to get them moving and take advantage of the short window they had before Amy was discovered missing.

He was just about to knock when the door opened. Kristine poked her head out. "I wasn't sure you'd still be here."

"Where else would I be? You two need to get out of here, and I know you're both badass dragons, but you still need someone to watch your backs. Have you packed yet?"

Kristine opened the door wider. "Almost finished. It's going to take my mother longer, I guarantee it."

Jayce stepped inside and pulled Kristine into a hug. "How are you doing, my love?"

She melted into his embrace. "I'm okay. I think my mother is more shaken up than I am. I'm just relieved that you found her—alive."

Jayce leaned back and gave her a quick kiss. "Okay then, you'd better get a move on. I'll be right here as your lookout. Yell if you need me."

"I will." She jogged down the hall and disappeared into her bedroom.

Amy wheeled out her suitcase. Thank God there was only one. Jayce had dreaded Amy taking an entire matching set of luggage in different sizes. Since the only place he had to take the women to was his minuscule hotel room, he pictured sleeping on top of their suitcases or on the bathroom floor. "I'm glad to see you're packing light."

"Oh, this is just the first one. I have a few more things…"

Kristine breezed out of her bedroom carrying a duffel bag over her shoulder.

"Mom, you can leave the rest. Think of it as an excuse to go shopping and replace your whole wardrobe."

Amy brightened immediately. "I hadn't thought of that. What a brilliant daughter I have." She winked at Jayce.

He couldn't help smiling, even though his anxiety level was rising by the second. "Let's get going. Hopefully, at some point you can come back. Right now you're not safe."

"I dare anyone to mess with the three of us," Amy said.

Jayce hoped she hadn't just cursed them. He reached for Amy's suitcase handle. "I'll take that."

"Thank you."

He gestured toward the door. "Ladies first."

The women hurried down the stairs. Finally at the bottom, Jayce maneuvered his way around them and opened the outside door, holding it for the ladies.

"What a gentleman you found, Kristine. Does he have any brothers?"

Jayce burst out laughing. The levity was a welcome relief, but he hoped he hadn't drawn attention to them.

"Only five or six," Kristine answered her.

Jayce set a quick pace as soon as the suitcase wheels hit the sidewalk. "I'll tell you all about my family after we get to my hotel. For now, we should just get the hell out of Hell's Kitchen."

The place was a good half dozen blocks away. The streets seemed relatively quiet, but appearances could be deceiving. Amy and Kristine chatted casually, as if the group were just out for a walk. All needed to remain vigilant, however.

Jayce wondered how Kristine was going to handle getting a leave of absence from her job. She wouldn't try to work while Donkey Pizzle was looking for her, would she? No. She had to know how foolish that would be. Still, knowing how she felt about her job…

A chill raced through him. Jayce decided to bide his time and wait until they were safely inside his hotel room before he brought up the issue. The last thing they needed was a loud argument.

At last they reached the hotel without incident. Jayce scanned the small lobby and saw no one about. He took them right to the bank of elevators and up to the seventh floor.

He walked off first, digging his key out of his pocket, and then waited while the women exited the elevator. The breath that whooshed out of his lungs seemed to work in tandem with the elevator doors whooshing closed.

When he got to his room and opened the door, the ladies were talking to each other and not paying attention. Before he could warn them that the bed was in the way, they both walked right into it.

"Oof!" Amy landed on her side with a surprised look. Kristine braced herself before her face hit the mattress.

"I forgot how little this room was," Kristine said.

"If you've been here before, Kristine, I imagine you were distracted," Amy said with a sly smile.

"Welcome to my suite," Jayce said, and the ladies laughed. "Allow me to make room."

The bed was a clever device that, with the push of a button, electronically folded almost in half, creating a couch of sorts.

"There. I'm afraid that's the best I can do. In bed form there's no room to walk. As you saw, the mattress almost met the opposite wall."

"Well, I guess we're staying up all night and talking." Amy collapsed on one end of the folded mattress/couch.

"Fine with me," Kristine said. "My nerves are too frayed to sleep now anyway." She glanced around and tossed her duffel bag into a tiny space between the couch and the wall that separated it from the bathroom. "I'm supposed to go in to work tomorrow."

Jayce leaned against the wall. "I was afraid of that."

"Afraid of what? That I'd have to go do my job eventually?" Kristine asked. "I don't have much of a choice."

Jayce gestured toward the couch for the ladies to sit while he parked the suitcase next to the door and slid down the wall to sit beside it. "I'm afraid this is where my plan ended. To get you both to safety was my whole goal. Now we need to talk about the next step. I don't want to have gone through all that just so they can grab Kristine next."

Kristine sighed. "I know you're worried, but I'll be ready for them. And it's not like I'm alone. I'll be surrounded by big, strong guys every minute I'm on the job."

Jayce folded his arms. "One of us is going to lose a job. I'm not leaving New York with you here. It makes more sense for you to come to Boston. My vacation is almost over."

"Some vacation," Amy mumbled.

Kristine gazed at him but remained silent.

He stared back at her.

Amy glanced back and forth between them, and then as if she couldn't take the silence anymore, she said, "Jayce is right, Kristine. We're not safe here. They know where we live. They know where we work…and they know what we are."

"But now that we know who *they* are, shouldn't they be just as worried about us going to the cops? Maybe they're the ones who should be on the run."

Amy shook her head. "Ah, my darling daughter. How naive you are. Why do you think they've never been caught despite breaking the law for decades?"

"Are you saying the cops know about them but are turning a blind eye? Or that maybe dirty cops are protecting them?"

"Both," Amy said. "They have guns, tranquilizer darts, plenty of people in their debt to do their bidding, and coldhearted, unforgiving natures. You'd be putting your fellow firefighters in harm's way if you expected them to protect you."

"I don't want that, and I don't want to be looking over my shoulder constantly, but I don't want to lose my job. Are you sure there's nothing we can do about these jerks?"

"Not without someone getting killed."

Jayce felt it was in his best interest to let Amy do the talking. She knew these guys were not to be trifled with. Kristine would have to come to the logical conclusion eventually. If he kept pushing for her to go to Boston, it would look like he was being selfish.

Kristine just stared out the window, worrying her lip. Jayce could practically see the wheels turning in her mind.

Amy reached over and took her daughter's hand. "And another thing, darling. I really don't want you anywhere near them because I gather there's some monstrous new project they're going to begin soon."

"New project?" Kristine prompted.

"Yes. Human trafficking. I saw them moving a giant cage in through the back doors and down to the basement."

"Are you sure? Maybe they're just getting a large pet."

Amy leveled an unbelieving look at her daughter. "Really?"

"Okay, okay. I give up. I guess I don't know what they're capable of because I don't think like a sociopath."

"I like that about you," Jayce said. He had hoped to lighten the mood, but it didn't seem to work very well. He cleared his throat. "I think your mother and I are both worried about the same thing. You could underestimate these guys and wind up dead."

"Or worse." Amy shuddered.

At last Jayce had to voice his opinion bluntly. "Something's gotta give, and if you're stubborn about staying, that something could be your freedom or your life."

"So, what are we going to do about not working but not getting fired?" Kristine asked.

Amy tapped her bottom lip. "I've been thinking about that. Perhaps I could fake an illness, use up my sick time, and figure out something from there. You could say you need a leave of absence to take care of me."

"But then people would expect us to be in our apartment. It's not like we can afford to move, especially if we're not working."

"Better yet," Jayce interjected, "you could take her to get medical treatment by specialists. Boston is famous for medical excellence."

"So, not just beans then?"

He smirked. "I think you'd like my fair city, hon. There's a lot I could show you there." He rose, crossed the two steps to reach her, settled in next to her, and framed her face with his hands. "The most important thing I can show you is how much I love you." He kissed her tenderly.

"Hmm, if you're expecting me to choose between gangsters and death on one hand or my boyfriend's affection, my mother's safety, and my life on the other hand, I have to admit you're making a compelling argument."

Jayce finally smiled for real. They could spend the rest of the night hammering out the details, but at least they were all on the same page at last.

Chapter 9

MEANWHILE, IN THE SCOTTISH HIGHLANDS, MOTHER NATURE watched a mountain climber. The little man was tired but trudging up a steep mountainside near Loch Ness, and she couldn't have been prouder of him. Oh yes, she knew the man by name and knew him by his other form too—he was one of her rare dragons.

Conlan Arish was making his way up the mountain without using his wings once. Of course, his supernatural strength aided him, but gravity was gravity, and a brave man-dragon he was.

She knew what he was looking for too…and that he was looking in the right place. Unfortunately he was in the wrong century.

"If only I weren't so softhearted," she murmured to herself. "I guess I'll have to go and tell him." It wasn't that she had a problem with his mission. She knew he was looking for a single female dragon in order to continue the species. She even knew who he was looking for; however, the family with the yellow mark in their widow's peaks had moved to Nova Scotia long ago.

Conlan had impressed her when he met her for the first time. He and his brothers from Northern Ireland were visiting his cousins in Boston. She was well acquainted with the Boston Dragons, Rory and Drake. Both were mated to her modern muses: Drake with Bliss, the muse of email, and Rory with Amber, the muse of air travel.

As far as Conlan knew, Gaia was just a friend of Amber's, staying for tea and pie. When he sat next to her and hit on her with his Irish charm, she almost laughed out loud. But Rory and Amber wouldn't let him humiliate himself and told him he was speaking with Mother Nature herself.

His shock was evident, but he treated her with the reverence she deserved immediately. In the end that's all she really wanted. To be treated with respect.

She watched him coming up upon a ledge. She didn't have to suddenly appear out of thin air or in the middle of a little tornado to announce her power along with her presence. So she transported herself to the top of the ledge and settled into a lotus position. To be sure he recognized her, she stayed dressed in her vine-belted white robe and left her platinum hair long and loose.

She heard him huffing and puffing before she saw him pull himself up over the top. He didn't see her right away, which was probably a good thing. She didn't want him to let go of the ledge in surprise. He threw his leg over one side, and with an "oof," he hauled himself up and rolled onto the flat rock, lying on his back.

When eventually his eyes fluttered open, he whipped his gaze toward the mountainside and saw her. Bolting upright, he stared and asked, "My Goddess, to what do I owe the honor of your presence?"

"I thought you could use my assistance."

"Sure 'n' I could! Do you usually help hikers as they climb? Or am I about to fall to my death and you thought you'd give me a warnin'?"

She laughed. "Neither, dragon. I'm here to tell you how proud I am of you for staying in your human form

and not calling attention to your paranormal abilities—
even though no one appears to be within sight. I also
thought, since you're being such a good boy, I'd let you
know you're not looking in the right place for what you
seek."

"Do you know who I'm searching for, Gaia?"

She rolled her eyes. "I know everything…or almost
everything. I know you're looking for the dragons
marked with a yellow stripe in their widow's peaks.
You're hoping to find a mate among them, and apparently you received a lead, bringing you here."

Conlan leaned back on his hands and looked discour-
aged. "A false lead, apparently. I guess you're tellin'
me I'm on a fool's errand and I should just give up and
go home."

"I'm not telling you that at all. You're looking in the
right place but at the wrong time. They *used to* live here
until humans spotted your distant cousin, Nessie, living
in the lake. Ever since then, the chance of discovery
made them vulnerable. So they moved to Canada."

Conlan furrowed his brow and crossed his arms.
"Seriously? I've come all this way for nothin'?"

"Yup. I'm afraid so."

He lay back down and let out a long, exhausted
breath. "I cannot believe me luck. It's the luck of the
Irish, all right. Bad."

"Oh, don't be so hard on yourself." She rose and
extended a hand to help him up.

"If you knew I was looking for them and you knew
where they were, why didn't you just tell me?" he asked
as he stood with her help.

"Where would be the fun in that?"

He studied her carefully. "Either you're tellin' me that you get off on watchin' us struggle and fail, or there's some kind of lesson we need to learn from workin' hard at a goal."

She tipped her head one way and then the other, considering his words. "Well, you're right and you're wrong. Watching humans try to improve their situations is indeed entertaining. I don't want you to fail, or in your case fall, but what kind of mother would I be if I didn't let you learn from your own mistakes?"

"So you would let me fall?"

She gazed at the sky. "Well, you didn't, so it's a moot point. The important thing is I am making an exception and getting involved where I probably shouldn't. I hope I don't regret it."

Conlan leaned toward her conspiratorially and asked, "How involved do you intend to be? Will you give me an address or merely point me in the right direction?"

Mother Nature sighed. She thought about it and realized that if he went to Canada, he would still be in the wrong country. *Should I tell him where she is?*

"So I'm to go to Canada then?"

Gaia chuckled. "I probably shouldn't tell you this, but you were closer when you were in Boston. But she's not in Boston…yet. I'm sorry to be so cryptic, but you wouldn't appreciate her if this were easy."

Conlan dropped to his knees and clasped his hands. "I swear I will appreciate her forever and always, even if you help me find her."

"Well, I'm not going to. A little guidance is all I'll give. Eastern United States. The rest is up to you."

"Why? With all due respect, of course…"

She tossed her hands in the air. "How do I know you

won't just give up if your mission becomes difficult? Don't you want to know how committed you are?"

Conlan gripped both sides of his head and shook it. "You're confusin' me. I know how committed I am. It's up to me to continue the species. Hell, I'm on the side of a bloody mountain in bloody Scotland. As long as I get down from here alive, I'll go to America and continue my search there. And I will not give up!"

The goddess nodded once. "Excellent. I wish you *good* luck."

And with that she disappeared. She watched from the ether as he took a deep breath and let it out in a whoosh. Then he scooted over the ledge, finding a place for his foot and anchoring his weight. He slammed his pickax into the rock and appeared more determined than ever as he climbed back down.

Jayce would have to fly back to Boston at top speed the next morning to make it in time for his shift. He watched from overhead as Amy and Kristine carried out their plan to get Kristine an emergency leave from work, and Amy some sick time from her job.

As far as he could tell, everything went well and the ladies made it to Penn Station safely. Soon they were aboard the first commuter train bound for Boston. Then he had to get moving.

The night before, Gabe had agreed to leave his window open and lay some clean clothes out for Jayce. By the time he arrived at work, he'd probably have a few more gray hairs, but if anyone noticed he'd blame it on hard partying on his vacation.

He was actually looking forward to getting back. He had a few questions for Drake, his dragon buddy. Specifically if there might be a way to have human off-spring with non-dragons. Drake had a son. There had to be a way.

He was greeted by his coworkers and welcomed back as he got his coffee in the firehouse's kitchen. As soon as he saw Drake, he cornered him. "Hey buddy, can I talk with you?"

"Sure, Jayce. What's up?"

"Uh… We should find a place where we won't be overheard."

Drake looked at him quizzically but followed him to the rec room. They closed the door. A large window allowed them to see if anyone was coming. It was prob-ably the most privacy they could find in a firehouse with a dozen people around.

"Have a seat," Jayce said.

Drake found an overstuffed armchair next to the couch and sat down slowly. "You're making me ner-vous. Is everything all right?"

"Yeah. I don't mean to worry you. I just need some information. I want to know a few things about your kind."

Drake studied him. "My kind?"

"You didn't think I knew about Chloe—my sister-in-law—being a dragon? Weren't you curious about whether the whole Fierro family knew her secret?"

"So Ryan told you?"

"Not exactly. He took our father to the paranormal club, and he said you were there. My dad spilled the news to everyone at Sunday dinner."

Drake nodded and then heaved a sigh. "How much do you know?"

Jayce smiled. "Enough to trust you. Especially since I have a secret too, and trust goes both ways. Let's just put our cards on the table. I'm a phoenix. You're a dragon. We both have an advantage when it comes to fighting fires…"

Drake nodded. "Okay. You got me. So what does Chloe have to do with this?"

"Nothing really. It's just the fact that my brother, a phoenix, fell in love with and married a dragon. Now I'm in love with a dragon too."

Drake's eyebrows shot up. "The hell you say. I don't know any other dragons besides the Arish family. Don't tell me you're breaking up a happy family! Or…are you involved with one of the male cousins?"

Jayce leaned back, open-mouthed. "No! It's not them."

"You found another family?" Drake's eyes rounded.

"Yes. A mother and daughter."

Drake smiled. "So which is the lucky girl, the mother or the daughter?"

"The daughter. But without getting into any more details about the family, I was wondering what you can tell me about dragons."

"What do you want to know?"

"For starters, why are there so few of you? I thought you were very hard to kill." Jayce hoped the info he'd been given about a dragon only being able to have children with another dragon was false.

Drake looked at him sideways. "Do not ask me how to kill a dragon. Or I'll tell you to shower us with cake and ice cream."

Jayce laughed. "Why would I ask you that? I love this girl. I was just wondering why there are so few of you. Is reproduction difficult?"

"Oh." Drake clasped his hands and leaned forward. "Our women don't get pregnant very often."

That doesn't sound like it can't happen… Huh. It made Jayce wonder about his brother Ryan and Chloe. When Chloe had been welcomed into the Fierro fold, it had been established that she and Ryan wouldn't be able to have children. But if both he and Ryan couldn't have kids, Mama Fierro wouldn't like it. She wanted grandchildren and lots of them, like yesterday.

Drake scrubbed a hand over his face. "Mother freaking Nature…" he muttered. "She thought it would be a good idea to make our females fertile only once every five years. If you miss the window, the siblings will be ten years apart—or fifteen. And then there's the little fact that a dragon can only reproduce with another dragon."

Oh no. It was true. Gabriella would freak.

Drake seemed to be watching his expression closely.

"Okay. That makes sense. I remember Chloe telling the family she couldn't have children, but I didn't know why."

Drake tilted his head. "Does that affect things for you?"

"It doesn't affect the way I feel about Kristine." Jayce suddenly realized something. "Wait. Your wife must be a dragon, because you have a son!"

He groaned. "No, but it's a long story."

Jayce was just about to ask him to explain when he saw the captain coming toward them. "It looks like we won't be alone much longer. I guess we'll have to save the rest of this conversation for another day."

They both rose and shook hands.

Then Drake surprised him by pulling him into a man hug and slapping him on the back a few times. "Hang in there, buddy."

Drake left the recreation room as Captain Madigan entered.

He stared at Jayce. "I'd ask if it was something I said, but I haven't had a chance to say anything."

"Don't take it personally. We were just done with our conversation. Hey, do you feel like playing pool? I could use a little cash after spending it all on vacation."

"Hell no. The last time we got a call in the middle of our tournament, someone took the cash."

"Shit. Did you lose a lot?"

"Doesn't matter the amount. It's the principle. It's hard to believe anyone would take advantage of firefighters when we're on a job. It'll be a while before the sting wears off."

"I know what you mean. That must've happened while I was on vacation. I don't remember hearing about it."

"Yeah, a few things happened while you were on vacation."

Jayce bet what had happened to him while he was in New York was a hell of a lot more interesting than what had happened back here at the station—no matter how many car crashes, multiple-alarm fires, or public assists they'd been involved in. He was pretty sure his weird rescue mission had them beat.

—◦◦◦—

Hoping she wasn't interrupting anything, Kristine called Jayce.

He answered with "Hey! I was about to call you."

"We're almost to Boston."

"That *is* good news." He sounded happy.

"My mother pulled off an Oscar-worthy performance at the station this morning. She ambled in like a zombie, found the captain's office, propped herself up against the doorjamb, said, 'I need my daughter—I'm ill,' and then slid to the floor."

"Wow. I'll bet the captain bought it."

"Oh yeah, he did. He wanted to carry her down the stairs to an ambulance. When I explained she had just been diagnosed with chronic fatigue syndrome and there was a specialist in Boston we wanted her to see, he urged me to take her. Amy insisted she'd be fine after a little nap…just like a real patient would. Then he said to take however much time I needed, and we'd work around a caretaker schedule when she got home."

"That's incredible."

Kristine was saddened slightly. "Yes, he really is a nice person down deep. I guess his sister had chronic fatigue syndrome, and doctors didn't believe her until she fainted at their feet."

"So he's seen this before."

"Oh yes, and he wants her to get all the help she needs. I feel a little guilty knowing she doesn't need any."

"Don't be. She *does* need help. It would be a miracle if she doesn't have PTSD. Unless you want to tell your captain she was abducted and you spent your days off negotiating with kidnappers—"

"No. Of course not. I know she needs this, if for no other reason than to get some peace of mind and a little sleep."

After a brief hesitation, Jayce added, "Hey, since you're taking the commuter rail, you can get off right in Back Bay. That's just blocks from the B and B. Much closer than South Station. I'm on duty now, and the B and B is not that far from the fire station, so I can be there as soon you get in and carry your things."

Kristine laughed. "Are you forgetting what we really are? We're strong enough to carry half of our apartment across town. If we're only a few blocks from the B and B and you're on duty, just point us in the right direction and give us the address. We can find our own way. It might help if you call your friends at the B and B and tell them to expect us. Do you think they'll have room?"

"From what I understand, they only advertise at the paranormal club next door, so they almost always have vacancies. They don't want humans mixed in with their paranormal guests. I'll explain the situation to them, and I'm sure they'll hold one or two rooms."

"Don't let them go to any extra trouble. We can stay at a hotel for a night or two. But my mother is very anxious to speak to these paranormals, especially the dragon."

"Why don't I call you back as soon as I've talked to them?"

"I can't wait to see you," she said, almost shyly.

"Same here."

"When do you get off the rotation?"

"We're here until tomorrow at 6 a.m. I'll bring breakfast."

"But doesn't B and B stand for 'bed and breakfast'?"

"Oh yeah." He laughed. "I'm an idiot."

"No, you're not. It's just good to know you aren't perfect." *Even though you seem perfect for me.*

"I'm sure Rory and Amber will take good care of you until tomorrow. I'll let Amber tell you what sort of paranormal she is. It's a great story. A little too complicated for me to explain, but she's a really good person and will welcome you with open arms."

After a brief pause, he whispered, "I love you."

Kristine said, "I love you too." And from a distance Amy called, "I love you too."

Jayce chuckled.

Kristine was just about to hang up when she heard the tones ring out on the other side of the phone.

"Gotta go," Jayce said, and the call disconnected.

The fire was along Charlestown's waterfront. Trucks rolled out, with Jayce and Drake in the back of Ladder 9. Jayce didn't recognize the address they'd been given. It could've been anything from a brand-new high-rise waterfront condo to one of the remaining warehouses. He just knew it wasn't the naval shipyard. The Navy took care of its own.

The firefighters spotted plumes of smoke before they arrived. The fire appeared to be near the docks... probably one of the old warehouses. The brick building was only four stories high, but as they pulled up, Jayce saw smoke pouring out of some broken windows on the second and third floors. Flames shot out of the first-floor windows.

As soon as the firefighters jumped out of the truck, they began grabbing their gear, anticipating Captain Madigan's shouted orders. The ladder truck's aerial was being raised, and all the firefighters who were planning to go in were putting on their air masks and tugging on their gloves.

Drake was directed to the roof with the big K12 saw, along with another two firefighters. Jayce and two others were told to check the upper floors while staying in constant communication. They needed to locate the seat of the fire and relate their findings over the radio.

"I can check four, and you guys check two. We'll meet on three." Jayce charged up two floors and was on the top story before the other two finished the lower level. He moved lightning-fast across the large expanse, smoke filling the area so quickly and so densely that even with his superior vision he was having a hard time seeing much more than his hand in front of his face. He picked his way along the floor. Having not found signs of any fire yet, he turned a corner and moved along in that direction until he had to turn again. He kept picking his way across the long warehouse floor, which was filled with large boxes. Shelving was about the only differentiation. The windows were high, and as a result barely any light reached him.

The air was getting hotter, and he knew he must be getting closer to the area of the fire, but he still didn't see any flames. The smoke may have been coming up through grates or the stairwell, but there was so much of it. He kept going, hoping there wasn't any fire on this top floor yet.

Jayce listened for the captain's voice over the radio. At last, the captain asked, "Fierro, have you got anything?"

"No, Captain. Just a lot of smoke."

Captain Madigan barked the same question to the other two firefighters. One of them on the third floor, Walters, had found flames. He was approximating his location at fifty yards in, but Jayce knew that with smoke clouding everything, it was difficult to precisely calculate where you were in a building. The heat grew more intense as Jayce crept forward, zigzagging his way through the various paths created by stacked boxes and shelving.

If he didn't find fire soon, he would guess that perhaps there had been a smoke bomb—or several—set off to cover the area and perhaps give the fire a chance to burn whatever evidence might be there. He had seen this once before in an arson case. It was a bitch to find anything when all you saw was smoke.

But since Walters found something Jayce decided he would backtrack and go help his buddy.

He bumped into the end wall of the building—how the hell had he gotten so turned around? Thankfully there was no fire on his floor, but the smoke was, if anything, worse than before. Then he spotted the vents and the floor grates that allowed smoke in from below. Smoke was pouring out of the grate near him. At least he knew where he was now.

It was time to lend his buddy a hand. He lifted the radio to his mouth. "Walters, are you on the third floor?"

The radio crackled. "Yes, third floor. Flames spreading fast here."

"Second floor too, Fierro," a firefighter named

Harmon added. "It looks like it started on two and spread up to the third floor."

"Fourth floor is secure. For now." Jayce said. "I'm working my way back to the stairs, and I'll meet you on the second floor, Harmon."

The captain called out, "No, Fierro. I'm sending hoses to the second floor. You go to the third floor with Walters. The workers are accounted for, but you may find a visitor. They think someone made a delivery on the third without signing in."

"You got it, Captain." Jayce rushed across the floor, thinking he was retracing his steps. Suddenly he was bumping into another wall. *Shit. Where did that come from?*

One of the worst mistakes a firefighter could make was getting turned around in a building full of smoke. As he realized he had made that mistake and was in very real danger of not being able to find his way out, he thought about Kristine. What if she and her mother arrived to find no one waiting for them? What would she think? He doubted her first thought would be that he had been reduced to ash and reincarnated. Then he would have to spend the next several weeks in phoenix form until he reached maturity so he could shift into his adult body. *Fuck*. If he shifted tomorrow, he'd be an infant and unable to tell anybody anything.

He stuck close to the wall and moved in the direction he thought would lead him back to the stairs. But after a couple of minutes, when he came to the adjoining wall, he realized to his horror he had gone further into the building and not toward the entrance at all.

"Goddamn it!" As much as he didn't want to admit he had made a mistake, he knew he should let his fellow firefighters know he wasn't coming—at least not as quickly as he would have liked to. He hoped they wouldn't panic and try to find him. They were mortal and would be putting their own lives in danger.

He bumbled his way along the other wall, seriously not knowing which way he was going. He figured he must be against the long wall. If he just moved away from the short one, then he would be heading back the way he had come. Thick smoke surrounding him made it impossible to see anything. The floor had heated to a point where he imagined it wouldn't be much longer before it reached its flashpoint.

He moved faster and hugged the wall, hoping he would find an opening quickly.

"Fierro, where are you?" It was Harmon speaking.

Jayce should have joined him by now. As much as Jayce hated to do it, he had to tell the truth. "I got turned around. I'm finding my way out against the long wall."

He heard the captain swear.

"Is there fire where you're at, or is it just smoke, Fierro?"

"Just heat and smoke, Captain," he said. "Don't send anyone. I'm almost out."

"How do you know? Can you see something? Is there light coming through?"

Jayce wished he could have said yes. He desperately wanted to get out of there on his own. "Almost out, Captain."

As Jayce rushed along the wall, he tripped over something and skidded into a pile of boxes—apparently some had fallen and not been picked up. Or whoever had set the fire may have left them scattered as a booby trap for unsuspecting firefighters. He'd heard of sick individuals doing things like that.

He pushed himself to his feet, felt around for the wall, and realized he had lost his bearings—again. After falling ass over teakettle, he didn't know in which direction he popped up. Now he was surrounded by smoke he couldn't see through, so he moved a few feet in each direction, feeling for the wall. Nothing. Back to center. A few more steps in another direction again led to nothing. He came back to the center, moved a few feet in another direction, and pawed at the air. He couldn't believe this calamity. Just when he thought it couldn't get worse, his low air alarm began chirping. Its warning told him he had five minutes—ten at the most—to breathe. *Shit, shit, shit.*

Jayce heard voices and turned toward those. Apparently the captain had sent someone after him even though he had asked him not to. He was never so happy to be second-guessed.

"Fierro! Where are you?" Drake called out from somewhere nearby.

"Stay where you are," he yelled. "I can hear you. I'm coming toward you."

"Well, hurry up. We've got a bitch of a fire on our hands, and we need you."

Jayce felt bad enough without being told he was part of the problem. He charged toward the voice, tripped again, and yelled, "Jesus Christ."

"You okay?"

"Yeah. I just feel like an idiot. Thank God it's you. I was afraid they sent someone…" He almost said the word *mortal*. That would've been hard to explain.

"Yeah, I know. Come toward my voice. And watch your feet this time, Grace."

Jayce laughed, even in the midst of his frustration and anger at himself. He slid his foot ahead a few feet and then pulled the other one up to meet it. In this way, Jayce sort of skated his way across the floor toward Drake's voice.

"I can see you."

Jayce squinted through the smoke and saw a dark shape a few feet ahead. "Yeah, I see you too. Almost there."

When he reached out, Drake grabbed his arm and dragged him in the right direction. "I've got ya, buddy."

Jayce let out a deep breath, never more grateful to hear those words.

Drake led him another dozen or so feet to the stairwell. "I've got him, Captain."

"Thank God. Get him out of there before he runs out of air. You all right, Fierro?"

"Yeah, Captain. I'm fine. Just got turned around when I tripped over something. Not a body—just boxes. We'll go and help Harmon now."

"No, Fierro, you're coming to me. Cameron can help Harmon."

Crap.

When Kristine and her mother arrived at the Back Bay train station, they heard their names being called from a distance. A handsome man was heading toward them. It wasn't Jayce or any of his brothers. Curious, Kristine and Amy headed toward the stranger who knew their names. When they reached each other, the guy introduced himself.

"I'm Rory, owner of the B and B where you'll be stayin'," Rory said with an Irish accent.

Kristine stuck out her right hand. "Hi, my name is Kristine Scott. This is my mother, Amy."

They all shook hands and exchanged pleasantries before he reached for the two heavy bags. They tried to stop him.

"You don't have to carry our stuff. We're plenty strong and can do it ourselves," Kristine said.

"Oh, I have no doubt of that. But how would it look if I strolled beside two ladies carryin' heavy luggage?" As they walked, he chatted away. "I've heard good things about you, Kristine. And this is your mother? She looks young enough to be your sister."

Amy tittered.

Kristine rolled her eyes. "Don't encourage her. You know what we are. Right?"

"Yes, Jayce told me. He thought you'd want us to know. Still, your mother doesn't look a day over thirty," Rory continued. "Our kind is lucky. I'm about a thousand years old meself."

Amy smiled. "I'm not far behind you then."

His brows lifted. "Really? And where might you be from?"

"Originally? Scotland. I was born there. Kristine is much younger, however. She was born in New York."

"Ah," he said. "Much younger, then." Rory continued. "I couldn't be more excited to meet another dragon clan! Me friend Drake can't wait to meet you as well."

"Is he a dragon?" Amy asked.

"I'm supposed to let guests reveal themselves if they

choose to—and I should let you know…we have a strict policy not to reveal our paranormal status to humans. But Drake isn't a guest. He's a member of the club next door and one of our resident firefighters, like yourself, Kristine."

"We'll be excited to meet him too," Amy said. "Is he single?"

"Ma!"

She giggled. "It never hurts to ask…"

"Alas, he is not," Rory said. "His wife's name is Bliss, and the couple couldn't be more blissful."

"A pity," Amy said. "Oh! Not about their happiness. I only wish I could find the same."

The two New York dragons followed Rory through the beautiful neighborhood called Back Bay. When they arrived at Beacon Street and took a left, Amy asked, "Is this the street you live on?"

Rory gave them a gleaming grin. "It is indeed."

"It's gorgeous!" Amy exclaimed.

Kristine had to agree. It seemed as if the Boston paranormals were doing quite well.

Soon they arrived at a magnificent brownstone. It was more of a light gray, but Kristine knew the term actually referred to any building of similar style, the common denominator being a front stoop.

As Rory ascended the stairs, Amy halted, caught her breath, and placed a hand over heart. "I'm gobsmacked. This is one of the most beautiful city homes I've ever seen."

Rory paused and gazed up at his home lovingly. "She is indeed. I won't pretend to be humble and say, 'Aw, it's nothin',' because, truly, it's a privilege to live here. Me sister and I restored the building to its original elegance. It was a labor of love that lasted about a year."

They no sooner had entered the beautiful home than Kristine's phone rang.

"Jayce! We're here!"

"Did Rory show up?"

"He arrived on schedule. We're at the B and B now."

Rory smiled at Amy. "Let me give you the tour. Kristine can catch up with us after her phone call."

Perfect. She wanted a little privacy to talk to her lover.

"I can't wait to see you!" Jayce said. "I'm getting off a little early. Can I take you out to dinner?"

"I'd like that." Then she lowered her voice. "Unless you want dessert first."

"Would I!" He laughed. "I can't wait."

Rory and Amy chuckled. *Damn. I thought they were preoccupied.*

As soon as Kristine and Jayce said their good-byes—or see-you-laters, as it were—she found the others. "I'd like to rest up a bit before Jayce arrives."

"Of course, luv. I'm sorry for tarryin'. It's just that we Irish love our stories and long introductions. But let's get you settled and feelin' right at home." He called up the stairs, "Amber?"

Home? Kristine didn't know where home was anymore. They couldn't go back to their apartment in New York. They'd have to move, and to be safe they should return only when they were sure the apartment was no longer being watched and they had a new place to go to.

Moving would be a nightmare. Amy had already complained about leaving so many of her special things behind—like her Tony award—even though she knew it was imperative to get out of New York as quickly as possible.

She'd definitely be going back for it, no matter how dangerous the situation was.

Chapter 10

JAYCE FOUND THE B AND B EASILY. IT WAS RIGHT NEXT door to the building that housed the paranormal club his father and brother had told him about. He jogged up the stairs and rang the bell.

A moment later, a young woman with honey-colored hair answered the door and opened it wide.

"You must be Jayce," she said.

"I am. I've come to see Kristine."

"Come in. Come in. My name is Amber, and I run this joint with my fiancé, Rory Arish." She stuck out her hand, and Jayce shook it, glancing up the stairs impatiently.

"Is Kristine here?"

Amber didn't have to answer because the sound of running footsteps was soon followed by his lover, who jumped off the third step and into Jayce's open arms. He caught her and held tight as she smacked kisses all over his face. He laughed and then puckered up, waiting for her lips to find his. They shared a long, languorous kiss.

Jayce barely heard Amber say, "Well, I'll leave you two alone. Maybe we'll see you at breakfast, Jayce." She snickered as her footsteps faded away.

"I'm so relieved to see you here and in one piece," Jayce said.

"You and me both. Let's go upstairs, and I'll show you my room."

"What are we waiting for?" Jayce asked, and they ran up the wide stairway hand in hand.

On the third floor, Jayce let Kristine lead the way. He followed her to the end of a long hallway and waited impatiently for her to unlock the door to her room.

When he stepped in, he couldn't help being impressed. The beautiful four-poster bed against the far wall sported an elegant brocade bedspread and loads of colorful pillows. The drapes matched the bedspread, and the sumptuous fabric was tied back with gold cords.

All he wanted to do was tear off their clothes and get horizontal, but the elegant furnishings made him think twice about carelessly tossing that bedspread across the room.

She draped her arms over his shoulders, and they shared another hot kiss. A few moments later, someone cleared his throat, and Jayce realized they hadn't closed the door. He managed to wrench himself away from Kristine and close the door on a grinning young man in the hall.

"Sorry. I didn't mean to provide an audience," Jayce said.

"I'm just as guilty of being overanxious." Kristine giggled.

Jayce picked her up, carried her to the bed, and set her down on it gently, tossing three of the five pillows.

Kristine grabbed the hem of her T-shirt, yanked it over her head, and tossed it on the floor. She wore a black lace bra. Jayce couldn't help wondering if she had panties to match or if she was sticking stubbornly to her granny panties. She moved and shimmied out of her jeans, silently answering his question. She was wearing, of all things, a black lace thong.

"I thought you didn't like floss."

"And I thought you liked nice surprises," Kristine said and gave him a seductive look.

When she turned around to pull the bedspread down, he almost died. The perfect globes of her bottom were right there for him to see or touch. He toed off his boots while removing his T-shirt and jeans. They followed Kristine's clothes onto the floor.

The moment Kristine turned around, facing him, he tackled her onto the bed. She laughed aloud as they bounced.

"Can't wait, huh?" Her turquoise-blue eyes gazed into his brown ones. There was a mysterious darker circle surrounding her irises, like especially deep parts of the ocean.

He rolled until she was on top of him. She wiggled, batting her eyes playfully. "I thought you'd probably want me."

His cock was throbbing for her. The Neanderthal in him wanted to spread her wide and pound his way to heaven; the rest of him wanted to crush her in a sweet embrace for all eternity. The rush of love that flooded through his veins silenced him.

"I love your chest." Her hands were wandering over his skin, softly exploring. She dipped her head and licked his shoulder, her tongue tracing a muscle that flexed there. "Love your body," she sighed.

Oh damn, he was going to explode on the spot!

There was no doubt he wanted her. Kristine could probably feel his iron-hard erection pulsing between them. Memories of the last time overwhelmed him. The friction of their mingled bodies, sending her screaming over the edge in bliss, had haunted his daydreams. Just the recollection was making him even harder. But Jayce was silent, clutching onto her for dear life, gazing into her eyes.

"Oh, Jayce!"

The tiny word released him. He was plastering kisses on her mouth, running his hands down her back over her ass and those sweetly pretty, hideously uncomfortable butt-floss panties she'd worn just for him. It had been a tease, but now her body burned. Her breath was ragged.

He was drowning in her silky hair, her soft skin, and her perfume; a sweet feminine scent that reminded him of flower gardens. She was the most beautiful creature he'd ever known, and he wanted her forever.

A swift movement pulled the thong down to her knees. A wriggle sent them flying to the floor. His hard flesh slipped between her thighs, encountering the welcoming dampness there.

"Don't wait," she gasped. "I want you right here, right now."

He leaned against her, reveling in her quivering body and her rasping breaths. She wanted him as much as he wanted her. He paused, knowing he'd treasure this moment forever.

Then he took her in one fierce move, piercing her core in a deep thrust. They fused together, arms folded tight. A moment later, they relaxed, and their bodies began their ancient dance in perfect harmony.

He could feel the heat inside her gather and wondered if her breath might turn to fire. As he dipped his head, his tongue flicked over a taut nipple. Her deep internal muscles clenched, flooding him with fierce delight. Their sensuous movements coupled with the rough colliding of bodies sent him soaring again. Each strong thrust seemed to push her closer to the edge of release.

Her skin was damp, her eyes heavy-lidded. Her legs crossed over his back, pulling him in close. She moaned, rising to meet his every thrust. Her need was driving his body and enveloping his soul. His balls tightened, his body taken over by shivers that drove him closer to his peak with each minute movement.

They clenched and shuddered together. Their breaths mingled in harsh gulps as they rose and fell, seeking their release. Her heated body was releasing waves of hot womanly perfume. She was biting her lip, moaning and gasping.

His fingers held tight to her upper arms as he pulsed into her in staccato bursts. Her hands gripped his shoulders, and her heels dug into him as she writhed and called his name.

A fiery thrust flashed through him, fanning the flame into an inferno. *Oh God, I'm coming hard.*

"I love you, Kristine!"

A slow arch and quiver turned their gasps to shudders. Their bodies tightened, soaring before shattering. They were groaning in harmony. Kristine raked her fingernails down his back. They pulsed in frenzied explosions of sensation. Loving kisses mingled with raw panting and newly made memories of glorious abandon.

They slowed to a shuddering halt, delighting in the aftershocks of almost violent ecstasy.

When Kristine and Jayce finally descended the marble staircase and made their way to the first-floor lounge, there was an animated discussion going.

Two women rested on the cream-colored couch, and two men sat in adjacent light-blue armchairs. When they all noticed the couple, the men jumped to their feet. Kristine recognized Rory but not the other young man.

"Kristine!" Amy exclaimed. "We found another dragon and possibly a relative!"

Kristine gaped at the young man she didn't know as Amy gestured to him. "This is Conlan Arish, Rory's cousin from Ulster."

He stepped over to her and shook her hand. "Ah... It's pleased I am to meet you. I see where you get your good looks." He glanced over his shoulder at Amy, who beamed at him.

Amber chuckled. "Beware of these Irish charmers."

"Are you saying be wary or be aware?" Rory asked as he sat down and patted his lap. Amber rose from her spot on the sofa and crossed to her fiancé, settling down on his lap to make room for Jayce and Kristine on the couch.

"Depends. But let's leave the teasing for now," Amber said.

"Indeed. It sounds as if there's more to talk about, like finding possible family that we thought were lost forever," Conlan said excitedly.

Jayce crossed to the couch, holding Kristine's hand, and the two of them sat close together. Jayce put his arm around her shoulder, and she cuddled into him. Amy remained on his other side.

"So, how are we related?" Kristine asked.

"We're not positive that we are. Apparently there's another dragon in town with the same yellow streak in his widow's peak that you and I cover with hair dye," Amy said.

Jayce spoke up. "You mean Drake?"

Amy's eyes widened. "You know him?"

"I work with him. Would you like me to call him and invite him over?"

Rory grinned. "I'm afraid we beat you to it. He said he's having dinner with the Mrs. and he'll be over directly."

Conlan reseated himself in the armchair next to the couch and gazed at Amy, who sat adjacent. It was hard to miss the chemistry between them. Kristine wanted to be happy for her mother, if she had finally found someone special, and another dragon meant they wouldn't have to explain themselves. That was always a big problem when a relationship with a human reached a serious point.

"So, tell us about yourselves," Conlan said.

Kristine took a deep breath and sighed. "I wouldn't know where to begin."

"Maybe we could start at the present and work backward," Amy suggested. "I've already told them we're from New York and that you're a firefighter and I'm an actress...perhaps a former actress," she said sadly.

"I understand you're in a spot of trouble," Conlan said. "But you never elaborated on what that might be. Mayhaps I can help."

Amy leaned back and gazed at the ceiling. "You don't ask easy questions, do you?"

"Forgive me. I don't mean to pry, but if there's anythin' I can do..." Conlan seemed genuinely concerned for their well-being.

Amy smiled. "That's very kind of you. But I think we've done what we had to do, mainly getting out of New York and finding a safe place to stay for a while."

"And how long is a while?" he asked.

Amy shrugged. She looked over to Kristine, who also shrugged.

Jayce cleared his throat. "I wasn't going to bring this up right away, but I was thinking perhaps Boston would be your home from now on."

Kristine leaned away from him, shocked. "That's quite an assumption on your part. Our lives are back in New York. My mother acts on Broadway and teaches at an acting school, and I don't think you have a branch here. After all that's happened, it's tempting to want to relocate, but I won't be run out of my city, and my firehouse, which I'm also quite attached to."

Jayce let out what sounded like a frustrated breath. "I knew I shouldn't have said anything yet." When the doorbell rang, he mumbled, "Saved by the bell, literally."

Amber jumped up off Rory's lap. "I'll get it."

Everyone waited quietly until they heard Amber welcome Drake. She escorted him into the living room, and he began shaking hands.

"I think you know most everyone here," Rory said. "But let me introduce you to our newest guests, Amy and Kristine Scott."

They both jumped to their feet. Drake walked over to Amy and shook her hand and then crossed to Kristine and shook hers as well. The usual pleasantries were exchanged but with a bit more animation. He did indeed sport the yellow streak in his widow's peak that matched their own.

"Kristine and I conceal our marks with dye, but if we didn't, we'd have the very same mark you do!"

"This is exciting," Drake said. "I thought I was the last of my clan so kept the mark visible, just in case. I thought I had lost every family member I had, and now, if I heard right, it looks like I may have found some again."

Amy pulled him over to the couch, gesturing for him to sit down next to Jayce, and she sat on the arm next to him…even closer to Conlan.

Amber said, "I'll get you another chair."

"I'll get it," Drake said.

A moment later he returned with two chairs from the dining room. Drake sat in one, and Amber settled in the other, while Amy returned to her spot on the couch.

Kristine leaned across Jayce, focusing on her mother. "Let's not get ahead of ourselves," she whispered. "We may not be related—"

"Aye. You're quite right," Drake said with a very slight Scottish accent. "We should compare facts first. My family came from Scotland many years ago and settled in Nova Scotia, Canada."

Amy's eyes widened, and she slapped a hand over her heart. "I was born in Scotland, and later I went to Nova Scotia before settling in New York. When did you go to Nova Scotia?"

Drake smiled broadly. "About four hundred years ago."

"And what is your last name?"

"Cameron," Drake said, hopefully.

Amy shook her head. "I don't know of any Cameron relatives."

"My parents met in Canada."

"And they were both dragons? What are the odds?" Amy wondered quietly.

Rory cleared his throat. "If I may…Conlan and I were wonderin' if we dragons *all* might be related. Conlan and I are cousins. Our fathers were identical twins. However, they had a younger brother as well."

Conlan added, "Apparently our uncle left for parts unknown."

"Why did he leave?" Amy asked. "And when?"

Rory cleared his throat and adjusted in his seat. "There was a bloody battle over the rule of Ballyhoo about a thousand years ago. Many died, but in the end my father defeated Conlan's father."

"Meaning he killed his own brother. All over a castle and a piece of dirt on the cliffs of the Atlantic Ocean. That's about all that was left after the battle." Conlan clasped his hands, as if in prayer.

The mood of the room turned somber. Rory took a deep breath. "We've put all that behind us now, right, cousin?"

Conlan nodded sadly. Then his countenance brightened. "Not without some good old Irish family drama, though."

Rory laughed. "Me sisters and I stayed in Ballyhoo, Ireland—we'll tell you about our cousins' return from Ulster another time."

"So what did *you* do, brave dragon?" Amber asked Rory. "Did you fight with your father?"

"No. I wanted to, believe me. But me father ordered me to stay below in the caves with me mother and sisters. He didn't want to leave the women alone and vulnerable."

Conlan laughed. "Aye. Me brother, Aiden, saw how

vulnerable a female dragon could be when he was fightin'
for his life with Rory's sister Chloe last summer."

Amber smirked. "I remember. But let's get back to
the original battle—the one between your fathers..."

"A few years after me father was declared victori-
ous, our parents left me in charge of a crumbling castle,
two young sisters, and a couple of humans in a caretaker's cottage."

"Meanwhile," Conlan added, "me brothers and I
moved north with our widowed mother and settled near
Belfast in Ulster."

"And you've done quite well there," Rory said. "They
own a distillery that makes some of the finest whiskey
you'll ever taste. Who would like a dram?" Rory rose
and walked over to the small bar in the corner.

"I think we could all use some...but only a little,"
Amber said.

"Why? Is it very strong?" Amy asked.

Amber shrugged. "One never knows what will
happen during Irish family reunions. I figure a little
whiskey might settle the nerves. A lot of whiskey might
have the opposite effect."

"Oh. And of course our Scottish families are so much
better behaved." Amy exchanged a grin with Drake,
who laughed.

"Ah, so we *are* related," he said.

"Let's figure this out," Amy said, animatedly. "What
do you know about your family, Drake?"

"I was told that my great-grandfather was the
dragon thought to be the last on earth. The one St.
George was credited with slaying—although it pains
me to call the man a saint. My great-grandmother

was pregnant with twins at the time and fled north, finally settling in the Highlands."

Amy gasped. "I was told something similar. Except the pregnant dragon was my mother—your grand-mother, Kristine. I was sired by a different father fifteen years after the twins."

"So, if my grandfather was the missing Irish uncle," Kristine said, "we could all be cousins—er, second cousins, or first cousins once removed... I don't know how it goes, but we might be related."

Drake cleared his throat. "I know I should never ask a lady this question, but how old are you both?"

"I'm about eight hundred or so. We didn't keep records in the Scottish caves. Kristine is twenty-six."

"I'm about five hundred. Like you, I have no real birthday recorded," Drake said.

The room grew quiet as everyone glanced at each other and tried to put some kind of extended relation-ship together.

"Why don't we throw out some names?" Rory asked.

Drake went first. "My mother's name was Mary, and my father's name was Faelen." Jayce had coughed when Drake said his father's name, and Kristine wasn't sure she'd heard right.

"Did you say his name was Fang?"

Drake laughed. "Actually, I said Faelen."

Amy shot to her feet. "Mine too! You must be my brother. My little brother." She began to cry. "No, wait. You were told Mary was your *great*-grandmother."

Conlan spoke up. "Sometimes what we're told and the truth are a wee bit different. When dragons move around, they often change their names to hide their longevity. Or they invent or eliminate knowledge of a generation altogether to protect their secret."

Drake looked like he was trying to choke back tears. He strode to Amy and pulled her into a tight hug. "I don't care what anyone says. I've found a sister."

The room was silent except for some sniffles. Rory and Conlan stared at each other. Kristine saw the look that passed between them.

"What is it?" she asked.

The elder dragons turned to her and smiled. Rory spoke up first. "Mayhaps we've all found each other at last."

"It was our uncle Faelen who left Ireland before the battle of Ballyhoo," Conlan added.

Kristine touched her widow's peak. "I don't know much about my father's lineage. So at this point I would guess that our yellow mark, which matches Drake's, probably belonged to his father—or his father's father— and the slight bit of orange I can see in Conlan's roots were probably indicative of his father's line."

Conlan rose, strolled to the mirror over the fireplace, and inspected his widow's peak. "I've been neglectin' me appearance while on me quest."

"Rory? Do you have a mark?" Kristine asked.

"Indeed. Me sisters and I all sport the red streak. Like you, we dyed it to match the rest of our hair. Chloe's hair is blonde. Shannon's is red—well, more like flame-orange. Not the soft strawberry-blonde hair you have."

Jayce finally said something. "Am I to understand that you're all cousins from some royal family long ago?"

Rory grinned. "It would appear so."

Amber said, "Let me try to put this together. Maybe a

thousand years ago there were a couple of dragons who miraculously survived the original St. Patrick's Day."

"More than a thousand, but yes," Rory said. "St. Patrick lived in the fourth century."

Conlan set his whiskey on the mantelpiece. "When St. Patrick drove all snakes and serpents over the cliffs, our grandparents managed to grab hold of a rock or two and scramble into a cave as they went over the side. Mayhaps a few others survived in similar ways."

"Our kin became king and queen of the cliffs, living simply and in secret," Rory said. "After St. Patrick died, they felt comfortable building their castle on the edge of that cliff over the caves. A few humans inhabited the castle aboveground, and only the dragons had access to the cliffs—flying at night to remain unseen."

"So the humans still thought all the dragons were gone?" Amber asked.

Rory nodded. "For the most part. A trusted few may have known the truth."

"Okay. So the survivors…" Amber continued. "The king and queen had three sons. One had a red mark in his widow's peak, one had an orange mark, and one had a yellow mark. Eventually, the twins—one with a red mark and one with an orange mark—challenged each other to take over as king when their father died or moved on or whatever. Right?"

"That is correct." Rory said.

"So what happened to your grandparents? Why was the crown up for grabs?"

"The same thing that happens to all dragons after a time. Humans became suspicious of their longevity. They had to say good-bye and settle somewhere else until all those humans passed away. Only then could they return—when they would no longer be recognized."

"Only they never returned," Conlan said and took a sip of his whiskey. He smacked his lips and said, "Ahhh."

"So the crown passed to the eldest." Rory adjusted in his seat. "Me father was assumed to be the eldest and ruled for many years. Then when the midwife became dotty with age, she seemed to think Conlan's father was born first. That doubt caused the rift between the brothers. Some human knights aligned with one and some with the other, hopin' to gain a powerful place in the court of the victor."

"I think we've gone over the rest," Conlan said with finality.

Kristine looked between her mother and now the men who were possibly her cousins. "So we're Irish? But our last name is Scott."

Amy looked at her and shrugged. "Not very original, but if my father was trying to hide his Irish heritage, changing his name from Arish to Scott would make sense."

Drake said, "My mother died not long ago, so I canna confirm all the information. All I know is that I have found two I can call sister and niece when I thought I had no family left."

He laughed. "So I guess you outrank me in this convoluted heir-to-the-throne business *if* your father is the mysterious dragon who disappeared from Ballyhoo, Ireland."

"Not so fast," Conlan said. "Rory's younger sister, Chloe, is queen and living in the castle that she and her husband are restoring as we speak."

"So how did Chloe become queen when she's not the oldest?" Amy asked.

Rory and Conlan glanced at each other.

"Rory is eldest, and I would be next in line…had everything gone smoothly," Conlan explained. "Chloe was third. Rory abdicated the throne in order to stay here in Boston and open this B and B with his ladylove, Amber."

The two of them gazed at each other and exchanged loving smiles.

Conlan continued, "Me brothers and I did not want to cause another rift like our fathers had, so we made no claim to the throne at Ballyhoo. We have our whiskey business in Belfast, and we live like kings there."

Amber gave Conlan a sly smile and wink. "And besides, the Ulster cousins have an important mission. They're in search of a single female dragon in order to keep the line going. As you know, dragons can only create life with another dragon."

Conlan glanced at the two female dragons. "Perhaps there's hope for the species yet."

Kristine held up her hands. "Don't look at me…"

"I'm not lookin' at *you*, luv." Conlan stared at Amy and Amy at Conlan.

"But we might be cousins," Amy whispered to him.

"But we might not be." Conlan waggled his eyebrows. Everyone in the room laughed.

"There's one more thing," Drake said. "My parents met in Canada. It's only a rumor or speculation, but I think my father's family made it to Greenland a few centuries after the St. Patrick debacle…with the Vikings."

Rory slapped his leg. "Of course! The Vikings! Mayhaps they scooped up some survivors. They were sailin' all around the North Atlantic. There's evidence of their having made it to Greenland more than a thousand years ago."

"I wouldna be surprised to learn that they found some displaced dragons on outlying islands and brought them along," Conlan said.

"And who could survive a cold, hostile environment like Greenland?" Drake asked. "Dragons! I've always figured that Scotland had to be the origin of my father's side simply because of my last name. And now my mother's side—Scottish, Irish, or whatever—could be sitting right next to me."

Amy and Drake rose and hugged each other. Then Drake held one arm out to Kristine. She stepped into the group hug. She let out a sigh of relief. Not just that she may have found some legitimate family—but that the word *legitimate* didn't come up in conversation.

"And what about your father, Kristine?" Conlan asked.

Suddenly Jayce jumped up and said, "I almost forgot. We have dinner reservations. If we leave right now, we'll just make it before they give away our table."

Kristine gave him a grateful smile and followed him to the coat closet.

"Quick thinking," she whispered.

"Actually, I was thinking about it all along but didn't want to interrupt. It didn't seem like the right time."

"Your timing was perfect."

—◦◦◦—

"So, Jayce," his father said at the next Sunday dinner. "How was your vacation?"

"It was great." Jayce shoveled a good portion of lasagna in his mouth and chewed slowly.

Antonio raised one eyebrow. "Is that so? You look like you need a vacation from your vacation. Do I see a little gray in your temples?" Everyone looked at Jayce, as if they were checking him out for the first time.

Jayce shrugged. "I don't know what you're inferring. We're all getting older, you know…"

"Oh, I know," Antonio said sardonically. "But you look like you've aged a few years in just a few days. You haven't been flying during your time away, have you?"

Jayce just shoved a bigger piece of lasagna in his mouth and chewed. All his family members seemed to be holding their breaths and watching him, waiting to hear what he would say. They never lied to their father when he asked a question point-blank. Jayce wouldn't either. He just hoped there would be a distraction…and yet the distraction that occurred was *not* what he wanted.

Sandra doubled over and cried out in pain. Miguel grabbed her shoulder. "Are you all right?"

"No. Something is wrong…with the baby." Her free hand was cradling her baby bump.

Gabriella Fierro shot to her feet. "Do something! We have six EMTs around this table. Surely one of you can help her."

Sandra leaned away from the table and glanced down. "Oh no…"

"What is it, honey?" Miguel's brow furrowed.

"I think something awful has happened. I'm bleeding," Sandra said with a shaky voice.

Three cell phones punched in 911 at the same time. Antonio held up one hand. "I'll call for an ambulance.

Get yourselves out on the sidewalk…and move your cars to make room for the ambulance."

"I'm not going anywhere," Miguel stated.

"Of course not," Gabriella said.

"*911, what is your emergency?*"

Jayce was just about to get up and join his brothers when his father put his hand over the microphone end. "Jayce. Stay put. You need to think about running the family when I leave, so you should see what it takes."

Jayce thought this was totally unnecessary but didn't question or disagree with his father. He was going to be in enough hot water when the old man remembered he'd never answered his question about shifting and flying.

"We have a pregnant woman in her second trimester, and she's experiencing sudden sharp pains," Antonio barked into the phone. "She said she's bleeding." Then he rattled off the address and gave his name and the name of the baby's parents.

Sandra was leaning against Miguel's shoulder, and he was rubbing circles over her back.

"Is there anything I can do?" Gabriella asked, wringing her hands.

"Not until the ambulance gets here," Miguel said.

"I was asking Sandra."

"I… I don't know. Could you get me a glass of ice water?" Sandra asked. Beads of sweat were popping out on her forehead.

"Of course, darling. I'll be right back." Gabriella dashed to the kitchen.

"No. Don't drink water in case they have to do surgery," Miguel said. "Just bring a cool, damp cloth, Mom."

Jayce felt helpless. His father was staying on the

phone until the ambulance arrived. Miguel tried to keep Sandra calm. Gabriella returned with a damp washcloth. She bathed Sandra's forehead and wrists with the cool cloth. He wasn't needed on the sidewalk to help the ambulance. Four Fierros were certainly enough there.

"It could just be Braxton-Hicks contractions," Jayce said hopefully.

Sandra gave him a sad smile. She probably knew it was too early for that.

The sound of sirens was never more welcome in the Fierro household. In only a few minutes, two EMTs and two Fierros ran to Sandra's side with a stretcher. Jayce and Miguel helped transfer Sandra from the chair to the stretcher. Blood on the chair didn't escape the notice of the first responders.

Noah removed her shoes and said, "Dante and Luca are standing in the parking spaces in front of the ambulance in case some numbskull decides to park there."

Gabe unfolded the blanket he held and laid it on top of her.

"I'm going in the ambulance," Miguel said.

The EMTs nodded. Jayce didn't know either of them, but they seemed to know what they were doing and didn't give Miguel a hard time. Jayce felt assured that Sandra would get the care she needed as soon as possible.

As they were wheeling her toward the front door, Jayce happened to glance over at his father. Antonio had put down his phone and gave Jayce a sad look.

Gabriella had her hands folded in front of her and her eyes closed. He imagined she was praying, so he didn't say anything that would interrupt her thoughts.

When the second EMT had closed the front door,

Antonio let out a deep breath. He rose and stood next to his wife as tears leaked from the corners of her eyes. As soon as she was finished with her prayer, she turned into his embrace and let the tears fall.

"She might not have lost it," Jayce said. "It could be any number of things. She might be put on bed rest for a few weeks and still carry the baby to term."

Gabriella swiped at the tears on her cheeks. Jayce handed her his napkin, which was still clean, and she dried her eyes. "I hope you're right, dear. She's only twenty-four weeks, but babies have been born that early and survived."

The amount of blood on Sandra's chair might suggest differently, but Jayce didn't want to worry his mother. Mr. Fierro glanced over at the chair, which Jayce subtly pulled out enough for him to see, and he shook his head. He was so much taller than Gabriella that she didn't see him.

Chapter 11

KRISTINE AND HER MOTHER WERE AT A NEARBY LAUNDROMAT, taking care of the few clothes they had brought with them. Kristine cleared her throat and launched into the conversation she knew they needed to have alone.

"I have to go home, Mom. Lieutenant Mahoney called and said there was a huge high-rise fire. Two guys were injured. They need me."

"Oh no, you don't. It's not safe to return yet. Is it?"

"If Donkey Pizzle and company are looking for us, they probably know that we're not in New York anymore." Kristine tossed her thong onto the pile of granny panties she usually wore.

Amy eyed the thong, and her eyebrows shot up. "Is that what I think it is?"

"Not a word."

Amy chuckled. Soon she became serious. "I hope you'll take a while to think about this. They're bound to be furious that I got away, and I'm sure they'll be looking for me."

"Well, they're not going to find you because you're staying here in Boston."

"But what about you? They could go after you next."

Kristine stuck her hand on her hip. "Let them try. I'm a freakin' dragon."

"You aren't thinking of doing anything stupid, like breathing fire in public, are you?" Amy folded her arms and stared at her daughter. "We don't have the power to erase minds."

Kristine was determined. Her fellow firefighters needed her. She was the only one who was fireproof, not that they knew that. But she was always able to pull them out of danger, and if worst came to worst, she could fly out of any situation and shift back in the smoke before anyone saw her. At least that's how it had turned out so far.

Amy sighed. "You have that look on your face."

"What look?"

"The one that says 'Don't bother...I know what I'm doing, and nothing you say will stop me.'"

Kristine chuckled. "Yup. You know me well."

Amy shook her head and went back to folding socks. "I don't suppose Jayce can go with you? Can he?"

"I doubt it. He's needed here in Boston. He just took a vacation, so I imagine he can't get away again for a while."

"I wish you'd reconsider... I know you can protect yourself but not without using your supernatural powers, and you know why we can't do that."

Kristine rolled her eyes. "Yes, I know. People will see us as a threat. Then capture and study us or just outright kill us. People are stupid."

"No, people are human. They fear what they don't understand, and trying to understand that dragons are real is beyond most modern thinkers. There's really no point in arguing this," Amy said. "It's the only hard-and-fast rule I've ever demanded of you. That hasn't changed."

Kristine dropped the T-shirt she had been about to

fold. "Seriously? I'm an adult now. You really can't tell me what to do or what not to do anymore."

"Oh yeah?"

Kristine ignored the comment and returned to folding her FDNY T-shirt. When she couldn't afford to finish college, the only saving grace was that she could become a firefighter. It was a noble calling, and it fulfilled her in a way she hadn't expected.

Still, a college degree would help her rise up the ladder. Not that she'd want to go so high she didn't see any action at all. But becoming a lieutenant would be nice. As it was, she would have to start all over in Boston, but she really thought she could make a difference if she had a little more clout.

Kristine had taken a few brave chances and demonstrated how valuable she was to her fellow FDNY firefighters. They had stopped questioning her abilities as a woman long ago, and she had proven herself many times over. She felt regretful for the high-rise getting so out of control. Had she been there, she might have been able to help. "I'm sorry, Mom, I have to go back."

Amy shook her head and remained silent.

"On the plus side, while I'm there, I can search for a new apartment for us."

Amy bit her lip but still didn't respond.

Kristine had to wonder what was going on in her mother's head. Did she want to stay in Boston, even though her job was in New York? She'd bet meeting Conlan had something to do with it. "So, should I look for a one bedroom or two?"

"I don't know yet."

Kristine slapped her hands over her eyes. "I don't

fucking believe this. You're the one who wanted to stay in New York. Your job at the acting school was so important to you, and there's nothing like that in Boston."

"That's where you're wrong. Amber was telling me about Emerson College. It's right down the street from the B and B. They have an exceptional arts program, especially when it comes to drama. With my credentials she thinks I'd be a shoo-in for a job there. And many Broadway shows come to Boston."

Kristine's eyes widened. "You're really thinking about staying here?"

Amy shrugged. "I don't know. It's a possibility."

"'It's a possibility…'" Kristine mocked.

"Don't be fresh. What's wrong with keeping our options open? I would have thought you'd like to be closer to Jayce."

"And it's just handy that you would be closer to Conlan and all his relatives."

Amy grinned. "That part doesn't suck."

Jayce and his father waited in the hospital lounge for news of Sandra and the baby. Miguel was with her.

"I wanted you here so you could see what it takes to run this family," Antonio Fierro said.

"I really don't understand what the big deal is, Dad. Anyone could sit here and wait for news."

Mr. Fierro straightened and stared at his son. "No, Jayce. Not just anyone. The head of the family needs to be responsive and available to any and all of our family members in times of crisis."

Jayce leaned back and folded his arms. "What if I'm

on the job? Am I supposed to just run off and deal with every family emergency that could possibly come up?"

Antonio scrubbed a hand over his face. "No. Having a wife can help with that...for the most part. If she works too, one of you should be able to respond at a moment's notice."

His father took a deep breath. "I wasn't going to say this, not just yet anyway, but there are those in high places who know what we are. Promotions to nine-to-five positions can be arranged when necessary."

"Are you shitting me?" Jayce asked.

"There are a number of things I need to teach you. Maybe you'll understand a little better why it's important that *one* of us knows all the particulars."

"And why should only one of us be privy to this information?"

"Now *you* must be shitting *me*... The more people who know these things, the greater the chance of a slip of the tongue or eavesdroppers getting hold of sensitive information they shouldn't have."

"Does Miguel know?"

"No. At this point, there's no reason for him to know anything about this. I've been thinking I could make you and Miguel co-heads. That presents a problem if disagreements come up. I'm still hoping that you will take over."

Jayce saw an opportunity to possibly introduce the subject of Kristine fitting into his life. "Are you still stuck on the criteria for the leader of this precious family?"

Antonio rested his elbows on his knees, leaned forward, and clasped his hands. "You really don't understand our importance, do you? If you are to take over as head of the family, you *absolutely* have to understand and accept the criteria—that you be married, living in our home in the South End, or somewhere nearby that can accommodate all of us at once. It's been that way for as long as anyone can remember. Just letting Ryan move to Ireland with his fiancée was a huge departure from protocol."

"So why did you do it?"

Antonio snorted. "Remember the big public funeral we had for him? Anyone who spotted him would think they were seeing a ghost. It was dicey, but because he was reincarnated as a child, I could make the excuse that he was no longer the eldest. That makes you the eldest now."

"Lucky me," Jayce said sardonically.

Antonio stood and began pacing across the room and back. "This is the reason I felt that you and Miguel would have to do this together. He's much more serious and, pardon me for saying this, more levelheaded. He's married and will *someday* have children—I hope."

"He's a little too serious, if you ask me."

Antonio nodded. "That's true. Having fun makes life worth living—not just an endless struggle. And the two of you together would balance each other out. But it would be so much better if I could trust you to meet the criteria. As you know, your mother refuses to leave Boston until all her sons are happily married. You're making it seem like that will never happen."

"Ah! That's what all this pressure is about. You want to sit on a Caribbean beach sipping piña coladas. Well, never say never," Jayce said.

Antonio swiveled and looked at his son. "Is there

something you're not telling me? Is it serious between you and the New York girl?"

Jayce didn't know how to answer that. Kristine had told him she was going to return to New York. He didn't know how to make this work. He *had* to stay in Boston. He understood that he was obligated to his family despite arguing with his father about it. She seemed to be adamant about staying in New York. Yet he didn't want anyone else.

Jayce Fierro rose to his full six-foot height and folded his arms. "I was going to tell you at dinner—until everything happened with Sandra today. Kristine is in Boston. I'd like her to meet you and Ma, but I don't know how open you would be to an out-of-towner. She's important to me, Dad, but we haven't worked everything out yet."

"What are you saying?"

Jayce threw his hands in the air. "That's just it. I don't know what I'm saying."

"Sounds like the usual."

Jayce huffed. "Thanks a lot. What I mean is that *if* things depend upon some kind of semi-traditional marriage, I have to convince her to move to Boston. That won't be easy. She loves New York. I have to rely on *you* to make her feel welcome. I don't have to worry about Mom. Just bringing home a woman who's marriage material will thrill her, I'm sure."

Antonio chuckled. "You got that right. You're also right about how badly I want to leave these crappy winters behind and sit on a beach in January, sipping cocktails. So I'd be pretty damn happy too."

Jayce and Antonio noticed Miguel standing in the doorway and immediately rose.

"How is she? I mean they?" Antonio asked.

"Sandra's okay. The baby is still hanging in there too."

Both Antonio and Jayce let out their collective breaths in a whoosh.

Jayce wondered how long Miguel had been standing there and how much he had heard. "What happened? Do they know?"

"The doctor called it placental abruption. It's when the placenta separates from the uterine wall."

"I'm not familiar with it. Is it serious?" Jayce asked.

"It can be. It's fairly rare, so I'm not surprised you've never heard of it."

"I guess your mother and I were lucky," Antonio said. "All seven of you gave her morning sickness, but that was about it. After the first trimester, everything went smoothly. So is there anything they can do?"

"Well, they can't reattach the placenta, but they're going to keep her here and monitor her for a while. She might be able to go home and stay on bed rest if everything is stable. They said there's medication they can give to help the baby's lungs develop in case she's a preemie."

Antonio's brows lifted. "She?"

Miguel smiled. "It's a girl."

"I'll be damned," his father muttered. "The first girl in three generations."

A boy would take over the family when the next generation was ready. Now that Jayce knew there were secrets involved, he had to know what they were. Was running the family a blessing or a curse? Would a daughter be allowed to do it?

~~~

Kristine had agreed to visit Jayce at his condo. She
had to tell him she'd be leaving Boston the next day.
He'd probably try to get her to stay and join the BFD.
As much as she wanted to be with him, she didn't want
to leave her buddies who needed her—or be run out of
her neighborhood.

She stepped up to the old brick building by the river.
Jayce had said to enter by the side door, which he'd
leave unlocked. Kristine tried the knob. It turned, so
she figured she had the right place. She opened the
door and was immediately looking at a staircase. She
walked up one flight of stairs and tried the knob up
there. That too was open, so she figured she had arrived
at the right apartment.

Striding into a kitchen, Kristine was greeted with a
shriek. A naked woman stood at the stove, stirring something in a frying pan.

They stared at each other wide-eyed. Was this Jayce's
idea of a joke? Or did Jayce have another girlfriend she
didn't know about?

Kristine recovered first. "Does Jayce Fierro live
here?"

The woman let out a deep breath and quickly donned
an apron. "Jayce lives downstairs. You must have just
come in the wrong door."

"Oh! I'm sorry. He said he'd leave the door unlocked,
and I just figured whichever one opened was his."

The woman chuckled. "Yeah, I told my boyfriend the
same thing. I was surprised when you weren't him."

Kristine smiled, embarrassed. "Oops. It looks like

you're planning some kind of a nice surprise. I hope I didn't ruin it."

"Not at all. I'll just turn the bacon down, and he'll be here any minute."

"Okay, I'll be going now." Kristine paused with her hand on the doorknob. She turned to the woman and said, "Don't you know you're not supposed to fry bacon in the nude?"

The woman laughed. "Yeah. It was an inside joke, but I guess the joke was on me."

Kristine grinned and jogged down the stairs, passing a young man on his way up. She called over her shoulder, "Have fun."

As soon as she reached the ground floor, Kristine tried the other door. This time she walked into an entrance with a few steps leading down. Jayce stood at the sliding-glass door, looking out at the river. He sauntered over and enveloped her in a warm hug.

"Did you have any trouble finding the place?" he asked.

Kristine laughed. "Oh, no. No trouble at all, unless you consider surprising your upstairs neighbor, who was expecting someone else, 'trouble.'"

Jayce laughed. "I thought I heard a scream."

Kristine ran her hands over his hard chest. "Well, I'm here now."

"And I'm glad." They shared a quick kiss followed by a long, tender one.

When they finally eased apart, she glanced around the place and noticed the apartment was orderly and clean with newish furniture. Nothing appeared too fussy or heavy, neither feminine nor masculine, but everything was attractive and modern. Sort of how she would have decorated the place had it been hers.

Come to think of it, she wouldn't mind it being hers. "Nice place. I expected it to be a little messier, since you admitted to being a slob."

He laughed. "You remember I said that, huh?"

"Yeah. I was almost afraid to come here. I didn't know if I was going to find empty pizza boxes on the floor, dirty laundry strewn around, or what."

"Yeah, well, I neaten up when I'm expecting company."

Kristine gave him another peck on the lips and strolled over to the sliding-glass door. "Nice view."

"Not as good as the view I have," he said, staring at her short denim skirt from behind.

She couldn't help smiling. A few boats floated by. "Do you have a boat out there?"

"Yeah. My brothers and I like to go fishing sometimes. You should come with us."

Oh boy. She had the opening she needed but just hadn't thought it would come up so quickly. "Yeah, about that. There's something I need to tell you."

"Dragons don't like to fish?"

"It's not that. I might go with you sometime, but it will be when I'm visiting from New York again."

Jayce stuffed his hands in his pockets. "I guess you're still planning to return despite everything that's happened—"

"Yes. I am. We've barely started dating. I don't think I should be ready to give up my independence just yet. I want to get a new place, and I need to get back to work."

He ambled over to her, placed his hands on her upper arms, and said, "I was thinking this could be your place and you could get a job in the area. There's an opening in the fire department, or you could go back to college, or whatever you want to do… As long as we're together, I'd be happy."

Back to college? Had he realized how badly she wished she'd finished? "Why do you think I want to go back to college?"

"Oh, I don't know…maybe because you told me you were a college dropout in the first five minutes of meeting me."

"You got me. I wanted to be a doctor, but with all the related expenses, I realized my mother and I would be bankrupt before I got my degree."

Jayce smiled. "You're already an EMT and smart as hell. I can see you as a doctor. Let me pay your room and board, and you can look for a school. There are some excellent colleges and med schools in Boston."

Kristine smiled shyly. "That's sweet of you. But don't you think it's too soon?"

Jayce shrugged. "It isn't for me. I'd even do my best to keep my place neat and clean for you."

Kristine giggled. "Well, that's a plus. But I really miss New York. And it bugs me that I'm being run out of my home when it's not my fault."

Jayce let out a deep sigh. "I wish…" He let go of her and stepped away. "Never mind."

"What?"

He shook his head. "It doesn't matter." Then his expression changed. He focused on her with an intense stare. "No. It does matter. I love you, Kristine. I want to be with you. I thought you felt the same way about me. Don't you?"

She wandered over to one of the chairs and sank down onto it. "I do. I mean, if you could only come with me back to New York—"

Jayce folded his arms. "You know I have family obligations here. Is your mother pressuring you to go back?"

"No. Not at all. In fact, she's had a change of heart—"

"You mean because of finding relatives here? Or possibly more? I thought I saw something between her and Conlan—"

"You're very perceptive. She hasn't totally made up her mind yet, but she is considering staying here—at least for a while."

"Why don't you both stay a while? I know you think you're safe in New York now, but—"

"Jayce, I'm a dragon. I'm safe wherever I am."

"Then tell me, how did they get your mother? It's not like she couldn't also just open her mouth and melt whoever laid a hand on her."

Kristine knew, but she wasn't about to tell him. They'd shot her mother with a tranquilizer dart. She said she'd felt a sharp pain in the back of her shoulder before losing consciousness.

Jayce squatted next to her chair and took her hand. "Please. I know paranormals are perceived to be invulnerable, but we're not. I don't want anything to happen to you."

Kristine was irritated with herself. She could see his side of the argument and even felt herself softening to him, but she really wanted to stand up for her own principles. Her own hopes and dreams and wishes. She had finally learned what her mother had been hiding from her all those years, but she hadn't had time to process any of it.

She didn't like how these so-called goons or mobsters acted like they were unstoppable. Weren't they just human? The thought of her mother caving to them bothered her. Amy wasn't like that. Were they controlling her simply by threatening her daughter? That bothered her too.

Part of her wanted to see the rest of the picture in this dangerous puzzle, but mostly she wanted these assholes out of their lives. Never able to threaten either her or her mother again.

Jayce rose and returned to the sliding-glass door, which he opened, letting in a soft breeze. "It's a beautiful evening. Would you like to go for a boat ride in the moonlight?"

Kristine sighed. She was at war with herself. It would be so easy just to slip into the comfort of Jayce, moonlit boat rides, and falling in love. But easy wasn't always right. Those bastards were still living in luxury on Long Island—wreaking havoc on innocent lives. No wonder they thought they were unstoppable. Who was stopping them? If the police were dirty, there was no one.

She left her chair and stepped into his space, lightly caressing his pecs. "It would be so easy just to forget everything that's happened, but I can't. I love you, Jayce, and if you love me, you'll wait until I'm ready to make the changes you want."

"I love you so much I can't see straight."

He leaned in and pulled her close, delivering a long, deep kiss that had her tingling from the tips of her fingers to her toes. She did love him. He was easygoing, strong, and handsome—just looking at him made her weak in the knees. Plus he cared deeply and had never deserted her in her time of need. She doubted he ever would.

She cupped his cheek and stepped away. "One boat ride. But then I have to go back to the bed and breakfast. I can't spend the night."

He nodded, took her hand, and led her out onto the small patio. Then he locked the door behind them and ushered her to his boat. Kristine had never been much for boats, but his looked like a nice one.

Gabriella was painted on its stern. "The *Gabriella*?"

"My brothers and I named her after our mother."

Nice. He helped her down the ladder, and she glanced around. She thought it was called a cabin cruiser because there was some kind of enclosed living space below. "Do you have a whole kitchen and dining area down there?"

A sly smile stole across his face. "All that and more. There are a couple of sleeping spaces too. One is under the hull, and the benches turn into a surprisingly comfortable bed."

She laughed. "I should've known…"

As Jayce untied the boat and started up the motor, he winked at her. They backed out into the open river. Then he pushed the lever forward, and they cruised past several other docks and private boats.

"You have a sweet setup here," she said.

"All the more reason to move in with me."

"I thought we agreed it was too soon."

His smile faded. "I don't know about that. Timing is a funny thing. You know Rory and Amber, your hosts?"

"Yeah…"

"They've been living together since the day they met."

Her confusion must have been apparent. "What do you mean? Did they have some sort of roommate arrangement made for them before they moved in?"

He laughed as he steered them into open water. "Not intentionally. To hear them tell it is a lot funnier, but from what I understand, it all started in the building next door to the B and B. There's a husband-and-wife management team for the apartments. She rented the only vacant place from the wife at the exact same time as he rented the same apartment from her husband. Neither manager could decide which potential renter should have the apartment, so they simply stated that possession was nine-tenths of the law and waited to see who reached it first.

"There was a mad dash down the stairs, with Amber in the lead until Rory vaulted over the railing, but they burst through the door of the apartment at the exact same time. Then they were stuck. Whoever left first was giving up possession."

"So neither one could leave?" Kristine giggled, picturing the conundrum they must have been in. "But they live together next door now. How did they get from one place to the other?"

Jayce shrugged. "I'm not clear how they managed to buy such pricey real estate together, but I know they lived in the little apartment while they fixed up the building next door. I guess it was in rough shape. But with a lot of love and hard work, it became the B and B you're staying in."

Kristine's mind wandered as they left the harbor and sailed out to open sea. She loved the smell of the salty ocean air and the cool spray whenever they hit a wave.

Boston wasn't so bad. Some people certainly liked it. Liked it enough to fight over a tiny apartment and then wind up with something infinitely better. Maybe sometime she'd ask Amber how that had happened.

Kristine had never been much of a fighter. Which was odd since *fighter* was part of her job title and description. But something was telling her she needed to deal with Donkey Pizzle once and for all. Sure, the mansion was probably well-defended, but her mother had confirmed exactly how stupid these criminals were.

Once Kristine and Jayce were out of the harbor, he set the controls and left the wheel. He strolled over to her and rubbed her arms. "You look so serious. What's on your mind?"

She smiled automatically to reassure him. "Everything's fine. I'm just going to miss you, that's all."

He pulled her into a hug and caressed her back. "I'm not going to argue with you, you know. We may just be getting to know each other, but I can tell when I'm fighting a losing battle."

"Please be patient with me. I have the feeling that something will change eventually."

Jayce chuckled. "My mother always says that the only constant is change. If you don't like something, just wait it out." He sat down and moved over to make room for her to scoot in beside him.

"Your mom sounds like a wise woman."

"She is. I want you to meet her. I know she'll love you, and I think you'll like her too."

Kristine shrugged. "She must be incredible if you named your boat after her. If things work out with us, I imagine we will meet eventually."

NEVER DARE A DRAGON   205

"Why wouldn't things work out between us? What aren't you telling me?"

Kristine snuggled into his side and rested her head on his shoulder. She knew he'd be upset if she were to tell him the truth, but honesty in a relationship was important. If their relationship couldn't survive honesty, then what did they have?

"Jayce, you're not going to like this. I'm going after Donkey Pizzle. Right now, while my mother is up here and safely occupied, I have a window of opportunity."

Jayce reared back and stared at her for a moment. "Is this just about revenge?"

"No. Not *just* revenge...although I'm plenty pissed off. These people need to be stopped. I know what they're doing to mere human beings. I have an advantage. If they try to order me into some windowless van, I can simply say, *I'm a dragon. Make me.*"

"Kristine, I can't let you do this alone. If something happened to you, your mother and I would both be devastated. We'd blame ourselves and have to live with that forever."

"You can't stop me, but I was hoping you'd say something like that because I could use your help."

He simply closed his eyes and waited for her to continue.

"You know where they live. I wasn't there when my mother escaped. You were. If I ask her where they are, she'll know I'm going after them. She can't stop me either, and I don't want her to try. If she knows I'm going after them, she'll worry or get in the way."

"But I have a job, and I've been away from it. Can we wait until I accrue some more vacation time? Then I'll be glad to help you."

"Now is the only time. I'm on a leave of absence, and my mother is safe."

Jayce scrubbed a hand over his face. "I don't know what to do, Kristine. It seems as if you've made up your mind."

"Trust me, please. That's all I ask. I swear I can and will take care of myself first and foremost. Those asswipes don't deserve my life or my happiness."

She stepped into his space, rested her hands on his chest, and stared into his eyes. She hoped he would read the sincerity there. He leaned down and rested his forehead against hers.

"There must be something I can do to help you if you're determined to do this thing. Can you give me twenty-four hours to come up with something else?"

She sighed. "Sure. But I'm doing this, no matter what."

For a few minutes, they remained quiet—staring at the sea.

At last, Jayce sat down hard. "I don't know the address, but it's in South Hampton. A white mansion with direct beachfront access."

"Any other way I can identify it?"

He shrugged. "Tall hedges on one side. Some woods on the other—it can't be seen by neighbors on either side. There's a large oval pool near the back of the house, about fifty yards from the beach."

"Is there anything I could recognize from the street?"

"There's a stone wall and two iron gates next to the street. A long driveway ends in a circle in front of the entrance. There are topiaries on either side of the front door. They're pruned to look like lions."

She threw her arms around his neck. "Thank you. You really do love me."

He sighed and pulled her onto his lap. "I guess this is why they call it 'madly in love.' I must be mad to let you do this, especially without me."

She lowered her eyes shyly. "I'm madly in love with you too."

Jayce placed a finger under her chin and tipped up her face to look into her eyes. He must have seen the love shining there. She couldn't and wouldn't hide it from him.

He gently pressed his lips to hers. They were soft, but his intent was unmistakable. Their mouths opened to one another automatically, and she sought his tongue. After a gentle swirl, he sucked on hers, and the resultant tug had her pulling him closer, needing more of him.

He lifted her in his arms and set her on the deck just long enough to open the hatch to the cabin below. "M'lady…" He gestured to the steps down with a sweep of his hand.

"Such a gentleman…"

"Oh, there's nothing gentlemanly on my mind, I assure you."

"Good." Her voice sounded raspier than she had intended. She scrambled down the wide ladder. Jayce caught up with her at the back of the cabin, where a smaller ladder led to the bed under the front of the boat. There was only about three feet of headroom. "I don't think there's enough room in here," she said. "At least not if I'm on top."

Jayce grinned. "Oh, so you want to be on top, do you?"

Kristine tipped her head and smiled coquettishly. "I was only saying there's not enough room for me to do that, if you want me to. Or I could just lie there…"

Jayce took her hand and led her back to the galley. "Watch this…" He pulled the cushions off the built-in benches, knelt under the small table, and flipped up the leg. Then he lifted the tabletop off its hinges and dropped it down to fit between the benches perfectly. He rearranged the cushions so they all laid flat. "Presto-chango. We have another bed—and plenty of headroom."

"Oh? And what are we going to do with that?" Kristine blinked innocently.

Jayce narrowed his eyes as a slow, almost evil smile spread across his face. "I'm going to let you fuck me, my love. Any way you want to."

She laughed. "You're going to let me?"

"Any way you want."

He stepped into her space and began unbuttoning her blue-and-white-striped henley top. To her relief there were only three buttons from chest to neckline. She was becoming so heated from the inside that she couldn't get the top off fast enough.

She held up her arms, and he pulled it over her head. She had on a pink bathing suit top, but one yank on the tie behind her neck, and it was almost off too.

She grabbed the hem of his navy-blue T-shirt and pulled it over his head, tossing it on the floor. His hard pectorals and abs glowed with a golden tan. She caressed the hard planes of his chest while watching his eyes darken.

"Jesus, Kristine. You could drive me crazy with lust."

"Don't worry," she said as she reached for his belt. "I'll put you out of your misery." A moment later, his pants hit the floor, and she kneeled in front of him. Ordinarily finding no underwear would have surprised her, but he was probably expecting sex. She took him in her hand and licked the tip of his hard erection.

He leaned back and groaned. She pleasured him thoroughly, enjoying his every reaction. Without warning, she wound up on her back. The cushions were soft enough, so her squeal only resulted from surprise, not pain.

Jayce leaned over her and divested her of her skirt and bathing suit bottoms. Now they were both gloriously naked. She couldn't remember being self-conscious in front of Jayce. She'd felt a twinge of self-consciousness when they were first together, but that was more out of habit than any true awkwardness. She'd usually had a shy moment with any guy who made it to her bedroom. But she'd always felt comfortable with Jayce—almost proud of her nakedness. They fit together perfectly.

As if to prove the fact, he reached under her arms and yanked her up so they were even, face-to-face, and then he wrapped a hand around her hip, pulling her close. She twined her legs with his and caressed his face. His dark eyes were so intense that they seemed to bore right into her.

"Kristine," he murmured. He kissed her lips over and over with tenderness and purpose. They opened to each other and played hide-and-seek with their tongues.

He moved to the column of her neck, laying kisses down to her collarbone. He licked and nipped her there and then kissed his way down to one breast. As he suckled, creating delightful visceral sensations, she arched and moaned. When she whimpered, he switched to the other breast and gave that one the same full attention.

"Don't torment me, Jayce. I need you, now."

"Don't worry, love. I'll give you what you need." He

scooted lower, and his fingers parted her folds. "You *are* ready for me. And so soon. Are you sure you don't want more?"

"Not necessary. Please…"

"Just another minute more. It'll be worth the wait. I promise."

He lowered his head and laved her sensitive bundle with his tongue. Sensations built quickly, and soon she felt herself taking off like a rocket. Jayce didn't let up. Her core grew white-hot, and her thighs trembled. Then she exploded. The powerful orgasm left her almost sobbing.

At last she floated back to earth. There was a roaring in her ears, and her heart was pounding. Jayce gathered her in his arms and just held her while she gasped for breath. "How did…you do…that?"

"A hummingbird can flap its wings fast, right?"

"Yeah…"

"Well, a phoenix can flap its tongue just as fast."

"Holy shit!"

Jayce laughed. He tucked an arm around her waist and rolled until she was on top of him.

She giggled. "Really? I can barely move, and you want me to do all the work?"

Jayce lay there and tucked his hands behind his head. "You were the one who wanted to be on top. I can wait—although you would think that, as a dragon, you'd recover faster than a human."

She pushed on his chest and lifted her torso. "Oh, you would, would you?" She shimmered and transformed.

He just grinned. She could tell she wasn't going to get a shocked reaction, so she shimmered back to

human form and straddled him. His staff was hard as
steel. Taking his cock in her hand, she rubbed it up and
down. The surface was satiny soft, contrasting with the
strength and hardness beneath. At last, she lowered herself onto him and began to rock. He rubbed her breasts
as she found her rhythm. A visceral tug shot to her core,
and they both moaned in pleasure.

She loved knowing she was bringing him pleasure.
She wanted him to experience the same kind of gratification he gave her. If only she could just stay here,
hiding away with him on this boat forever.

Chapter 12

JAYCE WOKE UP IN HIS CONDO THE NEXT MORNING WITH A smile on his face. Before he opened his eyes, he remembered making love to Kristine on his boat and again in this very bed—twice. He opened one eye and glanced over at the empty space across from him. The sheets were rumpled, and her pillow still showed the imprint of her beautiful head, but she was gone.

He bolted upright. "Kristine?"

When there was no answer, he feared the worst. He jumped out of bed, donned his boxer briefs, and checked the open bathroom door on his way to the main living area. "Kristine?"

Silence.

Dammit!

He grabbed his phone off the kitchen counter and brought up her number in his contact list. How long could she have been gone? Hadn't they just fallen asleep? *Shit*. It was almost 8 a.m.

"Hello?"

"Kristine? Where are you?"

"Oh, Jayce. I'm at the B and B packing."

"I don't understand. You were going to give me twenty-four hours." He began pacing and tried to modulate his voice to keep his anger from showing.

"I told you I couldn't stay and that I was going back to the B and B after our date."

He bit back a swear. "When you fell asleep in my arms, I thought you had changed your mind." She was silent on the other end, and his frustration mounted. "When are you planning to return to New York? Before or after my twenty-four hours are up?"

She let out an audible sigh. "Jayce, I need you to trust me."

"Trust you?" His voice rose, but he didn't care at the moment. "It's hard to trust someone who lies to you."

"I never lied to you, Jayce. I never said I was going to stick around while you spent twenty-four hours thinking. I never said I was going to stay for breakfast this morning. I can't help the things you assume if you don't ask."

Jayce pulled the phone away from his ear and counted to ten. Technically, she was correct. She hadn't lied, and he had made assumptions. But that didn't take the sting out of it.

He swallowed hard and asked, "So what's your plan now?"

After a brief hesitation, she said, "I'm heading to the train station as soon as I'm done here."

"Does your mother know you're leaving? Or what you're planning?"

"Yes. Well, no. Not exactly. It's a long story."

"Summarize it for me." He resumed his pacing and scratched his head.

"I told her at the Laundromat yesterday that I was going back to New York. This morning I paid for my room and left the key with Amber at breakfast. My mother was right there. She didn't ask what I was planning to do beyond returning to work, and I didn't bother telling anyone."

"She was probably engrossed in conversation with Conlan, right?"

"Like I said, you're very perceptive. You must also be a little psychic. That's kind of scary," she said, as if making a joke.

He didn't find it very funny.

"Okay. If that's how you're going to play it, I have to do a couple of things first, and then I'll meet you at the train station. You don't have tickets yet, right?"

"Uh…no. Not yet. But there's a kiosk at the station. You don't have to come with me, you know. In fact, I thought you were due back at the station tonight."

"You're not leaving me much choice. I'll have to call in sick."

"You have plenty of choices. You can go about your business and let me take care of mine. Or you can follow me around and drive me crazy. Or—"

"Kristine. You're not being fair."

"Fine. I'm not fair. Life isn't fair. I was going to talk to you before I left."

"Oh? How considerate."

"Geez. What do you want me to do? Apologize for doing what I said I was going to do all along?"

He wanted to throw the phone across the room. How did this get so out of control? If he went to New York now, he wouldn't be there long. He was supposed to go back to work tonight at six. He hadn't even had his coffee yet, so hoping for a brilliant idea was a bit of a stretch.

"Can you wait until I meet you at the train station? Which one are you using, by the way? Back Bay?"

"Yeah. It's only a few blocks from here."

"Don't buy a ticket yet. The Boston Public Library is right down the street. Why don't you meet me on the steps there?"

When she didn't answer right away, he imagined her trying to think of any reason she could wiggle out of meeting him. He was careful not to give her one. He wouldn't assume she would be there. He would make her *promise* to be there.

"All right," she said.

"Promise you won't leave before I get there."

"How long will it take you to pack and use public transportation?"

"Who said I'm doing either of those things?" He ended the call with a click. *Good, let her wonder what that meant.*

Gabe lived a lot closer to the train station, and he could grab some clothes there. Flying always freed up his mind so he could think. Still, he knew better than to assume his brother would be home. He hit the voice command on his phone and said "Call Gabe" a little more forcefully than he needed to.

———

Kristine sat on the front steps of the Boston Public Library, staring at Trinity Church across Copley Square. Boston really was a beautiful city—smaller than New York, not that that was a terrible thing.

She sensed Jayce before she saw him jogging toward her. He was as handsome as ever, but his devil-may-care smile was missing. She rose from her spot on the steps and met him at the sidewalk.

He gave her a quick kiss and said, "My brother says

you're more trouble than a broken monkey cage at the Franklin Park Zoo."

She chuckled. "I never asked any of you to get involved."

"It's too late for that. If anything happened to you…" He simply stared at the sidewalk and shook his head.

"So, now what? Did you come all the way down here to try to talk me out of this?"

He shoved his hands in his pockets. "No. I think we established that you wouldn't listen to me no matter how much logic I threw at you."

"My bags are back at the B and B. You see? I'm not too stubborn to give you a chance to speak your mind." She held out her hand and prepared to walk back to Beacon Street with him.

He stared at her hand a moment and then wrapped his around it and pulled something out of his pocket.

"It's not what you think. That comes later." He slipped a pretty ruby-and-diamond ring on her middle finger. He must have been leaving her ring finger free for "later." Thank goodness it wasn't an engagement ring. She wasn't ready for that.

"The ruby symbolizes love. The little diamonds on either side, well… Let's just say they'll grow, if nurtured."

She admired the beauty and sparkle—and the sentiments. "Thank you," she said softly.

He didn't answer and still seemed way too serious. Without letting go of her hand, he turned, and they strolled side by side to the corner. Yes, he may have thought she was a lot of trouble, but she saw it very differently. She needed to end this public threat. That was her choice, not his. Donkey Pizzle and his cronies hadn't just terrorized her family; they thought nothing of using other innocents to get what they wanted. Amy had told her about their using drug addicts to pull off crimes with promises of a fix. Gun running and drug smuggling— selling to anyone who could pay. Now they were going to try their hand at human trafficking.

"So did you come up with any brilliant ideas?" she asked.

He sighed. "I wish…"

They waited for a break in the traffic and then hurried across wide Boylston Street. At last they were able to take it a little slower, but they became quieter as well.

Finally Kristine broke the uncomfortable silence. "So, it's after nine in the morning, and you have to be at work at six. What do you think you can accomplish in less than nine hours?"

"Not much. That's why I have Gabe to call in sick for me. If anything happens and I'm not back in time, he'll make up some excuse to buy me some time. If I fly my hardest, I can be back in an hour and a half. I'll have Gabe leave his window open for me until five thirty when he has to leave for work. Fortunately we're about the same size, and I can borrow some clothes from him and jog to work."

"You told Gabe?"

"You can trust my brothers. Any of them. Completely."

"How much did you tell him?"

"Only what I had to. He knows you plan to go back to New York, that it might not be safe yet, and that I'm going to make sure you're not being reckless. Do you have somewhere else to stay? These scumbags do know where you live. You haven't forgotten that, right?"

"Of course not. And as for where I can stay, I've been

thinking about that. I had to crash at Donovan's place once. He might let me stay on his couch again."

"What are you going to tell him as far as a reason why you need to?"

"You know, the usual. The place is being fumigated."

"So Donovan is a male friend?"

"Yeah. We work together. Don't tell me you're the jealous type, because that could be a real problem—considering the fact that I work with all men."

"No. You don't have to worry. I'm not an asshole—well, not usually. But I'm curious how you managed to stay single with so many guys knowing what a catch you are."

She laughed as they ran across the next street during a break in traffic. Now they were in the middle of Commonwealth Avenue, where there was a green space with benches and a paved bicycle path. She had to admit this was a pretty part of the city. "Why don't we stop for a minute and talk where we won't be interrupted?"

"Good idea," he said.

They found an empty bench and sat. She took another moment to admire the ring he had given her. It sparkled in the morning light. "It's beautiful."

Jayce put an arm around her and gently rubbed her shoulder. "So are you."

I could get used to this. Kristine understood he was just concerned for her, but she wasn't a hothead. He needed to know that. "I don't want anything to happen to me either. I'm not planning to go off half-cocked," she said.

"Okay, so you're going off fully cocked?" He smirked at her.

She tried to tamp down her frustration. "Look, I don't

exactly know what I'm doing yet. But I want to reassure you I won't do anything stupid."

"What do you consider to be stupid?"

She just stared ahead. No matter what she said, it would sound monumentally foolish. Going after who knows how many goons in their own well-defended fortress—alone—would probably be the definition of stupid. But what option did she have? Amy said they had been at this business for years and had hurt or murdered countless innocent people. They had to be stopped, and Kristine was convinced she was the only one who could or would attempt to do so.

"Tomorrow night is a new moon. That means tonight I'll have total darkness. I can shift into my dragon form if I need to get away quickly. In fact, I might show up in dragon form from the start. There's not much they can do to me as a dragon."

"Are you sure? Didn't they live with a dragon for a few years?"

"Yeah. It sounds like they were all afraid of him. According to my mother, these guys are pretty dumb. I'd have to say from what little I know of them personally, I can certainly attest to that. Who actually writes out a contract for a contract killing? And then mails it to a legal office?"

Jayce's eyes rounded. "They did that? Is that what you had to retrieve for them the first time?"

"Yeah. You see? Dumbdy-dumb-dumb."

"You could also sing that to suspenseful background music in a horror movie." To demonstrate, he did so… in an intense, low-pitched voice.

"If you're trying to scare me, I'm terrified," she said with deadpan sarcasm.

"So, they're hit men?"

"That and a lot more. My mother said they own a fancy boat and use it to meet drug smugglers offshore. They sell guns to anyone who wants to buy them. And here's the kicker... They find homeless drug addicts down on their luck and use them to rob banks, jewelry stores, or whatever for the promise of an unlimited supply of their drug of choice and a mansion to party in. But if they don't perform, they kill them and assume no one will notice they're missing."

"Aren't the police aware of what's going on?"

"If they are, they haven't done anything about it. My mother said she remembered their posting bail for one of their drug addicts and then making it look like he committed suicide. As far as the cops were concerned, society had one less problem."

"Jesus," Jayce muttered. "I understand your wanting to take them down, and I admire your courage, but wouldn't your mother have put a stop to them if there was any way to do that?"

"You forget, she had *me* to think of. And we're very different people." She sighed. "Please, let me go alone. There's really nothing you can do to help anyway."

"Oh? I don't know about that... I can watch, perched in a nearby tree. And if you need someone to dive-bomb Donkey Pizzle and peck his eyes out, I'm your man—or phoenix—at that moment."

She smiled. "You're so sweet."

He laughed. The thought of pecking someone's eyes out as a sweet gesture must have struck him as funny. She had to join in the laughter.

An elderly couple strolled by hand in hand and gave them twin smiles.

It was a long train ride, but it gave Kristine time to think up a plan Jayce would agree to. As much as she resented his interference, she also realized he'd probably already saved her life.

By the time they had arrived at Penn Station, he had talked her out of going back to her apartment for any reason. Until the thugs on Long Island were taken care of, they'd look for her in the Hell's Kitchen area. The element of surprise would only be Kristine and Jayce's if they stayed away.

She was right about the new moon and the darkness that would ensue. Jayce called Gabe and let him know he wouldn't be back that night. They needed that darkness to cover their paranormal identities. He could disguise his tail feathers with dirt, but there was no way to hide an almost-six-foot dragon.

Because it was early afternoon, they had some time to kill. They decided to visit Ellis Island and the Statue of Liberty. This was where more than twelve million immigrants landed with hopes of a better future. Some of the displays there gave them pause. Boatloads of human beings, some barely alive, were funneled through an uncaring system.

The United States required all immigrants to possess the ability to read and write—at least in their own language. Many of the people who arrived were illiterate, and therefore deported... Or they went to Canada. How many dragons learn to read and write in caves in the Scottish Highlands? Not many, she imagined. It's a good thing they came over before the Pilgrims.

Having spent the afternoon exploring and appreciating her home city, she wanted to fight for it more than ever. Since it was now May, and it would be quite late before it got completely dark, she and Jayce finally made it to a Broadway play together.

It was hard to believe that just ten days ago, Jayce had walked into her firehouse to reconnect with her. It felt as if they had known each other for months or even years.

At dinner after the play, Jayce reached across the table and took her hand. "Are you sure you want to go through with this, love?"

She nodded. Then she took a large bite of her lo mein and chewed slowly.

"Hey, I use that trick when I don't want to discuss something."

"What trick?" she mumbled around the food in her mouth.

He just laughed and shook his head. "Never mind."

She knew what he meant. She was stalling for time—he was right about that. Nothing he could say would talk her out of doing this. Their plan was drastic and dangerous, but they couldn't think of anything better. And it just might work.

Walking up to the front door and asking to be let in wasn't an option. There had to be cameras for security all around the perimeter. The only place from which they could approach undetected was the sky.

The plan was for Jayce to check out the situation via flybys first. If all seemed quiet, he'd fly down the chimney, and if they'd left the flue open, he could double-check from the inside. He often flew down chimneys, dragging his tail feathers through the creosote on the way down and then doing a quick turnabout and coating the other side on his way back up. This was how he and his brothers hid their colorful tails with waterproof camouflage. Unlike normal birds, they didn't worry about the filth weighing them down. They were strong.

However, this time Jayce didn't need the disguise. Well, he might if anyone saw him and lived to tell about it. But they planned to let no one live. As drastic as that sounded, it was the only way to be sure Kristine stayed out of jail, countless innocents remained safe, and the mobsters ceased their illegal activities. Smuggling drugs and guns was bad enough, but human trafficking was the last straw.

If Jayce could guarantee everyone was upstairs first and then pinpoint the bedrooms of those in the house after all the lights went out, Kristine could target those areas with a stream of fire. Jayce would gather sticks from the nearby woods and lay them under each exit. If cameras were picking up his activity, it would only look like some dumb bird decided he was tired of getting wet and wanted his nest under a portico. Then Kristine would need to work fast to light the tinder, blocking the exits, and then set the rest of the place on fire.

In a way, it was karma. Kristine learned on the news that the home on Park Avenue—the one they'd tasked her to set on fire before her mother escaped—belonged to an elderly art dealer. The place had been burglarized, and the resident had been drugged. They'd wanted her to burn him alive while he was incapacitated.

Thank goodness Amy's escape removed the only leverage they had. Getting out of the city was another smart idea on their part. Okay…Jayce was mostly responsible for that. She had to admit her stubbornness might have cost her or her mother their lives.

Jayce had said more than once that he didn't know what he'd do if anything happened to her. Well, she felt the same way. If anything happened to Jayce… Her heart broke just thinking about it.

Jayce drove the length of Long Island and found the place in South Hampton easily. He and Kristine sat on a piece of driftwood and watched quietly from the beach until half an hour after the last light went out inside the ostentatious mansion. If anyone saw them, they would have appeared to be a romantic couple sharing the peace and quiet of the night.

If only that were the case.

He leaned toward her and whispered, "Last chance to back out."

She shook her head vehemently.

He let out a deep sigh. Apparently she was hell-bent on going through with their plan, and he would rather support her than let her try it alone.

They strode to the edge of the woods, stripped down, and left their clothing behind a rock. Then Jayce shifted and flew high above the building.

No smoke emanated from the chimney. That was good news. He landed on the chimney and peered down inside. It looked like the flue was open, so getting inside wouldn't be a problem. He decided to wait on that. For now it was enough to coat his feathers with creosote.

Once he was appropriately camouflaged, he began his flyby of the lower windows. Seeing no activity, he took the time to land on the windowsills where he could scan the inside of each room. When he was satisfied no one remained downstairs, he rose and circled the second-floor windows. Three individuals occupied those rooms, and only the master bedroom had any light in it at all…a night-light.

Donkey Pizzle sleeps with a night-light?

He didn't really know if the individual was or was not the guy who seemed to be running things. He had never actually seen Donkey Pizzle. But wouldn't that be ironic?

All the occupants seemed to be asleep. Just to be on the safe side, he pecked each window once. No one stirred. At last he circled the third floor. The rooms were smaller and empty. Some were used for storage.

It was time to share his findings with Kristine.

He swooped down to the edge of the woods near the beach where he had left her and shifted. She eyed him up and down. Large splotches of soot appeared randomly over his human body.

"What? You don't like my new paint job?"

She covered her smile with her hand and looked like she was trying not to giggle.

"I don't have to explain. You already know the drill. It looks like there are three occupants and everyone is asleep on the second floor. It's almost time to put phase two into play. First I want to fly down the chimney and look around inside to be sure we aren't missing anyone. I'll come back when I'm ready for you."

She nodded.

"They're all asleep. You don't have to worry about talking."

"Okay," she whispered. "Then I don't have to worry about kissing either."

He smiled. "No, you don't."

She stepped into his space, draped her arms around his neck, and then pulled her arms away quickly. "Sorry, I shouldn't erase your disguise." Locking her fingers behind her back, she leaned forward, kissing him like the figurine of Dutch children that her mother had among her tchotchkes. Now, why would she think of something so mundane when they were about to commit a heinous act?

Kristine had already gathered dry sticks for kindling and left them in a pile for him. She had picked up some logs to prop under knobs and hold doors closed if the fire took a few seconds to catch.

"See you in a minute," Jayce said and shifted. Picking up a beak-full of sticks, he flew them to the windowsills and laid them there. It looked as if the porch was made of timber and not some composite that wouldn't burn easily. He was grateful for 1920s construction.

As Jayce worked, Kristine blockaded the side door Amy had escaped from and propped the logs against the other exits. The front stoop was concrete, but the doors appeared to be solid wood. There were two of them, opening in the middle for a grand entrance. He pictured these asshats throwing open the doors to a well-lit foyer. He was fairly sure they would catch and burn too. The doors...not the asshats. Although that was kind of the point.

Now it was Kristine's turn. Jayce flew back to the woods, but she didn't wait for him. She was probably tired of his asking, "Have you changed your mind yet?"

She hovered in her beautiful dragon form—an

iridescent blue-green reminiscent of her eyes. Then, beating her wings vigorously, she flew at the back door at full speed. Not that he knew what full speed for a dragon would be. He imagined they couldn't fly quite as fast as a phoenix. Or maybe they could. He'd ask her, if they made it out of this alive.

She turned at the last minute, roared fire all along the back of the house, and then whipped around the side of the building and did the same thing. The wood caught easily, along with the plantings all along the foundation. Fire sprang up and spread.

He could only see the amber-colored light from the front of the house, but he imagined that must be burning vigorously too. She was nothing if not thorough… and angry. Soon she rounded the far corner, still blasting fire. *Holy hell, Jayce. Try not to make her mad—ever*.

She targeted the second-floor windows next. The sills caught first, which would certainly discourage anyone from trying to escape that way. But escape they might.

Jayce felt like he should be doing more. He figured he could fly down the chimney and perhaps trip anyone running for the stairs—or blind them with a well-placed peck to the eyes. A broken leg should slow them. He knew the chimney would be the last thing to burn, so he had a handy escape route.

He flapped his wings and rose above the house, diving down the chimney to the blare of smoke alarms. Yeah, they should be up and looking for an escape route any minute now.

He landed on the oversized crystal chandelier in the two-story foyer. From there he had a great vantage point of the grand curved staircase. Hopefully, he could describe the mayhem to Kristine after all was said and done. She might appreciate a blow-by-blow account of her enemies' demise.

Seeing the power his lover possessed, he had to wonder why Amy didn't use the same tactics to get away. Did she know them as friends when she'd lived there before? Did they not know she was a dragon? Kristine's mother had impressed upon her the paranormal law to *never* reveal herself to humans—just as *his* parents had dictated to him and his brothers.

But Kristine certainly wasn't worried about that now. He imagined the neighbors would be waking up and calling the fire department as soon as they noticed the formidable smoke and sparks rising over the woods.

Ah, here came the criminals at last. One was in his robe. The other two were shrugging into their clothing as they ran.

"Grab the tranq gun," the one in the lead yelled.

"But, boss…"

That must be Donkey Pizzle…saving himself first without regard to the others.

The leader didn't wait to hear the guy's objection. He just shouted louder over his shoulder, "The tranq gun! Get it! *Now!*"

Jayce couldn't let them get away. They knew about Kristine. They'd go after her, and apparently, they knew how to subdue a dragon.

He saw his opening. Jayce flew at the distracted leader as he reached the top of the stairs and was turning his head back to center. Aiming for Donkey Pizzle's left eye, his beak hit soft tissue, and the guy hollered. The tyrant began swearing and grabbing at the air.

Jayce managed to get away and flew at the second guy.

"Son of a bitch! What the hell is that thing?" he yelled and crouched in time to avoid the same fate. The third guy made an about-face and ran.

Jayce flew faster and latched onto the third guy's back with his talons, sinking his sharp beak into his neck. If he hit the right nerve, he could paralyze him or make him forget about getting that tranquilizer gun.

The guy sank to the floor, moaning.

Donkey Pizzle was making his way down the stairs, holding onto the railing with both hands. Jayce flew between the legs of the one who was now at the top of the stairs, hoping to take them both out with one trip.

The guy grabbed at him but missed. He also missed the step and stumbled. Snatching the rail, he managed to catch himself and avoid falling. Now Jayce's only option to stop their leader was to go after Donkey Pizzle directly.

Because the element of surprise was gone, he was taking a risk. Jayce thought about Kristine and what Amy had told her—about how these guys had no conscience. Contract killings, using the homeless and drug addicts to pull off heists, plus drug smuggling and gun running. Smoke filled the stairway, so he could probably sneak through Donkey Pizzle's legs from behind.

He tried it, but as soon as he brushed the leader's leg with his wing, a hand shot out and grabbed his tail feathers. It hurt, but he didn't care. He needed to stop this monster.

Unfortunately, the one who was stopped was Jayce.

"Get to the basement," the guy behind him yelled.

"Not until I fuck up this bird!"

Jayce struggled to get away. He turned and pecked the guy's hand, but Donkey Pizzle hung on tight. Then Jayce felt his body swing hard to the right—and the room went black.

Chapter 13

KRISTINE LANDED ON THE LAWN BESIDE THE WOODS AND shimmered into her naked human form. Before she sprinted for her clothes, she turned back to be sure they'd succeeded. The mansion was engulfed in flames. So far, no one had come out...no one. She glanced around, looking for Jayce.

Where the hell is he?

Perhaps he was perched in a tall tree or circling high above, watching. Regardless, she had to get dressed before the fire department showed up. They'd certainly be there, and soon. Someone had to have noticed and called them.

Once dressed, she began searching the trees and sky for her lover. "Jayce," she whispered loudly.

No response.

He had paranormal hearing, so he must have been far off—or... *Holy shit. He wouldn't have gone inside, would he? That wasn't part of the plan.*

The roar of sirens split the night, growing louder with every second. Kristine began to panic. She was supposed to meet Jayce on the beach, so she ran away from the fire and jogged beside the ocean until she was sure he couldn't have or wouldn't have gone that far.

By the time she returned to the scene of the crime, fire trucks and police cars had arrived. Oh yes, she had committed a crime. A big one. Arson.

But considering all the crimes she was stopping, she was convinced it was the right thing to do. Where the hell was Jayce?

Firefighters were unrolling hoses and sprinting toward the house. She heard orders being shouted and knew they were assessing the situation before charging into the building. Soon streams of water were attacking the fire from the outside.

The roof had caught, so they didn't have to worry about getting firefighters up there to cut a hole, letting out the toxic gases. A steady stream of water prevented a widespread cave-in. So far the captain hadn't felt comfortable sending anyone inside. Kristine's stomach knotted as she witnessed her thorough work. She didn't know whether to be proud or horrified.

At last enough of the fire had been extinguished so firefighters were able to work their way inside and look for survivors. Their shouts were not met with any answering cries for help. Jayce had said they were in there. Perhaps they were overcome by the smoke and were unconscious or already dead. Kristine hoped for the latter.

As she waited, she grew more and more concerned. If only she could shift and storm in there in dragon form. She'd be completely fireproof and safe. But what if they saw her?

At last the radio crackled, and a firefighter said, "We have some possible survivors in the basement. It looks like some kind of Battle Royale took place here. Four men, all beat to hell, bloody and unconscious. Oh, and one is in a cage."

A cage! Oh no! That has to be Jayce.

She grabbed her hair in her fists and closed her eyes. *Count to ten, Kristine. Don't do anything rash.* Before she got to five, she dashed off toward the woods where she'd left her cell phone. She knew her love could reincarnate in fire. She just didn't know *how*. His family would know—but she didn't know his family!

All she could think of to do was to contact the B and B and hope someone would know what to do. She found her fanny pack behind the rock and dug out her phone. Her mother was only a quick call away. Hopefully, she was at the B and B and not gallivanting around Boston with Conlan.

"Hello?" Amy sang on the other end of the connection.

"Mom! Please tell me you're at the B and B. I need help!"

"Oh dear. What kind of help?"

"The kind that needs to know how to reincarnate a phoenix, still in man form, and in a cage…in the basement of a building on fire!"

Her mother's voice dropped an octave. "Where are you? Long Island?"

"Yes."

"Crap. Hold on. Let me talk to Amber."

"Why Amber? Isn't she human?"

"Hold. On," Amy said forcefully.

Kristine tried to slow her breathing. She couldn't help anyone if she passed out. The three minutes she might have been waiting seemed like a lifetime. She edged her way toward the house and sneaked a peek at the scene on the front lawn.

A firefighter exited the building with a limp body draped over his back. EMTs rushed over with a stretcher. She watched as they did a quick examination and then shook their heads.

She felt a few taps on her right shoulder and jumped. When she whirled around, she was greeted by Amber. "Where did you come from?"

"I'll tell you later. Right now, I hear you may need help. What can I do?"

Kristine pointed a shaking finger toward the fully engulfed mansion. "Jayce is in the basement. In a cage! I don't know if he's alive—or what to do if he isn't. He's a phoenix, but I… I…"

Amber laid a calming hand on her shoulder. "It's all right. We'll figure it out."

A split second later they were in a smoke-filled space with concrete walls. Yet the room wasn't hot. She spotted a slumped-over body in a cage.

"Jayce!" Kristine cried.

A firefighter was making his way up the stairs with what must have been the last of the three criminals over his back. He didn't even turn around to see who had shouted.

Kristine tried to run toward the cage, but Amber grabbed her arm.

"Let me go! He needs me, and I'm fireproof."

"I'm well aware. Married to a dragon, remember? But we need to know how to help him. We're in the ether right now. Neither here nor there. A place between. I'll explain later. Stay here."

With that, Amber disappeared.

What the hell? Obviously, Amber had some big supernatural secret of her own. As mysterious as that was, Kristine gave it only a moment of her attention before returning to panic mode. "Jayce!" she yelled.

If the firefighter hadn't heard her from this "ether" she was in, Jayce might be unable to hear her too. Just because he didn't respond... Kristine's hope was dying as surely as her lover was.

"Amber!" she yelled.

An older woman with long, white hair appeared next to her. Not Amber. "Who are you?"

"I'll explain later."

Could no one answer her questions now? She needed answers NOW.

"I know," the woman said.

She hoped she meant she knew what to do. "Let me go to him! I'll survive."

"I know that too... And we're going to deal with this—hold my hand."

She took Kristine's hand, and they stepped out of what felt like a cloud, leaving its cool dampness, into the crackling heat of the room. As they stood before the cage, the woman said, "I'm Mother Nature. I know what you are, little dragon. And your phoenix here needs your help. Breathe on him."

Kristine wondered if she was actually out in the woods, hallucinating. Was this apparition telling her to do what she thought she was hearing? "Did you say to breathe on him? As in breathe *fire* on him?"

"Yes. Bathe his body in fire, and don't stop until there's nothing but ash...no matter what you see or how you feel about it. Understand?"

Kristine's mouth dropped open, but no words would come out.

The woman jammed a fist on her hip. "I'd suggest you use that mouth of yours. I didn't just create it for kissing, you know. He doesn't have much time."

She didn't have any choice but to believe the stranger and act.

Kristine held onto the hot bars of the cage, opened her mouth wide, pulled in a deep breath, and then she exhaled a blast of fire aimed right at the man she loved. It felt so wrong, and yet she'd been told his brother was reincarnated in fire—twice.

Jayce's body caught fire and burned brightly. Kristine felt tears sting her eyes but continued her onslaught of fire until she was tapped out and his size and shape were reduced to nothing but a pile of ash. She turned to the woman to ask if she was finished.

The woman who called herself Mother Nature was gone, but a hand reached out and pulled Kristine back. A second later, she stood next to Amber in the cool ether.

Out of the corner of her eye, she saw the ash stir. She watched as a glowing wing emerged slowly. She gasped and stared at Amber wide-eyed. "Can I go to him?"

Before Kristine could take a step in his direction, Amber said, "Don't try to touch him or stop him. He'll find his own way out."

"But…"

A moment later a brilliantly glowing bird rose up, flapped its wings, and easily slipped between the bars of the cage. He flew toward the stairs and disappeared into the smoke.

"Is he all right? How will he get out?" Kristine asked.

Amber set her hand on Kristine's shoulder, and the two of them disappeared and reappeared, still in the ether; however, now they were hovering near the caving roof.

A moment later, the bird—now sporting the familiar brown body and fire-colored tail—flew out of the chimney and up into the sky.

"What… Where… When can I see him? Can you get me home from here?"

"Where's home?" Amber asked with a sly smile. "Boston or Manhattan?"

"Wherever *he is*," Kristine answered without hesitation.

———ᴡᴡ———

Kristine found herself in the living room of the B and B. She and Amber were the only ones there.

"You probably need some explanations," Amber said.

Kristine snorted. A curl of smoke exited her nostril. "You could say that. We probably have at least an hour to wait for him, so if you wouldn't mind filling me in—"

"It'll be longer than an hour. I imagine he'll go to his parents first. And, um, he may not be able to talk for a while."

"Why? Are they going to ground him?"

Amber's expression quickly turned from serious to amused and then serious again. "Not exactly. Maybe you can talk to them but not him. Not yet."

"I hate to meet Jayce's family under these circumstances. I don't even know where they live. But someone should tell them what's happened."

Amber scratched her head. Then she snapped her fingers. "There are a couple of people I can think of who can help. Well, not exactly people…"

"Huh? Like who—or what?"

"Like Ryan, Jayce's brother—also a phoenix who recently went through this. He lives in Ireland, but I can go and get him for you."

"Seriously? You can do this poof, grab, and transport thing anywhere in the world?"

Amber chuckled. "Have a seat. I think you could use a drink."

"I'll say." Kristine walked over to the comfortable couch and sank down on one end, while Amber strolled over to the bar and took a bottle of wine out of the fridge beneath.

"Do you like chardonnay?" She opened the bottle and poured a glass.

Kristine nodded.

Amber poured another glass and then brought both over to the coffee table and set them down. She took a seat next to Kristine. "Here's the quickest version I can give you. I'll start with myself. I'm a muse. A minor goddess, recruited by Mother Nature because she needed a few modern muses to take care of technology that didn't exist in ancient times."

Kristine's eyes widened. "Seriously?"

Amber smirked. "Trust me. I know how you feel. I found this pretty hard to swallow when I heard about it. But as Gaia herself would say, 'I don't have time for your doubt. Just go with it, Girlie.'"

Kristine took a large gulp of her wine, and Amber forged on.

"I'm the muse of air travel. Usually I take care of airplanes in trouble. Actually, I'm more apt to help the pilot stay calm and make a safe emergency landing. I used to be a flight attendant."

Kristine decided she had seen and heard plenty of bizarre things in the past few days, and being, well, a *dragon* herself, why couldn't there be muses? "Okay. You're a modern muse. The muse of air travel. I didn't see you use an airplane to take me anywhere."

Amber patted her knee. "Right. You're doing fine. As a minor goddess, I can go wherever I want, and as long as I stay in the ether, I won't be seen. It's imperative that humans don't see me appear or disappear. The ether is that cool and foggy place we were in for a while."

Kristine nodded as if all of this made perfect sense. "Continue," she said and took another swig of her wine. She was going to need more than one glass if there were many more of these revelations.

"To make a long story short, I can go and get Ryan *if he's alone* right now. He works with the local volunteer fire department. Or I can get Chloe if he isn't. I think she's still decorating their home—a castle on the cliffs, overlooking the Atlantic Ocean. You'll have to see it someday. It's stunning."

Kristine scratched her head. "Sure, uh-huh."

"Are you okay with me bringing them here? Either one can explain a phoenix reincarnation to you better than I can."

Kristine took another generous swallow of her wine. Amber must've noticed because she rose and made her way back to the bar. Grabbing the bottle, she smiled in understanding and returned, plunking down the whole bottle on the coffee table.

Kristine took a deep breath and let it out slowly. "Yes, I'd like to talk to them. Maybe it would be better if I talked to Chloe first. As I understand it, she's Rory's sister and a dragon too. So she might understand it from my perspective."

"Good idea. Oh, and just so you're not too surprised, she's also a modern muse. The muse of fire safety. She does everything from alerting parents when their kids are playing with matches to suggesting people make sure their ovens are off. Even encouraging scientists who are working on better ways to prevent fires."

Kristine worried her lip. "I'm not sure. Wouldn't she—"

A pretty blonde woman appeared on the other side of the coffee table and startled Kristine.

"Did I hear my name? Is someone in need of the muse of fire safety?"

Amber rose and strode to her, clasping the woman in a warm hug. "Hi, Chloe. We do need your help but not in a professional capacity."

Chloe gazed at Kristine. "Who is this?"

Amber gestured toward her and said, "This is Kristine Scott. You two have a lot in common. She's a dragon and a firefighter who's in love with a phoenix. Ryan's brother, Jayce."

"A dragon, are you? And a firefighter also? What a fine thing. Do you work for the Boston Fire Department?"

"No. At least not yet." Kristine bit her lip. Should she have said that? She honestly didn't know where she was going to wind up. A lot of that depended upon Jayce— and she still had more questions than answers.

This muse Chloe seemed nice enough. She had a lovely Irish brogue and a sweet smile. Remembering Rory saying that she was a queen and could be prickly made Kristine a little nervous, but the royal seemed plenty down to earth.

"Ah. Well, we can talk about work later. What is it you called me for?"

"I need to know about reincarnation. Jayce just… I just…" Kristine cast a panicked look at Amber. "A little help here?"

"Let's all sit down." Amber placed her hands on Kristine's shoulders and steered her back to the sofa. Chloe sat in the adjacent armchair.

"Wine?" Amber asked Chloe.

"Thank you kindly, but no. I was using a nail gun. When I return, I want to nail the furniture, not me fingers."

"You're making your own furniture?" Kristine asked, incredulous.

"Indeed. There are custom touches needed in a castle—round rooms and such—and I enjoy doin' it. But let's get back to your story."

Amber took a seat next to Kristine and nodded to her to go ahead.

With a deep breath, Kristine said, "Jayce got into a bit of trouble and had to be cremated—temporarily, of course. I need to know what will happen now."

"What does 'a bit of trouble' entail?"

"Um...I kind of had to burn down a mansion, not realizing he was inside."

Chloe shot to her feet. "You *kinda* had to burn down a residence? Were there humans inside?"

"Well, yes. They were very dangerous psychopaths. It was the only way I could think of to stop them from hurting innocents."

"So, you want the muse of fire safety to, what...help you cover up your arson? Forgive you?"

Kristine hung her head. "No. None of that. I'm afraid what's done is done. But Jayce—"

"What about Jayce?"

"That's what I'm hoping you can tell me. He reincarnated into phoenix form and flew off. I want to see him, but all anyone will say is "not yet." I'm told that if anyone would know what's going on, it would be you."

Chloe sat down and groaned as she dropped her head into her hands.

Alarmed, Kristine sat up ramrod straight. "What is it? What's going to happen?"

"I apologize. I didn't mean to concern you." Chloe composed herself and patted Kristine's arm, which was resting on the end of the couch. "I was just remembering what it was like for me. You won't suffer like I did. I'll make sure of it." Her eyes narrowed and her lips thinned. "You see, nobody told me what had happened to my love. I didn't even know *what* he was, other than a firefighter who met his demise in a backdraft. I truly thought he was dead."

Kristine sympathized immediately. "That must've been horrible for you."

"Feckin' right."

Amber chuckled and then slapped her hand over her mouth. "Sorry," she mumbled.

Chloe took a deep breath and said, "I saw a glowing bird rise from the ashes. I thought I was hallucinatin'. We buried a coffin, but unbeknownst to me, Ryan wasn't in it. I waited over two months with *no* explanation from his family. None. I thought he was dead forever. I went through the following two months like a zombie."

"What? How could anyone do that to you?"

"Ryan perished in a high-rise fire. I was right there and saw him die but could do nothin' about it. It was the most awful day of me whole long life. Because it happened on the job, there was no way to hide it. His family had to pretend to be in mourning. Naturally, I didn't have to pretend. I mourned in earnest."

"Oh my God. I saw you at the firehouse after the funeral! You were devastated. I hardly recognize you as the same person." Kristine slapped herself on the forehead. "That's when Jayce started flirting with me. When I learned he was the victim's brother, I couldn't believe it. I thought he was being callous, cold, and uncaring."

"When in actuality," Amber interjected, "he wasn't grieving at all. He knew his brother was alive and well and in bird form for the next two or three months."

Kristine glanced between the women. "You've both mentioned two or three months. What happens then, and will it be the same for Jayce?"

"Indeed," Chloe said. "In phoenix form, he will mature at the rate of a normal bird. Something like a hawk. It takes about two months to reach maturity. If he comes back sooner, he could be a much younger human. That happened to Ryan—twice."

"Jayce told me Ryan was actually the oldest."

"Ryan should have known better, but he couldn't wait and came back a bit early—more like seventy-five days. Jayce really should wait about three months, or ninety days, in order to look like he's thirty."

"So, you're saying that I won't see Jayce—as an adult man—for at least two months?"

"At least."

"Damn," Kristine muttered.

At that moment, the front door burst open, and laughter emanated from the front hall. It sounded like Amy and Conlan. The two giddy dragons entered the living room with their arms around each other.

"Oh! Kristine! I'm so glad you're here. We have

some wonderful news." Amy grinned at Conlan, who was already grinning at her.

She held up her left hand, sporting a large diamond on her ring finger. "We're engaged!"

Kristine had mixed emotions but tried not to let them show. Amy had known Conlan for a shorter time than she had known Jayce. Yet Amy seemed happier than she'd ever known her to be. Of course, that rock on her finger alone could put a grin on her face. *Ginormous, ostentatious, gaudy…* Yup. Just the thing to make her mother giddy.

But Kristine was more miserable than she'd ever been in her life. And it seemed to be for the same reason. Love. What a bipolar emotion!

"Congratulations!" she said and rose to hug both her mother and stepfather-to-be. "When's the wedding?"

"I know it may seem rushed, but we want to be wed in three months," Conlan said.

Amy leaned toward her daughter and whispered, "I'll be fertile then."

Conlan added, "We want to start a family as soon as possible rather than wait five years."

Knowing how badly the Irish dragons wanted a new generation, Kristine understood completely. She could ask her mother if that's what *she* wanted later when they were alone. In the meantime, she'd just concentrate on being happy for them. "So I'll have a stepfather *and* a brother or sister soon."

"Or more. Twins run in both of our families." Amy giggled.

"How exciting!"

"Indeed, it is." Conlan leaned toward Amy. She tipped up her face, and they shared a tender kiss.

Chloe cleared her throat. "By the way, Conlan," she said in her Irish lilt, "did our grandmother gift you with a special stone at your birth?"

Grinning wider, if that were possible, he answered, "She did indeed. It was an aquamarine—exactly the color of me darlin' Amy's eyes."

Chloe smiled. "It's a happy day indeed, cousin. If you haven't a venue yet, may I offer our ancestral home for your nuptials? It's nearly finished, and it would give Ryan and me great pleasure to show the whole family our restoration."

Amy gasped. "The Irish castle?"

"Indeed," Chloe answered.

Conlan gazed at his bride-to-be. "By your reaction, I'd say you approve?"

Amy nodded enthusiastically.

He bowed to Chloe. "Thank you, your majesty. We would be honored. Is three months time enough to pre-pare for the invasion?" He chuckled. "I'm just havin' a bit of fun. We want to keep the guest list small. Just family and plus-ones."

Chloe gazed at Amber with mischief in her eyes. "Perhaps me brother can make an honest woman of you at the same time."

"Seriously?" Amber exclaimed. "This should be Amy and Conlan's day."

Amy walked over to Amber and grasped both her hands. "I'd love to share our wedding day with you!" She turned to Conlan. "You wouldn't mind, would you, darling?"

"I think it's a grand idea. Both clans tying the knot on the same day? Less trouble for everyone, if you ask me."

Amber sighed. "I have a few friends and family members who'd never forgive me if I didn't invite them. You probably wouldn't have enough room for everybody."

"If we haven't, we'll make more." Chloe winked and disappeared.

Kristine took a deep breath. Minor Goddesses like Chloe probably had no trouble making things happen.

A wedding in three months. Three months to wait for Jayce. *If only I can make sure those situations dovetail.*

"Mom, can you give me time to look into something before you pick an exact date?"

Amy's brows rose. "Is everything all right?"

"It will be. I'll explain later."

"How long do you think you'll need?"

"That depends on when I can talk to Jayce's family." As nervous as the idea made her, she had to do it sometime. It would be easier if Jayce were there to introduce her, but she'd be brave and introduce herself if it meant she could invite Jayce to the wedding.

Chapter 14

AMBER EXCUSED HERSELF, AND KRISTINE WAS LEFT with Amy and Conlan. "Mom, I need to talk to Jayce's family."

"Of course, dear. I imagine you'd want to talk to Jayce too. He'll be your plus-one, right?"

"That's just it. I need to invite him, but he's...um, unavailable right now." She hoped her mother wouldn't ask too many questions. Maybe she could distract her by changing the subject—using Amy's own tactics against her. Hopefully she wouldn't recognize what Kristine was doing.

"Conlan. So, you're to be my new stepfather. How do you feel about that?"

"Ah, darlin'. I couldn't be more pleased. To start a new life with a family I can already be proud of, well, it's a dream come true. And..." He gazed at Amy. "We hope to have a large family in the years to come. Best to get started early."

Amy grinned and then shyly gazed at the floor. "We haven't even talked about where we'll live yet."

"I have me business in Northern Ireland. But if you want to be close to your daughter, I can run the management remotely."

Amy threw her arms around his neck and hugged him tightly. "I'm so glad you feel that way. I do want to be close enough to my daughter to spend some time with her. We're not just mother and daughter. We're dear friends, and I enjoy her company. I would miss her terribly if we were to move so far away."

Kristine relaxed. "I'm relieved to hear that also. I would miss you too, Mom."

"We have a little work to do at home, Kristine. By we, I mean you and I."

"Really? What's that?"

"We need to purge and pack." Amy smiled at her daughter and grasped her hand. "I know there are things that may be special to you that I might not want. And vice versa. Let's try to pare down as much as we can without throwing away each other's sentimental items."

Kristine chuckled. "You're the one with all the souvenirs. I don't have much stuff I'm attached to. I could probably pack everything in two boxes."

Amy's brows lifted. "Are you telling me that you might move too? I know the place is expensive, but I think your salary should be enough. If not, I can supplement…"

Kristine hadn't really thought it through and needed time to talk to Jayce. "I don't know. I have so many things to figure out."

"Do you think Jayce might consider moving to New York with you?"

Kristine sighed deeply. "He really can't. He has family obligations here, he says." She didn't know exactly what he meant by that, which was one more reason she wanted to talk to the Fierros.

"Well, how do you feel about moving this way?" Amy asked.

Kristine sighed. "I really need to talk to the Fierros. Only one problem: I don't know where they live."

"Well, we can fix that." Amy opened her purse and extracted her cell phone. She typed for a few seconds, and then her eyes widened. "Oh dear, I'm afraid there are quite a few Fierros in the Boston phone book."

Kristine laughed. "I could have told you that. Jayce has six brothers, and as far as I know, only one of them lives far away. He also said something about uncles and cousins in the area who are also firefighters. I could probably walk into any fire station and yell 'Fierro,' and somebody would answer."

Amy gasped. "Don't do that! Don't you know that *Fierro* means 'fire' in Italian?"

Kristine's jaw dropped. "Oh!" Then she giggled. "Yeah, no. That may not be a good idea, especially since Boston has a large Italian population. So, how will I find him?"

"Amber might know."

"Of course. She must, and she can probably take me there in the blink of an eye."

Amber rounded the corner and said, "Did I hear my name?"

"Yes, dear," Amy said. "Kristine needs to find Jayce's parents' home. And none of us knows where it is."

Amber tipped her head. "I'm afraid I don't know either. I've never been there."

"Please don't trouble yourself," Kristine said. "I'll find them."

"How?" Amy asked.

Kristine shrugged.

Amber snapped her fingers. "I'll be right back." She disappeared, and a few moments later reappeared with a handsome, dark-haired Fierro brother—Kristine recognized the family resemblance immediately.

"That was quick," Amy said.

Amber just smiled. "Muses can fiddle with time a bit. I actually had to pull Ryan away from home and explain your situation."

"Oh. Sorry," Kristine said. "We didn't mean to interfere with your free time."

"No problem at all. I was just helping my wife with her latest home project. As Amber just indicated, I'm Ryan Fierro." He stuck out his hand and shook Kristine's first and then Amy's. He smiled at Conlan. "Good to see you again, cousin-in-law."

"And you, my queen's consort." Conlan laughed and extended his hand. They pulled each other into a man hug, slapping each other on the back.

"So, I understand you'd like to visit my parents," Ryan said. "It's been a while since I've seen them too. I imagine it would be easier if we went together. Are you all right with that?"

"I'd appreciate it. Not just because I need directions, but it would be nice to have an introduction by a family member."

Ryan nodded. "At your service."

Kristine followed Ryan up the steps to the family's South End brownstone. As soon as they walked through the door, a beautiful bird with a long, colorful tail flew over and landed on Kristine's shoulder. Ryan stopped in his tracks and straightened his spine. "Jayce?"

"I'm afraid so," Kristine said.

Before she had time to explain, a woman who resembled the rest of the family except for her height came around the corner, drying her hands on a dish towel.

"Ryan!" The older woman rushed over to him and reached up to give him a hug. She was only about five feet tall.

"Hi, Ma."

"I've missed you."

"Missed you too."

After another brief hug but without taking her hand off Ryan's shoulder, she turned toward Kristine and asked, "Who have we here?"

Ryan smiled. "Mom, I'd like you to meet Kristine Scott. She's Jayce's friend from New York."

The bird on Kristine's shoulder bobbed its head a few times, as if nodding.

Mrs. Fierro clasped Kristine's hand, and then she placed her other hand over it. "Welcome, Kristine. Perhaps you can explain what's happened to Jayce. We've been wondering, but first let's sit down in the dining room. Would you like some coffee?"

"Yes, thank you."

She followed Mrs. Fierro to the large dining room, and Ryan pulled a chair out for her.

"Can I help you in the kitchen, Ma?" Ryan asked.

"Sure. We'll be right back, Kristine."

While Kristine waited, Jayce, still on her shoulder, leaned in and rubbed his feathered face against her cheek.

"Oh, Jayce," Kristine whispered. "I was told it would be a couple of months before we could speak, but I want you to know I'm so sorry. Of course, I'll wait for you."

Jayce bobbed his head in agreement like before.

"Amy and Conlan are getting married in a few months. I'd like you to be my plus-one for the wedding."

Jayce squawked. Kristine couldn't understand bird talk, but she imagined he was probably saying something like "Tell them congratulations for me" or "Sure, I'd love to go." She wondered if Ryan would be able to translate.

Ryan rounded the corner with a plate of cookies. He also had some napkins and spoons in his hand and placed four of those around the table. For a brief moment, Kristine wondered whom the fourth set was for. Did they feed Jayce birdseed at the table?

She heard Mrs. Fierro call out, "Antonio! Come and meet Jayce's young lady."

Ryan smiled. "My dad is probably in the man cave watching ESPN."

A couple of minutes later, a large, olive-skinned, older man entered the dining room. Kristine stood and extended her hand. "Hi. I'm Kristine Scott. The FDNY guys call me Scotty."

The balding gentleman grasped her hand, pumped it twice in a hearty handshake, and introduced himself as Antonio Fierro. Then he strode to his son and gave him a man hug with lots of backslapping.

Mrs. Fierro rounded the corner with a tray holding a large coffeepot and four mugs and plates.

"I should have introduced myself before. I'm Gabriella." She poured a cup of coffee for everyone and then put the sugar and cream on the table between them.

When they were seated and settled, Antonio said, "Jayce just showed up here a few minutes ago. Maybe you can tell us what happened, Ryan."

"I have no idea. I was hoping Kristine would explain."

"Of course, although it's a long story, and I'm not sure where to begin."

"Well, Jayce told us a little bit about you. But we'd like to know more," Gabriella said.

"Let's find out what happened to Jayce first," Antonio interjected.

Everyone focused on Kristine intently, waiting for the story.

Maybe she could just hit the highlights. "As you can probably guess, the old Jayce died in a fire." She realized that wasn't enough to satisfy them, but she had her own questions too. "I'm not exactly familiar with what will happen from here on out. I hope you can tell me more. I know he's a phoenix and needs a couple of months to reach maturity before he can shift back into his human form."

Mrs. Fierro nodded. "That's correct, dear. You seem to know more about him than we do about you."

"I'm a dragon."

It seemed bizarre to say that out loud. She had never told anyone before—well, no one but Jayce. His brothers had witnessed her other form, but she doubted they'd talked about it. Still, Jayce's parents just sipped their coffee as if this were a normal conversation. Perhaps it was for them.

Ryan smiled. "Just like my wife. And you're a firefighter too. I don't suppose you're a queen also?"

Kristine chuckled. "No. As far as I know, my mother and I have no royal bloodlines."

"Pity," Antonio said. "Ryan got a castle out of the deal."

Ryan laughed. "Yeah, and I've been rebuilding it ever since."

"So what happened to Jayce?" Gabriella asked again.

Kristine grimaced. "Like I said, it's a long story, but here goes…"

She started with Jayce showing up at the fire station and their first date and ended with finding out her mother was missing.

"Kidnapped!" Mrs. Fierro leaned back and clasped her hand over her heart.

"What did the kidnappers want?" Mr. Fierro asked.

"They wanted me to do their dirty work. As a firefighter, I could gain access to some of the buildings in my area. As a dragon, I could set them on fire with my breath and leave no accelerant behind to indicate arson."

"Oh dear. That must have been awful for you," Gabriella said sympathetically.

"There was no choice at all. If Jayce hadn't been there, I might still be doing their bidding. I would do anything to protect my mother."

"What did Jayce have to do with it?" Ryan asked.

Kristine gazed longingly at the bird on her shoulder and gave his feathers a little pat with her finger. "Well, for one thing, he kept a level head and advised me what I could and couldn't do about the situation. He was the one who heard background noise when I was allowed to speak to my mother over Skype.

"I was so freaked out that I didn't even think to listen for other sounds. But after he mentioned what he had heard, I had to agree that there had been waves lapping against the shore in the distance and someone talking about the Coast Guard boarding a ship. If we didn't have supernatural hearing, we would not have heard even that much."

"Do they still have her?" Antonio asked.

"Oh, no. Jayce helped me find her at the same time she escaped."

Gabriella leaned back and let out a deep breath. "Thank goodness. Is she all right? Is she home now?"

"We're staying at the B and B on Beacon Street. I understand you know the owners through Ryan and Chloe."

"Yes. We've never been there, but we met them at Ryan and Chloe's wedding…if you could call it that." Gabriella gave Ryan the stink eye.

"Ma, a fast wedding in Ireland was the best we could do in a short amount of time. And don't forget, I was officially dead and had to get out of town before anyone saw me. Look, guys, this isn't about me. Kristine is telling us what happened to Jayce. Or she will if you stop interrupting."

Antonio turned his attention back to Kristine. "I'm sorry, Scotty. You were in the middle of your story. Please continue."

She took a moment to sip her coffee and organize her thoughts. She filled in a few details about the search for and eventual rescue of her mother.

Both Fierro parents stared at the bird they recognized as their son, Jayce.

"You shifted? And stayed in bird form for extended periods?" Antonio asked.

Jayce hopped off Kristine's shoulder and strutted over to his old man. He simply raised his beak and turned slightly so he could look him in the eye. There was no way to interpret that other than assent without remorse.

"I thought he looked older," Gabriella said.

"He certainly did. And now we know why." Antonio folded his hands on the dining room table. "Kristine, I don't know what you've been told about our kind, but we age much faster in bird form. Three days as a bird equals about a year as a human. If we fly, we age even faster. Last time we saw Jayce, he had some gray hairs we hadn't seen before, and he looked tired. How long was he… Never mind. I'm sure Jayce and I will discuss it later. Continue on with your story."

"Oh. I didn't know it was like that. I never would have expected him to shift if I'd known. Not that I asked him to." She gazed at Jayce, and he spread his wings as if to say "So what?"

"Thank goodness we found my mother when we did. Who knows how many other heinous things the kidnappers would have made me do?"

Ryan, who was sitting next to Kristine, placed a hand on her shoulder. "That must've been rough. I'm glad Jayce was there to help you through it."

"Me too."

"But how did he die?" Mr. Fierro demanded.

"He helped me set fire to the kidnappers' mansion. I guess he had some kind of fight with the criminals and wound up locked in a cage."

"A bird cage?" Mrs. Fierro asked.

"No. A man-sized cage. We think they were going to start using it for human trafficking."

"Oh dear lord!" Mrs. Fierro's hand was over her heart again as if holding it in.

"So, how long are you staying in Boston?" Antonio asked.

"I'm not sure. My mother has met someone, and she sounds perfectly content to stay for quite a while."

"And you?" Gabriella asked.

"I have a job, and I should be getting back to it. I took a short leave of absence to take care of my mother. Now she's out of danger, and I need to go back to New York."

Jayce strutted in front of her and cocked his head.

"I know you probably want me to stay, but I don't want to lose my job. Frankly, I don't know how you're going to explain staying away from your job for three months."

Gabriella and Antonio groaned at the same time.

"We don't often have to come up with excuses. Our sons are usually careful. This one—" Antonio pointed at Ryan. "This one caused us some panic around that very question. I didn't think Jayce would *ever* go down in a fire. Especially after seeing what we went through with number one son here."

"Thanks, Dad. We haven't heard about the fire yet."

Kristine sighed. "As far as how he died in a fire, some of this he may choose to tell you himself. I'll just let you know that it wasn't his fault. I needed to stop those criminals from ever hurting anyone else."

"In other words, you set the fire," Antonio said.

Kristine steeled herself for their anger. "I'm afraid so. Jayce insisted on helping, but he wasn't supposed to go inside."

"And he went anyway," Antonio stated. "Why am I not surprised?"

"I'm sorry," Kristine said. "I'm so, so sorry."

"It doesn't sound like you have anything to apologize for, dear. If anything, you did the wrong thing for the right reasons." Gabriella pushed the plate of cookies toward her.

Kristine smiled. It seemed as if Jayce's family understood. She never would have expected a firefighting family to condone her actions—for any reason.

"Did the bad guys die in the fire too?" Ryan asked.

"Yes," Kristine said. "I saw the local firefighters carry out their bodies and lay them on the ground. I watched as the EMTs checked them out and shook their heads."

Silence settled over the room for a few poignant moments. At last Kristine looked at Jayce and said, "I think that's all I can tell you from my perspective. Perhaps Jayce can add to it later. At least it's over."

Jayce bobbed his head. Then he flew the short span to her shoulder and settled there again. She sighed. "I'm going to miss you for the next two or three months."

Jayce squawked loudly.

"Do you know what he said?" She glanced at the others around the table.

"I'm afraid not," Gabriella said. "I'm entirely human." She gestured to her sons and husband. "They can understand each other in bird form, but they've been forbidden to shift."

"Again, I'm sorry. I didn't realize…"

"Didn't realize he was defying his family and putting himself in danger for you?" Antonio asked.

Kristine hung her head. "I didn't know about the rule. I *did* know about the danger. I'm so—" She choked up and couldn't finish her thought.

Gabriella got out of her chair and moved over to Kristine, giving her a hug. She wouldn't have been surprised if it was followed by a slap, but it was not. Gabriella pulled out the chair next to her, sank down, and then took both of Kristine's hands in hers.

"The men in this family are special, not just because they're phoenixes but because they're heroes—in every sense of the word. And, I swear, any one of them would throw himself on a fire to protect someone he loves. It's obvious that Jayce loves you."

Jayce bobbed his head.

Kristine gave him a sad smile. "I love him too."

Gabriella sat up straight and grinned. "That's the most wonderful thing I've heard all month. I'd say all year, except Ryan and Chloe confessed to loving each other this year too. All I want, all I've ever wanted, is for my boys to be happy."

Antonio smiled. "Well, at least we don't have to hold a funeral this time. Maybe he can come back to his life as it was."

"That's right." Kristine smiled, thinking about how she had given Jayce such a hard time. "No one knows except Amber. I'll have to tell my mother eventually, but she's a bit distracted right now."

Gabriella and Antonio stared at each other for a few seconds. "What do we tell the chief?" Kristine finally asked. "Jayce loves the job, and they depend on him. He can't lose his position."

"I don't know. I remember when one of my Arizona uncles said his son had had a religious experience in the desert, and he had to go on a vision quest."

"Wrong culture," Ryan said. "We don't do vision quests or walkabouts."

"Hmm…" Gabriella rubbed her chin. "Perhaps we

can say he heard a higher calling in church and had to go to Jerusalem to explore it. Then when he comes back he can say he realized there was no higher calling than the BFD."

Ryan and his father looked at each other and shrugged as if to say "It could work."

Jayce squawked.

"Never mind, you." Antonio pointed a finger at his son. "It's up to us to get you out of this mess, and hopefully in a way that you can keep your job. The only higher authority I know besides God is the chief."

Chapter 15

"SCOTTY, YOU'RE BACK!" DONOVAN EXCLAIMED. "I GUESS your mother must be doing better."

"Yeah, she's still in Boston, but getting much better, thanks. How've things been while I was away?"

"You know…same old. Except ever since that explosion, everyone smells gas."

"Yeah," Mahoney said as he joined them. "Then when you get there, it smells like a fish and a head of broccoli had a farting contest. People should really take their garbage out more often."

After they were through laughing, Donovan said, "We were beginning to think you moved to Boston permanently because the work was easier—either that or to taunt the Sox."

What could she say? She was still wrestling with the idea of moving, but they didn't need to know that yet. "There was no time for ball games, I'm afraid. And if I moved there, it would be because the BFD guys are better looking, but it's good to be back anyway."

"Ouch… I thought you didn't date firefighters. When did you change your policy?"

"Who says I did?"

"Oh, so we're just eye candy to you? Is that it?" Mahoney asked.

"Not *you*, buddy—or anyone else in this battalion." She'd missed their banter.

"So it must be the Ninth you're ogling," he persisted.

"No! There's no ogling! I was just kidding around. Forget I said anything about looks."

"Nope. Not forgetting it," Mahoney said. "You said the guys in Boston were better looking. You must have looked. You're human after all, Scott."

She let out a laugh. It was good to be back, even if it meant bearing the brunt of some teasing.

"You still studying for the lieutenant's exam?" Donovan asked.

"Of course." She hadn't thought about it in a week. It had meant so much just a short while ago. Would it be a wasted effort? If she moved to Boston, she'd have to start all over again—and not where she left off. She'd have to start at the bottom and go through training all over again. Then probie status. She almost groaned aloud. After nearly eight years in FDNY, could she humble herself like that?

Suddenly she noticed the guys staring at her warily. She needed some time alone.

"Excuse me, guys. I think I'll go upstairs and study."

On her way up the stairs, her phone rang. She dug it out of her pocket and didn't know the number but she did recognize the 617 area code. Boston.

"Hello?"

"Kristine? Darling?"

The female voice didn't sound exactly like her mother, but who else would call her darling?

"This is she."

"Oh, good. This is Gabriella Fierro. I'm sorry to bother you, but I was wondering when you might be able to come back."

She sat on her bed. "Back? To your house?"

"Yes, dear."

"Is everything all right?"

"Well, yes and no. It's Jayce."

Her mouth went dry, and a rush of adrenaline stabbed her in the chest. "Is he okay?"

"Oh, he's fine. I didn't mean to worry you. He's just despondent. I guess it could be any number of things. His sister-in-law, our dear Sandra, lost the baby—we're all terribly sad about that, but most likely, he's missing you. He eats very little and stares out the window all day."

Was this a guilt trip? How could she be in two places at once? Of course she'd like to see him, but without being able to talk, their time together was kind of…not useless, but frustrating.

"What did you finally decide to tell his chief?" Kristine needed a minute to process what she'd been told, and she was curious. She'd feel terrible if he were fired, knowing how much the job meant to him. How much it meant to all of them.

Mrs. Fierro was quiet for a moment. At last, she said, "We really had to come up with something better than a religious experience. He'd never just take off without a phone call. We thought about saying he went to rehab, but those who know him would highly doubt that explanation."

"So what did you finally go with?"

"This is going to sound stupid, but it seemed like the only way to explain his inability to communicate his own absence. We said he's in a coma."

Kristine gasped. "A what?"

Gabriella giggled. "I know. It's not ideal. We'll have to fake medical documents. The captain wanted to visit, but we talked him out of it. We said it would be a waste of his precious time, since Jayce wouldn't even know he was there."

"But according to some patients who've come out of it, they heard everything going on around them."

"I know. We thought of that. We also said he was in New York. We figured he may have said something about visiting you there, and that would lend credibility to the story."

Oh sure… Blame it on me.

"I guess I could come back to Boston after my three-day shift."

"Oh! I didn't realize you had returned to work. I thought you were just around the corner. Please, forget I said anything."

"It's pretty hard to forget something like that. I do love him, and I want him to be happy. I just don't know how to make that happen right now." *What can I do? Bring him his favorite birdseed?*

"Of course. That's not something you need to worry about. It's up to us, as his family, to look after him. I just thought if you knew… But no. Never mind."

Kristine worried her lip. "Tell you what. Let him know that I'm packing. That might help him perk up. It might be a week or so before I can get back up there because my mother and I have to go through our things and donate or toss whatever we can live without. She's coming down in a couple of days to start the process."

"That's wonderful! He'll be very happy to hear that. So am I. We're all rooting for you two."

After Kristine and Gabriella said good-bye and hung up, Mahoney entered the large sleeping quarters.

"I, uh…heard something about packing? Are you going somewhere?"

Shit. Kristine had to think fast. *What did I say that he could have overheard? My mother and I were purging and packing. And "he" would be glad to hear it. Yeah, that's about it.*

"My mother is getting married! Her fiancé is in Boston and can't wait until we get her packed and moved to his place. She has a lot of stuff. We really need to go through it all. I'll have to help since she's still convalescing and everything…" *Shut up, Kristine. You're babbling.*

"Oh. Well, congratulate her for me. I was afraid we were losing you too."

"Too?"

"You know that I'm moving to the 7th Battalion, right? They need a lieutenant. That leaves a spot for you."

"Oh, yeah." *Now what?* She needed another distraction. "So, what else is new with you?" *Lame.*

"Nuthin' much. The kid is graduating from high school."

She wasn't crazy about how he referred to his stepson, but she'd learned to mind her own business when it came to other firefighters and their families. "High school, huh? That's great. Does he have any college plans?"

"Yup. Columbia. I may have to work overtime more often."

The lieutenant rarely worked overtime, so she imagined that's why he sounded less than thrilled.

"You must be close to getting your degree," he prompted.

"Yeah. Another semester."

And there's another thing I might have to finish in Boston this fall—if they don't make me take their core curriculum just to get their money's worth out of me. Then it could take another year or two.

"Well, I won't hold you up anymore. I know you want to get to studying. I just wanted to welcome you back, and," he lowered his voice to a whisper, "let you know that unless you really fuck up the test, you're a shoo-in for my position."

She forced a smile.

———

Four days later, Kristine took the train to Boston. She both welcomed and dreaded the visit with Jayce's family...and Jayce.

She stopped by the B and B to drop off her stuff, but her mom wasn't there. Amber said she was probably off with Conlan exploring the city, especially since they were considering making Boston their home.

She tried to think of what to say to Jayce on her way to his parents' house. It was an unusually cool summer day, giving her the chance to walk to the South End without being all sweaty when she got there. By the time she arrived, her thoughts were completely jumbled. Should she bother opening the conversation about where to live? Was it fair when he couldn't communicate his thoughts on the subject?

Regardless, she needed to do this. If for no other reason than to show him she still cared. That she wouldn't desert him in his time of need. Ever.

Upon her arrival, Mr. Fierro opened the door wide and greeted her with a strong hug and surprising kiss on the cheek. "Please come in. Jayce has been eagerly anticipating your visit."

Kristine almost asked, "How would you know?" Fortunately, he told her before she had to ask. Antonio pointed to a Ouija board on the living room floor. There was no pointer, just the board.

"Look. We found a way to communicate."

Just then, Jayce flew out of the adjoining dining room and landed on her shoulder. He leaned into her cheek, and she leaned into him. Just feeling the soft feathers and warmth cheered her. He was alive and well, and that's what really counted.

"Hi, Jayce."

He squawked and then flew to the Ouija board and pecked the *H* and the *I*.

Kristine chuckled. "That's brilliant."

Gabriella Fierro entered the room, saying, "Thank you. It was my idea." She strode over to Kristine and gave her the same warm welcome that she had received from Antonio. "Please have a seat. Can I get you some coffee or tea?"

"Just some ice water would be marvelous." She took a seat on the couch. "I walked here from Back Bay."

"That's quite a hike," Gabriella said. "I used to walk all over the city, but now I have arthritis in my knees. I'd be aching before I made it to Kenmore Square."

Kristine almost forgot Gabriella was human. She'd borne seven sons, and they were all grown. It was hard to place her age, but Kristine would guess the matriarch to be in her sixties.

"I'll be back in just a few minutes with your water. Antonio, come and help me in the kitchen."

Mr. Fierro's eyebrows rose. "You need help pouring a glass of water?"

Mrs. Fierro tipped her head toward Jayce.

"Oh! I see. You want to give them some alone time."

Gabriella shook her head and sighed. "Men."

Antonio chuckled as he followed her out of the room.

Kristine smiled at Jayce. "How have you been?"

Jayce picked out the letters *L-O-N-E-L-Y*.

Kristine gave him what she hoped was a sympathetic look. "I've missed you too." What she really meant was she missed the *real* him. The tall, broad-shouldered man she fell in love with. "I wish I could give you a hug and a kiss. But I guess that will have to wait."

He walked to the upper corner and pecked the word *YES*.

She hardly knew what to say after that. They just stared at each other until Jayce walked to the *W* and started pecking out more letters. He spelled *WELCOME HOME*.

Shit. Was Boston home? She still didn't know. She sighed. "Home?"

Jayce cocked his head. When he didn't follow up, she went on to explain.

"Everything I have, everything I am," she amended, "is in New York. I live and work there. I don't think I told you how much I'd be giving up by leaving. I just took the lieutenant's exam. There's an opening in my firehouse. I was told that unless I massively screwed up the test, the job would be mine."

Jayce didn't move. He just continued to stare at her.

Uncomfortable, she continued to talk. "Also, I'm in my last semester of college. I'm about to get my degree in fire science. It would probably set my graduation back if I were to transfer here, not that I wouldn't do that if I had to."

Jayce toddled over to the letter *O* and pecked it. Then he continued pecking until he had spelled out the word *ONLINE*.

"I don't know if I can do that. I'll have to look into it. Or…since we still have a lot to learn about each other, we could just keep up the long-distance relationship until I finish."

Jayce sat on the board where he was. She didn't know what that meant, but she could interpret it to be a stubborn "no."

She rose from the couch and started to pace. "If things had gone normally, we would probably have taken our time, gotten to know each other, assessed our compatibility over time, and all that normal stuff people do before they commit to a big change."

Jayce rose and spelled out *NOT NORMAL*.

Kristine let out a frustrated breath. "I know. I know. This situation is not normal. But that doesn't mean we shouldn't try to restore some normalcy."

Jayce walked to the opposite corner to the word *NO*. He hesitated a moment and then pecked the word.

Kristine had hoped he wouldn't. He *was* being stubborn.

Kristine folded her arms and glared at him. He took off and flew out of the room. Exasperated, she threw her hands in the air.

A moment later, Gabriella hurried in with a tall glass of ice water. "Is everything all right, dear?"

Kristine sighed. "I don't know. I think we just had our first fight."

"Oh dear... I should remind you, Jayce is still a child at this stage. Whatever he said is probably what he would've said when he was only about three or four years old."

"Shoot. I forgot about that." Kristine accepted the ice water and took a refreshing gulp. "When will he be, I don't know, about eighteen or nineteen? Mature enough to see reason."

"Come. Sit down. Antonio is talking to Jayce now. He'll probably calm down after their conversation. Do you mind my asking what your fight was about?"

Kristine didn't quite know what to say. She *did* mind. But this woman might become her mother-in-law someday. It would not be a good idea to piss her off.

"I'm sure it'll all work out. Please don't worry about it."

Antonio walked in with Jayce on his shoulder. "As I'm sure my wife explained, we estimate that Jayce is only about four years old right now. It hasn't been that long since he returned, although we don't know how much flying he did. To tell you the truth," he laughed, "there are advantages to having him unable to interrupt or talk back."

"Well, I can understand that. We kept getting...distracted and still have a lot to learn about each other. I don't even know how old he was before the fire."

Both parents looked surprised.

"Seriously?" Antonio asked. Then a smile stole across his face. "Ah, yes." He glanced at his wife. "I remember those early days of 'getting distracted.' Don't you?"

Gabriella set her hand on his knee. "You hush." Then she focused on Kristine. "I can tell you how old all of our children are. Ryan, even though he looks about twenty-five, is actually thirty-three. And Jayce is thirty-one. Hopefully, he'll wait until he looks thirty-one before he shifts back. We've explained it's important to wait until we tell him it's time.

"Now here are the rest. Miguel is twenty-nine, Gabe is twenty-six, Dante twenty-four, Noah twenty-two, and Luca is just nineteen."

Antonio laughed. "I don't know how you keep them all straight, never mind knowing how old they all are. How do you remember all that, hon?"

"How? Because I'm a mother, and I've given birth to every one of them. That's how."

The two were smiling at each other, so Kristine figured this was just good-natured teasing between a couple who obviously loved each other very much. Knowing Jayce had grown up with their example, and was growing up all over again seeing his parents still in love, gave her hope. It also gave her pause.

"Perhaps I should come back in a few days." She mentally counted out how many days it would take before she could have a fairly reasonable conversation with him. Maybe a couple of weeks before he even reached the mental age of eight.

"We understand," Antonio said.

Jayce flew to the board and pecked the word *NO*.

"Now, Jayce," Gabriella said. "You know the nice lady has to go home and take care of things there."

Jayce hung his head and slowly walked over to the word *YES*. He pecked it, albeit reluctantly.

Gabriella smiled. "Good boy."

Kristine figured it was time to leave. She downed

the rest of her ice water and asked to use the bathroom before the long walk back to the B and B.

After she left, she raked her fingers through her hair. A couple of strands got caught in her ruby ring, and she inadvertently yanked them out. The sting faded as she worked the red strands loose and tossed them to the wind. She was sure the sting of this visit would fade quickly too.

"Have a seat. I'll tell you what I know. There was this rogue family of dragons in the Caribbean…" Drake knew Amy and Kristine were desperate for news of more dragons. They had the B and B to themselves since Conlan, Rory, and Amber were in Ireland for a few hours. Drake had promised to tell Kristine and Amy the story of how many of the older dragons, including his mother and uncle, managed to get sick and die.

"She who shall not be named, for fear she'll hear me and show up, removed all dragons' immortality for a while. She was trying to stop these Caribbean dragons from exposing themselves to humans. The two younger ones were spoiled rotten and had no intention of obeying the rules."

Drake shuddered as he remembered the silver-marked dragon who had decided he would be her mate whether he liked it or not. She was bat-shit crazy, and his true love Bliss was in mortal danger.

"Apparently, the brats' mother saw this coming and had a voodoo priestess reinforce her children's immortality so it could not be removed."

"Even by she who shall not be named?" Kristine asked.

"Especially by her." Drake sighed. "Unfortunately,

all the other dragons on earth were vulnerable during that time. My mother developed cancer. My uncle died of a heart attack in a Long Island jail."

Amy and Kristine stared at each other with wide eyes. Amy reached for Kristine's hand and held it tightly. "So the two of us were vulnerable during that fiasco?"

"Indeed you were."

Kristine blanched. "When was this? Recently?"

"Yeah. A couple of years ago."

The women stared at each other again. Something silent but meaningful was going on. Probably the shock of their mortality—even if it was temporary.

"I imagine you're thinking about Kristine fighting fires without her immortality. I hope you were wearing your breathing apparatus whenever you entered a smoke-filled building."

"Of course," Kristine said.

Drake smiled. "Then you should be all right."

"I feel fine. Mom? Did you have any weird symptoms, that is, when you weren't acting?"

"I can't think of any."

"Whew. I guess we made it through that time okay," Kristine said.

"So what happened to the Caribbean dragons?" Amy asked.

Drake groaned. "Well, I have to give credit where it's due. She who shall not be named sent her to Siberia with strict instructions that she was never to return or there would be hell to pay."

At that moment, a small whirlwind began in the center of the living room, and Gaia stepped out of it. She flicked her fingers, and the swirling air dissipated.

"Did you think simply by not using my name I wouldn't know that you were talking about me?" Mother Nature asked sweetly.

Damn. Drake forced a smile on his face. "Gaia! How nice to see you."

"Cut the shit, dragon." She folded her arms and glared at him.

Heat crept up his neck, so he inserted a finger in his collar to loosen it. "Am I in trouble?"

"What do you think?"

Drake searched his recent memory for anything he may have said that would have offended her. He wasn't sure, so he erred on the side of safety. "I'm sorry?"

"For?" she asked.

Dammit. She's not going to give me any chance to wiggle out of this. He shrugged. "I'm not sure. Was I not supposed to tell the other dragons what happened a couple of years ago?"

Mother Nature narrowed her eyes at him until he became uncomfortable and started fidgeting.

A sly smile crept across her face. "No, it's fine that you told them. Just don't tell them anything else they don't need to know." She pointed to her eyes with two fingers and then turned those fingers on him. "I'm watching you." And with that, she disappeared.

Drake let out a huge breath of relief. "She could have transported me to the epicenter of an earthquake or put me on a surfboard in a tsunami. She has threatened to do both of those things and more to paranormals who walked a little too close to the line."

"Wow! Can she?" Amy exclaimed. "Would she?"

"She can, and not all of her threats are empty. Case in

point—the dragon brat in Siberia. Let that be a lesson to you ladies. The all-powerful one is…" *Holy crap*. What could he say in case she was listening?

Gaia's voice supplied the rest. "Touchy? Prickly? Easily pissed off? Be careful what you say next, dragon."

Drake thought fast. "I was just going to say, 'The all-powerful one is always right!'"

Still without showing herself, Mother Nature laughed wholeheartedly. "Nice save. Now change the subject or do something else. I have a planet to run."

Everyone rose quickly.

"It's nice to, um…meet you?" Amy said, her voice trembling a bit. "I should go upstairs and pack."

"Yes, er, excuse me, I have to, um…" Kristine headed toward the downstairs bathroom.

Drake smirked. "I guess we're done here. I'll go home to my beautiful wife and son and count my blessings on the way."

—⁓—

Amy and Kristine rode the train back to New York. With three and a half hours to sit and talk, they processed a lot of what they had learned not only about their species but also about their extended family.

"So, are you okay with possibly being related to Conlan?" Kristine whispered, hoping no one would overhear their bizarre conversation.

Amy leaned back and sighed. "You'd think I'd be extra sensitive to that, but to be honest, I really don't care. If we are related, it's not that close. They have an orange marking in their widow's peaks, and ours are yellow."

"So, if you have children, will they have orange streaks or yellow streaks or orange-yellow?"

Amy chuckled. "I don't know. I guess we'll have to wait and see."

Kristine gazed at her lap. "So, I guess *my* father's marking was yellow like ours, right?"

"I never saw it. He probably dyed his hair regularly. It was quite dark, and I don't think that was natural. His complexion was like ours. Peaches and cream." Amy rolled her eyes. "He used to refer to himself as tall, dark, handsome, and humble."

"Geez, I'm kind of glad I never got to know him."

"You and me both."

The two of them laughed. *What a difference*, Kristine thought. Her mother guarded that secret so carefully for so long. It was freeing to have it out in the open now.

"So, Mom, do you really love Conlan?"

Amy smiled with a glow in her eyes. "I really do. He's the one I've been waiting for. He's thoughtful, generous, intelligent, and handsome, and he has a sexy accent to boot."

Kristine believed her. "I'm really happy for you, Mom."

"And how about you? Are you really in love with Jayce?"

Kristine thought about the night on the boat. He was exactly as her mother described. Thoughtful, generous, intelligent, and handsome, and even though his Boston accent wasn't sexy, the rest of him certainly was. His temporary immaturity could be forgiven. It was the result of sacrificing himself for the good of others. All because she was determined to go through with her plan, and he wouldn't let her do it alone. *What an idiot I was.*

"Without a doubt. I found the right man for me too."

Amy hugged her, and she returned the loving gesture.

"So, why don't the two of you share our wedding date?"

Kristine laughed. "Isn't it enough that you're sharing it already with Rory and Amber?"

"The more the merrier," Amy said with an animated grin.

Kristine smirked. "We're still getting to know each other and have a lot of things to work out. But I appreciate your holding off until August so Jayce can at least attend as a guest. A human guest."

"Well, the invitation is there. You two can decide what to do about it later."

Kristine remained quiet. Even if Jayce agreed, at this point he was still a little kid and didn't really know what he was agreeing to. She'd have to wait until he had his adult brain and power of speech so they could discuss it rationally as a couple.

"Let's not count on that. I'd rather focus on you and your special day. What are you going to wear?"

With a wistful, faraway look in her eyes, Amy described the designer gown she had seen in the Vera Wang window. It was long, silky, and sleek. It would hug her curves and, hopefully, not upstage Amber. "I think I'll have it made in aqua. Conlan loves the color of my eyes."

"That sounds perfect. And where are you planning to live?"

Amy turned to her with enthusiasm. "Didn't I tell you? We found out the baseball player and his wife who own the apartment building next door to the B and B are

expecting baby number two. They're moving to the suburbs, and since everyone in the building is paranormal,
we'd fit right in!"

Kristine's brows shot up. "You're renting the penthouse? Can you and Conlan afford that?"

She laughed. "With ease. Conlan will be importing
Arish whiskey to sell on this side of the pond, and I'll be
teaching acting at Emerson College. The drama department is right down the street!"

"Really? When did you apply?"

"Yesterday. They just had an instructor quit at the
end of last semester, and they jumped at the chance to
have a real Broadway actress and professional coach
take her place."

"That's fabulous! I had no idea!"

After another hug, she wondered what the penthouse
looked like on the inside. Outside, a lot of floor-to-
ceiling glass was visible, and it looked very modern. In
fact, it stood out in the old Boston area as if a spaceship
had landed on one of the roofs. "Are you going to bring
all your Hummel figurines to the fancy new place?"

"Maybe not. I doubt they'll fit in with the decor. But
there is some storage in the basement."

Amy looped her arm through her daughter's. "We
haven't had a lot of time for just the two of us to sit and
talk. I'm glad we have this long train ride in order to
catch up."

Kristine could have done without the commuter
train stopping at every Connecticut town of any size
along the way, but it was nice to have her concerns for
her mother's well-being put to rest. Now if she could
just figure out an amenable arrangement with Jayce.

Sadly, she doubted their cards would fall into place as easily as that. One of them was going to have to sacrifice everything.

Chapter 16

IT WAS THE END OF JUNE, AND JAYCE'S LITTLE BROTHER, Luca, was graduating from high school. Mrs. Fierro had invited Kristine to attend, and it did happen to fall on her latest three days off. As kind as it was for her to be included in their family event, Kristine just didn't feel right attending without Jayce.

She supposed she could go with him, letting him ride like a parrot on her shoulder, but looking like a pirate wouldn't exactly blend in. Instead she suggested that she visit with Jayce at their home, keeping him company while everyone else was gone. Jayce must be about fourteen years old mentally by now, so they might be able to have a decent conversation.

Before the family left for Boston Latin High School, Mr. Fierro took the front-door key off his key ring and handed it to Kristine. "If you need anything or just feel like going out for a walk, please lock the front door."

"Wow," Luca said. "You must really trust her, Dad."

"I trust her just fine. It's the rest of Boston I worry about walking in and helping themselves to our priceless treasures." He laughed.

"Come on, Antonio," Gabriella said. "We're going to make Luca late for his lineup. We need to leave now." She surprised Kristine by walking over to her and kissing her on both cheeks. "Thank you for staying with Jayce. I know he appreciates it."

Kristine thought if he appreciated it so much, he'd probably show up. He was nowhere to be found. "Where is he?"

"In the basement, dear. He tries to fly outside sometimes. So we close the door when he goes down there to eat."

That seemed odd to Kristine. "Isn't he old enough to understand that you want him to stay in?"

Gabriella sighed. "Jayce was always the rebel."

Antonio snorted and said, "And how. Where's Luca?"

"Already outside. I saw him leave while your backs were turned," Kristine said.

"Come on, Gabriella. You're the one who wanted to get going, remember?"

"Yes, yes. We'll see you in a couple of hours, Kristine, dear." And with that, she hurried after her husband and closed the door behind them.

Kristine had better let Jayce out. She strode over to the basement door and opened it.

Jayce must have been waiting at the top of the stairs because he flew out immediately and landed on her head.

She giggled. "I'm glad to see you too."

He hopped onto her shoulder and leaned in, laying his cheek against hers.

Encouraged, she looked forward to a conversation with him. A real conversation.

"Let's find your board so we can talk."

They started in the living room, looking all around for the thing. "Damn. They must've put it away," Kristine said when she couldn't find it. "Do you know where it is?"

Jayce did his best to shake his head. Basically, he

looked at her with his right eye, then his left, and then his right again.

"I'm sure it's around here somewhere." She moved to the dining room and tried opening the drawers at the bottom of the hutch. All she found was silverware napkins and tablecloths. "Not here." She moved on to the kitchen and began looking in drawers and cabinets there. No luck. "Well, without going through every room in your house, I guess we just better enjoy being in each other's company."

He hung his head.

"What, you don't like my company?"

He squawked and took off, flying in a circle around her. Then he landed on her shoulder again and leaned in to touch her cheek.

"I love you too."

She stroked his feathers. He made a different sound this time. Almost like a coo. Perhaps they could communicate a little bit if she learned some bird-speak.

"I've been thinking… One of us is going to have to compromise if we're to be together."

He squawked.

She wished she knew what he meant by that, but for now she'd just elaborate on what she said and perhaps that would give her more of a clue.

"If we want to stay with the fire service and each other, one of us will have to start completely over. I was thinking, since you're already a lieutenant, and I just took the lieutenant's exam in New York…"

She didn't have a chance to finish her thought. Jayce took off and squawked, squawked, squawked as he flew around the room.

"Are you upset because I took the lieutenant's exam? Or that I think I should be the one to make the sacrifice?"

He must've been totally frustrated and distracted because she hadn't really given him a way to answer both questions at once. He flew into the wall.

Kristine gasped and jumped up. By the time she reached him, he was already on his feet.

"I'm sorry. I didn't phrase that correctly. Are you upset because I took the lieutenant's exam in case I stay in New York?"

He took off again and squawked as he circled the room and then slammed into a different wall.

"Jayce! Are you doing this on purpose? Or do you just not know where the walls are?"

He righted himself and turned his head to stare at her with his right eye. She slapped herself upside the head. "Oh crap. I did it again. We need to come up with a code. How about if you look at me with your right eye for yes and your left eye for no? I'll try to remember to ask one question at a time."

Jayce just stood there, not looking left or right. Sheesh. What did that mean?

"This isn't going very well, is it?"

He looked at her with his right eye.

"Okay. Maybe we can do this. First, I should tell you everything that's been going on. Then we can make some decisions, if you feel you're ready to do that."

She waited for him to look left or right. He took the neutral position, facing her head-on. Well, she hadn't really asked a question.

"Okay, here goes. First off, my mother is engaged to a dragon she met here in Boston. She'll be living with him in the apartment building next door to the B and B. If she were returning to New York, I wouldn't be able to leave her. It's hard enough to trust this man she just met—correction, this *dragon* she just met. So, that means I would either live alone in New York and visit you periodically, or—"

Again, he didn't give her a chance to finish her thought. He squawked his head off and flew around the room, this time smashing into a window.

"Damn it, Jayce! Knock it off." She thought about what she just said, and before he knocked his head off, she quickly amended, "I mean, stop it! Sheesh!" *If a teenage human brain hasn't fully developed, a teenage birdbrain must really be a problem!*

He took off again, but she was having none of it. She grabbed the afghan off the couch and tossed it over him like a fisherman tossing his net, trapping him and letting gravity take him to the ground. He squawked once as if surprised.

What now? She couldn't just leave him there. But it was for his own good. Before he knocked himself out or did some serious damage. "I did this because I can't let you hurt yourself."

He just resumed squawking and thrashed under the afghan.

How could she make him more comfortable and yet not let him out completely? She wondered if she crawled under there with him whether he would welcome her presence or peck her eyes out. "Jayce would never hurt me," she muttered. With that hope, she crawled under the afghan, making sure she didn't create any spaces big enough for him to get out.

When she finally managed to wiggle her whole body under it, she sat up and let her head be a tent pole. Jayce stepped toward her and opened his wings once, as if stretching his arms. Then he waited quietly.

Kristine was afraid to say anything at all. At least anything that might set him off. He must've been a rough teenager. She wondered if he had smashed his fist into a wall when he was really pissed.

"Are you all right?"

He looked at her with his right eye.

"I imagine a normal—I mean, *ordinary* bird could have broken a bone or suffered head trauma...or worse."

He just sat there in the neutral position.

"You scared me."

He hung his head.

After a brief silence, she said, "I'm so sorry. You wouldn't be in this situation if it hadn't been for me and my vigilante justice."

He looked at her with his right eye, then the left.

She chuckled. "Yes and no. I get it."

He hopped over, jumped up onto her leg, and then he cocked his head.

"Ah. You want to know if I'll lift the blanket now?"

He turned his head to look at her with his right eye.

"I will if you promise not to lose your cool again—no matter what. Got it?"

He bobbed his head.

"Okay." *Here goes*. She gathered the afghan and threw it off. Thank goodness he stayed where he was.

She thought of a way to pass the time without letting her big mouth get her into any more trouble. "Would you like me to read to you?"

He bobbed his head and then used his right eye to signal yes. Lucky for her, she'd loaded up her phone with some great books.

"I'll be right back. I just have to get my phone out of my backpack."

What would a teenage boy want to read? She had a great variety of books from breezy chick lit to dark thrillers. Maybe he'd like a young adult novel?

They spent the next three hours engrossed in the start of a wonderful series. Before she realized how much time had passed, the Fierros—all of them—arrived back at the house.

Dante greeted her first with a saucy, "Hey, beautiful!"

Jayce flew onto her shoulder as if to stake his claim. The other brothers said hello but didn't try to goad Jayce. *There's a smart-ass in every bunch.* "Don't worry," she whispered to Jayce. "I'm all yours."

When Mr. Fierro Senior stomped into the house, she knew something was wrong.

Gabriella had to run to keep up with him. "Calm down, Antonio. Luca's young. He doesn't know what he wants yet."

Antonio whirled on his youngest son, who entered the house last, and practically roared. "Oh, he knows what he wants all right. He wants to be a cop!"

"For Chrissake, Dad. You'd think I want to sell drugs or guns without background checks. I want to be a peace officer. At least I'd get to go home every day."

Antonio mumbled under his breath, "Not to my home, you don't."

Luca tipped up his chin. "Fine. I'll move out."

Gabriella intervened by inserting herself between the

two of them. "Now, stop it. Both of you, before things are said that can't be taken back."

The wind went out of Antonio's sails. "You're right, hon." He glared at his son. "We'll discuss this later."

Luca breezed by them and disappeared into another room. Jayce flew off after him.

"If you're worried about a little family drama scaring me off, don't be," Kristine said. "Jayce and I had our own little drama, and I'm still here."

"Oh?" Gabriella said, wringing her hands. "What happened?"

"It's nothing we can't work out in a few more weeks. Let's just say that teenage Jayce wasn't much easier to deal with than four-year-old Jayce."

Gabriella burst out laughing and left the room. Her laughter followed her all the way to the kitchen.

Antonio smirked. "You got that right."

———— ⁓⁓ ————

Kristine and the elder Fierros had agreed that waiting until Jayce shifted to human again before the two reunited would be a smart idea. So she had returned to New York and worked her shifts. Since Jayce had to wait in phoenix form for another six weeks, Kristine arranged to take summer classes and finish her degree early. She missed Jayce terribly and was ninety-nine percent sure she'd be moving to Boston—even if it meant giving up her firefighting career. It wouldn't hurt to have the degree, no matter what she did.

She spent her off hours sorting through her belongings and donating what she didn't want. If anyone was going to make the sacrifice, she wanted it to be her. His family obligations were important to him, and now her only family would be in Boston too. She just had to be sure Jayce could get his job back—and that he still wanted her.

Apparently Antonio was close to the chief, and his friend had assured him that Jayce would be welcomed back as soon as he recovered from his—ahem—coma.

Finally, the day came when she could see him again. She had the next three days off and wanted to spend every one of them with Jayce.

She boarded the train for Back Bay Station, and the three-hour trip seemed to take ten. Then she grabbed her backpack and, for the heck of it, donned her Fitbit before running to the Fierros' home in the South End. She may have banged on the door a little too enthusiastically because she heard Jayce's voice calling out, "I'm coming. I'm coming. Hold your horses." It was the most beautiful sound she could have imagined.

He threw open the door, and with a grin on his face, he spread his arms wide. She jumped, and he caught her, pulling her inside and then spinning her around.

Without putting her down, he fused his lips to hers. She practically melted down his body until her feet reached the floor. When they finally managed to pull apart, she asked, "Where are your parents? I want to say hello." Then she whispered, "Before we get too carried away."

With a twinkle in his eye, he said, "They're off looking at colleges with Luca. We're alone."

"Did he decide to go to college instead of the police academy?"

Jayce closed the door and then grabbed her hand,

speaking as he led her toward the stairs. "They've reached a compromise. He'll look at colleges that have a good program in law enforcement. If he still likes it when he gets out, they won't stop him, and he'll be in a better position for promotions. My parents see promotions as meaning desk jobs, but Luca sees them as a way to become a detective faster."

"Everybody wins," Kristine said.

When they reached the basement, Jayce lifted her into his arms and carried her over to the L-shaped sofa. He threw off the pillows and laid her down. Then he crawled over her like a predator eyeing its prey.

Lowering his weight upon her, he asked, "Am I too heavy?"

She stroked his muscular biceps, enjoying the feel of their hardness under her fingers. "Well, I wouldn't want you sitting on my head or shoulder anymore. But I think I can handle the weight like this."

He grinned, looking at her with a soft glow in his eyes, and lowered his head to capture her lips. She threaded her fingers through the hair at the nape of his neck and opened her mouth to welcome his tongue.

Heat sprang up between them as their passion flared. They had both been waiting so long for this.

Jayce unbuttoned Kristine's jeans, and she returned the favor. They pushed, pulled, and scrambled out of their clothing until everything hit the floor except for Kristine's fitness tracker. She checked the number and said with a sly smile, "Let's leave this on, just for fun."

Jayce seem to understand what she wanted to do. The device would measure how many calories they'd burn by how much energy they'd expend. He laughed and then proceeded to devour each of her breasts like a starving man. She arched and moaned as the sensations created a visceral tug all the way to her core. Her womb fluttered and produced a feeling she'd never experienced with anyone but Jayce. "I love you," she murmured.

He lifted his head and stared into her eyes as he said, "I love you too. So much more than I realized." Then he crawled further down her body, planting kisses on her hot skin along the way. When he reached her pussy, he licked the folds and at last zeroed in on her clit.

Kristine almost jackknifed off the couch. He flicked her clit with his tongue until she came apart, screaming. There were no words to describe the ecstasy she experienced with him. Her chest was heaving as she gasped for breath.

Jayce grabbed his T-shirt. "Lift up your pretty bottom for me." She barely had the strength to move but managed to elevate her dead weight on rubber legs.

He stuffed his shirt beneath her and crawled up over her body until they were nose to nose. Then he kissed her again and positioned his cock at her opening.

He entered her reverently, pushing himself all the way to the hilt. His erection was long, thick, and hard as a spike. She moaned as she welcomed all of him. He began his rhythm of thrusts, and she matched it. Meanwhile he bore down on her clit with his pelvis.

The fluttering sensations started up again, and she lifted her hips to make the connection again and again. The ancient dance followed its natural course, each body rocking and connecting with the other as deeply as it could.

Kristine's sensations built again, and before she knew

it, she was on the precipice of another climax. As her orgasm exploded, her spirit took off and flew. It felt as if she had left her body.

When she finally returned to earth, she could hardly describe what had just happened.

Instead of worrying about it, she watched Jayce's reaction. He stiffened, and his eyes scrunched shut. His mouth open, he jerked into her several times. Then he let his head drop down, and he panted. When he finally lifted his face, he was grinning at her.

After only a brief respite, they made love again—and again.

When at last they were spent, Jayce asked, "What does your Fitbit say?"

Kristine checked the device on her arm and noted the number had changed dramatically. When she analyzed what that meant, she said, "We just expended enough energy to climb twelve flights of stairs."

Jayce laughed. "In other words, we just fucked each other up a high-rise."

Kristine joined him in laughter and hugged him close. "I love you so much, Jayce."

Jayce lifted his upper body enough to stare into her eyes. "I love you too. I'll love you forever." He carefully withdrew and moved to a kneeling position. "Marry me, Kristine."

Oh my God. When she could speak, she said something totally lame. "Don't you think we should clean up first?"

He shook his head. "I don't want to wait another minute. I've wanted to ask you since the night we went out on my boat."

She sat up and linked her hands behind his neck. His arms went around her back automatically. She paused for a moment to think of some poignant words. Jayce lifted his eyebrows, waiting.

"I will." It wasn't very eloquent, but it seemed to be what he wanted to hear—and, in essence, what she wanted to say.

He grasped her close and whispered, "I'll do everything in my power to make you as happy as you've just made me."

———————

Eventually, Jayce and Kristine got off the couch and decided to eat something before they starved to death.

Since he knew where everything was in the kitchen, Jayce offered to cook. Most firefighters knew how to prepare meals, since they rotated the responsibility of keeping their coworkers fed.

Jayce wanted to impress her with his cooking skills, but he didn't believe in wasting food, so he looked for the items that might expire before his parents returned. "How do you feel about an omelet? And what do you like in it? Meat? Veggies?"

Kristine sat at the kitchen table and rested her chin in her hand. "I'm easy."

Jayce turned around and flashed her a grin. "I like that about you."

She chuckled and didn't contradict his deliberate misunderstanding. He started pulling things out of the fridge: leftover steak, cheese, a green pepper, a red onion, and mushrooms.

"Can I help?" Kristine asked.

"Sure. You can wash the veggies while I whip up the eggs and season them with spices."

"You use spices?" Kristine asked.

"Yeah, don't you?"

Kristine shrugged as she wandered over to the sink. "Do salt and pepper count?"

It sounded as if she wasn't used to fancy fare. He'd hold back on some of the more exotic spices. Jayce found a colander and stuck it in the sink for her, piling the veggies in it.

"Wow. Are we feeding an army?"

He chuckled. "I could eat like one."

"Maybe I can make a salad with anything that's left over."

"Now you're talking." He grabbed a head of lettuce out of the fridge too.

They worked easily side by side and soon had not only a couple of fabulous omelets but also a crunchy salad to accompany them.

Kristine had already set the kitchen table and placed their salads beside their forks. Jayce brought the omelets over. As they ate, Jayce realized he had a few important things to tell her. He didn't know if he was supposed to yet, but if she was to be his wife, eventually she would have to know.

"Babe, I need to fill you in on a few things I learned recently. My dad had been trying to tell me some important stuff for a while, but we kept getting interrupted. So, eventually he had a captive audience—specifically, quiet Miguel and me when all I could do to interrupt was squawk. These are secrets, closely guarded by and known only to the heads of the family. Can you swear to me you won't tell anyone?"

She stopped chewing, swallowed, put her fork down, and asked, "Are you sure you want to tell me? Of course I can keep a secret, but I'm not the head of the family."

"You will be. We will be. As well as Miguel and Sandra. My father had thought it would be Ryan and his wife—and then he had to disappear because of that whole dying-and-funeral thing. Then he thought it would be me and my wife after I married because the leader's wife is an important part of the checks and balances in any decision-making process."

"So…Miguel and Sandra?"

"There for opinions only."

"Okay… How often do these decisions need to be made? Is it a daily thing? Are we expected to micromanage everyone's lives? Because that would suck."

"No. If something important comes up that the individual can't handle, he or she can call a family meeting. The head of the family makes any huge decisions that affect the others. Everyone is supposed to abide by that decision…not that I always did."

"And what am I? Your conscience? The tiebreaker?"

He smiled. "Not exactly. It was decided long ago that leaders need to talk things over with a more neutral party, just to be sure the decisions they make aren't rash or a knee-jerk reaction. I've been told I can be a bit impulsive."

Kristine smirked. "You don't say…"

"Be nice."

She giggled. "Sorry. So is that why Miguel has an opinion?"

"While I was incapacitated, Dad realized it would be nice to have a backup. He had been thinking of putting the two of us in charge together anyway. Miguel and I are very different, and we'd balance each other. Plus, if I never married, I would need Miguel and Sandra to intervene if necessary."

"Is there anything else I need to know?"

"Ha! I haven't even scratched the surface of the paranormal secrets. I'm glad you're sitting down."

She raised her brows, obviously anticipating a surprise. He wouldn't disappoint.

"As it turns out, Boston is teeming with paranormals. And not just us. For instance, a lot of cops are werewolves."

"How do they handle the full moon?"

"The people in charge of scheduling are usually werewolves themselves, and they have day jobs. We're supposed to keep our para identities under wraps, so it gets tricky. But the mayor and chief of police are in on it. Some of the district fire chiefs know too."

"Okay. What is it you want me to know?"

"Well, because Boston is a hotbed of paranormal activity, it's the favorite hangout of a goddess who keeps an eye on us. Not just any goddess…*the* Goddess. Gaia, sometimes known as Mother Nature."

When Kristine didn't react, Jayce thought either she was taking it well or she didn't believe him at all. He continued on, hoping she wasn't just humoring him. "Gaia not only likes her seasons in Boston, but she protects her humans from us. If they knew about the paranormal population, they'd freak.

"She watches what we're doing, making sure we don't reveal ourselves even by accident. She used to be very upset about a paranormal bar in the area, but now we have a more private place to socialize. In fact, the paranormal club is in the building next door to the B and B where you were staying."

"Uh-huh," Kristine said, almost sounding bored.

"No, really! My father and Ryan have been in it…and they've met Mother Nature herself!"

She smiled and said, "So have I."

After a stunned silence, Jayce asked, "Seriously? How? When?"

"She helped me get you out of the fire in the mansion. Amber is a modern muse and got me into the cellar, but she didn't know how to save you. She brought Mother Nature. It was Gaia who told me to incinerate you with my breath. If I hadn't known you were a phoenix or that this older woman was Mother Nature, I wouldn't have been able to go through with it."

Suddenly the Goddess appeared with her arms folded in front of her white toga. "*Older woman*? I've been told it's very difficult to guess my age."

Crap.

The Goddess laughed. "Don't worry about it, dragon, I'm trying out this odd communication style you call humor."

Jayce let out the deep breath he'd sucked in without realizing it.

"Actually, I can appear to be any age I like. Of course, the truth is I'm older than dirt…literally. One of my muses said that to me—and I let her live. I must be mellowing."

Jayce turned to Kristine. "You don't seem very alarmed. You're not even nervous."

Kristine shrugged. "If this was your big secret, I'm not really worried. Mother Nature has been very kind to me." Kristine rose and walked over to the deity. "I never had the chance to thank you. I appreciate how you helped us when Jayce was in trouble." She reached out her hand, and Gaia just looked at it.

The goddess rolled her eyes and then took Kristine's hand and shook it. "You should know, dragon, that when you do something to impact nature, there's always an effect."

Kristine straightened her posture. "Oh? What did I affect?"

One side of Mother Nature's lip rose. "Well, now you owe me a favor."

Jayce worried. *What kind of favor will she be expected to do for a goddess?* Whatever it was, it was his fault. Hopefully, he'd be able to help her with it.

"As a matter of fact, phoenix, you can help by encouraging her to take the job I'm about to offer her."

"Job?" Kristine asked.

"Yes, yes. As you know, I've recruited a few modern muses to take care of technology that didn't exist when the original nine, now useless, muses were created millennia ago."

"Amber told me something about that."

"And you were able to keep all of that a secret. I believe I can trust you, dragon. I'm prepared to make you a modern muse."

Kristine took a step back. "Me? What can I possibly help you with?"

Jayce rose and put his arm around Kristine's shoulder. "Whatever it is, she gets a choice in the matter. Right, Goddess?"

Mother Nature crossed her arms and frowned. "*She* does. You don't."

Okay then…

Gaia clasped her hands behind her back and began pacing. "Getting back to my current problem. I have noticed that everyone seems to be walking around blathering on these little rectangular devices. What the hell are those things?"

"Smartphones?" Kristine asked.

The Goddess looked impatient. "This isn't a quiz. Just tell me."

Kristine cleared her throat. "It sounds as if you're describing a mobile phone…or a radio. Firefighters use radios to stay in touch with each other during a fire. Cops use them in a similar way. But if you're talking about something more common, it seems as if everyone has a cell phone."

"Yes. I've noticed you using both devices expertly. That's why I would like you to become my muse of wireless communication."

"Really?"

"No. Not really." After a brief pause, Mother Nature snorted. "Of course, really. Do you think I recruit muses for sport?"

"No. Not at all. I'm just—overwhelmed. It sounds like an awesome responsibility, and I'm flattered, but what would I have to do?"

"Damned if I know. It seems that everyone is delighted with the thing until it doesn't work. Especially during emergencies. Then they throw them across the room."

Kristine blanched.

"Maybe you could keep them working just a little bit longer until the emergency is over or inspire inventors to make better ones… And not only that," Gaia continued,

"I notice they can be quite a problem when concentration is required. They can distract a driver and cause an accident. You could whisper, 'Hey dumbass. Put down the phone and pay attention!' Or—you know what I'd really like?" Her lips thinned, as if her frustration were growing simply by discussing the subject. "If people would set them down once in a while and have a conversation with the person right in front of them. You can just whisper in their ear, 'Turn off the damn phone and pay attention to your date, idiot.'"

Kristine quickly covered her mouth and looked like she might be hiding a smile.

"Can she think about it, Goddess?" Jayce interjected. Even if the deity got mad at him for interfering, he was going to look out for his bride-to-be. Like it or not.

The Goddess looked at the ceiling and sighed. "Why does everyone have to think about it? I offer the greatest of compliments, and the job comes with some incredible new powers, but still they have to 'think about it.'"

Jayce was about to explain the necessity of making informed decisions, taking one's time, going over the pros and cons—all the things his father impressed upon him—when Kristine put her hand in his. "I'd like to talk to Jayce and Amber first. Can you give me a day or so?"

"Sure. She's one of my best modern muses. Well, actually, she's one of my best muses period…since nobody gives a crap about the arts anymore. Damn fucking shame, if you ask me."

Kristine nodded solemnly. "I'll be sure to get in touch with her right away." Then she turned to Jayce. "Oh, you were in the middle of telling me something important. Was there anything else I should know?"

"Uh, no. I think we covered it." Jayce thought about how his little family drama paled in comparison to the news Kristine had just received.

"Oh, Gaia, wait!"

"Don't care." Mother Nature disappeared before Kristine got another word out.

"Jayce, I just remembered Amber's wedding! She's probably already in Ireland, planning for the big day."

Jayce smiled and squeezed her hand. "There's this great modern convenience called a cell phone…"

Chapter 17

ON THE CLIFFS OF BALLYHOO, IRELAND, STOOD A BEAUTIFUL castle. It wasn't huge, and part of its elegance was its modesty. There was only one turret and one arched opening with a beautiful wood door. Jayce had been told that the majority of the living space was built into the cliffs.

Kristine took his hand. "Shall we go inside?"

"I suppose so. If for no other reason than to drop off our wedding gift and then be told where to wait."

The two of them knocked on the beautiful door with its ornate brass knocker shaped like three dragons. A tiny window slid to the side, and a pair of dark-brown eyes seemed to light up with recognition. Then the window slammed shut, and the door opened wide.

Ryan pulled Jayce into a hug, and they slapped each other on the back. When Jayce stepped away, he clasped his brother's upper arm and said, "Damn, it's good to see you, Ryan."

Ryan glanced past Jayce and smiled at Kristine. "This beautiful lady is still putting up with you?"

Jayce let go of his brother and put a hand on Kristine's lower back, escorting her over to him. "Ryan, I'd like you to meet the future Mrs. Jayce Fierro, my fiancée."

"No shit?" Ryan then slapped himself upside the head. "I'm sorry, Kristine. That's no way to talk in front of a lady. What I meant to say was *congratulations* to you both."

Chloe came up behind Ryan and slipped her arm around his waist. "What were you apologizin' for, luv?"

Kristine chuckled. "He did nothing wrong. I've heard worse language every day at the firehouse."

Ryan grinned. "That's right! You're also a firefighter."

"All four of us are," Jayce said. "You two, Kristine, and me."

"You'll have plenty to talk about at the reception, since you're all being seated at the same table," a female voice said from behind Ryan. He stepped aside and revealed Amy Scott…soon to be Amy Arish.

"Mom!" Kristine said. "I thought you'd be getting ready by now."

"I was waiting for you, darling. Come with me." Amy grabbed her hand and practically dragged her into the castle and around the corner where Jayce could no longer see her. He did, however, notice the incredible view on the opposite wall. A large Palladian window looked out onto the Atlantic Ocean.

"Well, are you going to invite me in or what?" Jayce asked his brother.

"Of course. Come on in, and I'll give you a tour of my humble abode."

Jayce burst out laughing. "Don't even pretend you're being humble. You live in a frigging castle."

"Okay, you got me. I might be a little proud of my home."

Chloe folded her arms. "You mean *our* home, don't you? And we have a right to be proud, having done most of the work ourselves."

"Yes, dear." Ryan leaned close to his brother's ear

and whispered, "Learn those two words, and you'll have a happy marriage."

Chloe snorted. "It's a good thing I know me husband's teasin'. Jayce, can I get you something to drink?"

Before he had a chance to answer, she glanced outside and said, "Oh shite. The leprechauns are here. Who invited them?"

One little guy in brown and two in green approached. The brown one stepped up to the door. "No one invited us, me darlin'. But we believed it to be an oversight. We come bearin' gifts, and we'd be grateful for the chance to make up for our bad behavior in the past."

Chloe crossed her arms. "You realize we have a few humans here, Fagan. You aren't allowed to perform any of your leprechaun magic."

"And we won't, Your Highness."

Chloe rolled her eyes. "I don't want any of that 'Your Highness' nonsense. Just call me Chloe, like everyone else does."

"That seems fair, since I'm king of the leprechauns, and you insist on simply callin' me Fagan."

"Good."

"Fine."

"Grand," the other two chimed in.

Ryan said, "I was just about to take Jayce around and show him the place. Will you excuse us, love?"

Chloe smiled. "Of course."

Ryan leaned over and gave his wife a kiss before he clapped his hand on Jayce's shoulder and said, "Let's go this way." He steered him to a spiral staircase leading down.

Jayce followed his brother down the stairs, which

opened onto a large foyer. Another Palladian window looked out over the ocean. Hardwood floors matched the ones upstairs, and three arched doorways offered choices of moving left, right, or directly behind.

Ryan walked through the arch on the right and into a study with tall bookshelves and comfortable chairs. A desk faced the window. "Welcome to my office, library, or den, whatever you want to call it."

"Man cave?"

"Anything but that." He walked over to a piece of furniture that looked as old and ornate as the front door. "What can I get you?" He opened a polished rolltop to reveal a well-stocked bar.

Jayce smiled. "I don't suppose you have any of that Arish whiskey, do you?"

"Of course he does," Conlan said as he strolled into the room from the one beyond. "If he doesn't, we're not doin' right by our cousin."

Ryan lifted a bottle and used it to point toward Jayce. "Conlan, have you met my brother Jayce?"

Conlan laughed. "Jayce was there the day I met me bride."

"Really?" Ryan chuckled. "It seems as if few introductions are needed. Drake knew everyone too."

"Drake is here?" Jayce asked.

"Of course. He's Amy's younger brother…or something." Ryan offered Jayce a glass with two fingers of whiskey already poured.

Jayce took the whiskey and raised it as if giving a toast. "What is it you say here? Slant?"

Ryan and Conlan laughed. "*Slainte* is the word," Ryan said.

When all three of them had their glasses filled, Ryan raised his and said, "To family."

"*Slainte*," Jayce said.

"Cheers!" Conlan added.

The three of them laughed, clinked glasses, and sipped their whiskey.

"I was showing my brother around, but we didn't get very far," Ryan said.

Conlan groaned. "It's just as well. The women have taken over the bedrooms on both levels. Below us, the kitchens are filled with caterers. And your banquet room has been locked against all intruders. I guess Amy and Amber had it decorated just the way they wanted it."

"Speaking of the other bride, where's Rory, the other groom?" Jayce asked.

"Rory is visiting with his sister Shannon and her husband, Finn. They also have a few humans to distract while the paranormals are lectured."

"Lectured?"

"To keep their identities a secret."

"Ah," Jayce said. "I wondered how that was going to work."

"If history repeats itself, it won't work at all," Rory said as he entered the room.

Conlan laughed and slapped Rory on the back. "I see me fellow bridegroom is as nervous as I, but mayhaps for a different reason."

"How is that?" Rory asked.

"This place is, or was until recently, your home. With all the shenanigans that could happen when Irish families and paranormal friends get together, things could get ruined…not to mention if any one of us shows our paranormal abilities around a human, there will be hell to pay."

"Don't pay me," Ryan said.

"You realize he's talking about me." A disembodied female voice resonated around the room.

"Gaia!" Ryan exclaimed. "I didn't know you were coming."

Mother Nature appeared. "I'm not...but I'm watching. I don't want anything to ruin my muse's special day. It's bad enough she had to include two humans, but I understand they are her mother and sister. What I don't understand, Rory, is why your brother-in-law Finn, Father Joseph, and the owners of the pub have to attend. They're humans too."

"Beggin' yer pardon, Goddess." Rory bowed reverently. "The good father is officiatin', and I was the one who invited Finn. He's married to me sister, Shannon, and didn't faint when he learned about dragons and leprechauns. He should be fine. The O'Malleys are here to cater the dinner. As long as everything goes well during the reception..."

The Goddess closed her eyes and shook her head. "How little you know about weddings. That's when everything bad happens."

—∿∿—

Meanwhile, in the master bedroom, Amy slipped into her aqua silk dress. She couldn't afford the genuine Vera Wang, so she had a costumer she knew from her stage career make one like it.

"Conlon offered to pay for any dress I wanted, but I wouldn't hear of it."

"Why not?" Kristine asked as she zipped up the back.

"Soon enough my finances will be tied to his."

Kristine laughed. "Mother, you realize that's like saying, 'Soon enough I'll hitch my little red wagon to his Maserati.'"

Amy admired herself in the full-length mirror. "I guess you're right. I've never been able to depend on another person's income, and it feels strange. I know you helped me pay our rent all those years, but even then I knew that someday you'd move out to live on your own or with someone else—speaking of which, have you worked out where you and Jayce will live?"

"Not yet. We haven't had much time to just talk."

Amy burst out laughing. "Yeah, I'll bet. When the two of you come up for air, you probably have to make up for lost sleep."

Kristine felt her cheeks heat. She didn't discuss her sex life—especially with her mother! It was time to change the subject—or sidestep it a little.

"Jayce was cleared to go back to work. He offered to quit and move to Hell's Kitchen—despite how much his family wants him to stay in Boston. And now that my family will be in Boston, it would just be pigheaded of me to insist on staying in New York."

"So, you're giving up everything you've worked for? The lieutenant position?"

"It was either that or let him do all the sacrificing."

"He was really ready to give up his rank and his home and disappoint his family? All just to make you happy?"

"Yes. Amazing, isn't he?"

The women smiled at each other.

"What about your degree?" Amy asked.

"I managed to almost finish it over the summer. I can do the rest online."

"Oh, that's wonderful! Every woman should have a fallback." Kristine's mother sat at the dressing table and began combing her hair.

"Let me do that for you, Mom." Kristine picked up the brush and stroked her mother's long, shiny red hair.

"That's very practical of you...to have a fallback, I mean."

Amy closed her eyes and almost purred. She loved having her hair brushed, and Kristine wondered if she'd ever get the chance to brush it for her again. Probably not for a while.

"I've always been more practical than you think. Acting may seem like a frivolous career, but waitressing put food on the table, and acting made me happy. I'd like to think I was a better mother because I followed my dream as best I could."

"You absolutely were. You're still a good mother." Kristine leaned over and kissed her mother's cheek. "Do you want to wear your hair up? Like this?" Kristine wound the hair around into a French twist and held it up for Amy to look at.

"Yes, you do that beautifully, and I have a special comb to hold it."

Amy reached for her small white evening bag and extracted a beautiful gold comb with sparkling crystals and pearls.

"That's beautiful, Mom! Where did you get it?"

"It's from Conlan. Apparently his mother wore it before she passed."

"She had to be a dragon too, right?"

NEVER DARE A DRAGON

"Yes, she was. She met with a dreadful car accident a few years ago. It may have been during the same time that Mother Nature revoked our immortality for a while."

As Kristine inserted the beautiful comb, Gaia herself popped in. "Did I just hear my name?"

Kristine and her mother startled. "We didn't mean to call you away from your…whatever you're doing," Kristine said. "We were just discussing something, and your name came up."

"Yes, I know. I was about to come and see you anyway."

"Oh? What about?"

"I finally have someone to train you, Kristine. My modern muses are quite busy. All the more reason to have more. I thought it best to add her to the guest list so she can keep an eye on things and make sure the paranormals don't get out of hand. I'm much too busy to stick around in case of trouble."

Amy turned enough to look at both of them. "She found someone to train you? In what are you being trained, Kristine?"

"I wasn't going to tell you until after your honeymoon. The Goddess offered me a job as a modern muse. Specifically, the muse of wireless communication. Cell phones, radios, and the satellites that keep us in touch globally."

"A muse? Like Amber and Chloe? That's wonderful! I suppose you don't need another job in Boston now. It sounds as if you'll have your hands full."

"I imagine so. Did you say you have someone to add to the guest list, Gaia? Have you checked with Chloe?"

Mother Nature jammed a hand on her hip. "Of course.

Contrary to what you may have heard, I'm not totally rude, entitled, and pushy."

Amy rose. "Goddess, I've not heard you called anything of the sort, and if I did, I would have to disagree."

The goddess smiled. "That's sweet of you, but you'll learn. Meanwhile, Kristine, I'd like you to meet Brandee."

A pretty young woman with a different shade of long, red hair appeared. Not like Amy's bright-red or her own reddish-blonde color. She shook Kristine's hand, and without letting go, she looked over at Amy.

"Oh. My. Gorgeousness! You must be the bride."

Amy grinned and tipped up her chin in her regal pose. "That I am."

Brandee glanced between Amy and Kristine and back again. "I can't tell if you're mother and daughter or sisters."

Gaia waved. "Yes, yes. That's all lovely, but we have to cut the chitchat short. I need to go push a tornado out of the way of a house in, uh… Kansas. Yeah. There's a girl and her dog inside. If I don't get there in time"—Mother Nature disappeared before she finished her sentence.

Brandee gave them an apologetic smile. "I'm sorry to crash your wedding. Gaia thought that since Chloe would be busy playing hostess and Amber's time would be consumed with being a bride and all, a less involved muse to keep an eye on things would be a good idea."

"Oh, I'm fine with it," Amy said. "I just feel bad that we're taking you away from your muse duties."

Brandee laughed. "This is the best part of my duties. I'm the muse of film and digital images." Suddenly she was holding a very technical-looking camera. "Now I can *really* keep an eye on things."

"And we get wedding photos!" Amy exclaimed.

The wedding was magical. Two beautiful brides, one wearing aqua and one wearing ivory, took their vows in the castle courtyard with their handsome princes, who were each wearing a kilt of Arish plaid. The design was woven with midnight blue, shamrock green, and gold wool. The same colors of the blue-and-green flag with three gold dragons on it flying from the high turret.

They had been blessed with a perfect sunny day. Not a cloud in the robin's-egg-blue sky. When the wedding party and their guests descended the stairs to the kitchen and ballroom level, Jayce understood why it had been roped off before.

Opening the doors revealed an elegant room with one long dining table, set with white linens, crystal glasses, and silver flatware. Bowls of pink roses surrounded by petals graced the table every five feet or so. At one end was a kiddie table, set with the same decorations.

Jayce hadn't noticed any children. Then he realized in horror that the table must have been put there for the leprechauns. *Shit.* This was the first time he'd met any, but he had heard they were quick to take offense and never apologized, even if they were dead wrong. Did that include at weddings?

He spotted his and Kristine's names engraved on cards in ornate calligraphy and escorted her over to their places near the middle of the long table. Jayce held Kristine's chair for her and pushed her in. He left his

own chair out a bit just in case he had to jump to his feet
to prevent a brawl.

No one else seemed too worried. People were smiling, chatting, and laughing. All except the Arish cousins
seated across from them. Aiden and Eagan seemed on
the edge of their seats too.

Finally, in came the leprechauns. They glanced up and
down the long table, noting there were no seats left—
except for two on either end, for the brides and grooms.

Chloe rose and hastened over to the little men. She
bent down and whispered something, and pointed
toward the kiddie table. The one wearing brown seemed
too serious.

Uh-oh. This is it, Jayce thought.

When Chloe returned to her seat, she remained standing until all three leprechauns had found their places.
Meanwhile, the photographer moved around the room,
taking pictures from every angle.

Jayce didn't even realize he was on high alert until he
jumped when Chloe tapped her glass, interrupting any
ongoing conversations with a musical tinkle.

"Thank you all for coming. I have the honor of intro-
ducing the Arishes. First, me brother, Rory, and me new
sister, Amber…"

To the sound of enthusiastic applause, the happy
couple entered from a side door and were seated at one
end of the table. Jayce wondered if the humans hadn't
been present if they'd be referred to as princes and prin-
cesses—or clan leaders and ladies or whatever. Keeping
it simple was probably for everyone's benefit.

Then she introduced her cousin, Conlan, and his
lovely wife, Amy. More applause made Amy's grin grow

even wider. If she had taken a stage bow, he wouldn't have been surprised. As it was, she stopped and dropped a curtsy to Chloe, and Conlan offered a respectful bow.

It seemed as if all was well. At last he could relax and enjoy the festivities. Until…

Fagan rose, or at least he slipped off his chair. Clinking his glass, he announced, "May I have everyone's attention please?"

Jayce wouldn't have heard Chloe mumble *shite* if he didn't have paranormal hearing. Unfortunately, he did.

"Before we get started, I'd like to present our gifts to the happy couples. We have a bit of mischief to make up for, so we wanted our gifts to be special."

Rory mumbled, "Is that what being kicked out of me own country is called? Feckin' mischief?"

If Fagan heard him, he ignored it. The O'Malleys came out with champagne and began pouring everyone's glasses half full.

They did a double take when looking at the kiddie table full of little bearded men but politely continued on their way.

"One of our gifts is too large to show you here. It's upstairs in the courtyard."

Chloe rose, and everyone else rose with her. Fagan grinned as if very pleased with himself. He ran on his little legs to the door, with his two compatriots following. "Let's go," he called. The guests looked at each other, slightly confused, but followed politely. After climbing two sets of stairs, the leprechauns in green paused, one on each side of the big double door that led to the courtyard. Fagan waited until everyone had gathered in the grand foyer and then announced, "This is for Conlan and Amy." They threw open the double door and revealed a sleek, black Maserati convertible.

Some of the guests gasped while others made impressed sounds like "Oooohhh…"

Amy leaned toward Kristine and whispered, "Do you think they heard us talking?"

Kristine shook her head and shrugged at the same time.

Fagan focused on Amy. "Come here. Admire it."

Conlan took her hand, and they strolled over to it, making appreciative comments. Jayce noticed Conlan appeared hesitant.

"Where did this come from?" Conlan asked.

Fagan smirked. "Italy, of course."

He bit his lip, as if holding in his thoughts. Chances were he suspected something but was too polite to bring it up in front of their guests.

Chloe cleared her throat. "Well, that is very generous of you, but I'm sure the O'Malleys have dinner planned, and we wouldn't want it to get cold. So let's go back down to the banquet room."

Her subjects followed without question. The other guests lingered a bit, taking a longing look at the car and then trailing behind the rest downstairs.

The leprechauns jogged down the stairs to keep up with everyone. When all the guests arrived back at the ballroom and returned to their seats, Fagan and the other two remained standing.

Everyone lifted their champagne glasses.

"Wait. Before we begin the toasts," Fagan called out, "we want to present our gift for the other couple. We know you'll like it much more than a new car."

Ryan put down his glass.

Rory and Amber glanced at each other.

"Well… Come here." Fagan waved them over.

Brandee got herself in position to take a picture of their faces when they received whatever special gift they had coming.

Fagan spoke in a low voice so only the couple and those of paranormal persuasion could hear. "We know you can't have children, so we found the perfect gift for you." He swiveled, and when he turned back to them, he held a baby in his arms.

"Shite!" Rory said as he took a step back. Amber just stood there with her mouth and eyes wide open.

Jayce quickly glanced around the room and noticed the O'Malleys frozen in mid-step as they carried out trays of shrimp cocktail. The priest was frozen in place too. He checked on Amber's mother and sister and noticed both of them gazing in the same direction, smiling and unblinking.

Brandee snapped her fingers, and her camera disappeared. She marched over to Fagan and gently removed the baby from his arms. "Now, tell me where you found this child so I can return him or her."

Fagan looked deeply offended. "You would return our gift? Who are you to do such a thing?" He folded his arms and glowered.

Gaia appeared. "Thank goodness my muse was here to stop you from giving humans a glimpse into the paranormal world." She turned toward Brandee. "Give the child to me. I know right where she belongs."

Fagan bristled. "But the babe was in an orphanage. What kind of life is that for her? We were doing both her and the bride and groom a grand favor."

Mother Nature leaned over them and rose off the floor a few inches. "I know exactly what kind of life she'll have. In a few days, she'll be adopted by a loving family. Yes, they'll make mistakes, and she will probably wind up in therapy someday, but if she grew up as a human with paranormal parents, she'd be in therapy that much sooner."

Fagan sighed. "Well, this is embarrassing... I suppose we'll have to come up with something else now that we have everyone's attention."

Gaia frowned. "I'll deal with you later, leprechaun. My muse will turn back time just enough to erase the humans' memories. Now I'm off to do the same at the orphanage." With that, Mother Nature and the baby disappeared.

Fagan scratched his head. "Feck. I thought we had the perfect gift for you," he said to Rory.

Rory smiled. "It was a lovely thought. Fortunately, we have everything we need. Just that you hoped to do something special for us is all the gift we could want." He put his arm around Amber's shoulder, she slipped her arms around his waist, and they gazed at each other lovingly.

Fagan stamped his foot. "You see? You would have made very good, loving parents. I'm afraid I'm too upset to stay." He turned to his brothers and said, "We shall leave now." They nodded, and all three of them disappeared.

A collective whoosh of air suggested that more than one guest had been holding their breath. Various expressions of relief followed.

Brandee addressed Amber. "What now? How far should I back this up to cover the fact that they left?"

Amber sighed. "I wish we could back it up to before they came, but too many guests were already here and in mid-conversation. I guess we can back it up to the point where they closed the doors on the courtyard upstairs and everyone filed downstairs."

"Then just pop them back to wherever they came from and make an excuse that they had a family emergency and had to leave—if anyone misses them."

Suddenly Jayce and Kristine were descending the stairs again.

Jayce leaned over and whispered to Kristine, "Well, at least Amy and Conlan get to keep the Maserati."

Epilogue

JAYCE AND KRISTINE SNUGGLED ON THEIR COUCH, GAZING out at the sunrise colors reflected in the river. The still-twinkling lights and flow of the water mesmerized them. They wore matching white bathrobes, sipping their morning coffee. No words, television, or other entertainment was needed. They just enjoyed cuddling and being surrounded by their love for their condo and each other.

Startled by the sudden appearance of a platinum-haired woman wearing a flowing Grecian robe, Kristine recovered first.

"Gaia! What can I do for you?"

"The question is, my little dragon, what can I do for you?" The goddess folded her arms and waited.

Confused, Kristine sat up on the edge of the sofa and asked, "What do you mean?"

Mother Nature rolled her eyes. "You haven't heard? Whenever a modern muse offers her services to me and appears to be serious about performing her job well, I give that person a reward. So, what would you like? A new car? A house? A money tree?"

Jayce returned her puzzled stare. "Don't ask me. It's your reward."

Kristine pondered the question. At last she said, "I don't know what I want. I have everything I need. The man I love. A job I love. Enough money to live on. I really don't need another thing. Unless… No. Never mind. That would be impossible."

Gaia smiled. "Let me be the one to decide what's possible. I know what you want. You want knowledge and a little bend in the rules."

"Yeah, well… You can't do that."

Mother Nature glared at her. "What makes you think I can't? I can do pretty much anything I want. And I want to do something that will make you so grateful you won't renege on your commitment to me."

Oh, so that's what this is about. It's more of a bribe than a reward.

"I know what you really think, little dragon. Don't forget that. It's not a bribe. Try looking at it as a sign-ing bonus."

"Okaaay." Kristine racked her brain for anything nice that she would like as a bonus but really couldn't come up with anything special.

Mother Nature jammed her hands on her hips. "Seriously? You really aren't going to ask for what you want? I already told you it's not impossible."

Kristine's eyes rounded. "You mean to tell me I don't have to go back to the bottom of the ladder and I can be a Boston firefighter?"

"Not only that, you can be promoted if you want."

Jayce pulled himself up next to her and draped an arm around her shoulder. "Think about it. You can do the job you've always loved without losing a thing." Then he gazed up at the deity and asked, "You can plant the knowledge she needs into her brain? The policies she needs to know for the BFD?"

Mother Nature folded her arms, tipped her chin up,

and looked smug. "Not only that, I can make her your equal. A captain."

Jayce smiled at Kristine. "She has always been my equal."

"Well, equal but different," she said.

"That's for sure. I don't wear granny panties."

Kristine pulled her robe to the side a bit. "When I'm with you, I hardly wear panties at all."

"And I always remember to floss." He chuckled, and they shared a knowing grin.

The goddess shook her head. "I don't pretend to know what that means, and I don't want to. I'm getting impatient. Do you want this reward, or don't you?" She began tapping her foot.

"Yes. *Yes!*" Kristine cried. "I didn't know you could do that."

Mother Nature threw her hands in the air and snorted. "What have I been telling you? Never underestimate me. At least I finally know what you want." She strode over to Kristine, placed her hands on top of her head, and gave them a push. "There!"

The deity disappeared. Suddenly Kristine realized she knew things she hadn't known before. Excitedly, she spouted some of these facts to Jayce.

He laughed. "Yup, only an officer in the BFD would know any of that."

The phone rang.

"I'll get it," Kristine said. She reached over to the end table and picked up the cordless phone. The irony of having a landline when she was the muse of wireless communication didn't escape her.

"Hello?" she said.

"Scotty. This is Chief O'Brian. I have what I think will be good news for you."

She had never met him, yet the chief sounded as if he knew her.

"That's great, sir. I'm anxious to hear what you have to say."

"We can use a new captain in District 2. Your name came up, and I couldn't think of a better candidate. With your experience, both in New York and Boston, we feel you'd be a perfect fit."

Kristine wondered if he really knew what he was saying, but it seemed as if Mother Nature had performed her magic. *I'd better just go with it.* "Thank you, sir. I appreciate the vote of confidence."

"Anyway, the job is yours if you'll accept it."

"I'd be honored to serve in the capacity of captain in any Boston firehouse, and I'll do my very best to make you proud, sir."

"I know you will. After all, you're going to be a Fierro."

"Wait. Did I get this job because I'm related to Jayce? Or rather, I will be after Christmas."

"Not at all. You got it on your own merit. It's just nice to know there's another Fierro officer who we can count on. After your honeymoon, of course. By the way, will I be invited to the wedding?"

Kristine almost groaned. The guest list was already huge and still growing. But why not? She would be part of a large, noisy, sometimes rowdy family. Back when she was a little girl, she never dreamed her wedding would be such a well-attended event.

"Of course, sir. We haven't sent out invitations yet, but you can expect yours when we do."

They exchanged pleasant good-byes, and she hung up. She stared at Jayce. His eyes were twinkling, and he wore that sexy smile that she had fallen in love with.

"That's one hell of a signing bonus," Jayce said.

"It certainly is. And it seems as if we'd better hurry up and order invitations. A whole crapload of them."

Jayce laughed. "Yeah. Between your friends at FDNY, my friends at BFD, our families, our extended families, and our parents' long-time friends, we'll have to find a bigger venue too. If it weren't a winter wedding, maybe we could rent out Fenway Park."

"Well, I don't want to push off the honeymoon until spring. I'm looking forward to St. Kitts in late December and early January."

"Don't worry. We'll cram everyone into Emmanuel Church somehow. But you're right about needing to get on those invitations. Do you want anything special?" Jayce asked.

"I don't really care what the invitations look like. Just as long as you're standing beside me on our wedding day. It's you I want."

"You have me. And I'm thankful that I have you."

They shared a tender kiss and the promise of a bright future full of fun, laughter, and love.

Keep reading for an excerpt from

I DREAM OF
DRAGONS

Available now from Sourcebooks Casablanca.

THUNK.

"What the hell?" Rory picked himself up off the floor beside his bed, rubbing his sore hip. Three little men dressed in green stood by his bedroom door. One of them looked angry, and one of them was trying not to snigger. The other seemed like a neutral party with his hands in his pockets.

"Rory Arish, you're being charged with theft," the angry one said.

Rory blinked and stared at the little men. "Theft, is it? What is it I'm accused of stealin'?"

"Me gold. All of it."

Rory scratched his head. "Lucky, is it?" he asked, trying to put names to their faces.

"If you're talkin' about me name, it's Clancy. Lucky is me brother." The man with his hands in his pockets withdrew one and waved at Rory. "If you're talkin' about your day, I'd say this is the unluckiest of your whole long life."

The red-haired man who'd been trying not to laugh moved his hand, uncovering his short, red beard.

"Nobody steals from leprechauns and gets away with it—no matter how big you are."

Rory sighed. "There's been some kind of misunder-standin'. I haven't stolen anyone's gold—or anythin' else for that matter. Do you see anythin' worth stealin' here?" He spread his arms wide and swiveled, indicating the whole sparsely furnished room.

He and his sisters had moved from the crumbling castle on the cliffs to the caretakers' cottage a few years ago. The Arishes hadn't changed much, leaving the cottage about the same as when the caretakers had lived and died there.

"Move your arse, dragon," the angry one said. "March me to my gold!"

"I will not march anywhere," Rory said. "Especially when I don't know where your feckin' gold is."

Clancy balled his fists.

The gleeful one muttered, "Oh, *that* did it."

"Be quiet, Shamus," Clancy snapped. Then he focused his attention on Rory again. "Mr. Arish, I'm trying to be reasonable, but I'm not a patient man. Now, admit what you did and rectify the situation, or we'll be forced to end the treaty between our people."

Clad only in their nightgowns, Rory's sisters appeared in the doorway behind the little people. Well…behind and over them. Even at five foot five or six, the girls were easily twice the size of a leprechaun.

"What's goin' on here?" his sister Chloe mumbled as she rubbed the sleep out of her green eyes.

"Apparently I'm bein' accused of a crime I did not commit," Rory said.

His youngest sister, Shannon, piped up. "Crime? What crime?"

Clancy whirled on the girls. "Mayhaps one of you took me gold. We don't know if it was your brother or not, but it had to be the work of a dragon. Who else would have the strength to move it?"

Rory rubbed his forehead. "Now wait a minute. Me sisters didn't steal anythin' either."

Clancy pointed a finger at Rory. "Then you admit it! It was you!"

"I admit nothin'." Rory's annoyance was growing now. *Fine, wake me up. Accuse me of something I didn't do. But don't go pointin' fingers at me sisters!*

"It could have been any one of you...or all of you colludin' together. The punishment will be meted out to each and every one until somebody confesses."

"Punishment?" Chloe laughed. "I'd like to see you try."

Oh shite. That was probably the worst thing she could have said, but leave it to Chloe to poke the beast. Even though they came in pint-sized packages, leprechauns possessed powerful magic. Either Chloe didn't remember the treaty because it was signed when she was so young, or she didn't believe the leprechauns held the power to protect or expose her and her family. But how else could their castle in the cliffs have remained hidden from humans for all these centuries?

It's true that the bulk of it was built underground with entrances in the cliff's caves, but there was one turret, like a large rook on a chess board, in plain view. It was for the few humans brave enough to live near dragons, plus the royals had posted a sentry there to see anyone coming by land.

Clancy narrowed his eyes at the three of them. Finally

he said, "You leave me no choice! You will march to the cliffs—now. If one of you doesn't confess to the crime before you get there, I will cast you into the ocean and ban you from ever setting foot in Ireland again! In fact, you'll be banned from all of the United Kingdom!"

"Ha!" Chloe said. "Nobody's goin' anywhere."

Moments later, dragons Rory, Shannon, and Chloe Arish bobbed on a raft just off the western shore of County Kerry, Ireland. They had been marched, against their will, to the edge of the cliff, and then magically transported to the raft. Rory, head of his clan, shook his fist at the little bastards dancing and laughing on the cliff above them, right next to his clan's, now fully exposed, ancient castle.

"You can't do this! Our people have coexisted for centuries. You're violatin' the treaty signed by our ancestors," he roared.

Shamus, the most gleeful of the three redheaded leprechauns, yelled back, "We don't know who signed it. We weren't there. Maybe the dragons forged our ancestors' signatures."

"Why would they do that?" Chloe yelled. "We were protectin' each other. Your people with your magic and our clan with our might."

"Ha! Look who's high and mighty now," Shamus called back.

"This is the same as murder!" Chloe yelled. "You know damn well this raft won't make it across the ocean. And look what you're doin' to me poor sister." She pointed to Shannon, who was lying prostrate on the lashed logs, sobbing. The bastards hadn't even let her say good-bye to Finn, her intended.

Lucky elbowed Shamus. "She has a point."

"About a cryin' sister? Who cares?"

"Not that. About the murder part."

Clancy stroked his red and gray beard. "We should give them a worthy craft and enough food so they don't starve."

Shamus's delight faded fast. "You're not goin' soft on these thieves, are you? They took your gold!"

Clancy leaned in close, but Rory's superior hearing picked up what he thought was an admission of doubt.

"We didn't take your damn gold!" he shouted at the leprechauns.

"You did," Shamus insisted. "Who else but a dragon would covet our treasure?"

Rory set his hands on his hips. "Oh, I don't know… Everyone?"

Clancy finally addressed his brothers. "They should be kept alive. If we don't find the gold in their keep, we may have to question them some more."

Lucky nodded. "I agree."

Suddenly the dragons found themselves on a fishing trawler, probably large enough to make it across the sea *if* the weather was perfect the whole way.

"There. Now they have safe transport and all the fish they can catch," Clancy said.

Shamus let out a defeated sigh. "All right. I guess that covers our arses."

"Speaking of arses," Rory yelled. "What do you little shites expect us to do for money *if* we land somewhere? Are we to sleep on the docks and starve while we look for work?"

Lucky said, "Certainly not." He turned to Shamus. "There are women aboard."

Shamus rolled his eyes. "Fine."

A dozen plastic cards rained down on the dragons, bouncing off their heads.

"Ow," Chloe said. "You bastards did that on purpose." Then she picked up one of the credit cards and yelled, "Who the hell is Molly McGuire?"

Shamus shrugged. "Does it matter? She probably won't miss it for a bit."

"Surely we can have the treasure that you know belongs to us," Shannon pleaded. "All you're missin' is gold. We have jewels, antiques, silver…"

Clancy nodded and a jewelry box, a harp, and a silver tea set appeared on the deck. Suddenly the ship dropped a little lower in the water.

"There's more below," Lucky yelled.

"And what about our clothes?" Chloe called out. "Our instruments!"

Clancy tossed his hands in the air and said, "Do I have to do everythin'?"

"I'll get them," Lucky said. A moment later three small suitcases and their only means of income, the family's musical instruments, landed on the deck.

Suddenly Shannon shimmered off her nightgown, shifted into her dragon form, and flew at the cliff. Before either Rory or Chloe could scold her for changing in broad daylight, she bounced off an invisible barrier and landed in the sea, stunned.

Chloe gasped. "Shannon! Are you all right?"

A curl of steam escaped Shannon's nostril. She righted herself and flew at the cliff a second time—faster, as if speed could break through whatever magic barrier the leprechauns had created. Again she bounced off and landed in the ocean. This time her eyes were closed and her wings were limp as she floated on her back.

"You killed our sister," Rory yelled. He shimmered off his sweat pants, shifted into dragon form, and swooped down to grab his precious baby sister's limp body. After he'd returned her to the deck of the boat, he shifted back to human form and put his ear to the soft part of Shannon's scaly chest, listening for one of her two heartbeats. Rory always suspected her softer nature was a result of those two hearts. He sometimes wondered if she'd also gotten Chloe's, because his middle sister could seem a bit heartless at times.

He heard a few faint beats. *Ah, she's alive. Damn good thing too, or I'd have found some way around that barrier to toast every one of the little bastards and serve them as s'mores.*

Lucky and Clancy leaned over the cliff and appeared somewhat concerned. Shamus folded his arms and said, "If she's dead, she killed herself."

Clancy whirled on Shamus. "Shut your trap."

Shamus's back stiffened, but he didn't argue with his brother.

Shannon groaned and her eyes fluttered open. She shifted back to human form and touched her head. "Ow."

"What were you thinkin', Sister?" Chloe demanded as she rushed over with a tarp. "I get the first time, but the second? Did the first bump on the head knock the sense right out of you?"

"Finn... I need to see Finn. How will he know what happened? He'll think I've just run off and left him."

"No, he won't," Chloe said. "You two have been joined at the hip since you were sixteen. He'll know somethin' is drastically wrong."

"And that's supposed to comfort me?" Shannon moaned.

Chloe just held up the tarp while her sister shimmered back into her nightgown. Soon Shannon was bawling again.

Rory began fiddling with the controls in hopes of getting the boat started. He couldn't stand it when his sister cried. "Try to buck up, Shannon. I'll do whatever I can to get this vessel to a safe haven. From there you can call or text or whatever you want to do to him."

Chloe smirked. "I'm sure she wants to do more than that to him."

Shannon let out another wail, and Rory narrowed his eyes at his middle sibling. "You're not helpin', Chloe."

At last the engine caught and he pushed the throttle forward. They sped west. Eventually he'd figure out all the controls and possibly even hit Iceland.

Amber, along with the other flight attendants, boarded the plane from Iceland back to Boston.

She noticed a young red-haired woman with her adorable daughter—the resemblance couldn't be missed— seated in her first class section. She thought she heard the woman explaining to the little girl that she could have snapped her fingers and they would have been home instantly, but she didn't want the girl to think that was the normal way to get around. The little girl nodded and her big, blue eyes didn't blink, as if the explanation made perfect sense to her. It made no sense to Amber. She must have misheard.

All was going well until a bit of turbulence ruffled the plane's smooth path. Amber happened to be standing next to the mother's and daughter's seats.

The captain announced over the intercom, "Sorry, folks. We seem to be experiencing a bit of rough air."

At that moment the plane bounced dramatically, and Amber braced herself against the passenger's seat and the overhead bin. "No shit," she muttered under her breath.

The woman giggled as if she had superior senses and had heard the inappropriate comment over the engine noise.

"Please be sure your seat belts are fastened," the captain continued. "Flight attendants, return to your seats and buckle up. It's going to be a bit bumpy."

The woman seemed to be glancing at Amber a little more frequently than she'd expect—almost sizing her up.

Oh well… If she's going to lodge a complaint against me, it will take the decision to quit or not to quit out of my hands.

Amber had been flying the skies ambivalently for several years. After high school, she didn't have the money for college and didn't know what her major would be, so rather than waste her mother's hard-earned money, she'd decided to go to work. She figured as soon as she discovered her passion, she could go to college and by then she'd have a bunch of money saved up for school. Maybe it was time…

A few hours later they made a safe landing in Boston, and Amber waited to deplane after everyone else.

The redheaded woman and the adorable mini-version waited until they were the very last passengers.

Amber couldn't help being a little nervous. Did the woman want to confront her on her language? Chastise her privately? She wouldn't blame her. The little girl didn't act as if she'd heard Amber swear, but using such language was inappropriate nonetheless. Yup, it was definitely time to think about finding another job. This had to be a sign of burnout.

Ah, good. The woman walked past her and disappeared into the crowd. Amber headed for the airport bathroom.

When she entered the restroom, the redhead was washing her hands.

Damn it. She hadn't seen the woman enter, but here she was. It must be a sign. Amber would have to stop trying to avoid her and just face the consequences of her stupid remark. Or maybe the woman wasn't upset at all. Better to keep it casual and see.

"What a beautiful little girl," Amber said.

"Thank you," the woman responded, beaming. "She really is a great kid."

The little one giggled and nodded.

"Awww… What's her name?"

"Nikki," the mom said. "And I'm Brandee." She extended her clean and now dry hand to shake Amber's, so she grasped Brandee's hand for a firm handshake. Brandee held it a little longer than necessary and a smile spread slowly across her face.

What was that about?

A woman in a crisp business suit joined them and stood next to Brandee. She seemed happy to see her. It wasn't unusual for travelers to bump into people they knew at the airport, so Amber didn't think anything of it until…

"I might have a candidate for you," Brandee whispered to the businesswoman, who gave Brandee a smile.

"Do you now?"

Brandee tipped her head in Amber's direction, but she was already on her way to a stall. When she turned to close the door, she saw the woman pat Brandee on the head and say, "Good girl. I'll take it from here."

Brandee didn't seem to mind the businesswoman's condescending behavior. She simply smiled and then addressed her child. "Is it time for a diaper change, honey?" The toddler nodded.

When Amber exited the stall, Brandee and Nikki were gone and the businesswoman was washing her hands…again. *Must be a germophobe.*

She observed the flight attendant until Amber glanced at her and smiled. She was about to tell the woman to have a good day when suddenly she wasn't there. The whole restroom wasn't there! *She* wasn't there. She was surrounded by fog and couldn't see a thing. *Where the hell am I?* Suddenly the fog cleared and she was alone. What. Just. Happened?

—⁘—

By some miracle, Rory and his sisters made it to Iceland. They stood on the shore, shivering.

"I need a coat and a place to get out of this wind," Shannon said.

"We're *all* freezin' our arses off," Chloe snapped.

"At least the leprechauns gave us our clothes," Rory said. "Jeans and sweaters are better than your nighties."

Chloe snorted. "To be sure. That was so feckin' nice of them."

Rory's teeth chattered. "I spotted a cave off the south coast. We have our own source of heat. If the place is private, we'll be safe. But as far as coats are concerned, if either of you have a suggestion, let me know."

Chloe withdrew a credit card from her pocket. "I think Molly wants to go shopping."

"You can't!" Shannon said. "That doesn't belong to you."

"These are desperate times, Shannon," Chloe hissed out between her teeth.

"Look," Rory said. "The credit card company will reimburse Molly. I'll take Shannon to the cave I saw, and we'll get a fire going. Then I'll come looking for you. Where do you think you'll be, Chloe?"

Chloe bit out some kind of oath. "Sure. Baby our baby sister some more. That'll really help her get along in the real world."

Rory set his hands on his hips. "If we split the chores, we'll be comfortable that much sooner. We can stand here and freeze to death while we argue, or you can give me a direction so I can come find you in an hour or so."

"Fine," Chloe said. "I'm headin' northwest." She pointed a long, un-manicured finger at a building right off the dock. The place looked like a clothing store with all sorts of outerwear in the window. "What size do you wear?"

Rory rolled his eyes. "Just buy me somethin' extra large and extra warm."

"You can send Molly whatever-her-surname-is a check to cover it later," Shannon said.

Chloe laughed. "Yeah, I'll do that. I'll be sure to give the police our return address too."

Rory grabbed Shannon's wrist before he started swearing and marched off in the opposite direction.

"You don't have to drag me, Brother. I'll come willin'ly."

He sighed and let go. "Thank the gods. At least one of you can be reasoned with."

Although she had to run to keep up with his long-legged strides, she caught him. "Chloe's not really upset. It's just her way."

"Well, I'm glad you're not that way. Otherwise I'd probably be an only child by now."

Shannon laughed.

It was the first smile he'd seen from her since they'd left Ireland. He knew she hadn't accepted their lot. It was just a tiny truce until the next hissy fit. He also knew better than to bring up the name Finn Kelley or she'd begin to weep again.

How had he wound up in these circumstances? They hadn't done a thing. The leprechauns had hidden their castle from humans for centuries, and for the last several years, while the castle crumbled, they'd lived quietly in a cottage on the property far down the dead-end road, away from prying eyes. Suddenly they had been dragged from their beds and marched against their will to the castle, which was no longer hidden but standing—albeit crumbling—on the cliffs in plain sight of the ocean.

When the leprechauns demanded that the Arishes produce the gold that was missing from their coffers, Rory had thought they were daft. Apparently Clancy had discovered the loss and had convinced his cronies that the dragons' love of treasure had finally gotten the better of them.

When Rory and Shannon reached a deserted part of the coast, they found a large cave in which they could make a temporary home. Dragons weren't seafaring creatures, and he was glad to be on solid ground.

Shannon's face screwed up and tears glistened in her eyes.

Oh no. Here we go again.

"What it is, luv?" he asked, dreading the answer.

"Is this what we've come to? Livin' in some hard, dank cave? I miss our peat fire and our lovely flowered sofa. There's not a comfortable spot anywhere."

Rory patted her shoulder. "I need you to make it as homey as you can. Just start a small fire and keep it goin'. I have to fetch Chloe and show her where we are. The three of us will put our heads together and come up with a better plan soon."

Shannon's gaze dropped to her feet. Not long after, he saw shivers rack her body and a fat teardrop fall from her chin. "I hope Chloe gets us some warm boots—I mean Molly."

He thought he'd pull out every last hair on his head if he had to put up with his soggy sister much longer. "Come now. How can you start a fire if you're just goin' to put it out with tears?"

She took a few deep breaths, and he could see her trying to wrestle herself under control.

"That's a good lass. I'm sure you can warm the place a bit while I'm gone. Just don't move so Chloe and I can find you again."

"What am I supposed to keep burnin', Brother? Rock?"

Do I have to think of everything? "We'll bring some newspapers and branches back as fuel and give you a break. For now, just heat the rocks with your breath. That may produce a bit of steam, but it'll warm the air."

Shannon sighed, then took a deep breath and blew out a stream of fire aimed at the cave walls.

"Perfect. Thank you, luv. I'm off to fetch our surly sister." Before Shannon could think of anything else to complain about, he rushed out the cave's entrance and picked his way over the rocks toward town.

———∿∿∿———

When Amber finally reappeared in the airport bathroom, she mumbled, "I need a vacation," and went straight home to her apartment building. She thought she must be losing her mind and just wanted to lie down—after having a much-needed drink. She ignored the sign on the elevator door. It was in small print and official looking. Probably a notice that the landlord would be spraying for bugs or something. She spied the same notice on each tenant's door as she fumbled with her keys. At last she let herself into her apartment and grabbed the notice, intending to look at it later.

Dropping her flight bags outside the kitchen, she took a mini wine bottle out of the fridge. She glanced at the notice on her way to the living room and almost dropped the bottle of Chardonnay. *An eviction notice?*

"Holy mother!"

"I'm right behind you," a woman said.

That caused Amber to whirl around and repeat herself loudly.

"I said, I'm right here!" The white-robed woman

slapped her hands over her ears. She had long, thick, white hair. Her robe was belted with a vine of ivy.

"Hey, aren't you the woman from the bathroom? Brandee's friend?"

"Sheesh. Have a seat, girlie. We need to talk."

Amber hesitated. The woman wasn't carrying a weapon, although something about her seemed ultimately threatening. As if to affirm the feeling, thunder rolled and the sky outside the window darkened. Amber stumbled backward and sat down hard on her beige linen sofa.

"That's better," the woman said. "I'm aware you don't know who I am, so I'll introduce myself. I don't have time for your disbelief, so save me the trouble and just go with it. Okay?"

Amber nodded woodenly.

"Good. The truth is, I'm Mother Nature. Those who know me call me either Goddess or Gaia. That's my title and my name. You should begin by calling me Mother Nature just to drive the point home."

Amber heard herself say, "Okaaay," in a little girl's voice.

"Here's the good news. You won't have to worry about that eviction notice. I have a job for you, and it won't matter where you live. I know you're getting disenchanted with your job as a flight attendant."

"How do you know that?"

The woman smirked. "Really? I'm Mother freakin' Nature. I know just about everything. If people were meant to fly, I'd have given them wings." She cocked her head. "Why did you become a flight attendant anyway?"

"I—uh. I wanted to see the world."

"You mean you wanted to meet a rich businessman

and do a little traveling before you settled down. How's that working out for you?"

Her back went up. "He doesn't have to be rich."

"But relationships with men in general aren't working out. Right?"

She sighed. "Not so much. Every guy I get close to assumes I'm cheating when I'm out of the country and eventually finds a 'backup,' or he's just pissed because I'm not around much. And don't even get me started on the pilots."

"So, how much of the world have you actually seen?"

Amber grimaced. "Pretty much the same routes over and over again."

"So…nothing but the same foreign airports and hotels."

"You may have a point."

"Of course I have a point. I always have a point. I don't chat with mortals for my health. Speaking of my health, spreading all that noxious jet fuel so close to my ozone layer is the most harmful thing you can possibly do to me. Did you know that?"

"Um…not really. Is it?"

"Sheesh. How dumb can you be? You blow a hole in my sunscreen, and you think I won't get burned?"

"I…I don't really make those decisions."

Mother Nature—or whoever she was—rolled her eyes and sat down on the chair across from Amber. "Well, you may be able to make those decisions in the future. I want you to be my muse of air travel."

Amber's brows shot up. "Huh? You're offering me a job? As a…what?"

Mother Nature sighed. "I knew you'd have a hard time believing all of this. I gave you a trusting nature but also let you develop some healthy skepticism. Look, I don't have time for a lot of chitchat. I'm in desperate need of some modern muses. You've met one of them. Brandee is my muse of photography."

"I thought muses took care of poetry, dance, and other ancient arts."

The woman let out a groan. "Exactly. The original nine are useless in this modern age. I tried to get them to reeducate themselves in new areas, but it's been a disaster. I can't even get the muse of epic poetry to rap—or the muse of dance to crunk. And forget music videos! Technology is way beyond them, and I can't wait any longer for my muses to catch up. Your world is growing too fast. Therefore, I've begun the task of finding a few modern muses. Any questions so far?"

"Um, yeah. A few hundred…"

"Well, hold your questions for the end. I'll pair you with someone who'll have the patience to answer them. In other words, not me."

Amber wanted to throw her hands in the air and say something sarcastic, but she still wasn't sure how crazy this woman was—or *she* was, so she just waited.

"Good. Let's see now…" Gaia tapped her chin as if deep in thought. "I know. I'll pair you with Brandee since you've already met and she's the one who recommended you. That way if she doesn't answer your questions thoroughly and you screw up, it'll be all her fault."

This insulting woman was trying Amber's patience. How could she get the woman out of her apartment? Playing along with her was getting old.

"Why don't you give me Brandee's phone number? I'll give her a call sometime."

Mother Nature frowned. "You still doubt me, glitter tits?"

"What did you call me?"

"Look down."

Amber was bare to the midriff and indeed her breasts were covered in glitter. She gasped and tried to cover herself with her hands.

"Relax. I've seen them before. Heck, I made them."

Amber was struck dumb. If she protested, who knew what the woman…or goddess would do. "I—I…"

"Mother Nature" waved her hand and Amber was wearing her uniform blouse again. Then the self-proclaimed deity shouted at the ceiling. "Brandee, I need you."

To Amber's shock, the redheaded passenger from her latest flight appeared in her living room.

"Yes, Gaia. How may I be of service?"

"This is the woman you recommended for the muse of air travel, correct?"

Brandee turned to Amber and offered a friendly smile. "Yes. I liked her immediately and thought she'd fit in with the others. As you know, I can sense people's innate goodness and I'm a very good judge of character."

"Well, she needs to talk to someone like you or Bliss. One of my modern muses. She has questions, and I don't have the time or patience to answer them."

"Understood," was all Brandee said.

The woman looked relieved and smiled. "Thank you. As a reward for your help, I'll send an influential customer to visit your gallery tomorrow."

Brandee grinned. "Thanks! We're doing quite well, but I can always use more—"

"Yeah, yeah." Mother Nature disappeared into thin air and Amber let out the breath she'd been holding in a whoosh.

"Where did she go?"

Brandee shrugged. "Who knows? She likes to hang out in her office building on State Street, but she could be creating natural disasters like floods or earthquakes. You just never know with her."

"Is she really…"

"Mother freakin' Nature? Yeah, she is." Brandee chuckled. "You probably pictured someone wearing rainbows as a halo and patting kittens, didn't you?"

"Well, no, but I didn't think…"

Brandee sat next to her and lowered her voice. "You didn't expect a sarcastic crone with the patience of a gnat, am I right?"

Amber chuckled. "Well, no."

"You'll get used to her. You should meet my friend Bliss."

"She mentioned something about a person named Bliss."

"Yeah. She's rather famous among us muses, having been the only one gutsy enough to refuse Mother Nature's generous offer."

"Generous offer? I never received any offer sounding remotely generous."

"Really? Huh. I guess you didn't get that far. Gaia never expects her muses to work for nothing. She rewards us handsomely—usually with our greatest desire. But Bliss…" Brandee shook her head and sighed. "She stood up to Gaia and said no, even with a money tree growing right in the middle of her man's living room."

"Her man, huh?" Amber mumbled.

"Ah!" Brandee said. "Could that be what you want? A boyfriend?"

Amber snorted. "No. I've had plenty of boyfriends. What I'd like is a stable guy who won't cheat on me. I don't seem to be having much luck finding one of those."

Brandee set a sympathetic hand on Amber's shoulder. "We've all had our share of failed romances. If it isn't one thing, it's another, but both Bliss and I are now 'blissfully' happy, if you'll pardon the pun. So, if what you want is a wonderful, faithful man to love, marry, or live with, I'll mention that to the goddess."

"No! Oh no. Don't do that yet. I think I'm leaning more toward Bliss's reaction than yours."

Brandee raised her eyebrows. Then she smiled and seemed to relax. "You know what might be a good idea? If we include Bliss in this conversation."

"Ugh. Please don't. I can't stand any more people popping into my living room. I'm quite convinced I'm losing my mind as it is."

"Oh. Sorry. I forgot what it was like in the beginning. Of course your head is probably spinning. It's natural to doubt your own eyes and sanity. Why don't I give you my address on Beacon Hill? Let the dust settle and meet me there tomorrow. I'll ask Bliss to stop by, *if* you actually show."

"If I say I'll be there, I'll be there. Unlike some people, I can be counted on to keep my word."

Brandee winked. "I knew I liked you for a reason. Here's my gallery." She held out an empty hand, and then a business card appeared.

"Whoa. Neat trick."

"I'm not a magician. I'm a minor goddess. Take the card and turn it over."

Amber did as she was told. Brandee pointed to the card and a different address appeared on the blank side. "That's my home address and phone number on Mount Vernon Street."

"Fancy."

"We like it. Come by at noon. I take a lunch hour at home to feed the baby. Although I'll be meeting an important client tomorrow, and I don't know the time yet." She waved away the thought. "If I'm late, my husband will let you in."

"Are you sure? I mean, Mother Nature mentioned someone influential kind of offhandedly. Do you think it'll really happen?"

"She keeps her word too. Well, except when she's bellowing empty threats. Then we're just as happy she doesn't." Brandee smirked. "Well, toodles. I'm going to meet my family for lunch and will leave you to doubt your sanity for another twenty-four hours."

And with that, she disappeared.

Amber *was* doubting her sanity. Just out of curiosity, she peeked down the front of her blouse. "Yup. Covered in glitter. I'll be damned."

Acknowledgments

Major thanks to the Boston firefighters who were kind to this curious writer and generous with their knowledge, especially Captain Coleman Connolly, all those on Engine 22, and Hazmat Mindy. I was even allowed to borrow Mindy's jacket and join the guys on a couple of ride-alongs.

Also, thanks again to another Massachusetts firefighter, Tom Madigan, who beta-reads all my scenes involving firefighters on the job. He has kept me from straying too far from the truth through three books, and is already helping me with another one. No, it's not a coincidence that I made him a captain in this book!

By the way, I owe a big thank-you to my New York editor, Cat Clyne, for catching my gaffes regarding Manhattan, which would have certainly given me away as an out-of-towner.

About the Author

Ashlyn Chase describes herself as an Almond Joy bar: a little nutty, a little flaky, but basically sweet, wanting only to give her readers a satisfying experience.

She holds a degree in behavioral sciences, worked as a psychiatric RN for fifteen years, and spent a few more years working for the American Red Cross. She credits her sense of humor to her former careers since comedy helped preserve whatever was left of her sanity. She is a multi-published, award-winning author of humorous erotic and paranormal romances, represented by the Seymour Agency.

Ashlyn lives in beautiful New Hampshire with her true-life hero husband who looks like Hugh Jackman with a salt-and-pepper dye job, and they're owned by a spoiled brat cat.

Ashlyn loves to hear from readers! Visit ashlynchase .com to sign up for her newsletter. She's also on Facebook (AuthorAshlynChase), Twitter (@GoddessAsh), and Yahoo groups (ashlynsnewbestfriends), and ask her to sign your ebook at authorgraph.com.